The HEAT of the SUN

The
HEAT
of the
SUN

a novel

Louis D. Rubin, Jr.

LONGSTREET PRESS, INC.
Atlanta, Georgia

Published by LONGSTREET PRESS, INC.,
a subsidiary of Cox Newspapers,
a subsidiary of Cox Enterprises, Inc.
2140 Newmarket Parkway
Suite 118
Marietta, Georgia 30067

Printed in the United States of America

1st printing, 1995

Library of Congress Catalog Number 95-77242

ISBN: 1-56352-233-0

This book was printed by Maple-Vail Book Mfg., York, PA
Electronic film prep by Advertising Technologies, Inc., Atlanta, GA

Jacket design by Laura McDonald
Book design by Jill Dible

For Jay and Ann Logan

Sauve qui peut

Author's Note

Although this story is set in a particular time and place, it is because they are the only such that my imagination as a novelist knows. What follows is fiction all the way, and based on nothing that to my knowledge took place in that time and place, either then or later. Anyone who lived in Charleston at the time and who believes that he or she can recognize any of the protagonists or remember any of the events is mistaken.

L.D.R
Chapel Hill, North Carolina
February 15, 1995

The HEAT of the SUN

Fear no more the heat o' th' sun
    Nor the furious winter's rages;
Thou thy worldly task hast done,
    Home art gone and ta'en thy wages.
Golden lads and girls all must,
As chimney-sweepers, come to dust.

— SHAKESPEARE, *Cymbeline*

1

THE NEW BOAT was thirty feet long, wooden, and painted white. She was named the *Gilmore Simms*, and she rested on a cradle at the head of a marine railway at Elzey's Boatyard in Charleston, South Carolina. Her super-structure had been garlanded in maroon and white crepe paper, and a stepladder was in place alongside her prow. The marine railway led down to a creek that opened upon the Ashley River.

The owner of the new boat, who was standing near the ladder and talking with some of the several dozen persons gathered there for the ceremony, was Dr. Lancelot Augustus Rosenbaum, professor of English at the College of Charleston and known to his friends as Rosy. He was a large, somewhat plump man in his early 40s. A native of Charleston, he had been on the faculty for twelve years — which is to say, since 1928.

The launching party itself was the inspiration of Dr. Rudolf Strongheart, professor of zoology at the College and Rosy's colleague and friend. He and Sara Jane Jahnz, the College librarian, sent out the invitations, and came over to the boatyard that morning to bedeck boat and premises in the College colors.

A thin, wiry little man with a high furrowed brow, Dolf Strongheart stood by in growing excitement, attired for the occasion in a seersucker suit with red bow tie and a flat-brimmed straw hat, clutching a bottle of champagne wrapped in a towel.

"Are we ready now?" he asked the boat yard proprietor.

"Might as well put her in," the proprietor said. "Tide's up pretty good."

"Splendid! Remember, the instant you see the bottle break, turn her loose."

Handing the bottle and the towel to Sara Jane Jahnz, Dolf began to ascend the stepladder. "Be careful," Sara Jane cautioned. "It's pretty wobbly."

"Fear not." He climbed the rungs until he was six feet or so off the ground, his head at a level with the top of the bow. Then, carefully shifting his feet, he turned around so that his back was to the ladder. "Friends!" he called out. "Ladies and gentlemen! May I have your attention, please?"

The ladder rocked slightly, and he reached back with one hand to take hold. The onlookers assembled about the bow of the boat.

"Good friends," he began, "we are gathered here upon this auspicious occasion to celebrate the launching of our distinguished colleague's new acquisition."

"Hear, hear!" someone called out.

"As we all know, Rosy informs us that the boat has been built solely in order to further his Civil War historical researches."

"The War Between the States," somebody objected. "Get it right!"

"The War of the Rebellion," Dolf declared. "Whether or not such an assertion is indeed the truth, the whole truth, and nothing but the truth, is not for us to decide today. Suffice it to say that as we all know, the pleasures of scholarship can be both numerous and various. Let us, therefore, wish our colleague joy and happiness in his new role as captain of the good ship *Gilmore Simms!*"

"Hear, hear!"

"In this connection, I have here a telegram —" he searched inside his jacket. The ladder swayed, and Rosy reached out to steady it. "I have here a telegram from our beloved president and his good wife, who as you know are vacationing in Maine and so cannot be present to celebrate with us." He held a piece of yellow paper in his hand, and flipped it several times until it opened. "'Regret we cannot be with you on this historical occasion. Best of luck and smooth sailing for captain, crew, and ship. Page and Tennie.'"

"Hear, hear!"

He replaced the telegram in his pocket. "I shall now proceed to break a bottle of wine across the bow, and with it we consign the good ship to the waters of the harbor, with our prayers and best wishes. Godspeed!"

Sara Jane held up the towel-wrapped bottle to his reach. Taking hold of it through the towel and by the neck, Dolf grasped the ladder with his other hand and gingerly turned himself around, so that he was facing the boat.

"I christen thee *Gilmore Simms!*" he declared, and rapped the bottle against the prow. It failed to break.

He drew the bottle well behind him. The ladder wavered. "Watch it now, Dolf," Dr. Rosenbaum cautioned.

"I christen thee *Gilmore Simms!*" he declared again. This time he swung the bottle decisively against the prow in a wide arc. There was a clunk, and golden wine oozed through the towel and onto the prow of the boat. The stepladder swayed precariously, and Dolf grabbed hold of the bow with his free hand.

At that instant the boat began rolling down the inclined railway toward the water. Dolf dropped the towel, grasped the bow with his other hand as well, just as the ladder fell away. Holding on for dear life, he was borne down the marine railway toward the creek.

The boat slid into the creek. Letting go of the bow as the water rose around him, Dolf dropped off, stern first, his legs thrust out in front of him like sticks. For an instant he disappeared beneath the surface of the water, but promptly emerged.

"Man overboard!" someone yelled. "Call the Coast Guard!"

Dolf scrambled to his feet in creek water up to his chest, then began to make his way toward the wharf. Meanwhile the boat drifted out into the creek, where its movement was arrested by lines from the dock.

"Your hat, Dolf!" his wife Linda called from the dock. "Get your hat!"

Dolf's straw hat was engaged in floating away. He changed directions, reached out and retrieved the hat, shook it, and replaced it on his head. Then he resumed his progress toward the dock. "This mud is soft as turtle shit," he announced.

"Watch your language!" Linda said.

"Beg your pardon. The texture of this mud is as insubstantial as turtle do-do." He slogged his way through the water over to the edge of the dock, where outstretched hands waited to extricate him.

To the applause of all present, he was lifted onto the dock. There he stood, creek water streaming from his pockets and dripping from his hat, and with shoes, socks, and the lower portions of his trouser legs coated with black pluff mud. The lenses of his steel-rimmed eyeglasses were fogged over. He reached into a side pocket and extracted a very wet handkerchief.

"Here, take this." Rosy handed him a dry handkerchief.

He dried his glasses, held them up to the light, and replaced them on his face.

"Get that halibut out of your ear, Strongheart!" somebody suggested.

"Are you all right?" Sara Jane Jahnz asked.

"Yes, I'm all right." He doffed his straw hat, shook more water from inside, then looked around him. "What could have happened to my trident? I must have dropped it."

"You were supposed to christen the boat," someone else said, "not baptize it."

"We Jews hold with total immersion," Dolf responded. "As in Jonah."

"Yes, but not walking on the water."

"One of our boys did that, too."

"Mommy, why did Daddy go swimming with all his clothes on?" Benjy Strongheart asked.

"Because he wanted to make a great big splash," Linda told him.

The boat yard workers pulled the *Gilmore Simms* further out along the dock and cleated down the lines. Everyone walked out to where she lay and stood around admiring her.

The boatyard owner came along the dock, bearing a sump pump with a length of water hose and a coil of electric line attached.

"You ought to mount that pump on Dolf," someone suggested. "He needs it worse than the boat."

"Yes, and if you don't shut up I know where I'm going to stick the end of the hose," Dolf replied.

"Why do you need a pump?" somebody asked. "Does the boat leak?"

"They all leak some at first," the boat yard owner explained, "until the planks swell up." He climbed aboard the boat, lifted a section of decking in the cockpit, placed the pump inside the hull, led the hose over the side and secured it to a cleat. Then he stepped back onto the dock, wrapped the end of the electric cord around a post several times, and plugged it into a receptacle. The pump began humming and there was the sound of splashing water.

"She'll take in some water for a few days," he told Rosy. "After that she ought not to leak a drop."

THE NEW BOAT was to be berthed at Adger's Wharf on the Cooper River, rather than at the new municipal yacht basin on the Ashley River. Rosy justified the decision to do so on the fact that the charting work he would be doing out in the harbor was more accessible from the downtown waterfront. This was true, but it wasn't the real reason. Adger's Wharf was a commercial wharf — two, in fact, a north and a south — and most of the craft moored there were workboats, including tugboats, shrimp trawlers, cargo launches, and the like. That, and not a marina whose docks were loaded with sailboats, yachts, runabouts, and pleasure craft in general, was the ambiance that Rosy liked. He wasn't sure exactly why, but there was something utilitarian and unpretentious about workboats that appealed to his sensibilities.

There were disadvantages to the choice. On the north wharf, across the way from where the *Gilmore Simms* would be berthed, was a packing operation, under a tin roof and open on four sides. Shrimp from the trawlers were hosed down, sorted by size, loaded into tins, and iced down for shipment by truck. The aroma was pungent and, especially on summer days when the sun bore down on the discards and debris strewn about the wharf and overboard, formidably redolent. Sea gulls, attracted by the provender, were in raucous attendance. Just up the way from the north wharf, too, was Thelning's Marine Yard, and repair operations there could get quite noisy. A railroad spur led past the wharf, and on occasion a small but very smoky steam locomotive showed up to spot boxcars alongside nearby warehouses. Tourists frequently came by the wharf to photograph the multi-hued shrimp boats with their nets. The location was, in short, nobody's quiet haven. No matter; Rosy liked it.

Rosy had grown interested in the wartime defenses of Charleston harbor from reading about a floating artillery battery supposedly designed by the antebellum novelist William Gilmore Simms for use in the Confederate bombardment of Fort Sumter in 1861. It had last been reported as lying half-sunk in a tidal flat near Fort Sumter in 1864. Rosy had rented an open boat with an inboard engine and, using grappling hooks, sought to locate the wreck, but without success. During the process he had discovered that there was considerable confusion about the locations of most of the wartime batteries, so he decided to write a little book about the harbor defenses. This involved going out in the rented boat and determining the trajectories of the various batteries.

Linda Strongheart had another explanation for both Rosy's harbor defense project and the building of the boat. They constituted an oblique way, she said, for Rosy to enjoy the company of

Sara Jane Jahnz. For Sara Jane almost always took part in Rosy's expeditions about the harbor to search out and chart the wartime defenses. It was she who kept the charts and recorded the bearings while Rosy manned the transit and called them out.

"Well, if that's what's involved, what the hell's he waiting for?" Dolf demanded. "Why does he think Sara Jane goes along? Just because she likes boat rides?"

"Dear one, you can be awfully obtuse sometimes," Linda said. "Of course not. But boats aren't called 'she' for nothing."

THE SEAMS SWELLED; the *Gilmore Simms* ceased to take in water. The boat builder took her out for her sea trial; an hour's run past Fort Sumter and back turned up no flaws. She was now Rosy's, to have, to hold, and to maintain.

To take her around from the boatyard to Adger's Wharf, a run of four miles or so, Rosy invited Sara Jane and Dolf to come along. "Old clothes will do," he told Dolf. " Don't dress up. If you intend to go swimming again, wear your bathing suit."

"Up yours, comrade," his friend replied.

They left the boat yard, proceeded under the Memorial Bridge, and headed downstream, past the new yacht basin at Bennett's Mill, past the tidal flat where the hulk of the old ferryboat *Sappho* was moored, past the entrance into the Inland Waterway at Wappoo Creek, around the Coast Guard station at the foot of Tradd Street with its red and black buoys on the dock and the tenders *Cypress* and *Mangrove* tied up alongside, and along the sea wall of Murray Boulevard. It was a hot day with little breeze, and Rosy, at the wheel, felt highly gratified by the performance of his boat as she moved cleanly along the channel, the gasoline engine humming steadily. Sara Jane and Dolf sat out in the stern in the roofed-over cockpit.

Up ahead, along the port side, was the white six-story bulk of the Fort Sumter Hotel, the green trees of White Point Gardens, and the High Battery at the tip of the peninsula. To the starboard was a belt of marshland and the tree-lined shore of James Island. Straight ahead, six miles distant, was Fort Sumter and the entrance to the harbor.

They rounded the buoy off the High Battery, turned to port, and followed the ship channel up the Cooper River waterfront, past the sea wall and the Carolina Yacht Club, with Castle Pinckney to starboard, and up to where the three red tugboats of the White Stack Towboat Company were tied at the end of the south wharf at Adger's Wharf.

At low speed they steered for the entrance between the two piers. The assigned slip was located two-thirds of the way up the pier. As they drew abreast of it, Rosy threw the engine into reverse.

The stern had traveled no more than a few yards when it became evident that they were backing in the direction of a launch in the next slip. The stern was swinging toward the slip, but not enough. They were not going to clear the bow of the launch.

"Keep her off the boat!" he called to Dolf, who was standing on the fantail, a line held in one hand, as the stern edged toward the launch.

Dolf dropped the line and grabbed hold of the bow of the launch with both hands.

Rosy ran out onto the stern. The stern was drifting away from the launch's bow, and there was a yard of water between them, with Dolf, still retaining his hold, suspended over it, his hands grasping the top of the launch's bow while the toes of his shoes were pushing against the lip of the fantail in an effort to keep the boat from drifting further, and with Sara Jane Jahnz's arms wrapped around his knees to keep him from going overboard.

Rosy grabbed him by the belt of his trousers. "Let go!" he yelled, and hauled him back onto the fantail.

In the slip on the landward side a blue-hulled sailboat was tied. A man was standing on the bow holding a boathook, grim-faced, as if prepared to fend off boarders.

Rosy returned to the controls. They went forward a few yards, then he began backing again. This time they were coming squarely in under the launch's bow. He took the transmission out of gear and hurried back onto the stern, mounted the fantail, and as they drifted against the launch, reached out and shoved the stern away and toward the piling. Slowly they moved off. He grabbed the side of the launch's bow again, pushed some more.

"What can I do to help?" Dolf asked.

"Nothing. Just don't grab hold of anything."

The stern was now close to the piling. Sara Jane handed Rosy a line and he looped it around the piling. Then he shoved the boat away from it.

"Here, take this!" the man on the sailboat called. He heaved a line, Sara Jane grabbed it, Rosy pushed the stern away from the piling, and the man pulled them across the slip.

After more pushing and pulling the *Gilmore Simms* finally lay in her slip, bow lines secured to the pilings, stern lines cleated on the dock.

THEY SAT OUT in the cockpit, and Rosy poured drinks.

"The prows of boats," Dolf said, "seem somehow to hold a fatal appeal for me. Is it possible that in a previous reincarnation I may have been a Rhine Maiden?"

"I would say more likely a snapping turtle," Rosy said. "Once you take hold of something you don't seem to want to let go."

"The boat ran very nicely," Sara Jane said.

"What I've got to remember," said Rosy, "is that boats don't go back in a straight line, like automobiles. I haven't got the hang of it yet."

"I confess that I still don't quite understand the fascination that you find in boats," Dolf said. "Compared with you, Captain Ahab was a model of sanity and reason."

"At least I don't keep a boat in my office." Dolf's office and laboratory at the College were lined with aquaria and with animal and reptile cages.

Sara Jane laughed. "Neither of you is without obsessions," she said. "Rosy, what are you going to do with your boat when a hurricane comes?" Dolf asked.

"I don't know. I haven't thought about it."

"We haven't had one in years," Sara Jane said. "The last one was in 1927, wasn't it, Rosy?" In her early thirties, like Rosy she was a native Charlestonian.

"I don't remember. I was still in New Haven at the time."

"Well, I remember it. A limb blew down from an oak tree and knocked in a stained glass window of St. John's Church, right above our pew. Aunt Ruth had a conniption fit, because the prayer book she was given when she was confirmed was soaked beyond repair. She still talks about it."

"This city," Dolf declared, "is marked for destruction. You had an earthquake, two years ago there were those tornadoes, and you have these hurricanes. Don't you think maybe God's trying to tell you something?"

"Whom the Lord loveth He chasteneth," Rosy told him.

"That's the New Testament," Dolf declared. "Don't tell me they're using that at Beth Elohim now." As an Orthodox Jew, Dolf liked to claim that the Reform Judaism in which Rosy was brought up was a disguised form of Protestantism.

"No, and they've also stopped making sacrifices to the moon goddess."

"Boys, boys, do behave!" Sara Jane said. "No theological disputes, please."

"When are the Carters due back?" Dolf asked after a moment. The College's president and his wife, both avid sailors, had missed the boat launching because they were off in Maine crewing for the Bar Harbor-to-Annapolis offshore race.

"They're back now," Sara Jane said. "Page stopped by the library yesterday. He wanted to know how the launching went."

"You told him swimmingly, I hope," Rosy said.

"I didn't have to. He'd already heard."

"Pah!" Dolf said.

"He and Tennie don't really approve of powerboats," Rosy remarked. "They can't understand why I didn't get a sailboat." The Carters lived across the Ashley River on James Island, and kept a 40-foot ketch moored out in a creek in front of their house. "They consider it unnatural and immoral to use an internal combustion engine on the water."

"But don't they have one in their boat?" Sara Jane asked.

"I think they do have an auxiliary engine in it, but only for use in emergencies."

"I don't see the point of using sails," Dolf said, "when an engine can get you where you're going faster and without depending on whether the wind's blowing."

"It has to do with aesthetics," Sara Jane said.

"Aesthetics aeschmetics. Just so long as it looks pretty."

One of the White Stack tugboats at the head of the wharf cast off its lines and headed out into the channel. They watched it move upstream until it was out of sight behind the Clyde Line wharves.

"Now that's what I call beautiful," Rosy said. "Ever since I was a child I've always wanted to own a tugboat."

"You could always give this one a coat of red paint and string some old tires around it," Dolf suggested.

"Good idea. I'll think about doing it."

"Oh, no, Rosy!" Sara Jane said. "Leave it white, just like it is. It's such a pretty boat!"

"Especially when a certain member of the crew is along," Dolf said, gesturing to Sara Jane with his hand to show who he had in mind.

"Why didn't I think to say that?" Rosy asked, verbalizing a thought.

THAT EVENING AT his rooms at the St. John's Hotel, Rosy made a list of projects he wanted to do aboard the *Gilmore Simms*, and he also reread Admiral DuPont's account of the failed attempt of the Union ironclads to run past the defenses of the outer harbor in 1862. The remains of the ironclad *Weehawken* were said to be still visible off Cummings Point at low tide. It would interesting to track them down, and also to figure out, from the reports of the various captains, just how far each ironclad had reached before being forced to turn back. Now that they had the boat, the harbor seemed to be a mine of possibilities, with dozens of interesting projects they could undertake in the months ahead.

He was preparing to undress for bed when he heard the rumble of thunder from beyond the open windows. Was the *Gilmore Simms* properly secured? He couldn't remember whether he had closed the forward hatch, either. He decided he'd better go and check. He grabbed a raincoat from the closet and hurried out.

To the accompaniment of ever-louder claps of thunder he drove down Broad Street to the waterfront. When he arrived at the wharf the fronds of the palmetto trees along the Tradd Street sidewalk were bending in the wind, and drops of rain were already falling. A streak of lightning flashed across the sky to the south, followed closely by a loud clap of thunder. He hurried along the wharf; tide was very high, and the moored boats, riding up, were swaying at their lines. He stepped onto the stern of the *Gilmore Simms* just as the full downpour began, hurried into the forward cabin and lowered the hatch cover, then went back out onto the stern cockpit, grabbed the seat cushions and folding chairs, and pulled them under the overhanging roof. But the rain was blowing in almost horizontally, so he took them into the cabin and closed the door behind him.

Rain was pouring down, rattling on the cabin roof, thunder was crashing all around, and repeated flares of lightning lit up the interior of the cabin. The *Gilmore Simms* was tugging at her mooring lines, but they seemed secure enough. He went up into the forward cabin and looked through a cabin port. The recurring lightning illuminated the boats across the way on the north wharf as they rocked and tossed.

After a time the force of the wind decreased and the rain was coming straight down. The cabin windows were fogged over. He opened the door and stepped outside under the cockpit roof. Other than a light on the dock nearby he could see almost nothing. There was no point in trying to get back to the car until the rain slackened. He returned to the cabin, got a folding chair, and sat down next to the motor box to wait in the darkness.

His eyes had become more accustomed to the dark, and the rainfall had diminished enough so that now he could make out the light up in the White Stack office at the head of the wharf, and the masthead lights of the tugboats as they swayed in the harbor current. His uncorrected eyesight was poor and the thick lenses of his glasses kept fogging up. The center of the storm had moved across the harbor; the flares of lightning were off to the east, and the intervals between them and the thunder were longer now.

Presently his ears picked up a humming sound. It appeared to be coming from down the harbor beyond the south wharf. He stood up and looked. He could see nothing. The sound was growing louder. It seemed to be an engine of some kind, but with a noise more like a metallic whine than a roar. It was almost as if were an aircraft engine, but no airplane could be that low to the water. Now he could see something white on the water, out in the channel off the yacht club. It was the bow wave of a boat of some kind, moving along at considerable speed.

As he watched, he thought he could make out the outlines of a boat, low in the water, coming along the channel. It was planing atop the water at high speed, faster than he had ever seen a boat travel, while the whine of the engine grew in volume. In no time at all it drew even with the tugboats at the head of the wharf, then vanished from sight behind them. He turned his head just in time to catch a glimpse of the speeding boat out in the channel, long and low, as it hurtled across the space between the north and south wharves, then vanished again, heading up the waterfront, trailing a thin white wake behind it. The noise of the motor receded; soon it was a low droning hum in the distance.

What was it? It was like no other watercraft he had ever seen. It was almost as if he had imagined it. Yet the *Gilmore Simms* was rocking beneath him from the waves of its wake.

He listened. He could still hear the sound, faint now, off to the north, and then more toward the east, as if the boat had rounded Hog Island and was out in the Rebellion Reach channel across the harbor. The rain had slackened until it was no more than a light drizzle. In the sky to the west he could even see a few stars. The air was noticeably cooler; the thunderstorm had brought some needed relief to the muggy weather of the last few days.

He placed the folding chair back inside the cabin, and stepped up onto the dock. A lantern shone at the head of the dock, and the White Stack night watchman came into view, walking toward him.

"Did you see that boat go by, Dr. Rosenbaum?" he asked.

"Yes. What was it?"

"Damn if I know. Must have been doing forty miles an hour!"

"Did you get a good look at it?"

"Not much. It was there and gone before I knew it. It was long, and black, with a sharp pointed bow, and all covered over except for a small cockpit, with somebody standing in it. Must have had one hell of an engine to go that fast. Didn't sound like a piston engine, though; something like a whine. I'm glad you saw it too. I thought I might have been losing my mind or something."

"I saw it, all right," Rosy assured him.

"I've seen a lot of things out on that water," the watchman declared, "but nothing like that. It reminded me of one of those hydroplanes they race out there sometimes, only it didn't sound like an outboard, and it was a lot bigger."

Rosy walked back to his car, thinking about what he had seen. Perhaps it was some kind of supersecret Navy craft. But it hadn't come from the direction of the Navy Yard up the river, and he was fairly sure that he had heard it heading around Hog Island and toward the outer harbor.

ooooo

LATER, AS HE lay in bed, the sound of a ship's whistle out in the harbor came through the open windows, grave and stentorian. He fell asleep. Sometime that night he dreamed that he was driving in the mountains, and tried to park his automobile on a hill with a steep downward slope. Every time he thought he had it properly lined up so that he could back the car into the appropriate space, the engine would cut off. Sara Jane Jahnz was with him, and she laughed and laughed.

2

MICHAEL QUINN SAT on the front porch of his fiancé Betsy Murray's house on Murray Boulevard watching the sailboats go by in the Ashley River. The Murrays — the street wasn't named for them, Betsy said — had gone to church. They were Episcopalians. Mike was a Roman Catholic.

It had all happened very quickly. He met Betsy at a fraternity party in Lexington in February — not his fraternity; he didn't belong to one. By early March they were engaged to be married. He had sent off letters to a number of newspapers looking for work. To his delight, he was offered a job right there in Charleston, Betsy's home town. It was almost, he thought, as if the hand of destiny had been at work.

Betsy was a beautiful girl, so much so that it was still amazing to him that she was going to marry him. She was small, with a trim figure, dark hair, and an olive complexion. She had been a drama major at Sweet Briar College. Her ambition had been to become an actress, and she had appeared in student plays, but she had given it up. She wasn't good enough for a career on the stage, she said. "All I want to do now is to be your wife and go where you go," she told him. She would be taking courses in shorthand and secretarial skills at Rice Business College over the summer, and would begin work at her father's office in September. They were going to be married sometime next spring.

What he liked most about her was her enthusiasm for things. There was a spontaneity about her; she enjoyed so many activities. She seemed to have the ability, when she was doing something she enjoyed, to put everything else out of mind, as if she were a child. Occasionally, when crossed, she became grumpy, but such moods passed quickly. She loved to dance, which was not something he was very good at, although he liked to listen to good jazz. Classical music was his favorite. She was a good athlete — they played tennis sometimes, and she often beat him. In a glass case out on the sunporch there were a dozen loving cups, medals, and ribbons that she had won as a horseback rider. She had given up riding, she said, because too much drinking went on at the shows and meets.

MIKE READ THE war news. It was all bad; the Nazi blitzkrieg had destroyed the French army, old Marshal Pétain was taking over as premier of France, and was expected to surrender to Hitler. The Italians had joined in the attack. President Roosevelt had denounced the move as a stab in the back, and pledged help to England, which now awaited German invasion. He also called for large expenditures for U. S. defense, and there was talk of a military draft. If there were one, he might quite possibly be taken into the Army; he was twenty-two, unmarried, no longer a student. The Republican convention would soon begin, and a man named Wendell Willkie was said to be a likely candidate to run against Roosevelt.

It was a pleasant day, with a breeze blowing in off the water. He had been there for perhaps half an hour when he saw somebody coming along the sidewalk who looked familiar. It was a boy named Rhett Jervey, a junior at Washington and Lee, who was from Charleston, and who did most of the photography for the college newspaper. He called out to him. Rhett came up onto the porch. "I thought that was a W&L sticker on that car," he said. Mike's 1933 Ford V-8 coupe was parked in front of the house.

Rhett sat down, and they talked for a while. He lived around the corner on Gibbes Street, and knew the Murrays, he said, though not well.

"Do you ever do any sailing?" Mike asked.

"Not much. What I like is fishing. Do you fish?"

"Not really." Mike shook his head. "I've never gone fishing in salt water."

"I'll take you some time. Are you staying with the Murrays?"

"No, I've got a room over on Montagu Street. I'm starting in at the paper tomorrow morning."

"I can reach you there, I guess," Rhett said. "Hey. See that boat coming along there?" He pointed out toward the river.

A launch, painted white with an American flag prominently displayed at the stern, was moving down the channel, not too far from the sea wall. It was a jaunty-looking craft, more like a workboat than a yacht, and Mike could see two people seated out on the deck.

"The guy that owns that is an English professor at the College," Rhett said. "He just had it built."

"'Build me straight, O worthy Master! Stanch and strong, a goodly vessel . . .'" Although he had majored in journalism at W&L, Mike had taken numerous literature courses, and was given to quoting verse.

While they were talking, Betsy and her parents arrived back from church. Mr. Murray was affable, even jovial, more so than Mike had previously seen him. He joked to Rhett about Betsy's having a boyfriend who didn't even know how rice was supposed to taste, and had never smelled pluff mud. "We'll have to civilize him!" he said, chuckling. Mrs. Murray apparently belonged to the same garden club as Rhett's mother, and she spoke of her as if they were familiars. Mike had the feeling that they were trying to impress his friend, for what reason he had no idea.

At dinner that afternoon, which was served by a Negro maid in a light gray uniform with white collar, Mrs. Murray did most of the talking, mainly about various people they had seen at church. It was odd that the Murrays, despite their wealth and prominence and Mr. Murray's even being the mayor pro tem of Charleston, seemed to be so intent upon knowing certain people. The citing of names, he thought, was not so much for his benefit — they meant nothing to him — as for each other's.

AFTER DINNER HE and Betsy went driving with her parents. The Murrays had three cars: a large black Packard sedan, a Cadillac which Mrs. Murray used, and Betsy's new Buick convertible, which her parents had given her for a graduation present. Mr. Murray drove the Packard through town and onto the Cooper River Bridge, an enormous cantilever structure with two spans that crossed high above the harbor; from the top of either span he could see the entire harbor and the ocean beyond. Afterward they drove through a town called Mount Pleasant and then over a low drawbridge to Sullivans Island.

As they crossed over the bridge, the harbor was in full view. Two destroyers were coming into port. "They ought to be out practicing sinking German submarines," Mr. Murray declared. He believed in a strong national defense. On the one hand he condemned President Roosevelt and the New Deal for what he said were socialistic programs, favoritism to labor unions, and wasteful spending policies. At the same time he advocated heavy expenditures for defense, and he railed against the isolationists; we needed an Army and a Navy second to none in the world, he declared, and we ought to give immediate aid to the British and take over patrolling the sea lanes off the North American coast. He'd told Franklin exactly those things, he said several times.

"Do you know President Roosevelt personally, Mr. Murray?" Mike asked.

"I'm talking about Franklin Poinsett," Mr. Murray said. Mike wanted to ask who Franklin Poinsett was, but Mr. Murray's tone of voice implied that everyone ought to know that.

On Sullivans Island was Fort Moultrie, where the Americans

had driven off the British fleet in 1776, and which the Federal troops had evacuated just before the Civil War broke out, crossing over to Fort Sumter. Mr. Murray drove through that part of the island rapidly. East of the Fort were block after block of beach houses, most of them built high off the ground. Several times they stopped so that Mr. Murray could inspect new houses which his company was building, and which bore signs reading "Another New Home by Murray" and, in smaller letters, "Murray Construction Co. phone 2-1365."

The people for whom one of the houses was being built were on the scene, and Mr. Murray went over and talked with them for a while. Mike couldn't hear what was being said, but there was laughter, and Mr. Murray was obviously quite jovial and good-humored.

"Who are they?" Mrs. Murray asked when he returned to the car and they drove off.

"Fellow named Saperstein. Runs a clothing store up on King Street. Made his money selling to niggers. It's getting to be a damn ghetto out here."

They drove over a narrow bridge across an inlet with white sandy beaches. Beyond it was the open ocean. "They're going to have to put in a better bridge if they expect to do much out here," Mr. Murray said.

"Isn't this where the British tried to cross over during the battle of Fort Moultrie?" Mike asked.

"I don't know," Mr. Murray said.

They were on the Isle of Palms. The road led past high sand dunes fringed with sea oats, and with occasional glimpses of the ocean between them. They arrived at an area with some stores, a boardwalk, an amusement park, and a pavilion. "Let's go for a stroll on the beach," Betsy proposed.

No, Mr. Murray said, he wanted to drive around. "You all go for a walk." He looked at his watch. "It's 3:45. I'll pick you up here at 5:00."

The Murrays drove off, and Mike and Betsy walked along a

wooden footpath between some dunes and down to the beach. It was broad, with a long, gentle slope. Beach umbrellas and beach chairs were everywhere, with towels laid over the sand, people talking and reading, bathers in the surf, children playing in a gully, and some young people engaged in a game of softball. Beyond the breakers the ocean was flat and calm. To the west, several miles away across the water, was Fort Sumter, and the low shape of another island, with a black-and-white striped lighthouse on it.

Up the beach there were far fewer people. They walked in that direction.

"Who's the Franklin Poinsett that your father keeps talking about?" he asked Betsy.

"He's our Congressman. He's very influential in Washington," she said. "He and Daddy are close friends. They went to Clemson together. He's my godfather, in fact."

There were no houses or buildings on that part of the island. He climbed the soft sand of a dune and looked; the palmetto trees, matted thickets, and vines looked like a tropical jungle. He halfway expected to see bananas and coconuts growing on the trees and paroquets visible in the foliage.

He watched the green Atlantic Ocean, stretching out before him to the horizon, and the breakers as they rolled ashore. In a way, he thought, the whole area, the city of Charleston and the surrounding islands alike, reminded him of the way that the West Indies were supposed to look. It wasn't just the palm trees and the beaches; there was a kind of untrimmed, sprawling, fecund look to everything. It was very different from the mountains around Roanoke — hotter, wetter, more unkempt. The air had a salt tang about it. The light dazzled off the surface of the water. Off to the west, a towering mountain of cumulus cloud was building, the lower clouds dark gray at the center, indicating that a thunderstorm was brewing. Did it rain regularly every afternoon during the summer, and did the sun shine so glaringly off the water? He wouldn't be surprised. It was unlike any other place he had ever been.

"I should have brought my sunglasses," Betsy said.

"'Fear no more th' heat o' the sun, Nor the furious winter's rages.'"

"It's not the heat. It's so bright that it hurts my eyes."

A cloud drifted over the face of the sun and the face of the ocean darkened. "'For this relief, much thanks,'" Mike said.

"Oh, you and your poetry," Betsy declared.

HE REPORTED FOR work shortly before noon on Monday. There were five other reporters on the news staff of the *News & Courier*, along with a sports editor, a telegraph editor, an assistant city editor, a city editor, and, in charge of all, a managing editor. All were male — the society pages were produced by women, but their activities were conducted elsewhere in the building — and all were older than Mike, although a couple of reporters were still in their late twenties.

He was given a desk with an old Underwood typewriter, and for the first several days his work consisted of rewriting obituaries and taking news of club meetings and the like over the telephone. His workday began at one P.M. and usually ended sometime between nine and ten P.M., Monday through Saturday. Three or four nights after work he drove over to Betsy's, and they spent a couple of hours together, sometimes going for drives out to the beach, where they went walking along the shore in the dark, and sometimes just sitting out on the sunporch of her home, listening to the radio and dancing a little. Her parents usually went to bed in the early evening, so that they were by themselves.

They spent a good deal of time necking. Several times during the first couple of weeks things got very torrid, and he had the feeling that he could have continued right on past the customary boundaries, but he was sure that Betsy was a virgin, and he didn't want to take advantage of her affection and trust. He had done it only once himself, with a girl at a weekend party up at Mountain

Lake when they had both had too much to drink.

Betsy had numerous friends, and several evenings after he got off work they went to parties. There was dancing, and no small amount of drinking. Most of the men worked in law firms or insurance companies, or sold real estate. Her friends talked a great deal about such things as the movies, automobiles, and sports, but very seldom about their work. He was surprised to find, too, that nobody seemed to have any interest in local history and the Civil War. Most of them appeared to be involved in horseback riding, and even though Betsy had given it up herself she still took considerable interest in what they said about it.

Her friends were amiable enough; out for a good time, they showed no particular tendency to make judgments and discriminations. Any friend of Betsy's was welcome. If she had come back from college engaged to some boy they didn't know, and knew nothing about, and who was a newspaper reporter, of all things, that was all right with them.

He enjoyed the company of the reporters on the paper far more. Several of them usually went out for dinner together, and often after work one or more of them stopped in at the Porthole, a tavern on Market Street near the waterfront, for a few beers. They seemed to know everything that was going on in town, and had irreverent things to say about the local politicos, the editor of the newspaper and the members of the family that owned the paper, and just about everything else. They also teased each other a great deal. Various people stopped by their table at the Porthole to chat, and there was much banter.

The only person on the staff that Mike didn't like was the assistant city editor. He was a moon-faced man in his thirties, named Moore, and he was absolutely humorless and devoid of imagination. Ordinarily he was not in a position to bother any-one, but occasionally when both the managing editor and city editor were absent, he was in charge of the news desk, and was given to finding all kinds of supposed flaws in style and usage in copy that was turned in. Among the reporters he was considered something of a joke. "Pay him no heed," Mike was advised. "If he tries to give you a hard time, just ignore him."

HE WORKED IN the office for a couple of weeks, doing rewrites, taking stories over the telephone, and being sent once to cover a civic club luncheon meeting. Then one day the managing editor told him to drive out to James Island and talk with a man named Frampton. It seemed that a road was scheduled to be cut through the ruins of the Confederate fortifications on the Secessionville battlefield, and Frampton and some residents of the area were trying to prevent it.

Mike had never heard of the battle of Secessionville until then, but he read several accounts of it, called the man, and arranged to go out to talk with him that afternoon. The area in question was on the road to Folly Beach, west and south of the Ashley River, about ten miles from town. He had driven out to Folly Beach at night with Betsy, but never before during the daytime. The country was flat, with enclaves of salt marsh and tidal creeks everywhere about, and with groves of palmetto trees and some oaks here and there. Some of the terrain was in farmland.

Mr. Frampton was a man in his sixties, who lived in a white two-story house with tall chimneys. He showed Mike a photograph taken during the Civil War, with the house clearly visible along with some earthen ramparts. In June of 1862 the Union army had attempted to move against the Confederate defenses at Fort Johnson, at the mouth of Charleston harbor, by landing a force southwest of the city. There had been a battle at Secessionville, and hundreds of men were killed on both sides before the invaders were driven off.

What was happening now was that a group named the Stono Hunting Club had bought an island immediately to the southeast of the battlefield, and was planning to build a lodge on it. To get out to it a causeway was to be constructed, and the route lay across a corner of the battlefield. Mike went out with Mr.

Frampton to look at the site. Although grown over with trees and shrubs, the outlines of the Confederate ramparts, which had been called Fort Lamar, were still clearly visible. A line of stakes, indicating the route of the road leading to the causeway, ran directly across the ramparts.

The day was hot, with the sun beating down upon the flat, sandy terrain and on the bordering marshland. Here and there were duckblinds. Tide was out, and the black mud of the exposed creek banks was inlaid with oily pools and pockmarked with the dens of fiddler crabs. White wading birds with long sticklike legs moved about in the shallows. There was no breeze; the air was thick with insects. He had seen some of the Civil War battle-fields in Virginia, including Chickahominy Swamp near Rich-mond, but compared to this one they appeared neat and tidy. It must have been thoroughly miserable to have waited behind the ramparts, in the scorching sunshine, for the coming of the Yan-kee invaders. "But 'twas a famous victory." It was amazing to him, too, that unlike those in Virginia, this was unmarked; no highway signs called attention to it, and no explanatory markers were in place.

Mr. Frampton and some of his neighbors were circulating a petition calling upon the county authorities to prohibit the road-way from being cut through the earthworks. So far they had some fifty signatories. There was no law on the books which for-bade the destruction of historic battlefield sites as such, but what they hoped was that the county could either persuade or order the hunting club to build their lodge elsewhere. The property containing the earthworks and the island belonged to an out-of-town corporation named Island Properties, which was located in Greenville, South Carolina. The corporation had been written to, asking that no easement be granted, but no response had been forthcoming.

Mike talked at length with Mr. Frampton, who showed him some wartime maps and let him copy a letter that his grandfather had written to a friend just after the battle, describing what happened. Then he drove back to Charleston, excited over what he had seen. He wanted to write a story that would arouse public interest in saving the battlefield.

He told the managing editor what he had found out. It would make a good feature for Sunday's paper, the managing editor said. He was to write the story, then arrange with the staff photographer to go out to James Island tomorrow and make some photographs of the scene, preferably with Frampton and one or two of his neighbors in them.

Mike telephoned several other people who had signed the petition and got comments from them. He called Greenville Information and tried to get the telephone number of the corporation that owned the land, but no such company was listed. He did get hold of the president of the Stono Hunting Club, however. "The whole thing is ridiculous," that worthy declared. "Nobody ever goes out there. It's all overgrown, and hasn't been used for years."

Mike wrote his story. In the lead paragraph he described how the weed-grown ramparts that had once stood fast against Union assault were now in danger of being breached and overrun in order to build a road for a hunting lodge. He told about the petition, quoted Mr. Frampton and others on why the site should be preserved and the hunting club president on why not, described the battle of Secessionville, and included most of the text of the letter by Mr. Frampton's grandfather.

Neither the managing editor nor the city editor was on duty when he finished the story. The assistant city editor, Moore, was manning the desk. He read the story and began objecting to various things in it. The lead paragraph, he declared, was biased; Mike was to present the fact that the petition was being drawn up, and omit reference to such things as weed-strewn ramparts that stood fast against Union assault, and now in danger of being breached and overrun, and so on.

Mike was taken aback, but he rewrote the lead. Moore objected to the revision as well; he was not to refer to "saving" the fort, for that constituted editorializing. He wrote the lead a third time, making it as flat and as impersonal as he could. Moore changed several words in it, then placed the story in the hold basket for Sunday. "If you want to write for a newspaper," he told Mike, "you have to learn to keep your personal opinions to yourself."

Later that evening the city editor was back on the desk. He picked up Mike's story, read through it, and called him over. "This is pretty good," he said, "but can't you liven up your lead some? It's awfully pedestrian. Get something in there about the fort withstanding attack, or the like."

One of the reporters, Jim Igoe, had observed the whole process. Put your original lead back on it, he advised. Mike substituted the lead paragraph he had first written, and turned it in. "That's much better," the city editor said. "Now you're giving the sense of what it's all about."

The assistant city editor, whose desk was next to the city editor's, gave no indication of having heard the exchange. He did not look up, but only continued working away.

THE STORY APPEARED at the top of the second section of Sunday's paper. There was a photograph of Mr. Frampton and two other men pointing to where the road would run through the earthworks, along with the wartime photograph showing the ramparts next to Mr. Frampton's house. Atop the story, in boldfaced type under the headline, was his byline: "By Michael Quinn." At breakfast Mike read the article through several times.

Betsy's father had also read the story, and he was not nearly so pleased with it. "You let that old guy Frampton take you in," he told Mike. "The damn property's been sitting out there collecting weeds and not doing anybody any good all these years, and now when somebody tries to get some use out of it, they get all worked up and start circulating petitions. What about the property owners? Don't they have the right to earn some revenue from their property? What's wrong with putting a clubhouse out there?"

"They don't object to the clubhouse on the island, Mr. Murray," Mike said. "They just don't want the road to it to go through the old earthworks."

"Where the hell else is it supposed to go? If they had to run that causeway all the way through the marsh from the highway, it'd cost them a thousand bucks just to haul in the fill dirt!" If the local residents wanted to preserve the earthworks, he said, they should have bought the property and fixed it up. "Hell, nobody even knows it's there. It's nothing to see — just a little line of mounds out in the marsh."

It was getting so, he declared, that you couldn't dig a hole in your own backyard without somebody complaining about it. "You can't preserve everything that ever happened. You'd think the county was nothing but a damn museum." Whenever anyone tried to do anything worthwhile, he said, there was always a bunch of do-gooders on hand to object. "Some guy who's never done a day of hard work in his life starts sounding off, and the papers play him up like it was Jesus Christ come back to raise the dead."

Mike pointed out that more than one person was involved; there were at least fifty names on the petition. Mr. Murray snorted. "People will sign anything if you ask them. How about the property owners, and all the people in the hunting club who'll be using the lodge? Don't they have any say?"

He was irate. There was no point in trying to discuss the matter rationally with him. Mike went out onto the front porch and watched the sailboats in the river.

"Don't argue with Daddy," Betsy said afterward. "Just let him talk."

THE NEXT EVENING, at the Porthole, he mentioned Mr. Murray's reaction to his story to several of the reporters. There was laughter. "You know who's got the contract to put that road through and build that clubhouse, don't you?" Jim Igoe asked.

Mike shook his head.

"The Murray Construction Company, that's who."

Mike was amazed. "How do you know?"

"I ran into Allen Grimball at City Hall this morning, and he was talking about it. He says Turner Murray would put a filling station on the High Battery if he thought he could make some money on it."

It turned out that the reporters on the paper all knew a great deal about Betsy's father. If Mr. Murray appeared to dislike and disapprove of newspapers and newspapermen, for their part Mike's colleagues did not care for him, either. "Whenever Turner Murray smiles," somebody said, "it always reminds me of the silver handles on a coffin." "Turner Murray," another reporter remarked, "gets what he wants."

Mike was surprised to discover that despite their wealth, their imposing home on Murray Boulevard, and Mr. Murray's status as mayor pro tem of the city, the Murrays were by no means solidly positioned within the community's social establishment. Not only were they not originally from Charleston, but their status as communicants of St. Michael's Church was of relatively recent date. "They used to be Baptists," Mike was told. "They turned Whiskeypalian and joined St. Michael's about ten years ago. Since then he's given them a bunch of money for this and that, just like he's given money to the Gibbes Art Gallery and the College. What he wants is to get invited into the Yacht Club and the St. Cecilia Society. He's trying hard, but they've got a long way to go yet."

Mike recalled the way Mr. and Mrs. Murray had seemed to be buttering up to Rhett Jervey. Rhett was a Deke at school — the right credentials. Doubtless the Murrays weren't exactly thrilled when Betsy announced that she was going to marry a boy from Roanoke, Virginia, who didn't even belong to a fraternity and was a Roman Catholic to boot. The Murrays would just have to learn to live with it.

Still, it was hard on Betsy. No doubt she was being placed under considerable pressure — more than he had realized. It was up to him to try to minimize the cleavage between him and her father, to the extent that he could. But he could not and would not compromise his integrity and independence as a journalist. No indeed. Not for all Mr. Murray's money. Not even for his daughter.

3

AT THE CHARLESTON Library Society on King Street, tea was served each afternoon at five, typically with Allen Faucheraud Grimball featured. He was not an employee of the library, but he was often to be found there doing antiquarian research, and whenever he was present at a social gathering he held center stage, with his thick black beard, booming voice, and dramatic gestures.

On an afternoon in late June, Rosy and Sara Jane Jahnz were at work in the library, making notes on the activity of Civil War blockade runners from a harbormaster's record book that Sara Jane had tracked down, and when tea-time came they joined the group in the anteroom off the librarian's office.

"How do you do, Rosy?" Allen Grimball called out as they came into the room. "I trust things go well for you?"

Rosy's acquaintanceship with Allen Grimball went back to their childhood years. Their families had both resided on the same block of Pitt Street. They had been classmates at the College of Charleston. Allen had taken a law degree at the University of Virginia, but had never practiced. Descended from early Carolina settlers, he made of his colonial ancestry and social prestige a way of life, and was renowned in local circles for his encyclopedic knowledge of colonial and early national plantation architecture, and of local antiquarian lore in general.

"Pretty good, Allen. What do you hear from Gwen these days?" Gwen was Allen's sister.

"She's still out there in California. I don't see how she stands it. I'd just as lief live in a nudist colony. By the way, I understand you've taken to the water. You must let me conduct you on a tour of the Cooper River plantations aboard your boat some time." He had edited a book chronicling the early low-country plantations and their proprietors, most of whom were related to him in one way or the other.

"That's an idea." Rosy and Sara Jane were handed cups of tea by the librarian and took seats over by the window where Allen joined them.

"I see," Allen declared, "that the chairman of your board of trustees has once again demonstrated his consummate regard for safeguarding our historical heritage."

"Who, Turner Murray?"

"Didn't you see the story in Sunday's paper about cutting a roadway through the ramparts of Fort Lamar, out at Secessionville? It's Murray's company that's going to do that work."

"I didn't realize that. Did you, Sara Jane?"

Sara Jane shook her head. "No. I didn't, either."

"I assure you it's so," Allen Grimball said. "It is astounding that a boor like that could be associated with an institution of higher learning, in any capacity other than that of janitor. The law specifying that an elected official shall be chairman of the College board of trustees was enacted during an era when only gentlemen were eligible for public office. Nowadays, when the merest wastrel is considered fully capable of voting, the law needs to be emended."

"He's been pretty generous to the College, though," Rosy said. "He's given us several nice gifts." Rosy didn't especially care for Murray, but when Allen began sounding off he liked to play the devil's advocate.

"You mean bribes, not gifts. He hopes Page Carter will put him up for the Saint Cecilia. I don't believe the man has ever given away a dollar bill in his life without an ulterior motive."

"At least he gives it away. That's something."

"Let him keep on, however," Allen said. "I'll fix his wagon properly. The next time he comes up for reelection I'm going to prepare and to distribute a pamphlet showing that he is lineally descended from a family of mountain grills, the lowest of the low, whose male members were not only deserters from the Confederate Army but made a living distilling pizen whiskey and selling it to both sides."

Rosy laughed. The notion that a pamphlet on Murray's supposedly lowly ancestry would influence most local voters was typical of Allen Grimball.

"And I'll tell you this, too," Allen continued. "In these days of debased standards and sham gauds, money may go a long way indeed. I personally have never felt the lure of it. With wealth comes care, and I prefer my independence. But so long as I am able to cast a ballot, there will never be enough money printed or coined to secure W. Turner Murray's admission into Hibernian Hall on the night of the Saint Cecilia Ball! Why, one might as appropriately induct the Three Stooges!"

Afterwards, Rosy drove Sara Jane home. "Do you suppose Allen really believes all that?" she asked.

"I don't think believes is quite the right word. Allen doesn't live a life; he lives a novel, and he's the principal character."

"Was he like that as a child?"

"Pretty much. We all played together — Allen and his sister Gwendolyn, and the two Magwood boys, Edward and Henry, and a boy and girl , and Buddy Ostendorff and myself. We were all between eight and ten. Allen tended to be stuck on himself even then, and Gwen, too. But we took it out on them. You know how kids have names, euphemisms, for bodily functions? Well, instead of saying Number One and Number Two, we used to say we had to do Gwen B. and Allen B. It got to be second nature. We'd say it without thinking."

Sara Jane laughed. "I must admit," she said, "that I share his opinion of Turner Murray."

"I know you do. But that's Page Carter's problem, not ours."

Rosy thought about Allen Grimball and what he had said. Why, he wondered, had Allen felt quite free to go on about Turner Murray's ambition to be invited into the St. Cecilia Society, and how he intended to keep Murray out? As a Jew, Rosy was ineligible for such membership; Allen knew that very well. One might think that he would therefore refrain from discussing such matters in his presence.

The truth was that Allen considered the social distinction he possessed to be so thoroughgoing and absolute that no normal, rational person who lacked it would ever remotely aspire to it. Therefore he could discuss the impudence, as he saw it, of Turner Murray's desire to enter that lofty social orbit without for a moment offending Rosy. It was as if he were a Roman Catholic commenting upon the forthcoming election of a Pope to a Protestant or a Mohammedan.

What was amusing about Allen was not merely the importance that he placed upon ancestral caste, but his assumption that everyone else shared his valuation of it. Never for a moment did it enter his mind that either Rosy or Sara Jane, who as a Lutheran of German descent was also not part of the city's social establishment, might not be unduly concerned over who might have owned a particular Cooper River plantation in 1789.

"Are you going to let Allen take you on a plantation tour of the Cooper River?" Sara Jane asked.

Rosy laughed. "Of course! On one condition — you've got to go along, too."

"Never! Think of being penned up on a boat with him and having to listen to ancestral history!"

"Would it be worse than having to listen to me on the harbor defenses?"

"Much worse," Sara Jane said. "At least you don't talk about who General Beauregard married."

ooooo

IN THE DAYS that followed, Rosy spent much of his time aboard his boat. More accurately, he spent comparatively few of his waking hours elsewhere than on his boat. He brought some books aboard. He used the dinette table as a desk to answer his correspondence. There was much work to be done on the boat and the dock. The normal tidal range in the harbor was five feet or more, so that at low tide considerable agility was required to climb down from the dock to the boat, and vice versa. One of his first projects, therefore, was to construct a ladder and anchor it firmly to the wharf. He also built a bookshelf to go into one corner of the cabin, a cabinet to keep belongings aboard, and another, over the sink, for supplies.

Several times he took the *Gilmore Simms* out for runs about the harbor, and he practiced backing into the slip, but mostly he stayed at the dock. He liked being aboard the boat. He enjoyed working on her; it had been years since there had been any occasion for such physical labor — not since his father had died and he had sold the house on Pitt Street almost a decade earlier. His muscles were sore, and there were little cuts on his hands and bruises on his arms, but he was pleased with himself and his boat.

"THAT'S NOT JUST a boat Rosy's got," Dolf Strongheart remarked to his wife Linda after dropping by Adger's Wharf one afternoon to see how the operation was going. "It's a religious experience."

"Surely he can't keep working on the boat forever," Linda said. "Eventually he's going to run out of projects."

"He can always get a bigger boat."

"What does Sara Jane have to say about it?" Linda asked.

"I think it amuses her. She always finds it very funny the way that Rosy gets going on a project and spends all his time and energy at it."

"It's too bad that Rosy doesn't think of Sara Jane as a project."

"It's too bad," Dolf said, "that Sara Jane isn't a boat."

THE CAMPUS OF the College of Charleston was tranquil in the summer. There were a few classes being held, mainly of the makeup variety, but otherwise the corridors of the main building, and the lawn and cistern in front of it, were free of students. Oak trees, with long limbs draped in Spanish moss, shaded much of the lawn from the direct sunlight.

On a morning in early July Rosy strolled through the gate-house, along the shell-covered pathway, and walked up the stone steps of the library building annex. Sara Jane Jahnz, at work behind the circulation desk, looked up as he entered.

"I'm surprised to see you over here during the day," she said. "I thought you'd joined the merchant marine."

"The carpenter's union would be more like it," he said. "Would you like to go out for a run this evening after work? I'll ask Dolf if he and Linda can come along."

"That would be nice."

The door to the library opened and a tall, thin man entered. "Good day to all!" he said. Thomas Lowndes was associate professor of history at the College. He had a long face and carefully trimmed moustache, and he was dressed in a tan Palm Beach suit with bow tie. From his somewhat balding head he removed a straw hat with dark green band, and held it in his hand. "Have you heard the news?" he asked. "It seems that we now have a dean."

"A dean?" Rosy asked. "Who?"

"A gentleman by the name of McCracken. That is, I trust he's a gentleman. There's a letter from our good president in the mail announcing his advent."

The College had never had a dean. There had seemed no need for one. Such administrative direction as was needed was provided by the president.

"What do you suppose a dean will do?" Sara Jane asked.

"Whatever it is that deans usually do," Lowndes said. "He'll find something to do, never fear."

"Where is he from?" Rosy asked.

"Greenville, originally. But he's been at one of those Midwestern schools. Illinois, or Indiana, or Iowa— one of those 'I' places."

"Are you sure he's not from one of those 'O' places, Tom?" Sara Jane asked. "Oberlin, Ohio State, or Oxford?"

"I was just kidding," Tom replied. "He's a psychologist."

"A psychologist? But we don't even have a psychology department," Sara Jane objected.

"Then he'll set one up. Perhaps that's his mission."

A LITTLE LATER Rosy walked over to the main building. There were three letters in his mailbox, one from a student asking him to write a recommendation, another from a book company announcing publication of a freshman English textbook, and one to the faculty and staff from President Carter:

Dear Colleagues:

On behalf of the Board of Trustees it is my privilege to announce that on July 1 Dr. N. Joseph McCracken will join us as dean of the faculty and professor of psychology.

Dr. McCracken comes to us from Iowa State College, where he has been associate dean. He is a native of Greenville, South Carolina, and holds the B.S. degree from Furman University, the M. Sci. Ed. degree from the Virginia Polytechnic Institute, and the Ph.D. from Western Reserve University. He has taught at Concord State College, Muskingum College, and Iowa State.

I am sure that all of you will join Mrs. Carter and myself in welcoming Dr. McCracken, his wife Artesia, and their children, Sibyl Ann, Goldie, Joseph, Jr., and Floyd, to our midst.

Cordially,

Page Burwell Carter
President

A strange business. The background of the dean — degrees in psychology and science education — seemed to be quite unlike anything that he should have thought would appeal to Page Carter. It was as if the president, a passionate sailor and commodore of the James Island Yacht Club, were suddenly to give up sailing and announce the acquisition of a houseboat.

Rosy pondered the matter as he walked across Greene Street to the onetime residence that served as Dolf Strongheart's zoology laboratory and office. Dolf's lab contained a number of aquaria and cages. Turtles were his specialty. When Rosy entered, Dolf was standing in front of a large glass case, open at the top, intently observing its contents. The floor of the case was mainly water except for a bank of soil at one end. There were several small pieces of tree branches lying on the bank and leading down into the water, and a plant of some kind with broad leaves. On one of the branches a small turtle with a smooth gray shell reclined, and the head of another turtle was thrust up above the surface of the water. "What have you got here?"

"*Sternotherus odoratus,*" Dolf said. "Stinkpot to you."

"That's what Tennie Carter calls motorboats. Why do they call the turtles that?"

"Because, beloved colleague, when annoyed it emits an effluvium that makes sun-ripened limburger seem like Chanel No. 5. It can also bite the shit out of one's finger, if one is not careful."

Rosy watched the turtles for a minute. "Where did you get them?"

"Out in the woods. They're all over this part of the country."

"Seems a bit cruel to keep them penned up in there like that."

"Cruel? From a turtle's standpoint," Dolf declared, "it is pure Elysium. It's got nice muddy water, a limb to bask on, the equivalent of three square meals a day, a partner of the opposite sex for purposes of venery, a place to lay its eggs — no troubles, no foes, no vexing cares and concerns. What more could a turtle ask in life?"

"Freedom, perhaps?"

"What is freedom to a mud turtle? Do not anthropomorphize Mother Nature's creatures."

"I came by," Rosy said after a moment, "to see whether you and Linda would care to join Sara Jane and myself for a boat ride this evening."

"I should think so," Dolf said. "I'll call Linda, and see if the maid can stay on. What time?"

"Any time after five. When Sara Jane gets off work. Can you give her a lift?"

"Certainly." Dolf walked out toward the front door of the building with him. "What do you think of the news about a dean?" he asked.

"Astounding. Did you have any idea it was in the works?"

"None whatever."

"And a psychologist to boot," Rosy said. "When we don't even offer courses in psychology. Tom Lowndes thinks Page may have decided that his faculty needs psychological therapy."

"He isn't that kind of psychologist," Dolf declared. "He's a behavioral psychologist — a rat runner. They're not interested in people. All they care about is how rats behave in mazes."

"You mean he'll do experiments with rats?"

"With white rats. Plain, ordinary rats won't do."

"Where will he get them?"

"He'll order them," Dolf said. "They'll be kept in cages, and the students will give them names. Eventually a few will escape, and take up with the local rats, and your native city's long tradition of selective miscegenation will be honored anew in our time."

"I believe I prefer your turtles," Rosy said.

"Think of it. Importing rats into Charleston, South Carolina," Dolf mused. "Talk about coals to Newcastle — the next thing you know, somebody will start importing cockroaches."

THE STRONGHEARTS AND Sara Jane arrived at the wharf a little before 5:30. Rosy helped them down onto the deck. Linda

Strongheart had not seen the *Gilmore Simms* since the day of its launching, and then only from outside. She was much taken with the arrangements — the dinette table which converted into a sofa, the sink and ice chest, the stove, the enclosed head, the vee-berths in the forward cabin. "It's divine!" she declared. "It would be just perfect for a couple to take a trip. Don't you think so, Dolf?"

"Yes indeed," Dolf agreed.

"Why, you could live aboard it!" Linda said. "You could go wherever you want, stay as long as you like, and be captain of your boat and your fate! Of course," she added, "you'd need a mate."

The lines were freed and the *Gilmore Simms* nosed out from her slip and turned toward the harbor. The late afternoon was sunny, with no overcast and very little breeze. Rosy listened for the throb of the engine. He was always nervous upon first operating a boat. At the boatbuilder's suggestion a rebuilt Dodge truck engine had been installed in the *Gilmore Simms*. It turned seventy-five horsepower, quite enough to move his boat through the water at a comfortable nine knots.

The 130-foot-high Town Creek span of the Cooper River Bridge lay a mile ahead. The freighter *Shickshinny* was tied up alongside Union Pier, a skiff at her stern aboard which two men were applying black paint to rust spots along the hull. Upriver by the Standard Oil Company wharf the tug *Barrenfork* nosed against the side of a tanker.

They cleared the buoy at the north end of Drum Island, turned eastward and then southeastward, and moved down the channel off Hog Island along Shutes Reach and Folly Reach. Up ahead Rosy noticed something in the channel. At first he thought it was a floating log. Then it disappeared, only to reappear again a few yards away.

He called to Dolf, who was out in the cockpit with Linda and Sara Jane. "Take those glasses" — he pointed to a pair of binoculars in a wooden box affixed to the bulkhead — "and see what that thing in the water up there is."

"Where?" Dolf held the binoculars to his eyes and focused them. "Over there to port, about a hundred feet away."

Dolf swung the binoculars. "I don't see . . ." Then, after a moment, "*Caretta caretta*! Stop the boat! It's an enormous loggerhead!" He hurried out onto the stern. Rosy took the engine out of gear and followed him outside.

Dolf leaned over the side of the cockpit and peered through the binoculars. "A huge loggerhead turtle!" he said. "Just ahead!"

Linda and Sara Jane came over to look. "I don't see anything," Linda said after a minute.

"It's gone under. Keep an eye out. It'll come up again."

"There it is!" Sara Jane said, pointing just off the port quarter. The head and part of the neck of a large turtle was thrust out of the water, not twenty feet away, its oval-shaped eyes gazing at them. They could see its body just beneath the surface, cream-green in hue, and its flippers. It appeared to be a yard in length at the very least.

"What a splendid carapace!" Dolf declared.

Linda tossed a cracker toward the turtle, upon which it promptly disappeared under the water. "I don't think it likes Ritz crackers," she said.

"There it is again," Sara Jane said after a minute. The turtle's head was in view some fifty feet beyond the stern.

"I thought it lived out in the ocean," Linda said. "What's it doing in Charleston harbor?"

"Turtles," Dolf explained, "haven't changed their way of doing things in two hundred million years, so can you think of a city where a turtle would be likely to feel more at home?"

The turtle disappeared beneath the surface of the water again. "Do you want me to try to follow it?" Rosy asked.

"No," Dolf said, "I had a good look. Wish I'd brought my camera, though. Magnificent creature. I've never seen one quite that large. He must weigh three hundred pounds. Or she."

The cruise was resumed. They moved down the Rebellion Reach channel until they were almost at the mouth of the harbor, then turned westward and proceeded along the south channel toward the city. The James Island shoreline lay off to port, beyond the marsh. The Carters' place was back along the shore, on one of the creeks leading through the marsh. The masts of their forty-foot ketch and a white boathouse were visible over against the line of trees.

Tennie Carter — her given name was Hortense —was scathing on the subject of powerboats, particularly speedboats with outboard motors. There were several hydroplane races held out in the harbor each year, and she likened the noise of the outboard engines to saxophones, a musical instrument that she despised. "It's as if several hundred tenor saxophones, all playing the same note, were honking around in your front yard for three hours at a time," was the way she described the races off the Battery, across the river from her house.

She was a marvelous hostess; she could give a reception for a hundred guests and make them feel at home and at ease. She also liked to entertain small groups of her friends as well. In the company of those she could trust, she was outspoken and irreverent. A New Englander, she had delicious things to say in private about the local mores.

Rosy thought again about how out of character it seemed for Page Carter to be bringing in the new dean. There had been no announcement of the fact that they were even looking for such a person. The appointment of a dean was an administrative decision, but one would have thought that the question of offering courses in psychology would have been taken up at a faculty meeting first, before anyone was brought in to teach them. He could think of several members of the faculty who might object strongly to the idea of courses in psychology being added to the curriculum for the new dean to teach, without a faculty vote on whether to do so.

He turned the boat toward the waterfront and they moved past the Battery and the Carolina Yacht Club toward the wharf. The cargo launch was gone from the slip next to his, which made things easier. This time he managed to put the stern into the slip. Sara Jane lifted a line off the piling, attached it to a cleat, and the *Gilmore Simms* was guided into place with relatively little difficulty.

Afterward they sat around on the stern, sipping drinks and talking. Dolf discoursed on the subject of sea turtles. The one they had seen in the harbor, *Caretta caretta*, or loggerhead, was a coastal turtle, which could grow up to four feet long, and weigh as much as half a thousand pounds. An even bigger sea turtle in the area was *Chelonia mydas*, known as the green turtle, which lived out in the ocean. It could grow to as much as five feet or more in length, and live to be a hundred years old or even longer.

During the hot months of the summer, he said, the females come ashore on beaches at periods of high tide to lay their eggs in the sand. What was remarkable was that even though they might swim thousands of miles out in the ocean, they always returned to the beaches where they were originally hatched. They clambered up the slope of the beach beyond reach of the tides, using their flippers to push themselves along, dug pits and deposited their eggs, then covered up the eggs with sand and returned to the sea.

"How can they remember which beach to come back to?" Sara Jane asked.

"No one knows. But they always do."

"Does this happen on the beaches around here?"

"Yes indeed."

"Let's go out to the beach some night and watch them," Sara Jane proposed.

"They're not likely to come to a beach where there are homes," Dolf told her. "It has to be one that's not built up. You know," he said, turning to Rosy, "you could take us to one in your boat."

"At night?" he shook his head. "I wouldn't think of trying to find my way behind some island at night."

"We could go during the day," Linda said, "and bring tents and camp out for the night, and come back the next morning."

"Why not?" Dolf declared. "What could be more romantic? A night under the stars, on a deserted beach, watching *Chelonia mydas* fulfill her maternal role. She is waiting at the shingle! Won't you come and join the dance?"

"What fun!" Sara Jane declared. "Let's do. I'll bring the mosquito lotion!"

"There must be a beach nearby where you can take us in the boat," Dolf insisted.

"I'll have to look on the charts and see," Rosy said.

"We've got a couple of tents," Linda said. "And we can borrow more."

"You provide the boat," Dolf told Rosy, "and we'll bring everything else."

ROSY CONSIDERED THE matter that night. It was all very well to talk about finding an island where those turtles might come and lay eggs, and camping out on the beach, but taking a boat into water that he didn't know, where he could easily run aground, was another matter. And even if he could find such an island, would there be enough water alongside to get close enough to the shore? Suppose the engine broke down when they were out there. How would they get back? They could be stranded for several days.

If they were to go on the turtle expedition, it was good that Sara Jane would be along. Unlike Dolf, she knew how to handle herself aboard a boat.

THE NEXT MORNING Rosy found a navigation chart showing the harbor and the surrounding area and spread it out on the dinette table. The Inland Waterway ran behind a chain of barrier islands along the coast. There was an island just beyond the Isle of Palms, with an inlet showing deep water between them. It was only a mile or so from the Inland Waterway. He knew nothing at all about the island, which was named Dewees, but he could ask around. Captain Magwood, who operated the White Stack tugboats, would probably know all about it.

Sea turtles laying eggs on a moonlit beach. What a curious business!

4

TO MIKE QUINN'S disappointment, no public outcry followed the publication of his story about the projected roadway through the ramparts of Fort Lamar. The principal result of its appearance was the breach in the relationship between Mike and his fiancée's father. If until then Mr. Murray had not seemed overjoyed at his continued presence in the house on Murray Boulevard, now he was no more than barely polite.

"He'll come around," Betsy told Mike. "He's just got to be handled the right way. Don't worry about it."

On a Saturday night in July they went out to the Folly Beach Pier to go dancing with several other couples. Jan Garber, "the Idol of the Airwaves," and his band were performing. Mike didn't finish work until after nine o'clock. They drove out in Betsy's convertible to join the others. He did the driving.

The pier was built out over the water. Jan Garber's band played in a shell midway down the roofed-in pier, and couples who were not dancing sat at tables around the dance floor. It was warm, but there was a breeze off the ocean. Unlike the bars and clubs in the city, there was no bar selling drinks, but set-ups were available, and everybody had brought bottles in paper bags.

Betsy's friends were already in high spirits when they arrived. They danced for a while, and sat around listening to the music. The conversation mostly had to do with horses; the other couples were enthusiastic riders, and they were recounting the doings at the Carolina Cup at Camden that spring. "You should have been there, Betsy," somebody said. "Elliott Mikell was taking the jumps like clockwork. At the hunt breakfast somebody said he must have been practicing long and hard for the race, and he said, 'Not me. I don't need to practice. I just naturally rise to the occasion!'"

They laughed, although Betsy did not seem to think it was particularly funny.

"Betsy, what did you ever do with that little black mare you used to have?" somebody asked. "Didn't you take her up to school with you last fall?"

"I sold her last spring."

"Who to?"

"A man in Charlottesville, Virginia."

Betsy had told him that she used to ride at home, but he had-n't realized that she had taken horses up to Sweet Briar with her. If she had sold the horse in the spring, that was after they had begun going together.

The band was back on the stand after an intermission. The Idol of the Airwaves waved his wand, and the music began. "Oh! 'I'll Never Smile Again'!" Betsy declared, jumping to her feet. "Let's dance!"

They went out onto the dance floor. Betsy loved to dance. It was not one of Mike's favorite activities, and he was not good at it. She didn't seem to mind, however. She sang as they danced:

> *I simply can't concede*
> *You aren't in love with me*
> *My heart will always need*
> *Our love that used to be*

The floor was filled with dancing couples. The saxophones, wide-throated and reedy, burbled away. The Idol of the Airwaves swung his baton lightly. A female vocalist, tiny, with jet black hair and a low-bodiced gown, moved to the microphone and warbled the lyrics. Betsy rested her head against his chest as they danced, his arm around her body and shoulder. Her body was so small and supple, and her light olive skin firm and beautiful.

The song ended, and everybody applauded. The band began another number. "This one's too fast for me," he said, and they made their way back to the table. "The Gypsy Man is looking for you," Betsy sang as they sat down. Another couple came back to join them. The girl sat down across from them. "Betsy, let's you and me dance this one!" said the boy, whose name was Billy Hugenin. She jumped up and they headed for the floor.

"I'd ask you to dance, but I'm not up to anything beyond a foxtrot," Mike explained to the girl, Annie; he couldn't remember her last name.

"Oh, that's all right. I'd just as soon listen."

They watched as Betsy and Billy Hugenin danced away, deftly and rapidly in time to the fast beat, swinging out and then in.

"How did you come to meet Betsy?" the girl asked.

He told about about encountering her at a fraternity party in Lexington. "I called her up the next week and asked her for a date," he said.

"What fraternity did you belong to?"

"I didn't belong to one," he said. "I just happened to be invited to the party. Lucky for me, she was there."

The girl seemed to be shocked that he wasn't a fraternity member.

Betsy and Billy Hugenin came back to the table. The band members were leaving the bandstand for intermission. "Care to go out and look at the water?" he asked Betsy.

"Okay."

They walked outside the partly enclosed dancing area and onto the deck. It was dark, and various couples were standing along the railing. Down below he could see the edge of the land where the last wave had fanned out before retreating. "Let's go further along," he said. They walked toward the ocean, the surf twenty-five feet or so below them, breaking and curling in irregular gray-white fringes. They could hear it roaring even over the blare of the music inside. The beach nearest the water seemed jet black, with the light from the pier reflected back from the moist sand.

The roof of the pier extended out over the railing, so that the area of the deck nearest the walls of the dance floor was in complete dark. There were giggles and whispered voices; more than one couple were taking advantage of the blackness.

The ocean stretched out before them. They stood at the railing. As his eyes grew accustomed to the darkness, he could see that out beyond the surf, the surface of the water was lifting and falling in long, low waves. Here at the ocean's edge it was a long way from the mountains of Virginia.

"I like the smell of the ocean. Don't you?" he asked.

"I don't know. I guess so. Why?"

"No reason in particular. You probably don't notice it, because you're used to it."

He drew her to him. Well out to sea there was a light of some kind, a ship probably. Or was it? "When I look at the ocean at night I always think I can see lights, or shapes of some sort," he said. Betsy's firm body was pressed against his own. He felt himself growing hard. He thought of suggesting that they step back into the shadow next to the wall. He felt sure Betsy wouldn't object. Just then the band inside the pavilion began another set.

"Listen! They're playing 'In the Mood'!" Betsy declared. "Let's go inside!"

He removed his arm from around her, and they walked back into the dance floor. The lights seemed blinding. He blinked his eyes. "That's pretty jumpy music for me to dance to," he said.

"Oh, come on," she told him again. "Don't be a wet blanket all the time! Try it!"

He followed her out on the floor, and did his best to keep up with her, but it wasn't really his kind of music.

ooooo

ON THE DRIVE home from the dance he steered with one hand, his right arm around Betsy's shoulders. She was still humming the last number the band had played, Count Basie's "One O'Clock Jump." He hadn't dared try dancing that with her.

"Wasn't the band divine!" she said.

"It was okay." In point of fact he hadn't thought much of the music. It was too saccharine, and the lively numbers too jerky and squeaky.

"I wish you'd dance more."

They pulled up before the guard rails and stopped. He shut off the motor. The drawspan of the bridge began swinging out in the darkness, a red light on the end. He looked up and down the creek. To the west a searchlight was playing on the edge of the marsh. It was very bright. After a minute he could make out the throbbing of an engine. Apparently a tugboat was pushing a barge.

He drew Betsy to him and they kissed. The tip of her tongue brushed his lips. His insides were quivering, and he could feel Betsy's firm breast under his hand. One of her hands lay along his thigh, and her fingers were pressing into his flesh. Then the chrome rim of the convertible windshield flared bright from the headlights of another car which pulled up behind them.

"Hey, Betsy, watch it up there!" a male voice called out, and there was laughter. It had to be the two couples with whom they had gone dancing. Betsy giggled. She disengaged herself from his arms, and turned around and waved.

"You want a beer?" the voice called.

"Sure!" she called back.

There was the sound of a car door opening, and after a moment Billy Hugenin came up alongside them. "Here you are," he said. "Nice and cold!" He held out two bottles of Pabst.

Mike handed one to Betsy. "I better not," he told Billy. "I'm driving. Thanks."

"It'll keep till you get home. Take it!"

He sat, holding the open bottle in his hand, until the tugboat and barge passed through the draw and the drawspan returned to position. After a minute the guard rails swung up and the traffic lights changed to green. He handed the beer to Betsy and started the engine. The last thing he needed just then was a beer. He had already had more to drink than he should. They drove across the bridge and on to Charleston.

By the time they reached Murray Boulevard she had finished the beer and drank part of the one she was holding for him.

"Oh shit!" Betsy said as they were driving up to her house.

"What's the matter?"

"Nothing, I just don't feel well."

He parked the convertible at the side door of the house. "Shall I come in?" he asked.

"No, I'm feeling sick. I'll see you for dinner tomorrow."

They kissed goodnight, and Betsy went inside the house. As he drove off he wondered what would have happened if Betsy's friends hadn't pulled up behind them while they were waiting at the bridge. Betsy had seemed very passionate. It must have been that last beer that had made her sick. It was too bad that he didn't like to dance more than he did.

THE NEXT MORNING, as he dressed and left for early Mass at St. Mary's, he felt depressed. It was a sunny day, and the female churchgoers were dressed in pastels and light colors; the men wore seersuckers. He had the sense of being shut off, removed from everything around him. He didn't like going out with Betsy's friends. It was his fault, in part at least, that he didn't particularly enjoy dancing. But it wasn't just the dancing as such; it was the syrupy band, the sitting around, the drinking, the meaningless chatter and inanity of the whole thing.

When Mass was over he drove over for breakfast at the chili parlor on the corner down from the newspaper office. He bought a paper and read it while he waited for an order of hotcakes. The front page was filled with war news. The Germans were continuing their bombing of England, and the Royal Air Force was launching night attacks on Germany. The election was heating up. The Democrats were preparing for their convention next week. The President had made no announcement yet about whether he would run for a third term, but the Republican candidate, Wendell Willkie, was sure that he would, and was attacking him for wanting to do it.

The two local Congressional candidates had both made speeches. The race for Congress was between the incumbent, Franklin Poinsett, who was Mr. Murray's friend, and a man named Howard Wade, who lived in the town of Moncks Corner, about twenty-five miles north of the city. The Democratic primary, which was what mattered, was scheduled for late July. There were rallies, speeches, advertisements in the newspapers and over the radio; along the highways, on the sides of buildings, in the windows of unoccupied stores were posters proclaiming the virtues of the two candidates and displaying their pictures: SEND FRANKLIN POINSETT BACK TO WASHINGTON. EXPERIENCE COUNTS; and VOTE FOR HOWARD WADE FOR CONGRESS. THE PEOPLE'S CANDIDATE.

As he was reading, Jim Igoe walked into the restaurant and joined him. "Except for a paper-thin wafer and a sip of tap water, I haven't had a goddamn thing to eat or drink since suppertime yesterday," he declared as he sat down. A short, stocky, profane man in his late thirties or early forties, Igoe was the *News & Courier's* police reporter. He was a bachelor, and like Mike a Roman Catholic.

He asked Igoe who he thought would win the Congressional election. "Franklin Poinsett," Igoe declared. "He's a shoo-in. Sitting on that Military Affairs Committee, and people know there's going to be a war — they're not about to send somebody else up there. Give him a couple of more years, with the war coming on, and he'll turn the city into a garrison town. Defense jobs by the thousands. Nobody's in his right mind's going to vote against that."

"Do you think we'll actually get in the war?"

"You damn right we will," Igoe said as he waded into his scrambled eggs. "Not a chance we'll stay out. I give it two years at most, depending on what the Japs do out there."

"Betsy's father and Poinsett are supposed to be good friends," he told Igoe.

"No fooling! Where'd you get that idea?"

He reported what Betsy had said.

Igoe grinned. "I'm just kidding you, kid. Everybody knows Turner Murray and Franklin Poinsett are buddies from way back. They say when either one of them belches, the other farts." He laughed. "You're marrying into a family with connections, my friend."

Igoe had a fund of stories about goings-on, local and otherwise, and in voicing his opinions was no respecter of the city's political and social hierarchy. "What you got to remember," he had told Mike one evening at the Porthole, "is that this is a wicked old seaport city. It's been like it is for two hundred goddamn years, and it's not going to change any time soon."

NOT LONG AFTER he arrived in Charleston, Mike had come upon an oddity. One Sunday the Murrays were out dining with friends, and he and Betsy had eaten dinner at Henry's Restaurant. The waiter had asked whether they might like anything to drink, and he had ordered a glass of beer.

"Sorry, sir, but we can't sell beer on Sundays," the waiter told him.

"What do you have, then?"

"Most anything you like," the waiter said. "Martini, whiskey sour, Manhattan, gimlet. . ."

He had ordered Scotch and water, and had puzzled over the customs of the community. When he told Jim Igoe about it, his friend had a ready explanation. "They don't want to lose their beer license, that's why. The hard stuff's illegal to begin with, so that doesn't count."

"But how can they sell whiskey, if it's against the law, but not beer?"

"Because," Jim Igoe said, "there's a state law saying that selling beer's okay except on Sunday. That's enforced. But the law doesn't allow selling whiskey. So they pay off to keep from being closed up."

"Closed up by whom?"

"By the state."

Mike didn't understand. "Who do they pay off to?"

"The city. The cops. There's a regular scale. You pay a certain amount per month to the city not to get raided."

"But if it's a state law, how can the city keep the state from enforcing it?"

Jim Igoe shook his head. "Hell, you don't think the state police could stage a raid in Charleston without the city police knowing it was coming, do you? The word comes down, the cops notify the bars and grills, they stash the stuff away, and there's no evidence. They tried it once or twice when Olin Johnston was governor, then they gave up."

"There's certainly nothing like this where I come from," Mike said. "Not in Virginia."

"You come from Roanoke, don't you? Ever spent any time in Norfolk?"

"No, I haven't."

"Try it sometime. I tell you, seaports are different. I bet you don't have a red-light district up there in the hills, either, do you?"

"Not as such," he said. "You can pick them up, down near the market."

"That's what I mean," Jim Igoe told him. "It's on an individual basis. There's no streets like West or Beresford where you can walk down the goddamn block at night and there's red and blue lights in the windows and slots in the front doors. But in Virginia Beach or Norfolk now, they can fix you up. And if you don't know where to find it, just ask the nearest cop." He laughed.

"You got a lot to learn about this area, kid. They might call it the Holy City, but Sodom and Gomorrah's also within the corporate limits."

MIKE LOOKED AT his watch. It was almost noon. He wondered how Betsy was feeling after last night. She'd had quite a lot to drink. If she had gone to church with her parents, he would sit out on the porch and watch the sailboats, which were out in force on the river.

He drove over to Betsy's house. When he arrived Betsy was in the living room, in her bathrobe, reading the paper.

"How do you feel?" he asked.

"Blah." She looked wan.

They sat in silence for a while. She was obviously hung over. "I think I'll go for a little walk," he said after a time. "Want to come along?"

"I'm not dressed."

"I'll wait for you. Go get dressed. Come on, it'll do you good."

She shook her head. "No, I don't feel like it."

He went out of the house and walked across Murray Boulevard. The tide was low, and there were banks of oyster shells in view all along the rocks. Out in the river sailboats were maneuvering around a buoy. He had never done any sailing. If he lived down here very long, he would have to learn. He walked along the sidewalk next to the railing toward the Lighthouse Station. It was a bright day, with a brisk wind; the sailboats were heeled far over.

Across the river he could see the trees on James Island. Somewhere over there was the entrance to Wappoo Cut, where they had waited for the tug and barge to go through. Betsy's mistake was probably drinking that beer, after the whiskey they'd been drinking at the dance. How did it go, beer on whiskey — or was it whiskey on beer? Whichever it was, he wished that Billy Hugenin hadn't given her the beer.

When he returned, Betsy had dressed, but she still seemed subdued. "Let's go out for dinner," he told her.

"No. I don't want to."

They sat for awhile. "Look," he said finally, "is anything the matter? Did I do something wrong?"

She shook her head.

"Well, what is it then? Did you have too much to drink last night?"

She grabbed a magazine and threw it to the floor. "Shit!" she said. "It's my *period*! You're so damn dense!"

He was stunned.

She said nothing. They sat in silence.

"Is there anything I can do?" he asked.

"No. I'll be all right. Just leave me alone." She stood up. "I'm going upstairs and lie down."

"That's a good idea," he said. "I hope you feel better. I'll call you tomorrow."

Betsy went into the house. The screen door slammed behind her. At least he wouldn't have to eat with the Murrays. He drove off, still in a state of shock. That her menstrual period was making her so cross had not entered his mind. He knew that it was supposed to be worse for some women than others. And all that booze didn't help, he thought.

"You're so damn dense!" he repeated to himself.

HE CALLED HER the next afternoon. She was feeling better, she said. He apologized again for his insensitivity. "Shall I come over after work tonight?" he asked. No, she told him, she was still feeling somewhat played out. Tomorrow night she had to go to a meeting. "Let's do something special Wednesday night," she said.

"RUN OVER TO Sullivans Island," the managing editor told him when he came in to work on Tuesday, "and see if there's been any effect out there on business now that the Eighth Infantry's gone. Al Myers is on vacation. Talk to a few store owners and realtors." Al Myers was the reporter who ordinarily covered the news east of the Cooper River. The Army's Eighth Infantry Regiment, which had been stationed at Fort Moultrie since the end of the World War, had recently been transferred to Fort Benning, Georgia.

He drove across the Cooper River Bridge and through Mount Pleasant, then across to the island. He stopped in at several grocery stores and rental agencies. The proprietor of Wurthmann's Pharmacy had most to say about it. Few of the army families had left yet, he said. Most of them were planning to move in August or early September, in time for their kids to start school in their new homes. The impact wouldn't be felt by the merchants until then, when the summer beach season was over.

He talked to several other people on Sullivans Island, then drove over to the Island of Palms to see what the situation was there. He needed some gasoline, so he pulled into a service station, and while the tank was being filled chatted with the owner, who had pretty much the same story to tell.

While they were talking, a large black Packard automobile rolled up to the gas pumps. Mr. Murray got out, along with another man. It was Congressman Poinsett.

Mr. Murray did not seem enchanted to see him, but he introduced him to Poinsett. He was a wiry little man, with a full shock of light brown hair. "You're a lucky young man!" the Congressman told him. "That's a mighty fine girl."

Thinking that Poinsett might have a comment to make, he told Mr. Murray and the Congressman about the story he was working on. He was right. "There's no need to worry about that!" Poinsett declared. "You can be sure that there'll be plenty of people looking for homes to rent all over the area. I can promise you that Charleston's going to be in the forefront of our national defense effort. This is just the beginning."

"May I quote you?" he asked.

"Yes, indeed. Charleston's strategically situated to play a major role in the defense of the hemisphere, and I intend to see that its advantages are fully utilized. Isn't that so, Turner?"

"That's right," Mr. Murray said.

The Congressman went inside the station to shake hands with the employees. Mike paid for the gas and drove back to town.

Before he wrote the story he asked the managing editor whether he ought to feature what Poinsett had said. "No, I don't think I'd do that," the managing editor told him. "Get it up into your story, but don't lead off with it. That'd make it a political plug. He's been saying that every speech he gives, anyway."

While he was at work on the story the telephone rang. It was Mr. Murray. "When you write about what Franklin said, don't say that I was with him," Mr. Murray told him. "I don't want it to look like I'm involved in the campaign."

Mike had no intention of including Mr. Murray in his story anyway, but the request, the order really, annoyed him. Mr. Murray seemed to think he could tell him, not ask him, to omit mention of his name.

Besides, if what Jim Igoe said was correct, Turner Murray's ties with Franklin Poinsett were common knowledge.

ONE OF THE reporters on the newspaper told about a night club out on the Folly Road, the Beachcomber, which he said had a first-rate jazz combo. It seemed like something Betsy would enjoy, so he called her Wednesday and they made plans to go after he got off work.

When he arrived he was glad to find that she was in high spirits. They went in his car, driving out along the Folly Road and found the place. There were a number of cars parked in front. They went inside and were shown to a table against the wall. They ordered a pitcher of beer. The combo was black — tenor sax, trumpet, drums, and piano. It was a hot night, and the room was smoky, and the music seemed to fit the occasion.

They were every bit as good as reported. It was exciting to

hear and to watch. They played one number after another, took a break, then came back for more and yet more. He and Betsy sat against the wall close to each other, sipping beer, sometimes holding hands, and taking in the music as if it were air they were breathing in. It wasn't music for dancing. At one point the sax man did announce that they were going to do the next numbers just for that purpose, and they played part of a set in easy tempo. Mike went out onto the floor with Betsy and they danced, but even then the music had a clarity and line to it that made him want to not do anything except listen.

The evening went by. The heat kept them thirsty, and the cold beer was sweet, but since he was going to drive home he made himself hold back. Betsy drank several glasses to each one that he sipped. She was having a marvelous time, laughing and drumming her fingers to the music and sometimes grasping his hand tightly. It was like it had been after they were first engaged, only more so.

When it was time to go and they got back in the car, his clothes were sticky and drenched with perspiration, and when he held Betsy's arm it too was hot and moist. They drove off, with Betsy snuggled against him, humming and singing "Perfidia." "Oh, they were so good!" she kept saying. This time there was no hold-up at the bridge, and they headed for the city. He drove down the other side of Murray Boulevard, made a U-turn around the grass divider, and then up to the front of her house.

"Park in the back," Betsy said.

"How come?"

"My parents are in Greenville and I don't want the neighbors to talk."

The whole thing began to look very exciting. "Maybe I ought not come in at all," he said.

"Don't be silly."

He steered around her convertible, which she always parked in the driveway under an overhanging roof at the side door entrance, and into the backyard. They got out, went up the stairs to the back porch in the dark, and she removed a key from her

Louis D. Rubin, Jr.

purse and opened the door. The house was dark. They went into the kitchen. "Don't turn on the kitchen light," she said. She stepped across the room and into the hallway, and turned the hall lights on.

He took off his coat. The damp shirt clung to his skin. "I'm soaked through," he said. He felt a little chilly, even.

"Me too. Would you like a beer?"

"What I'd like is a tall glass of water. I'm dehydrated."

"I'll fix it. Go on into the living room."

He went into the living room, laid his hat and coat on a chair, and sat down on the couch in the partial darkness. His shirt was sopping wet. After a minute she joined him, a glass of ice water in one hand and a beer in the other. He took the glass and drained it. Betsy drank a sip of beer, placed the bottle on the coffee table, and immediately turned into his arms. They kissed, then kissed again. He felt the tip of her tongue against his. They locked in an embrace. His tongue sought the roof of her mouth. He was very hard. We'd better stop now, he thought. They held each other for a minute, his hand cupping her small, firm breast. He felt Betsy's hand removing it, then guiding it down, deliberately placing his hand between her thighs. He pressed his fingers into the hollow, deeper, then after a minute pushed back her skirt, felt the sheer of her hose. What were they going to do? She was drunk, he thought. She continued to press against him, and he kept holding her.

Then Betsy pulled her lips away from his. "Let's go upstairs," she said. She stood up, took his hand and pulled him to his feet. He followed her up the staircase and into a room. He was so hard that it was difficult to walk. He felt awkward as they stood there in semidarkness before the bed. The only light was from the hall downstairs. "Just a minute, sweetheart," she whispered. She opened a door and disappeared behind it.

In scarcely any time at all she emerged from beyond the door. She wore only a short, almost transparent nightgown that came barely down to her knees. Even in the half-light the nipples of her breasts were visible through it. He put his arms around her, and

60

she kissed him. "Don't you want to get out of those wet things?" she suggested. Clumsily, his insides trembling, he undressed. She climbed into the bed, then reached her hand down to take hold of him, and they lay against each other. "Oh, sweet lover, I want you," she whispered, and they began to make love.

IT WAS WELL after three in the morning before he drove home. He felt drained. He had made love to Betsy, in her own bedroom, and not once but twice. They had slept together. And she had wanted to. She was not drunk. The whole thing was changed now. They were lovers.

He parked the car, unlocked the front door, went up to his room, and began undressing. His clothes were still damp. What had happened the second time was incredible. After they had made love, he had felt so sticky and perspiring that he had asked whether he could take a shower. He had gone into her bathroom, stepped around her things on the tile floor and into the shower stall, and was standing under the shower with the water pouring down on him, when the curtain was pulled back and Betsy had stepped right into the shower with him, naked. She hadn't said a word. They had stood together, holding each other, for a minute, with the water splashing over them, then she had reached down and taken hold of him. They turned off the shower, dried themselves, and returned to the bed. It had been wonderful.

While they were lying in her bed after the first time, he had thought about what would happen if her parents suddenly put in an appearance, even though they were supposed to be in Greenville. Obviously that hadn't worried her for a moment. That was Betsy's way, to act spontaneously.

He thought about the possibility that she might become pregnant. He had nothing to use. Surely the thought must have occurred to her too, before they had gone too far. But she loved him so much that she must not have cared.

5

ROSY PARKED HIS car on East Bay near Broad Street and went into the Carolina Savings Bank to deposit his salary check. Broad, or that portion of it from the Post Office at Meeting to the Old Exchange building fronting it on East Bay, was the city's legal and financial district. The pace of life along the thoroughfare was unhurried. At almost any given time one could find the sidewalks on both sides of the street, from Meeting to East Bay, lined with clusters of conversationalists.

Emerging from the bank, Rosy spied Herbert Simons and Edward Kohn engaged in conversation in front of Demos' Restaurant, and he crossed over to ask where the poker game was to be held Saturday night. Customarily it convened at Simons' house on Versailles Street, but during very hot weather they sometimes drove over to Ray Larrabee's summer place on Sullivan's Island to play.

Simons, a realtor, was a small man with mischievous eyes that twinkled when he made witticisms, as he often did. Edward Kohn was city editor of the afternoon newspaper; his expression was always grave, but he too could get off amusing remarks.

"Rosy, I wanted to ask you a favor," Simons said as he came up. "A few years ago I was on a boat out in the harbor, just this side of Fort Sumter, and I dropped a cigarette lighter overboard. The next time you're out there in your boat, would you mind seeing if you could find it for me?"

They laughed. He was always amused to watch how much Simons enjoyed his own witticisms. "Is your boat large enough for the poker club to play on it?" Simons asked.

"It would be a pretty tight squeeze. There's only so much room inside the cabin, and we couldn't very well fit all eight people out on the deck."

"Oh, that's all right," Simons came back immediately, "we'll bring our own deck!" His eyes twinkled as he laughed.

"Where are we playing this week?"

"Over at Ray's."

It was agreed that either he or Dolf Strongheart would pick up both of them up for the drive across to the island — probably Dolf, since his automobile was a sedan. "I'll call Dolf," he told them.

Dolf always drew tremendous pleasure from the poker game. There was a delightful enthusiasm, and a kind of naiveté, to everything he did. In certain ways, too, he was extremely gullible; Simons and Kohn in particular sometimes led him on with cock-and-bull stories. He always took them in good humor, however. Introducing Dolf to the Saturday night poker club when he moved to Charleston five years ago was one of the better things he had ever done.

Simons and Kohn departed up Broad Street, and Rosy was about to return to his car when Allen Grimball came walking around the corner of East Bay. "Come and have a cup of coffee," he proposed. "I have good news."

Rosy followed him into Demos' Restaurant and they found seats in a booth near the door. "You'll be delighted to know," Allen said, "that Alastair Wystan has accepted our invitation." Allen was president of the Poetry Society, of which Rosy was the vice president. Alastair Wystan was a British poet now living in New York.

"That's fine. When can he come?"

"The first week in November. We'll have to take him up to see the Cooper River plantations."

"Are you sure he'd like that?"

"How could he not?" Allen demanded. "He's a poet."

Rosy was about to suggest that not all poets might be interested in old plantation homes, when Jim Igoe, a reporter on the morning paper, came into the restaurant, in company with a young man whom Rosy didn't know. "Come join us," Rosy said to Igoe.

The reporter introduced his companion, whose name was Mike Quinn. He was also a reporter on the *News & Courier*, Igoe said, having just joined the staff. He was tall, dark-haired, and thin.

"I believe that you," Allen told the young man, "wrote the story about the Secessionville battlefield, did you not?"

"Yes, sir, I did."

"An excellent piece of writing, in yet one more hopelessly lost cause," Allen said. "I drove past there the other day; the road has been cut right through the ramparts. Absolutely disgraceful. One might as well attempt to roll back the ocean as to preserve an historical site in Charleston County from the greed of the nouveau-riche."

"Mike," Jim Igoe said, "is engaged to Turner Murray's daughter Betsy." Jim had obviously spoken up at once to forestall embarrassment.

"Did you work on another paper before you came to Charleston?" Rosy asked the young man, in order to change the subject.

"No, sir. I just graduated from Washington and Lee University in June."

"Oh." Rosy asked him whether he had taken any course from Francis Pendleton Gaines.

"No, sir, Dr. Gaines doesn't teach classes. He's the president."

"You might know Gaines's book on the Southern plantation," Rosy said to Allen Grimball.

"Oh, I do indeed," Allen said. "An interesting work." With that Allen was off and running. He talked about the plantation, cotton and rice culture, and the ruinous impact of cheap lands in the Old Southwest upon antebellum Southern plantation society. "We blame the Yankees," he declared, "and I hold no brief for them. But the seeds of our destruction lay within.

Ownership of a plantation and slaves was an institution for gentlemen, and by making it possible for every log cabin-born mountain grill to buy a few slaves and set up as a planter we laid ourselves wide open to the enemy."

"Wasn't Jefferson Davis born in a log cabin, Allen?" Rosy asked. Amused as always at Allen's version of history, he couldn't resist sticking in an occasional barb.

"There are exceptions to any rule," Allen said. Undaunted, he went on about *noblesse oblige*, the honor of the gentleman, and the erosion of traditional Southern society before the leveling forces of democracy and materialism. With easy money from cotton profits in the Deep South came greed, he declared, and an end of public virtue.

"What did you think of the movie of *Gone with the Wind*, Allen?" Rosy asked, as if he hadn't already heard Allen on the subject several times.

"A preposterous farrago of every cliché about plantation society ever uttered. An appalling falsification. Neither David O. Selznick nor that female sentimentalist who wrote the novel knew anything about Southern society before the War. By comparison *The Wizard of Oz* is sound historical documentation!"

While Allen was orating, Rosy glanced over at Jim Igoe, who winked at him. Igoe was also enjoying the spectacle. The young newspaperman, Mike Quinn, a puzzled expression on his face, was listening intently to what Allen was saying.

"All set for the hurricane season with your boat, Rosy?" Igoe asked when Allen Grimball next paused for breath.

"As ready as I'll ever be, I suppose." He really ought to find out what precautions to take, Rosy reminded himself, now that it was getting well into July. August and September were the prime hurricane months.

"Well, we've got to be going," Jim Igoe declared, and stood up.

"Me, too," Rosy said. "I'll be seeing you, Allen. Keep me posted on the plans for November." He followed Igoe and the young reporter out of the door.

"Old Faithful. Never fails to spout on schedule," Igoe said, laughing, as they left. "That's part of your initiation to Charleston," he told the young man. "Along with pluff mud and cockroaches. Right, Rosy?"

"Absolutely."

ROSY CROSSED THE street, walked half a block down to his car, and drove over to the campus. He parked on Greene Street and went into the main building and upstairs to the administrative office to check his mail. Page Carter was there, looking tanned and fit from his sailboat racing in New England. They chatted for a few minutes, and Page went into his office. Rosy looked in his mailbox and found there a cream-colored envelope containing a printed invitation.

> *President and Mrs. Page Burwell Carter*
> *and the Board of Trustees*
> *of the College of Charleston*
> *request the pleasure of your presence*
> *at a reception in honor of*
> *Dean and Mrs. Nathan Joseph McCracken*
> *Sunday, the twenty-second of September*
> *at four o'clock*
>
> *Grand Ballroom*
> *The Fort Sumter Hotel*

The Grand Ballroom.

He wondered whether the new dean was on the scene yet. The secretary, Miss Mouzon, reported that he was due to arrive at any time.

He walked across Greene Street to Dolf Strongheart's laboratory. In the somewhat larger building, also at one time a private residence, next door to the small building housing Dolf's entourage, there was the sound of hammering and sawing.

Dolf was seated at a table looking through a microscope. "Just one minute," he said. He adjusted a knob on the microscope, peered intently into it, then wrote something on a yellow tablet.

"What's up, comrade?" Dolf asked.

"What are you looking at?"

"*Rana clamitans* has had a blessed event, and I'm taking a census." He produced a pair of eyeglasses from his jacket pocket, held them up to the window, breathed on the lenses, extracted a handkerchief from a pocket in his trousers, and wiped them clean.

"Who's Rana whatever-it-is?"

"A green frog. I keep them outside in a pool. There will be tadpoles in a few days. Want to see?"

"No thanks. I suppose you got an invitation to the reception?"

Dolf nodded.

"What's going on next door?"

"That's where the dean's rat lab's going to be located," Dolf said. "The house has probably got more rats in it now than he'll ever need for his experiments. Tell me, have you been able to find an island where we can observe *Chelonia mydas* in action?"

"There's a possibility. I've got to find out some more about it."

"Please do. If we camp out overnight, would it be all right if we brought the kids along?"

"By all means. I assumed you would. If we can figure out a way to get there."

HE STOPPED IN at the library. Sara Jane Jahnz was standing behind the counter talking with Tom Lowndes. As always he was dressed immaculately. Today he wore a dark green jacket, striped flannel trousers, and a bright plaid bow tie that matched his hatband. Rosy felt sure that Lowndes must own a dozen straw hats. They chatted for a little while. "Well, I must go and see what the mail has produced," Lowndes said. "Ta-ta!"

Sara Jane had likewise received an invitation to the reception.

"The unveiling of the new dean!" she said. "The Grand Ballroom, too."

"Shall we go together?"

"I'd be delighted. Dolf came by earlier today," she said. "He's very eager to go out and watch those sea turtles laying eggs."

"Dolf thinks we can just pull up to an island and go ashore, without worrying about going aground or good holding ground or anything. I've got to find the right place. Do you know anything about Dewees Island?"

"It's the one just beyond the Isle of Palms, isn't it? People go out there to watch birds, I believe."

Rosy promised to check into it.

HE TALKED ABOUT Dewees Island with Captain Tunker Magwood, who operated the White Stag tugboats, and learned that the inlet between it and the Isle of Palms was frequently used by shrimp boats and was amply deep. The current, however, was quite strong, and Rosy would do well to anchor his boat in the creek just in back of the island and row ashore. As for a rowboat, he was welcome to borrow the skiff tied alongside the wharf and used only infrequently for work on the tugboats' hulls. The island itself was uninhabited, Magwood said; people went over there sometimes to fish in the surf or watch birds. There was no dock of any kind.

Rosy asked about hurricane procedures. What most people did was to take their boats up one of the nearby rivers or creeks, tie up close to shore where the land and trees screened off the full force of the wind, and ride out the blow.

Rosy found the prospect daunting. He had no idea where to take the boat, and he certainly did not wish to remain aboard while a hurricane was in progress. He could only hope that the occasion would not arise.

FRIDAY NIGHT HE took Sara Jane to dinner at Henry's. He told her about Allen Grimball's performance at Pete Demos' restaurant, and of his automatic assumption that because Alastair Wystan was English and a poet he was certain to be interested in plantation homes.

"He'd better be," Sara Jane said, "because with Allen as his host, he's going to get the full treatment, ancestors and all."

"Allen wasn't so bad when Carl Sandburg was here last spring."

"Sandburg was from the Midwest, and a Swede to boot. Allen probably decided he was a hopeless case to start with."

Rosy told Sara Jane that he was planning to resume his work on the harbor fortifications. If it wasn't too hot on Sunday morning, would she be free to go?

Yes, she would, Sara Jane said.

On the way home they drove through a thunderstorm, with lightning and thunder blasting all about. It was still raining hard when they pulled up in front of the house on Logan Street in which her apartment was located. While they were waiting for the downpour to slacken, Rosy reported what Captain Magwood had said about the course of action to be taken in the event of a hurricane.

"That's all very well if you're a commercial waterman like the other people who keep their boats at Adger's Wharf," Sara Jane said, "but it doesn't sound like anything you ought to do. I think you'd just have to tie the boat with good strong rope right there at the wharf and hope for the best."

"Maybe I can get Allen to come along and help me."

Sara Jane was amused at the idea. "I'm afraid that after a few hours of being cooped up with Allen's ancestors, you'd be sorely tempted to abandon ship."

Rosy laughed. "It'd be like 'Old Ironsides':

> *Nail to the mast her holy flag,*
> *Set every threadbare sail,*

And give her to the god of storms,
The lightning and the gale!

"Speaking of which," Sara Jane said, "I think I can make a run for it now. You needn't walk me to the door, I can manage. I'll see you on Sunday morning."

"Ten o'clock?"

"I'll be ready," Sara Jane said.

SATURDAY EVENING ROSY was waiting in front of the hotel when Dolf Strongheart arrived shortly before seven P.M. They drove out to get Herbert Simons, who lived at the far northwest end of the city. Dolf was delighted with the news about Dewees Island. They would go on Sunday a week, it was agreed, if the weather forecast was good.

Herbert Simons's house had been built in the 1840s, and was located on a bluff overlooking the marsh and the Ashley River. There was a grove of huge oak trees to one side of it. As they pulled into the circular driveway, several limbs were lying on the ground. Last evening's thunderstorm, Simons said after getting into the back seat of Dolf's car, had felled several branches. It was dusk, there was a breeze rustling the oaks, and the early evening sky was clear.

They headed downtown. As they passed the baseball field at College Park a small tree, obviously recently transplanted, lay on its side next to the sidewalk. "Any news about the hurricane?" Simons asked.

"What hurricane?" Dolf asked.

"The one off the coast."

Rosy was about to say that the nearest hurricane was reported to be in the Windward Islands, more than a thousand miles away, when he felt Simons's hand jabbing him in the back. He remained silent.

"You mean there's a hurricane off the coast?" Dolf asked.

"That's what the radio said," Simons replied.

"When's it due to come ashore?"

"They don't know. It could be any time, or it might not come at all."

"Too bad I don't have a car radio," Dolf said as he drove along. Rosy felt Simons nudge him in the back again.

"Do you think we ought to go out there on the Island?" Dolf asked after a few minutes.

"We'll see whether Edward has any further word about it," Simons told him.

They turned off Rutledge onto Bennett, passed the side of the Charleston Museum, where there were a number of brown palmetto tree limbs on the grass that last night's storm had knocked loose, and drove up to Edward Kohn's house. He was seated on the front porch waiting for them. As he climbed into the back seat, Herbert Simons asked, "Did you hear anything more about the hurricane?"

"No further developments," Edward Kohn said. "They're keeping a close watch."

Rosy wondered whether Simons and Kohn had planned it out ahead of time. He decided that they probably hadn't; Kohn had known instinctively what to say.

They drove across town toward the Cooper River Bridge. "How did your boat do during the storm last night, Rosy?" Simons asked.

"All right."

"If this hurricane hits, I hope you've got it tied down good," Kohn said. "I remember the 1911 hurricane. There were boats stacked all up and down East Bay Street before it was over."

Dolf Strongheart was more than usually quiet as he drove. They turned off Meeting Street onto Lee. The steep approach to the bridge lay ahead. As they neared it, a gust of wind blew a piece of newspaper across the street.

"The wind's beginning to pick up," Simons said.

"It looks like it," Kohn agreed.

"The worst hurricane," Simons said, "was back in 1893. There was no warning whatever. It killed more than a thousand people out on the islands between here and Savannah."

"In 1911 the mosquito fleet was caught offshore," Kohn said. "Before they knew it, it was on them. Some of them made it back, but not all, and even after they reached the harbor several more boats were lost."

They drove up the incline of the Cooper River Bridge. There was always a breeze blowing atop the bridge. "Can you hold it on the road all right?" Herbert Simons asked Dolf.

"So far it's not bad at all," Dolf said.

They reached the top of the west span. The illuminated waterfront lay below. Several miles to the southeast the lights of Sullivans Island were visible.

"Do you see anything?" asked Dolf, his eyes trained on the roadway ahead.

"I'm not sure," Edward Kohn said. "It's getting very dark off to the south."

As they drove down the slope of the west span three cars passed in the opposite direction, headed for the city.

"Looks like they've started to evacuate the Island," Herbert Simons said.

At the base of the span, where the roadway led across Drum Island, they saw a Navy destroyer moving seaward along the Cooper River channel. "They're heading out to sea to ride it out," Simons declared as they began the climb up the east span.

They topped the span. "How does it look now?" Dolf asked. Again Rosy felt Simons nudge him.

"It's getting darker," Kohn told him.

"It doesn't seem so bad up here," Dolf said.

"These things can come up very suddenly," Simons remarked. "One minute it's perfectly calm, and then it's on top of you before you know it."

They passed several more city-bound cars. "I don't blame them for leaving," Kohn remarked. "The island's no place to be during a hurricane. In 1927 the water was four feet high all over the first two rows of houses."

"It was worse than that in 1893," Simons said. "People were trapped in their houses for six hours, until the tide receded. It's the tidal surge that does the damage."

At the far end of the slope lay the toll booth. Dolf braked to a stop. "Here," Edward Kohn said, handing him a couple of dollar bills. Dolf thrust his head out of the window. "Round trip," he told the attendant as he gave him the money. "What's the latest on the hurricane?"

"I don't know anything about it," the attendant replied as he handed him a ticket and a fifty-cent piece in change.

"That damn fool! He doesn't even know there's a hurricane!" Dolf declared as they drove off.

Rosy bit down on his lip.

Dolf was driving noticeably faster as they passed through Mount Pleasant. Several more cars went by. "You don't suppose they've already left, do you?" he asked.

"Unless they've been listening to the radio, they may not even know about it," Herbert Simons said.

When they reached the causeway leading out to the bridge over the waterway behind Sullivans Island, people were graining for flounder, and several bright lights were visible out in the marsh. "What's that?" Dolf asked.

"They're firing off rockets," Edward Kohn told him.

There were small red lights at each end of the drawbridge platform. "They've got the warning lights on," Herbert Simons said.

"Yes. Look up on the water tower," Edward Kohn said. "They're on there, too." Atop the high water tower of Fort Moultrie a red aviation warning light blinked on and off.

They crossed the low bridge and drove eastward along the road, several times passing cars headed in the other direction. The oleanders along the roadside swayed and dipped from the sea breeze as they sped by.

"I wouldn't go too fast, Dolf," Herbert Simons cautioned. "The way things are tonight, you can't tell when a car might pull out in front of you." The light wind from off the ocean was causing the branches of the palmettos along the road to lift and toss. "It's really blowing now," Simons commented. "This thing sure came up fast."

They reached Station 24, turned into a side road, and drove along it until they came to the driveway to Ray Larabee's summer house, set back behind the dunes along the beach. Dolf turned into it. Two other cars were already there. Ray and several of the regulars were standing on the landing of the back stairs.

The low roar of the surf out beyond the dunes in front of the house was audible. Dolf pulled to a stop, threw open the car door, and leaped out. "Come on!" he called to the men on the landing. "We've got to get out of here before the hurricane hits!"

"Hurricane? What hurricane?"

It was a cloudless night. The stars were twinkling in the clear dark sky. Palmetto fronds rustled softly. The surf rumbled its monotone.

Herbert Simons and Edward Kohn began laughing. So, too, did Rosy. "You sons of bitches!" said Dolf Strongheart after a minute, looking at his companions, then at the sky overhead.

"You bunch of lousy, cocksucking bastards!" He looked at the sky again. "You goddamn shitheads!"

Then after a moment he began to laugh, too.

SUNDAY MORNING ROSY and Sara Jane took the *Gilmore Simms* out to the point off Fort Johnston and spent several hours charting the approximate artillery trajectories. Rosy called out the ranges and Sara Jane recorded them. Rosy told her about the trick that Herbert Simons and Edward Kohn had played on Dolf.

"That was cruel!" she said, but she laughed and laughed. "Dear old Dolf. He *is* suggestible, isn't he?"

"He's better on turtles than on hurricanes," Rosy agreed.

ON MONDAY MORNING Rosy stopped by Dolf Strong-heart's lab. "Been in any good hurricanes recently, Dolf?" he asked.

"That's all right," Dolf retorted, "I got all three of you bastards back good and proper." Dolf had won all the money at the game Saturday night, thoroughly cleaning out Herbert Simons and Rosy and taking several dollars off Edward Kohn.

They went over plans for the expedition to Dewees Island. All was subject to the weather. If rain was predicted the expedition would be put off until another time. Dolf was enthusiastic; he was particularly anxious, he said, to take some photographs of *Chelonia mydas* in the process of digging a nest.

"Have you met the dean yet?" he asked.

"No. Is he here?"

Dolf nodded. "In the flesh."

"What do you think?"

"I'll let you find out for yourself."

"Is there something mysterious about him?"

"Not exactly mysterious," Dolf said. "But you make up your own mind. I don't want to deprive you of the privilege."

ROSY DID NOT have long to wait. When he went into the office to check his mail, a man was standing behind the counter, talking with Miss Mouzon. He was of medium height, with the beginnings of a pot belly. His face was full, with prominent cheeks; he was bald except for a fringe of red hair at the temples; he sported a set of ferocious eyebrows; and he was lobster-pink-complexioned.

"This is Dr. Rosenbaum, Dr. McCracken."

"Ah! It's so good to meet you. I've heard so very much about you!" McCracken extended a long arm toward him in awkward, almost wooden fashion, and they shook hands. "Now you're in . . . zoology, isn't it?" He grinned, displaying a set of large teeth and breathing out in a kind of hissing sound as he did.

"English," Rosy said.

"Oh yes, to be sure. I look forward with the utmost pleasure to working with you!" The new dean grinned and hissed again. He had an odd way of speaking; the diction was formal, yet the way that he pronounced the words seemed a little off-register.

"Are you all moved in yet?" Rosy asked.

"In a manner of speaking, yes. We've engaged a residence on Tradd Street, and our furniture arrives tomorrow. With luck, we'll have everything shipshape by the time that classes commence. I am most eager to resume my laboratory activity." He flashed yet another grin and hiss. He didn't exactly pronounce laboratory with the emphasis on the second syllable, in English fashion, but he stressed each syllable almost equally: *Lah-Boh-Rah-Toe-Ree*. It was as if the new dean had taken elocution lessons, Rosy thought as he walked over to the library.

Sara Jane was at work at the card catalog. Rosy described his meeting. "Definitely no run-of-the-mill variety," he said.

"Tom Lowndes thinks he must have passed a Dale Carnegie course with highest honors," Sara Jane told him.

"There's something peculiar about him. It isn't just his appearance or the way he talks, or even the grin-and-hiss. I can't put my finger on just what it is. "

"He talks as if he'd swallowed an unabridged dictionary," Sara Jane said, "and was having great trouble digesting it."

Rosy laughed. "Now don't be unkind."

"We're treating him like one of Dolf's laboratory specimens, aren't we?" Sara Jane agreed. "When we don't really know anything about him."

"You pronounce that *Lah-Boh-Rah-Toe-Ree*," Rosy corrected her.

"Now who's being catty?"

"True. We mustn't be jumping to conclusions. There's no rea-son to believe that anything's going to be different."

"Not with Page Carter still in charge," Sara Jane said.

All the same, Rosy thought, everyone *was* concerned. Into a known and bounded situation, an unknown had been introduced, like a hurricane looming up in what had until now been a largely tranquil ocean. In which direction might it spin?

6

"THAT, MY FRIEND," Jim Igoe told Mike Quinn as they walked along Broad Street after coffee at Demos Restaurant, "was a Charleston institution which might possibly help you to understand how the Civil War got started."

"He's amazing. Does he live on a plantation?"

"Allen Grimball? Not at all!" Igoe laughed. "His father ran a grocery store over on Wentworth Street. They lived right down Pitt Street from us. He's about seven years older than I am. I don't doubt he may be descended from half the signers of the Declaration of Independence, but he lives in an apartment on Lamboll Street. He inherited some money from an uncle in the lumber business in Oregon, so he's got enough investment income so he doesn't have to work, but he's no plantation nabob. Did you notice the way he affects to despise money? I expect that's because he'd like to have a great deal more of it than he has.

"I'm glad you heard that," Igoe added, "because it makes you understand what somebody like Turner Murray's up against. Not that I'm a cheerleader for your future father-in-law's way of doing things, you understand. But if Allen Grimball had his way they'd still be auctioning off slaves on Chalmers Street, and reading by sperm whale oil light."

"Why do you suppose he's so down on *Gone With the Wind?*"

Igoe laughed. "I've heard him on that topic more than once. Because it makes the plantation owners around Atlanta aristocrats, i.e., gentlemen. As far as Allen's concerned, the gentlemen all had their plantations down on the sea coast. The upstate planters were common people, riffraff — in other words, nineteenth-century versions of Turner Murray. Of course he doesn't like the idea of Rhett Butler being from Charleston, either. Wasn't that funny about Gerald O'Hara being nothing but a shanty Irish cardshark?"

"I kind of liked him, though," Mike said.

"I do too," Igoe said. "Allen's so preposterous that he's funny. Consider what was going on there. Here he was, having a cup of coffee with two fish-eaters and a Jew, and he's delivering a lament for the decline of the old aristocracy and the rise of the common man!" He laughed again. "When I said that it showed what Turner Murray was up against, I didn't mean Allen himself — even though he doesn't have any use for Turner, while Turner doubtless thinks he's a fool. I mean that some of the attitudes that you see comically exaggerated in Allen are still very much in circulation around town."

"Dr. Rosenbaum didn't seem to mind him."

"Oh, Rosy knows Allen from way back. They grew up together. Didn't you see him wink at me a couple of times?"

Mike remembered Rhett Jervey pointing out a launch out in the Ashley River and saying that it was owned by a professor at the College of Charleston. "Is Dr. Rosenbaum's boat painted white?" he asked.

"I believe so." Igoe told him about the the Civil War harbor expeditions. "He and the librarian at the College, Sara Jane Jahnz, go out there on a boat and take ranges on where the artillery batteries were located."

"That sounds like fun. I liked him."

"He's a good guy," Igoe said. "Call him sometime and get him to take you along. You could write a good story about it."

ooooo

MIKE WAS STILL overwhelmed by the developments with Betsy after they had gone to hear the combo. He kept going over what had happened in his mind. Not only had he never enjoyed sex like that before — compared to it, his one previous experience had been next to nothing — but as far as he was concerned it placed his entire relationship with Betsy on a new and more intensely intimate basis. She had given herself to him, held nothing back. The bond between them now would surely set aside her parents' objections to him as of no importance.

When he went over to see her the next day, he had felt a little awkward. But what had taken place seemed to have made no difference whatever, either in her behavior or her attitude. There was no sense that she thought anything of transcendent significance had occurred.

During the next couple of weeks they made love several times more, out on the sunporch late at night— not with the same freedom as the first time, to be sure, since her parents were upstairs asleep. But she knew exactly how to handle the matter. There was no clumsiness, no confusion. She had simply reached up and turned out the lamp over the sofa, and at the proper moment made room for him.

After that first unexpected time when her parents were out of town, of course, he came prepared. If the possible consequences of the risk they had taken were of concern to Betsy, she gave no sign of it. However, the next time they made love she did ask him if he'd brought something to wear. For his part, *he* thought about it a great deal. If she was pregnant they would have to get married right away, and live on his $30-a-week salary until she finished her typing and shorthand course and began working.

It occurred to him that his earlier surmise, that Betsy was a virgin, had almost certainly been wrong. Obviously she must have known what she was about. But what might or might not have happened previously in her life was unimportant. She was his now, and he was hers. He felt quite sure of that.

ooooo

AT THE NEWSPAPER office the forthcoming Democratic primary was the center of attention. The general election in November was merely a formality for local and state offices; the Republican Party scarcely existed. Both candidates for Congress were issuing confident statements, but the signs were all that the incumbent, Franklin Poinsett, Mr. Murray's friend, would be reelected.

Five days before the primary, the Army announced the purchase of a five hundred-acre tract adjacent to the old Remount Station in North Charleston, upon which an Army Air Corps weapons supply facility, employing as many as 400 civilian workers, would be built. The tract was being bought from Island Properties, Inc., the same corporation that had owned the land on the Secessionville battlefield.

The announcement was made via the Congressman's office in Washington. The opposing candidate, Howard Wade, issued a statement charging that the timing of the announcement was politically motivated. He claimed that Poinsett, through his membership on the House Military Affairs Committee, had deliberately arranged to have it made on the eve of the election.

ON ELECTION NIGHT Mike was given an assignment. "Go up there to Wade headquarters and stick around until he makes a concession statement." The headquarters were located in the Francis Marion Hotel, at King and Calhoun. The room was festooned in red, white, and blue crepe, there were several oversized photos of Howard Wade on the walls, and, lettered on a long banner across the back of the room above a platform, the words "The President Needs Our Help. Send Howard Wade to Congress."

People were standing around talking. Drinks were prominently in evidence, but the mood was far from celebratory; faces were long. The telephones kept ringing steadily, the returns were coming in, and Howard Wade was trailing the incumbent by a two-to-one margin. Mike talked with a few people. One campaign worker was still irate about the weapons facility announcement.

They were going to demand an investigation, he declared, into the timing of the announcement, which he said constituted "a flagrant attempt to influence the voters of this Congressional district. We intend to get to the bottom of the collusion between Franklin Poinsett and the War Department!" He took down the statement and got the man's name.

Shortly before ten o'clock the defeated candidate came into the room and issued a concession statement. Copies were handed out. Nothing was said in it about the weapons facility. Mike drove back to the newspaper office. He told the city editor about what the campaign worker had said. Should he feature it in his story? "No," he was told. "If Howard Wade said it, that would be different. Just because somebody else says they're calling for an investigation doesn't mean anything."

By midnight all the local races had been decided. There were no surprises. Apparently this had not been one of the more hotly contested local elections. Mike had enjoyed it. It was fun to be in the newsroom on election night, with telephones ringing, precinct totals being called in, people coming and going, an air of excitement over the proceedings, and to be a part of what was happening.

After it was all done, he went over to the Porthole with Jim Igoe, Frank Blades, and several others. He told about the incident of the collusion charge. "They'll make some waves, but it won't amount to anything," Igoe declared. "Nobody in Charleston gives a damn. As long as Poinsett can provide the defense payrolls, he'll continue to get elected, with no questions asked."

Frank Blades, who covered city hall and government offices, was not from Charleston, though he had lived in the city for some time. "The people around here," he said, "sure don't worry about the threat of war. Back home" — Blades was from Ohio — "a lot of people are all worked up because they think that Roosevelt's deliberately trying to get us into the fighting. Not around here, though. You'd think South Carolina was still a part of the British Empire."

"Well, a great many people in town *are* for the British," Jim

Igoe said. "And almost everybody's against the Germans, including most of the old German families. They hate the Nazis, they despise the Japs, and as for the Italians, they don't much care, but they're on the side of the Nazis so they're against them too. And as far as Roosevelt's moving the country closer to war is concerned, that doesn't worry them. They're in favor of it."

"You're probably right," Frank Blades said. "But I'll tell you this. The fact that the more we do get involved, the more jobs there'll be at the Navy Yard, certainly doesn't hurt anybody's feelings. As witness tonight's election results."

"Right," Igoe agreed. "Keep in mind that there is one fundamental assumption shared by the voters of the First Congressional District of South Carolina. It is, that with the forces of totalitarianism menacing the democratic institutions of our hemisphere, this is no time to be casting a vote against Santa Claus."

MEANWHILE, THE MORE that Mike Quinn had to do with Betsy's father, the more difficult it was to get along with him. Several days after the election he remarked that he was sure Mr. Murray must be pleased with the results. The response he got was, "Yes, and small thanks to your paper, too!"

"I don't understand. The *News & Courier* didn't endorse Howard Wade, did it?"

"It doesn't matter who they endorse; nobody gives a damn about that. You played up the other fellow throughout the campaign, and let him get away with all kinds of lies about Franklin."

"If a candidate makes a public statement, we have to report the news, whether or not we agree with it."

"Yeah, that's always the excuse. It's nothing but yellow journalism, dealing in hearsay and gossip!" He was so prejudiced against newspapers that he could not accept the fact of routine news coverage.

"Why do you insist on arguing with him?" Betsy asked afterward. "You know how he feels."

"I wasn't arguing with him, I was just citing the facts. What was I supposed to do, just stand there and let him claim that we're printing lies, when all we're doing is reporting the news?"

"What does it matter to you what he says? Just ignore it."

He left Betsy's home that evening feeling very uneasy. What worried him was not only that Mr. Murray didn't like him, and didn't approve of his choice of vocations, but also and perhaps even more importantly, that Betsy didn't seem to think it mattered. She appeared to believe that so long as *she* got along with her father and with the man she loved, that was all that was necessary.

It concerned Mike that when Betsy completed the business courses she was taking, she would be going to work at Murray Construction Company. It not only would keep her too dependent on her father, but would put her even further into Mr. Murray's orbit.

She was well along in her courses by now. Mike did bring up the possibility of her looking for a position elsewhere, perhaps even at the newspaper if anything were open there, but Betsy wasn't interested. She had worked in her father's office the previous summer, she said, and her father expected her to do so again. "Besides," she added, "in another job I might not be able to take days off when I want."

AT THE NEWSPAPER, everything seemed to be going reasonably well, with the single exception of his dealings with the assistant city editor, Moore. There were always little complaints from him about whatever Mike wrote — an adjective here, a sentence construction there, never anything of major importance but always calculated to annoy. Moore considered himself an authority on English grammatical usage, and could understand and accept only the most literal, unmetaphorical writing. A word that was out of the ordinary, a metaphor or figure of speech, and if Moore was on the desk when he turned in the story, Mike would be called over. "What's this mean?" he would be asked.

Whenever possible he avoided placing stories in the copy basket when the city editor was not on duty, but frequently in the late evening there was no way to get around it. Mike noted that the man almost never questioned anyone else's copy. Obviously he knew better than to try. With Mike, however, he thought he could get away with it.

ONE EVENING ABOUT eight o'clock, several days after the Democratic primary, a man came into the news room bearing a cardboard shoebox with holes cut into it, and asked to see the editor. It was a light news night, the managing editor had gone home, the city editor was on vacation, and Moore was in charge of the desk. The man opened the box on the desk and showed him a freak toad — two fully developed bodies, each with legs, head, and eyes, but joined together, one above the other, like Siamese twins.

The double toad was about four inches long, warty, reddish-brown, with a light streak down the back. Its two bodies were identical, except for the throat of the upper body, which was darker. The man had discovered the double toad on the front lawn when he went out to get the evening paper. He was obviously very proud of his find. In the morning, he was going to take it down to the museum and present it to them.

The assistant city editor was greatly impressed; this was his idea of what a good feature story should be. He told Mike to write a piece about it, and called the photographer to get a picture. The photographer took several pictures, and the man departed, bearing his prize zoological possession.

The whole thing seemed a little bizarre, even repulsive. Mike didn't care for freaks of nature. If the story had to be written, he wanted to stress the scientific aspect, and he proposed to wait until tomorrow, when he could call someone on the museum staff to authenticate the find and provide the relevant scientific explanation.

The assistant city editor would have none of it. Readers know what toads are, he declared; there was no need to ask a scientist to give the toad a bunch of Latin names and all that. Besides, the *Evening Post* might find out about it tomorrow morning and beat them to the story. So Mike wrote the story the way Moore wanted it written. With the accompanying photograph of the double toad, it appeared on the inside front page of the next day's paper.

WHEN HE ARRIVED at the office the next day, everybody was grinning. It seemed that the city desk had received a telephone call from the professor of zoology at the College of Charleston, Dr. Rudolf Strongheart, advising that the supposed double toad was actually two toads, male and female, engaged in the act of coition. The one on top, the professor said, was the male, identifiable by its dark throat. Soon afterward the curator at the Charleston Museum, E. Burnham Chamberlain, called with the same information, and thereafter at least a half-dozen other people had called.

Mike was embarrassed. "I should have checked on it first," he told the managing editor. "I'm sorry."

The managing editor said that it was his understanding that he had wanted to wait and ask the Museum people about it in the morning, but that the assistant city editor had insisted on running the story that night.

Later Mike was told by Jim Igoe that when confronted with the information about the supposed double toad, Moore had refused to accept the fact. He didn't believe it, he said; he had been familiar with frogs all his life, and there was no way that what he had seen could be a male and female toad making out. It was joined together too firmly. At that point, Igoe said, the telephone rang and the managing editor answered it. He had listened to the caller. "Thank you very much for calling," he said.

"That," he told Moore after replacing the telephone on the

hook, "was the fellow who brought in the toad. He said he wanted to report that at eleven o'clock this morning, the toad on top got off."

THAT EVENING IN the newsroom, after the managing editor had gone home and the assistant city editor was presiding at the desk, there was a recurrent calling out, sepulchrally, resonantly, of the words *Knee-Deep!*, as if from a bullfrog in a pond. The first several times it happened, the assistant city editor looked up from his desk and tried to identify which of the reporters was doing it. He — or they, for there may well been several culprits — was never spotted. The sports editor, Joe Harris, a tall, cadaverous man with red hair, was suspected, but could not be caught in the act. After a time Moore gave up, pretended not to hear, and concentrated on his work.

Throughout the evening, the call came, *Knee-Deep! Knee-Deep!*, at intervals spaced sufficiently far apart to remain unexpected and unpredictable. Each time the reporters sniggered, and the assistant city editor kept his gaze trained upon the copy he was editing. All evening long, interstitially, it was

Knee-Deep!
Knee-Deep!
Knee-Deep!

The next day's paper featured, in a box on the first page of the second section, a retraction:

CORRECTION

Tuesday morning's edition of The *News & Courier* contained a story and a photograph of what was identified as a freak double toad. In actuality the photograph was of a male and a female toad mating. We apologize to our readers for this error both of zoology and good taste.

THERE WAS ANOTHER development with Betsy. She had decided, she told him, to resume her riding. She was rejoining the hunt at Middleton Place Plantation across the Ashley River. "You're at work every evening except Sunday, and it's something for me to do in the afternoons," she said.

"What will you do for a horse? Can you rent them?"

"I could, but Daddy's giving me one for my birthday next month."

Even though he had no objection to the horseback riding as such, it was something in which he would not be sharing, and the fact that her father was giving her the horse emphasized the separateness. Moreover, keeping a horse, he had gathered from remarks he heard when she and her friends talked, was an expensive affair. Once they were married, even with Betsy earning a salary to go with his, they would scarcely have money for that. What was the point, then, in her acquiring a horse now, only to have to give it up in the spring?

The trouble was that Betsy was so accustomed to having all the money she needed that it did not cross her mind that after they were married this would no longer be so. Unless, of course, her father continued to subsidize her doings, and Mike didn't care for that prospect.

"I thought you said you didn't like riding because of all the drinking," he said.

"Just because others do it doesn't mean that I have to," she replied. "Does it?"

"No."

The awareness that he disapproved obviously annoyed her. "Don't you think I know how to take care of myself?" she demanded.

"Of course I do. I was just remembering what you told me."

"Well, stop worrying about it! Why do you resent the idea of my getting a little pleasure out of riding?"

"I don't."

"Well, you certainly act like you do!"

She was very angry, more so than the occasion itself would appear to warrant. Whenever her wishes were contravened, whenever she did not get her way, she was apt to sulk. Yet from Mike's standpoint, this time more was involved than Betsy's merely being balked. In accepting her father's gift, and resuming her riding, in effect she was downgrading the importance of the portion of her life in which he was part. That she would do this at the very time when she had given herself physically to him made it all the more dismaying. She seemed to be both committing herself to him, and at the same time asserting the separateness of their interests.

To what extent was Betsy aware of what she was doing? He could not tell. Her way of doing things on the spur of the moment, which ordinarily he found so refreshing, had its drawbacks. She didn't take consequences into consideration, didn't think things through.

But she did love him, just as he loved her so much. If he had any doubts of that, they should have been assuaged by the way that they made up after their quarrel, and what she had done. Her parents had gone upstairs to bed. They listened to the radio on the sunporch and danced a little, and he had drawn her to him and they kissed deeply. "I can't tonight," she whispered, "I'm having my period." But then she reached into his pocket, removed his handkerchief, and without saying a word, brought him to climax. It was marvelous. She had known exactly what to do. "Now you owe me a good one," she said, and giggled. She was his; her love was for him.

Why, then, when he drove back to his room on Montagu Street late that night, was he feeling depressed?

HE WALKED BACK into his room, undressed for bed, and turned on the radio. There was a program on a station in Louisville, Kentucky, that he often listened to, an hour of classical music. His mother taught piano, and at home in Roanoke he had heard music being played all the time. He got into bed and read for awhile, then switched off the reading lamp and lay there in the dark, with the radio playing.

He thought about Mr. Murray, and the fact that Betsy had begun riding again, and would be going to work for her father. What would have happened if he had gone to work elsewhere? He wouldn't then be writing newspaper articles to be read and disliked by Mr. Murray. Once they were married she would have to leave her family, come to where he was located, find a job there. All she had wanted to do, she told him, was to be his wife, and go where he went.

Would things go better if he were not on the scene all the time? Had he made a mistake in coming to Charleston in the first place, locating a job there? But if he hadn't done so, they would probably have had to wait until they were married to make love as they were now doing. What she had done that evening had been a thrilling thing for him. Yet that remark she made seemed to disturb him, he wasn't sure why. "Now you owe me a good one." She had meant it, of course, as a joke. He had no reason not to trust her love for him completely.

The music had been playing, but he had paid little attention to it. Then abruptly certain notes registered in his consciousness. A piano was playing, *Für Elise*. It was a piece that his mother frequently taught to intermediate students. How many times, lying in bed in his room upstairs on Saturday mornings and on days in summer, had he heard it, coming from the parlor downstairs! He knew each note, anticipated each progression. When, as often happened, the pupil playing the piano was first learning the piece, and there were false notes or errors in tempo, he waited for them to be corrected by his mother, waited for *Für Elise* to come out right, to be played as it should be. He had never learned to play it himself; he had set out to learn to play piano one spring, had taken lessons and practiced during the spring and summer — Beethoven's Minuet in G, the Happy Farmer, Humoresque — until school had begun in the fall, and the school newspaper, and there was not enough time for the piano lessons, so he had stopped. Stopped for good; he doubted that he could even find the chords for the key of G any more.

Materializing out of the little radio into his rented room, in the darkness, four hundred miles from his home in Roanoke, the piano music of Beethoven made him think of his parents, the house he had grown up in, his own room with the pictures of Mel Ott and Stonewall Jackson on the walls, the furniture, the bookcase, the desk, the wrought-iron bedstead. His room was unoccupied now, waiting for his return even though he would probably never go back other than on visits — so near really, only a single long day's drive from Charleston, yet separated in time, two months back in the past, and seeming much farther away than that. The subtle thief of time.

What if he were to get out of bed, dress, pack his suitcase, go outside, get into his car, and head northward? Leave Betsy and Mr. Murray and Charleston, put them behind him, return to the mountains, back to his room in his parents' home?

But no, things would work out for the the two of them. Of course they would.

Hearing the piano music seemed to calm his heart. When it was done he switched off the radio, turned on his side, closed his eyes, and heard the deep-voiced whistle of a ship baying somewhere out on the water, an automobile horn, the siren of a police car wailing, the clock of a church tolling the hour, off in the night, here in a different room, far from home.

7

THE TURTLE EXPEDITION was set for Sunday and Monday. Rosy watched the weather reports, halfway hoping that the weather would turn bad so that there would be a legitimate excuse to call off the boat trip. But the prognosis was for fair skies and light winds.

The Stronghearts and Sara Jane arrived at Adger's Wharf shortly before noon on Sunday. The children, Benjy and Joyce, were already wearing life jackets. "Are you going in swimming again, Daddy?" the younger, Benjy, asked. Sara Jane laughed.

"Not unless the captain backs into a mine sweeper," Dolf answered.

"What's a mine sweeper?"

"Daddy's just kidding," Linda Strongheart told the child. "Now you and Joyce can go and look at the boats while we get ready. Be careful not to stand too close to the edge of the dock."

They loaded the tents, mosquito netting, sacks of groceries, bags of ice, and assorted paraphernalia into the boat and stored it away. Everyone except the captain was in high spirits; Rosy was apprehensive. Malfunctioning engines and anchors that failed to hold were on his mind. Why did he allow himself to get into situations like this?

What situation? he asked himself.

It was ridiculous.

They got away from the wharf without undue incident, although the engine growled sourly several times before it caught, and there was a moment when he feared that the line attached to the borrowed rowboat was going to snag the bow of a trawler. But it stayed free, he secured the rowboat in tow off the stern, and they set out across the water.

The sailboats were out as they moved along, past the Battery, past the Quarantine Station, across the Rebellion Reach channel and the mouth of the harbor, and toward the Waterway entrance behind Sullivans Island. They continued along the Waterway, with green salt marsh on both sides and the houses on Sullivans Island in view on the starboard side. The rowboat towed easily. Schools of porpoises came by several times, which the Strongheart children out in the cockpit found very exciting. A little later they threw crackers to the seagulls, with the result that for a time the air off the stern of the *Gilmore Simms* was filled with dozens of diving, soaring, and careening birds, until the supply of crackers was exhausted.

They moved along the Isle of Palms, and after a time drew near the numbered marker indicating the point at which they would leave the Waterway and enter the inlet flowing between the Isle of Palms and Dewees. From where Rosy now watched there seemed no gap between the two islands, but only a continuous solid line of trees and marsh grass. Up ahead across the marsh was a shrimp boat, its drying nets extended out like the wings of a butterfly, seemingly moving atop the reed grass. Then they rounded a bend, the creek widened, and he could see the inlet and the white sand shore and the ocean beyond.

Dewees Island was set well in, with the shoreline of the Isle of Palms thrust out much further out into the ocean to the south. On the chart Rosy had marked a place on a smaller creek where it appeared to be possible to anchor between a stretch of marsh and the beach, well away from where the inlet opened into the ocean. They moved up into it and he lowered the anchor overboard. The boat drifted back toward the inlet, then the line grew taut and the boat stopped drifting. He watched the shoreline; the anchor appeared to be holding firmly.

The *Gilmore Simms* was swinging easily in a wide creek. The white beach of the island lay a hundred yards off, curving along the edge of the inlet for several hundred yards before it disappeared from view behind the palmetto trees and underbrush. Across the inlet, a quarter-mile away, lay the eastern tip of the Isle of Palms. The sky was high and blue, with a few white clouds. The breeze was coming steadily in off the ocean — and a good thing, too, Rosy thought, for otherwise the mosquitoes were likely to be on the beach in overwhelming force.

He rowed over to the beach, making several trips to bring everything ashore, and they chose a camping spot. Dolf Strongheart began setting up the tents — one for Linda and himself, one for children, and one for Sara Jane. Rosy would sleep aboard the boat.

The children were excited. They ran along the shoreline and up to the edge of the woods, picked up shells and driftwood, and chased a few shorebirds. At one point their shouting disturbed a large brown-and-white-feathered bird, which soared out of the nearby woods and took off across the marsh. "Look, an eagle!" the little boy, Benjy, cried.

"No, that's an osprey," Dolf told him. "*Pandion haliaetus.*"

"Where are the turtles, Daddy?" the girl, Joyce, asked.

"They'll be along after dark."

"When will we see the turtledoves?"

"What are you talking about?"

"You told Mama you hoped we'd see some turtledoves as well as turtles on the beach before we went home."

Linda laughed. "Maybe we'll see some by the time we're done, dear," she said.

They walked along the shore to where the dunes began. Along the ocean front, stretching eastward, was a white sand beach. The incoming surf threw up a mist that blurred the shoreline. The children ran along the water's edge, while the adults strolled over the dry sand further up the slope.

"Under that sand, ladies and gentlemen," Dolf announced, pointing up the beach, "are dozens of turtle egg nests, waiting to hatch out. Waiting for them to do so, up in those woods, are numerous raccoons, and along the dunes thousands of ghost crabs in little caves. You can bet, too, that the local gull population is keeping an eye out. What the turtle hatchlings will try to do is to make it to the water before all are devoured by the raccoons, crabs, and gulls. Only a few will survive. It is nature red in tooth and claw out here." He swatted at his ankle. "Damn! Hand me the bug lotion!"

They stopped and coated themselves with oil of citronella. Dolf called to the children to come over. "Anoint them with oil, my dear!" he said.

Linda Strongheart applied citronella to all exposed surfaces, and the children took off again, heading for a gully near the edge of the shore. The beach was wide, with gullies, and completely deserted.

"I'd better go back and see how the boat's doing now," Rosy said after a few minutes. "The tide's changing."

"Oh, come on, Rosy," Dolf told him. "Just relax and enjoy the beach. If the boat floats away you can always chase it down in the rowboat."

Sara Jane laughed.

IT WAS WELL after the light had receded from view beyond the Isle of Palms and night had come on that they set out to look for the sea turtles. Before supper the Strongheart children had been dispatched to a tent for a nap, so that they could stay up late. Rosy had rowed out to the *Gilmore Simms* and checked the anchor to make sure it was holding properly. He also turned on the anchor light. Now all of them walked along the beach in the darkness. The moon was out, low above the water, and as their eyes grew accustomed to the dark they could see along the beach for some distance. Tide was coming in, and the surf was booming. The oncoming waves, their crests white and phosphorescent, crashed away, so loudly that they could scarcely hear themselves talk as they went.

They had walked several hundred yards when Dolf Strongheart stopped, turned, and held out his arms, motioning them to be quiet. He trained a flashlight up ahead, on what appeared to be a rough place of some kind in the sand. The beam of light moved along it and illuminated a moundlike object fifty yards away and halfway up the slope of the beach.

One of the children started to say something. "Shhh!" Linda said.

Dolf turned off the light. Placing a finger before his lips to signal for silence, he led the way, stepping carefully. They followed him. There was a noise, a kind of gasping snort, from up ahead. Dolf stopped, and they drew up alongside him. Ten feet in front of them was a turtle, fully four feet long and wide.

In the moonlight they could see her clearly as she labored, raising the forward portion of her heavy body and then shoving herself onward with her hind flippers. She moved a few feet ahead, gasping as she struggled to propel the weighty bulk of her carapace along the slope, then paused to rest, her neck thrust out and the eyes in her knobby head looking about. Her long foreflippers raised her body, her hindflippers shoved against the sand, and she lurched ahead again, a couple of feet at a time. Behind her a dark furrow marked her toilsome progress up the beach from the sea.

"*Chelonia mydas*," Dolf whispered. "A green turtle."

The turtle looked more brown than green. After a while she appeared to have reached the place for her nesting, for she stopped, and for several minutes lay motionless on the sand.

Then she began to dig. Her foreflippers pushed sand away. She began rocking from side to side, and her rear flippers dug in to the sand and began throwing clouds of sand out from behind. It was as if a tiny whirlwind were in place, with sand shooting out in all directions. Deeper and deeper she dug, the soil tossed out in clusters as she worked.

When the pit was both wide and deep enough to accommodate her body, she changed her tactics. Now only her rear flippers were in action, digging away in turn, one of them removing a clump of sand and depositing it at the side the nest, the other thrusting it further away. With each act of excavation she raised herself with her foreflippers, while her rear flippers dug deeper. She was a long time at it, so long that the children grew restless and Linda took them down to the edge of the shore for a while.

Finally the turtle settled down on her pit, and eggs began to drop into it. Dolf turned on his flashlight and illuminated the rear of the turtle. The brightness seemed almost blinding. "That's the ovipositor," Dolf said, indicating a tubelike extension that protruded from the turtle's body, and from which eggs began to emerge.

"Fascinating!" Sara Jane said.

Dolf called out to Linda to bring the children, who came running up to them. They looked on for a moment. "What's she doing?" Benjy asked.

"She's laying eggs," Dolf told him. "Some day they'll be little turtles."

"Doesn't she mind us watching?" Joyce asked.

"No, she doesn't even know we're here now. Until she finishes laying her eggs, nothing else matters to her. Look." He walked over to the turtle and thumped his knuckles against her shell several times. The turtle paid no heed; it was as if he had struck the side of a boulder.

Dolf began assembling his camera and flashgun. Then he moved around the turtle, taking pictures. The flashes of light were dazzling in the darkness. Oblivious, the turtle continued to deposit eggs into the pit.

"How long will she be at this?" Linda asked.

"Until she's all done," Dolf told her. "It could take an hour or more."

"The poor dear," Sara Jane said.

They watched for a few minutes. Dolf trained his flashlight up the beach. "I think there's another one over there," he said. "Let's go see."

A hundred yards further up the way and closer to the water there was a dark, domed shape on the sand. They walked down to the edge of the water and approached it from behind. Another turtle, somewhat smaller than the first, was moving up the slope. Her coloring was lighter and more yellowish, and her carapace was encrusted with barnacles.

"*Caretta caretta*," Dolf whispered. "A loggerhead. See how she walks?" Unlike the first turtle, this one was having an easier time of it, raising herself off the sand and using all four flippers at once in a slow, waddling gait.

"All things considered," Sara Jane said, "I think I'd prefer to be a *Caretta caretta* instead of a *Chelonia mydas*."

"All things considered," said Linda, "I'd rather be a male turtle."

AFTER A WHILE the first turtle had completed her egg laying, and was engaged in pulling sand down atop the eggs. Her flippers worked away, the foreflippers dragging sand into the nest, her hindflippers pushing it into the egg pit.

"I'm going to take the kids back," Linda said. "You be sure to come along in a little while, Dolf."

"Oh, I will, I will," Dolf said. "Never fear."

Sara Jane, Rosy, and Dolf watched the turtle cover up her nest. She shoved more sand into it, turned around atop it in a circle, raked in more sand, turned around on it some more. Next she began tamping the sand down with her body, raising herself up, dropping onto it, and slapping it with her flippers.

At length the turtle seemed satisfied that the eggs were properly buried and protected, whereupon she climbed off the nest and looked around. It was as if she saw them for the first time, for at once she turned toward the ocean and began shoving herself toward it. Down the slope she moved, steadily and determinedly. They followed her toward the ocean. Eventually she reached the water's edge. She rested a minute while the water swirled around her, then pushed off again, until she was all but covered by the water and, after a moment, afloat in it. In no time at all she had disappeared into the incoming waves.

"Before the summer's over she'll be back again with another batch," Dolf declared.

"The poor dear," Sara Jane said again.

"Well," Dolf said after a minute, "I'm going to head back to give Linda a hand. Here, you take this." He handed Sara Jane a flashlight.

"I've got one," Rosy said. "There's plenty of light to see by."

"Ah, but it's the light of the moon, my friend," Dolf declared. "Who knows what strange and wonderful things moonlight can do to seemingly rational people? 'That orbèd maiden, with white fire laden, Whom mortals call the moon.' Take care!" He walked away singing, "'By the light-light-light-light-light of the silvery moon.'"

THEY STROLLED ALONG the edge of the water. Once again they stepped over the track of a turtle, and Rosy flashed his light to see where the turtle had gotten to. "The place is crawling with fertility tonight," he said.

"Yes, it is."

They walked along in the part-darkness, the roar of the breakers booming out in the surf, and beyond them the open ocean, the waves lucent in the moonlight. The moon was now halfway up in the sky. Several times they heard sea birds out in the dark, above the noise of the breaking surf. Rosy thought of some lines of poetry. "Reminds me of Whitman," he said.

"What's that?"

"'With angry moans the fierce old mother incessantly moaning. . .'"

They continued walking. "It's a lovely night," Sara Jane said after a while.

"It's as if we were all by ourselves at the edge of the world," Rosy said.

"Yes."

Out beyond the breakers the reflection of the moon along the black surface of the water seemed like the wake of a ship. Rosy thought about his boat, rocking in the current back where it was anchored. Out of the cradle, endlessly rocking. Don't rock the boat.

"I wouldn't want to be out here during a hurricane," he said. "There's one down in the West Indies now."

"Is it coming our way?"

"It's too early to tell. If so it's at least a couple of weeks away. Of course, it's not like it used to be, when there was no radio to give advance warning. All they had to go on was the way the sky and the water looked."

"Yes."

"Think of how it must have been for the people living on Folly Beach or Sullivans Island, not to know what was going to happen."

"Yes."

"Of course there was the barometer. But that still wasn't much advance notice."

"No."

"'Last night the moon had a golden ring. Tonight no moon I see. / But the skipper he blew a whiff from his pipe, and a scornful laugh laughed he.'" Rosy quoted. "Longfellow. 'The Wreck of the Hesperus.' Did you have to memorize that in the seventh grade, too?"

"Yes. 'It was the schooner *Hesperus* that sailed the winter sea, / And the skipper had taken his little daughter to bear him company.'"

Rosy laughed. "I remember that I thought the lines about 'her bosom was white as the hawthorn bush that blooms in the month of May' were dirty."

Sara Jane laughed.

"Radio communication has made it different now," Rosy said

after a minute. "Ships at sea can report on the conditions around them. The weather moves in patterns, you know. They can tell what it's going to do by where the various fronts are."

"Oh."

"During the war, the blockade runners used to run close in along here to get around the Union fleet, you know. But not on nights like this. They waited for moonless nights, so their silhouettes couldn't be seen against the beach."

Sara Jane said nothing.

"The wrecks of several blockade runners are right off Breach Inlet, the other side of the Isle of Palms," Rosy said. "Maybe we could locate them some time with a grappling hook."

"Yes."

They watched the breaking surf and the moonlight on the water. Far out to sea a pinprick of light could be seen. Or could it? A ship? A buoy? The reflection of a star on the black ocean? Rosy watched for a while. He wasn't sure. The breeze was balmy, fragrant almost. He thought of another line of poetry. "For the gentle wind does move / Silently, invisibly." What was that from? It was familiar, but he couldn't think of the title.

"I guess we'd better be getting back," he said after a while.

"I guess so."

They turned and walked back down the beach, past the turtles laying eggs in the sand.

"It's amazing," Rosy said, "to think that these turtles live far out in the ocean, and then return to the same place to lay their eggs, through sheer biological instinct."

"Yes."

"Think of the urge that can make a turtle swim several thousand miles in order to come ashore on a particular beach, and never any other. Instinct can be a powerful and mysterious force sometimes."

"Yes, it can — sometimes."

The breeze blew in off the water, the incoming tide surged and lifted. Overhead the sky was bright with twinkling constellations. The lights of Charleston were a dim glow to the west.

"You don't really see the stars until you're away from the city," he said. "It's only when you get out here that you begin to realize how much you're missing in your life."

"That's true," Sara Jane said. "And sometimes not even then."

THEY MADE THEIR WAY back to the tents. From all indications the Stronghearts were sound asleep. "Better make sure your mosquito netting's tucked in all around you," he said. "See you in the morning."

"Goodnight."

The anchor light of the *Gilmore Simms* glowed out in the creek. Rosy walked over toward the skiff, untied the line from the tree, took off his shoes and placed them in the skiff, shoved it out into the water, and stepped in. He rowed over to the boat, tied the skiff alongside, and climbed into the cockpit. He sprayed the cabin in case any mosquitoes were about, and sat outside for a little while to give the spray time to subside. Then he went up into the forward cabin. He draped netting over one berth, removed his shoes, brushed sand off his shirt and trousers and feet, applied some citronella oil to his neck and arms, and climbed into the berth.

All was quiet, except for the lapping of the creek water against the wooden hull and, in the distance, the rumbling of the surf. The current was endlessly rocking the boat. Sara Jane had seemed rather subdued, he thought. "For the gentle wind does move / Endlessly, silently." What were those lines from? William Blake? He felt oddly depressed.

SEVERAL TIMES DURING the night he had been awakened by the sound of engines, and had looked out the port to see the running lights and the dark shapes of shrimp boats passing by out in the inlet. Now when he awoke it was broad daylight. He got up, went up into the main cabin, and looked through the windows. Sara Jane and the Stronghearts were walking along the edge of the shore with the children. Smoke was trailing up from a campfire not far from the tents.

His skin felt grimy from the citronella. He pumped some water into the sink and washed his face and hands, then changed into fresh clothes. It was a little after eight o'clock. The surface of the inlet was calm, with almost no waves. The *Gilmore Simms* had behaved well. His apprehension had been for nothing. With luck, they should be back at Adger's Wharf before noon.

He decided to let the engine turn over a little. He went to the console and turned the switch. The engine growled several times, but did not catch.

He tried again. This time there was only a faint clicking noise. The battery was dead.

Rosy waited a little while, worked the throttle a few times, and tried it again. More clicking. He removed a panel from the bulkhead and jiggled the battery terminals to see whether they might have worked loose. Again he tried the battery, without success. That was why it had not responded at once yesterday when they were leaving the dock. It was running out of juice.

He went out onto the deck and looked down the inlet and across the marsh. If a boat came by, he might be able to get a jump start. But there was no sign of another boat anywhere. He climbed into the skiff and rowed over to the shore with the bad news.

THEY DISCUSSED THE options. They could wait for a boat to come along. But that might not be for a day or more. He could get into the skiff, row over to the Waterway a mile away, flag down a passing craft, hitch a ride back to Charleston, and find another boat to come and get them. But it would take all day and well into the night. The other option was to row across to the Isle of Palms, and walk down the beach to the built-up area, four miles or so away. There he could telephone for help, or buy another battery and try to find someone with a motorboat who would take him back to Dewees. Of the three possibilities, that seemed the best.

"If you do that, how will you get the skiff back?" Dolf asked.

"I'll go over with him and bring it back," Sara Jane said.

"I'll go with you," Dolf said. "It's a long way."

"No, I can row perfectly well," Sara Jane insisted. "I've been doing it all my life."

Rosy rowed across the inlet to the Isle of Palms shoreline, slung his shoes over his shoulder, stepped out into the shallow water, and held the skiff steady while Sara Jane changed positions. He helped turn the skiff around, shoved it off, then went ashore. He sat down on the warm sand and put on his shoes, while watching Sara Jane, facing in his direction, her back to her objective as she worked the oars, move out across the inlet. She rowed very well.

ROSY SET OFF along the beach, keeping to the area just above the reach of the water where the sand was firm. This part of the island was uninhabited. It was going to be a hot day, and without much in the way of a breeze off the water. There was a bank of clouds off to the northwest, above the dunes and the trees beyond.

He might have known something would go wrong.

He looked up the beach. Nothing but sand and dunes and ocean. There were sea turtle tracks in several places. So they could have driven out here to see the turtles, and not had to bother with the boat at all.

Sandpipers, or some variety of little wading birds, were running along the edges of the water. The line of surf stretched up ahead, with a haze above it. Out in the ocean, gulls were working.

He heard a noise behind him, and looked around. A truck was coming along toward him; maybe he could hitch a ride. As it drew near he stuck out his thumb. The truck pulled up alongside and stopped. The words MURRAY CONSTRUCTION CO. PHONE 2-1365 were lettered on the door. He opened the door and took a seat. The truck moved off.

The truck was bound for Sullivans Island. Rosy got off at the service station boat rental at Breach Inlet and went inside. The man at the counter said he could sell him a new battery, and could take him over to Dewees in his own boat. He went back into a storeroom, and emerged after a minute with a large battery. "I'm going to have to put this thing on charge," he said. "It'll take about an hour."

Rosy bought a soft drink and some Nabs, and sat outside near the boat dock under a canopy to wait.

IT WAS THREE P.M. before they pulled up to the *Gilmore Simms*. The Stronghearts and Sara Jane were aboard, with the skiff tied alongside. The dead battery was removed and the new one installed. "Try it now," the man said.

He turned the switch, and the engine roared into life. The sound of the running engine was highly satisfying.

The man inspected the engine. "Here's your trouble," he said after a minute. "One of the generator wires come off. Wasn't charging."

THE JOURNEY BACK was uneventful. The *Gilmore Simms* made no more trouble. Midway through the two-hour run Sara Jane came into the cabin. It had been extremely hot and sticky out on the island, especially after the ice in the thermos jug melted, she said. The children had begun to squabble. Fortunately she had remembered the icebox on the boat.

They crossed the harbor and Rosy backed the *Gilmore Simms* into her slip. Sara Jane made the stern lines fast.

"Comrade," Dolf said, "it's been a voyage to remember."

He told Dolf about seeing the turtle tracks on the Isle of Palms. "Ah, but there wouldn't have been the same feeling of solitude, of being all alone on a deserted island."

"Daddy, how come we didn't see any turtledoves?" Joyce asked.

"They probably stayed out of sight in the forest," Dolf said. "They're very shy."

AFTER ALL THE paraphernalia had been removed from the boat and the Stronghearts and Sara Jane had departed, Rosy went back into the forward cabin. The mosquito netting was still in place over the berth he had slept in. He removed the pillow from it, placed it on the other berth, and lay down. The boat was rocking; tide was coming in. "'O captain! my captain! Our fearful trip is done,'" he thought to himself. He was very glad to be back at the dock. For a while at least, he thought, he would confine his boating expeditions to places within easy reach. It was then that he remembered the title of the poem about the wind blowing silently, invisibly. It was by Blake; the title was the same as the opening line. "Never seek to tell thy love, / Love that never told can be."

Don't rock the boat.

8

SEVERAL WEEKS AFTER the Democratic primary the rivalry between Congressman Franklin Poinsett and his recently defeated challenger, Howard Wade, flared up again. Wade called a press conference at his office at Moncks Corner, twenty-five miles north of town, saying that he had some very important news to announce. Frank Blades, the *News & Courier's* political reporter, was on vacation, and since Mike Quinn had been at Wade headquarters on election night, he was told to drive up to Moncks Corner and find out what it was all about.

Mike was the only newspaper reporter present. The *Evening Post* hadn't bothered. Information had been brought to his attention, Howard Wade said, that at the same time that the announcement of a new Army Air Force weapons facility was made — one week before the Democratic primary — similar new defense facilities were also announced for four other congressional districts. Of the five new facilities, four were in congressional districts whose representatives were members of the House Military Affairs Committee. The War Department had obviously timed these announcements in order to help the congressmen running for reelection. Accordingly, he was requesting the Ethics Committee of the U. S. House of Representatives to launch an official investigation of flagrant collusion between the War Department and Congressman Poinsett and the other Congressmen.

All five of the new defense installations were located in the

South, Wade pointed out. "You can't tell me that the Army isn't planning new defense facilities in other parts of the country. Why weren't any others announced at the same time? The answer is obvious — because the South was the only section of the nation where the Democratic primary is what matters, and that's held in July."

"Do you have any evidence that the congressmen asked the War Department to do it?" Mike asked.

"It stands to reason," Wade said. "Why would the War Department do it that way if not asked to do so? The only persons who stood to gain from the timing were the incumbents."

WITH FIVE U. S. congressmen involved, four of them on the Armed Services Committee, it was a big story, of considerably more than local import. The evidence might be circumstantial, but the coincidences were striking. He told the managing editor and the city editor about it.

They talked for a while about how to develop it. The Associated Press would be asked to check with the War Department in Washington and get a statement from the office, as well as descriptions of the other defense facilities concerned. The newspapers in each congressional district involved would be called; in return for the story, they would be asked to get comments from the congressmen and the defeated candidates in each election. Franklin Poinsett would be asked to comment.

Mike was to write the main story. "You turned it up," the city editor said. "So you write it." A major front-page news story! He was thrilled.

There was, he knew, one person who was certain not to appreciate reading what he would write, but that couldn't be helped.

The newspapers in the other congressional districts involved were quick to cooperate. Information about the recently completed primary elections was exchanged, and defeated candidates were asked for comments. Over the Associated Press teletype came a story providing descriptions of each of the defense installations, comments from both the War Department and the chairman of the House Military Affairs Committee denying any collusion, and disclaimers from all of the incumbent congressmen.

He telephoned Congressman Poinsett's office, spoke with an aide, read Wade's statement, and asked for a comment. An hour later the telephone rang and the aide read him a statement by Poinsett denying any pre-knowledge of the announcement, as expected. Not only had he been unaware of the announcements made in other congressional districts, he said, but no pressure had been exerted either by himself or, to the best of his knowledge, by any other Congressman to have the new installations made public before the Democratic primary date.

Mike wrote the story in takes. The city editor suggested some revisions in the way he said things, and he made them. This was the kind of newspaper reporting he had imagined himself doing. He wanted to call Betsy and tell her about it, but she would scarcely share his elation, knowing as she would that her father was certain to be irked at him for writing it.

Should he ask the city editor not to give him a byline? No, he couldn't do that. The newspaper wouldn't like the idea that he wanted to let personal considerations get involved with his work. Besides, he *wanted* the byline, no matter what Mr. Murray would think.

He waited around the office that evening until the paper came off the press. There was his story, with his byline, at the top right of the front page, along with the Associated Press story about the statements from Washington and the descriptions of the other elections.

WHEN HE SPOKE with Betsy on the telephone the afternoon after the story appeared, and proposed to come by after he got off work, Betsy told him to wait until ten o'clock or so before showing up.

"You mean until after your father's gone to bed, because he's so angry that you're afraid what might happen."

"He *is* angry. What did you expect?"

"I was assigned to write the story. Why can't he understand that?"

"Let's not go over all that again," Betsy said. "Just come by a little after ten. I'll be waiting."

IT WAS 10:15 P.M. when he arrived at the Murrays' house. Betsy was out on the front porch.

"Is the coast clear?" he asked.

"Yes. But let's go for a ride in my car," she said. "You drive."

He took a seat behind the wheel of the convertible, backed out of the driveway and into Murray Boulevard. "Where to?" he asked.

"Folly Beach," she said. "Is that all right?"

He turned into Rutledge Avenue and headed for Cannon Street.

At first Mike thought that Betsy might have wanted to discuss the situation between him and her father, but it was soon evident that she had nothing of the sort in mind. She had brought a thermos chest, and she sipped a beer as they sped along. Mike always enjoyed driving the big Buick convertible. The engine, so much more powerful than his little 1933 Ford's, had a satisfying snarl to it as they crossed the Ashley River Memorial Bridge and headed out along the Folly Road. She seemed in high spirits. She had finished her business school course, and next week she would begin work in her father's office. She had selected the horse he was giving her. Her birthday wasn't until September, but it was to be delivered to the stable on Friday.

"How much will it cost to keep your horse out there?" he asked.

"Oh, let's not worry about anything like that tonight. It's too lovely out!" They were in open country now, passing through fields and marshland. The moonlight was bright on the tidal flats and the road. Off to the left was the beam of the Morris Island lighthouse, sweeping on and then off again in regular sequence as it revolved. The breeze was salty and warm.

They topped the last high bridge and rolled onto Folly Island. Some of the stores along the highway were still open, and the amusement park across from the pavilion, in front of the pier, was operating, with the throbbing, pumping music of the merry-go-round audible, and overhead the lights of the ferris wheel. "Drive down the beach," Betsy said.

They rolled down the ramp, which at low tide was quite wide, and turned eastward, crossing underneath the dance pier, past the amusement park, then along the beach, past the lighted cottages behind the dunes and beyond the built-up area. The moonlight was so bright that Mike turned off the headlights and they drove along in the half-dark, the receding surf fifty yards away on one side, the sand dunes on the other. The lighthouse was ahead in the distance.

Mike was driving, watching the beach ahead, thinking about the way that the moonlight lay atop the sand like a sprinkling of snow. "'The moon lies fair upon the straits,'" he recited. Then he felt the pressure of a hand on his thigh, and then sliding across it, ever so lightly, touching the tip of the erection it evoked.

He eased the convertible to a stop in the darkness. The stretch of beach was deserted. There were no houses anywhere nearby. "No, let's go outside," she said when he reached for her. "I've brought a blanket."

The blanket was in the back seat. They stretched it out on the sand, took off all their clothes, and made love in the darkness. Then they went bathing in the surf; the water felt chilly only for a moment. They dried themselves — she had brought towels as well — and made love again. Then they dressed, got back in the car, and drove home, with the car radio playing dance music by Harry James and his orchestra, from the North Pompton Turnpike, New Jersey.

She was so good at it. He thought of her naked body, cool to the touch as they stood holding onto each other in the waves, her small breasts with the dark nipples glistening in the moonlight. She was built for pleasure, and she knew it and managed it so well. He hadn't been the first, but he was the one she had chosen for her lifelong partner.

It was after midnight. He switched the radio channel to WHAS, Louisville. The music was from *Tannhaüser*. They listened for a little while. "What are they playing?" Betsy asked.

"It's from *Tannhaüser*. The Venusberg. Do you like it?"

"Not really. Turn it back to Harry James."

He switched to the dance music again, and they drove across the Wappoo Creek bridge and through Windemere with the radio playing "Frenesi." Betsy didn't like Wagner; she didn't care for classical music. No matter. Venusberg meant mount of Venus; the *mons veneris*; the mount of love. And it was his mountain to climb. "A gentil knight was pricking on the plain." He chuckled at the thought.

"What's funny?" Betsy asked.

"Nothing," he said. "I was just thinking of a line from a poem."

"Instead of reciting your old poetry, I wish you'd learn to dance. I mean, something besides just a fox trot."

"Maybe I will some day."

They pulled into her driveway and to a stop underneath the side portico. The radio was playing "In the Mood," and they listened until it was done. It was Betsy's favorite tune.

WHEN MIKE BROACHED Jim Igoe's suggestion about doing a story on Dr. Lancelot Rosenbaum and his harbor project to the managing editor, he was encouraged to pursue it. So he arranged to interview him aboard his boat early the next afternoon.

The professor's boat, which was named the *Gilmore Simms*, was tied up at Adger's Wharf, on the waterfront. No one appeared to be on board when he arrived, so he walked along the wharf looking at some of the boats moored there. Except for Dr. Rosenbaum's boat and the tugboats at the end of the wharf, most seemed much in need of paint.

The tide was out, and along the shore there were wide mud-banks, with hundreds of fiddler crabs on them, just as there had been out at the Secessionville battlefield. The mud was viscous and jet black, with little pools of oily water here and there. There was a sharp, pungent odor everywhere, not exactly objectionable but very formidable. The lower portions of the dock pilings were covered with barnacles and oyster shells; they reminded him of the pantaloons that Scarlett O'Hara wore in the movie.

He was about to walk over to the north wharf and watch what appeared to be a shrimp sorting operation going on under an open tin shed, when he saw Dr. Rosenbaum coming along the wharf. They climbed down a ladder onto the stern of the boat. Dr. Rosenbaum went into the cabin, opened some windows, then brought out two folding chairs.

He asked why the boat was called as it was, and was told that it was for a Charleston writer by that name — his first name was William, the professor said — who had lived before the Civil War. Dr. Rosenbaum explained that he had written his Ph.D. dissertation on Simms, and told about how it was Simms who may have come up with the idea of the floating artillery battery that was used in the defense of the harbor.

They went inside the cabin, and Dr. Rosenbaum spread out the papers he had been carrying, which were nautical charts, on a table. He was shown the place where the floating battery was last reported seen. There were pencil marks all over the charts, and lines, and places where the wartime forts were located. Dr. Rosenbaum explained how not all the exact locations were known, and how he and a friend were using ranges, artillery trajectories, the known locations of some forts, and a few photographs in books that were taken during the war to try to determine just where everything was.

Dr. Rosenbaum showed him around the boat, and explained that a set of little sockets on the stern were there to keep the surveyor's transit he used to mark the ranges from slipping and falling when the boat rocked.

They were going out on Sunday afternoon if the weather was good, Dr. Rosenbaum said, and he was welcome to come along. They would be working off Fort Ripley, which used to be located in the center of the harbor not far beyond Castle Pinckney but had since been torn down.

"Would it be all right if Betsy Murray came, too?" Mike asked.

"Of course. But she might find what we're doing is boring."

Later he told Betsy about the interview. She thought she had met Dr. Rosenbaum once at a reception. There was a Jewish professor at the College who was supposed to be a world-famous authority on turtles, she said; she believed he was the one. She wasn't especially excited by the notion of accompanying him on the harbor expedition, but she agreed to go along.

SATURDAY NIGHT BETSY went to the movies with Billy Hugenin and his girl, and after he got off work Mike met them at Fiorello's, a nightclub on Meeting Street. When they weren't dancing, they were talking about horses and riding. He felt thoroughly left out of the occasion — so much so that he was almost grateful when it was time to dance. The music was utterly undistinguished, a six-piece combo playing arrangements.

He tried not to feel resentful; it was not Betsy's fault that he knew and cared nothing about riding. But Billy Hugenin was close to being brainless, or in any event idea-less, and his girlfriend, Annie Holmes, was pleasant but a cipher. The evening wore its mostly tedious way onward. When at last it was over, and he and Betsy were driving home, he couldn't refrain from remarking something to the effect that it was too bad they couldn't have brought their horses along.

Betsy flared up. "Just because you're not interested in riding, we're not supposed to talk about it?"

"I didn't say that. But that's all you talked about, all evening long."

"Oh, I'm *so* sorry you find my friends boring, and not up to your high intellectual standards. I'll drop them immediately and try to find some others that you approve of!"

"For God's sake, Betsy, I didn't say anything about your friends! But try to put yourself in my place. I don't know a thing about horses and riding. I could have been somewhere off in Timbuktu and it wouldn't have made any difference to the three of you."

"Well, if maybe you had a decent job with civilized working hours, like other people, you could find out something about them!"

"Thanks. I'm glad you approve of my career."

"You make me so mad, criticizing my friends and the things I find to do," Betsy said, "when you're at work every afternoon and every evening, six days a week. What do you want me to do, stay at home and listen to the radio and read books?"

"Of course not. That's not what I want at all."

"Then what *do* you want?"

IT WAS A FAIR question, and he was hard put to answer it. For it was quite true: the hours he kept as a newspaper reporter meant that except for Sundays, when he was not working, they could not be together and do things until nine or ten P.M. And Betsy was an outdoors person; she liked to play tennis, ride, swim. When he had first arrived in Charleston they had played some tennis in the mornings, before he went to work, but once she began business school, that had ended.

If Betsy could find a job that approximated his hours, that would help, but she was going to work for her father, and the construction business didn't operate in the evening. From Betsy's standpoint, she was being asked to give up most of the normal and expected activities that she might ordinarily be doing, in order to be engaged to him. And Betsy Murray wasn't used to denying herself.

They made up that evening, and each promised to try to understand the other's needs better. They sat out on the sunporch talking and listening to dance music over the radio, and they made love, and Mike felt better about things. But later on, in bed in his room, he thought again about what Betsy had said about a "decent job." She had been angry when she said it, and that doubtless had caused her to exaggerate her feelings, but it must have represented something of her attitude. Certainly it was what her father thought.

Yet she loved him, enjoyed his company, made love with him, was going to marry him. What more could he ask of her?

What they needed to do was to be married. He needed to get her away from her parents' house, away from the customary orbit she had moved in since childhood, get her living together with him. Once that could happen, things would be much better. Until then, until next April or May when they were married, he would just have to try to live with the situation and not make it even more difficult than it already was.

9

"IT DIDN'T WORK," Linda Strongheart said to her husband a week or so after the trip to Dewees Island. She and Dolf had given a dinner party for Sara Jane, Rosy, Tom Lowndes, and several other friends, and now were preparing for bed.

"How do you know?"

"Nothing's changed."

"Are you sure?"

"Yes. I could tell. No turtledoves."

"Too bad," Dolf said. "If a moonlight night on a deserted island with turtles laying eggs all up and down the beach couldn't do it, what can?"

"I don't know," Linda said. "We'll just have to keep trying."

"Maybe you ought to hint to Sara Jane to play hard-to-get. She lets Rosy take her too much for granted."

"I've thought of it," Linda said. "But it's not exactly the sort of thing one can say to Sara Jane very easily. Maybe what Rosy needs is some competition. That might wake him up."

"Do you have anyone in mind?" Dolf asked.

"How about Tom?"

"Tom? He's not interested in girls — as girls, that is. You know that."

"He's not — that way, is he?"

"Not so far as I know," Dolf said. "He's more the asexual type."

"Well," Linda said, "if that's so, maybe he might be willing to help."

"You mean, run interference? Fake a courtship, for Rosy's benefit?"

"Something like that."

"Hmm. Interesting idea."

"You don't think," Linda asked, "that there'd be any risk of Tom's playing John Alden to Rosy's Miles Standish, do you?"

"Oh, no. Not Tom. He's not bashful. If he were interested in Sara Jane, he'd have done something about it long before this. It's not like Rosy, you know. Tom enjoys her company, but he doesn't depend on her the way Rosy does. I'm sure of that."

"Then why don't you have a little talk with him?"

"Maybe I will."

Linda got into bed. "Turn out the light in Joyce's room, will you?"

"Okay," Dolf said. "The poor son of a bitch. He doesn't know what he's missing."

IT WAS UNFORTUNATE that on Labor Day Sunday, in early September, when Rosy resumed his mapping of the harbor defenses, the Carolina Yacht Club was holding the annual C. S. Pitcher Cup Regatta. The buoy signifying the reaching mark of the triangular race course had been placed less than fifty yards off the harbor beacon marking the shoal where Fort Ripley had once been located, which happened to be precisely where Rosy had prepared to set up his operations.

The result was that every ten minutes or so, successive waves of sailboats in assorted sizes came heading pellmell for the reaching marker. Most of them rounded it and set off for the next buoy, but not a few made the turn well away from the marker and close to the *Gilmore Simms*, while there was always the occasional sailboat that attempted to cut the course too closely and was forced to come about and try again — which was likely to place it squarely in the immediate vicinity of Rosy's activity. There was a brisk breeze blowing, and twice there were knock-downs just off the buoy, followed by strenuous struggles by the crews to right the boats.

All in all, it was the nautical equivalent of Grand Central Station off Fort Ripley, and Rosy's efforts to identify, sight along, and call out the artillery ranges, and Sara Jane's efforts to record them, were notably hampered. The wind and current repeatedly moved the *Gilmore Simms* away from the marker beacon.

Rosy did explain to the young newspaper reporter, Mike Quinn, what was involved, where the various wartime batteries were located in the harbor, where the Union ironclad flotilla had come in its unsuccessful attempt to force an entry, where the blockade fleet was stationed, and where the Confederate blockade runners entered and departed from the harbor. Meanwhile, Betsy Murray, Quinn's fiancée, when not watching the personnel of the water traffic, sat out on the fantail and read a magazine. The occupants of a sailboat that was not in the race recognized her, whereupon they drew so close alongside that the sails blocked the view of the range Rosy was taking with the transit. They conversed with her for a while, then they moved off. Not long afterward another sailboat, its crew also acquaintances of Betsy, came past and stopped to talk.

A little later a handsome ketch, dark-green-hulled and with gleaming winches and trim, came along the channel from the direction of Fort Sumter, sailed over toward them, and swung alongside. "May we offer you a tow?" someone aboard called. It was Page and Tennie Carter. The president of the College deftly maneuvered the 40-foot-long boat until it was no more than a few feet away, and they exchanged greetings and felicitations, after which the Carters bore off on a long reach across the channel toward the James Island shoreline.

No sooner had the Carters left than a runabout, mahogany with a pennant on its bow, came blasting past, bound for the outer harbor, and sending up a considerable bow wave. Once it passed the *Gilmore Simms*, however, it executed an attenuated 180-degree turn and came over to them, bouncing through its own wake en route. There were several young couples aboard, drinks in hand. They too were friends of Betsy's, and they exchanged pleasantries for a time before roaring off to the east. Rosy decided there was some validity to Tennie Carter's views on speedboats.

The *Gilmore Simms*'s mission survived for little more than an hour. "I think," Rosy concluded, "that we'd better call it quits for today. I can't get an accurate range."

"I think you're right," Sara Jane agreed. "Unless Fort Moultrie has been moved into the lobby of the Francis Marion Hotel, the last set of ranges you called out make no sense at all."

While driving Sara Jane home afterwards, Rosy remarked to her that the young newspaperman appeared to have enjoyed himself.

"A nice kid," Sara Jane said.

"His girlfriend didn't seem very interested, though."

"I thought she was a chip off the old blockhead." Sara Jane did not care for the chairman of the College's board of trustees. "The only time she showed any interest was when her friends came by. I think she'd have been happy to go off with them in that speedboat if they'd suggested it. Did you notice how she stayed out on the stern the entire time in full display, instead of sitting in the shade?"

"I thought she was enjoying a sunbath."

"I must say, it certainly worked like a magnet," Sara Jane said. "I feel sorry for that kid; he's in for a hard time, I think."

"WILL YOU HAVE dinner with me this evening?" Rosy asked when he drove up to the house where Sara Jane's apartment was located. They almost always had dinner together after the harbor expeditions.

"I'm sorry, but I'm doing something."

"Too bad. I'll give you a raincheck."

"All right. Bye bye."

She's probably having supper with her aunts, Rosy thought as he drove off. Yet, when she couldn't go somewhere or do something with him, she always explained why. This time she had volunteered no explanation.

THE FALL TERM was about to get under way. The campus of the College of Charleston, somnolent all summer, was once again a place of activity. Returning students gathered about the old cistern in front of the main building and in the hallways of the ground floor, comparing notes on their vacation doings. Faculty members who had been away during the summer months were back in town and exchanging the latest gossip.

The advent of the dean was, of course, the prime topic of faculty conversation. All were puzzled; auguries were sought. A faculty meeting had been called for the afternoon before registration day, almost certainly for the purpose of authorizing the dean to teach a course in experimental psychology. It was evident that approval would not be automatic. The appointment had caught everyone by surprise, and the way it had been done — without consultation or even explanation — caused resentment. That Page Carter, of all people, would have managed things in such fashion was baffling to everyone; for hitherto no one could have been more tactful, taken greater care to observe the precedents and amenities, and been less likely to act in arbitrary or cavalier fashion, than the president.

Rosy's colleague in English, Horace Hewitt, stopped by his office. A small, impeccably attired man with a handsome profile, he had taken his graduate degree at Balliol College, Oxford, where he had acquired a British accent and a belief that the study of literature properly concluded with the poetry of Tennyson and Browning.

"Did you have a good summer?" Rosy asked him. The Hewitts had always spent the summer months in a thatched cottage in England; the previous summer they had been forced to beat a hasty exit home when war broke out. This year they had gone to Biddeford Pool.

"So-so, so-so. Alas, I'm lost without access to the Bodleian. I fear that I shan't be able to complete my edition until this dreadful war is ended." Ever since Rosy had known him, Hewitt had been at work on an edition of the poems of William Wordsworth.

Hewitt was outraged at the advent of the dean. "The man is a churl!" he declared. "Have you talked with him? I can't for the life of me imagine why Page could ever have hired him."

"He must have had some reason for doing it."

"If so, he has failed to communicate it to anyone."

"Maybe he'll do it at the meeting tomorrow afternoon."

"Possibly. But I can tell you this: if Page or anyone thinks that this faculty will consent to the man's being permitted to offer courses in whatever it is that he supposedly teaches — psychology, is it? — without prior deliberation and approval, he is very much mistaken."

ROSY, SARA JANE, Dolf Strongheart, and Tom Lowndes had lunch together at George's, a small restaurant across the street from the campus. "That's where the battle lines are going to be drawn, all right," Tom observed after Rosy had described Horace Hewitt's response to the dean's appointment.

"And rightly so," Dolf declared. "What goes into the curriculum is the faculty's business."

"Still, it's going to be embarrassing for Page if the dean isn't allowed to teach a course in his field, don't you think?" Rosy said.

"He should have thought of that last spring," Dolf said. "That was the time to do it. "

"I don't think that Page knew the dean would be joining us last spring," Sara Jane said. "I think it all happened this summer."

"Why makes you say that?" Tom Lowndes asked.

"Because Page Carter doesn't make that kind of mistake. If

he's doing things this way, that can only be because he didn't have an alternative."

"That's what I think, too," Rosy said. "The question is, why?"

"Right. Why?" Dolf agreed. "Why suddenly bring in a dean, without preparing the way, without any warning, knowing that it's bound to set off storm signals?"

"And why *this* dean, of all possible choices?" Tom Lowndes added. "Why someone who works in a field that we don't even offer courses in? And is so very odd, to boot, with that strange way of pronouncing words, and that hissing grin? It doesn't make sense. Why did Page do it?"

"I think," Sara Jane said, "that it might not have been Page's doing."

"Not Page's doing? Then whose doing was it?" Rosy asked.

"I have the hunch that the chairman of the board of trustees was involved."

"Turner Murray?" Tom asked. "Why do you say that?"

"I'm not sure," Sara Jane said. "Call it intuition if you'd like. But there's something about the way it's all been done, and the way they've acted, that makes me think so."

Rosy looked at her. "If that's so, then we'd all better begin worrying, shouldn't we? If Page isn't in charge, anything could happen. Who's going to see that things are done properly?"

"I trust Page," Sara Jane said.

"I do, too, when it comes down to push and shove," Tom Lowndes said. "But he's certainly handling this one in highly uncharacteristic fashion."

ON THE WAY to the campus the next morning Rosy stopped by Luden's Marine Supplies on East Bay Street to buy several hundred feet of three-quarter-inch line. "You're the fifth person that's come in for line so far today," the clerk told him. The morning newspaper had reported a hurricane in the vicinity of Turk's Island in the southeast Bahamas, north of Haiti, and was believed to be moving west-northwest. The report said that it was of only moderate intensity, but hurricanes had a way of picking up strength as they went.

Captain Magwood had told Rosy that what the owners of boats at Adger's Wharf usually did in the event of a hurricane's advent was to go well up one of the rivers and tie up close to the shore where the land would serve to screen off the wind. Rosy had looked on the harbor charts and tried to identify possible places to go, but he didn't know the water and, besides, he had no relish for staying aboard the boat and riding out a hurricane. Perhaps he could take it around to Elzey's yard on the Ashley River; at least that was somewhat better protected than Adger's Wharf, which lay open to the harbor.

Page Carter would certainly have some suggestions. What did he plan to do with his boat? When Rosy arrived on the campus he headed for the president's office. Page was talking with Dean McCracken, Miss Mouzon said, and she had no idea how long the conference might last. She would call him, she said.

Rosy went to his office, and was preparing a syllabus for his course in the modern novel when a student, José L. Lopez, Jr., entered. A poet, he read and wrote verse constantly, and always brought his creations by for Rosy to look at and criticize.

What was unusual about him among student poets was not only his technical sophistication, but his ironic approach. He enjoyed satirizing the romantic high-mindedness prevalent among his youthful contemporaries. Last spring he had conducted a vigorous feud with the editors of the college's literary magazine, which was controlled by the Tri Delts, the campus's elite social sorority, whose more literarily-inclined members preferred poems that rhymed "truth" and "youth," "love" and "above," and generally offered uplift and inspiration. When they had declined to accept a sonnet sequence of Lopez's parodying Elizabeth Barrett Browning and beginning "Why do I loathe thee? Let me count the whys," he had published them himself. Rosy had helped by buying a number of copies and sending them to various friends.

Lopez had spent the summer, he reported, working aboard an Army Engineers dredge, and he was compiling a Low-country bestiary in verse. "Here's one about crabs," he said, and handed Rosy a copy:

BLUE CRAB (*Callinectes sapius*)
The crab is not foredoomed to dwell
Forever within a single shell,
But yearly swaps its carapace
For more expansive living space.
Not so with human beings; we grow
Ever more hidebound as we go,
And proffer to the world without
The same sad look, the same sour pout.

"And here's one on the blue heron." José L. Lopez, Jr., handed another poem to Rosy.

GREAT BLUE HERON (*Ardea herodias*)
OR, 'ONE IMPULSE FROM A VERNAL WOOD'
Yon stiff-legged heron by that log
Delights in playing clever tricks.
So still it stands, a passing frog
Mistakes its legs for sticks.

The heron dines, becomes a meal
Itself an instant later
When massive jaws ope to reveal
Not log but alligator.

Thus Nature ever documents
The burthen of the mystery
In acts of blessed innocence —
Bound each to each by natural piety.

Rosy laughed. "Horace Hewitt won't care for that." As a Wordsworth scholar, Rosy's colleague in English literature didn't like anyone poking fun at his favorite poet.

"I've signed up for your sophomore survey," José L. Lopez, Jr., said.

"What do you want to do that for? You've read most of that stuff, haven't you? I can get you exempted from the requirement."

"Yes, sir, but I think I'd like to read through all that poetry systematically."

"It's all right with me, then," Rosy told him. There were few students who knew what they were doing the way that Lopez did. The Morrison girl in his American literature seminar, one or two others. . . it was a pleasure to have such students around. If he were teaching at a large university with graduate programs, there would be more such. But Charleston had its abundant compensations.

THE TELEPHONE RANG, and Rosy was informed that the president was free. Outside the administrative offices he encountered Dean McCracken. "Ah, good morning, Dr. Strongheart!" the dean declared, with a hiss and a grin.

"Er, it's Rosenbaum."

"Oh, of course! Forgive me. So much is going on these days, now that classes are commencing, that I find myself making mistakes though I know better. It is so good to be resuming our mission of instructing the young, isn't it? We'll be seeing a great deal of each other, I'm sure!" McCracken flashed him another toothy grin and headed down the stairs, while Rosy went into the president's office. What an odd bird the dean was, he thought; perhaps José L. Lopez, Jr., should include him in his bestiary.

Page Carter seemed somewhat harassed. He too had been following the progress of the hurricane, he said. His advice to Rosy was both simple and comforting. If and when the hurricane's descent upon the area seemed imminent, the *Gilmore Simms* should be taken across the harbor by her captain and up into the creek to where the Carters kept their own sailboat, and which was protected on two sides by a bluff. "Once you hear that there's a strong chance of it hitting, bring your boat over then and there," he told Rosy.

What he should do when he got there, the president said, was to set two anchors off the stern, with plenty of scope, then take two lines ashore from the bow and secure them firmly to large trees. Page drew a diagram to show what he meant. Rosy should also wrap the lines with cloth at the point where they led through the chocks. "Have you got plenty of line?"

Rosy said he thought he had about four hundred feet.

"You'll need every bit of that."

The president said nothing about the forthcoming faculty meeting.

WHEN ROSY WENT to lunch with Sara Jane, Dolf, and Tom Lowndes, he found that the first two were now quite angry with the dean. McCracken had presented himself at the library that morning, and handed Sara Jane a list of professional journals and books to be ordered at once. The cost — and the dean wanted complete sets of the journals, with all back issues — would come to almost a fourth of the library's meager acquisitions budget for the school year.

"When I told him that we couldn't afford to order all the back volumes right away," Sara Jane said, "he informed me that he required them — that's the word he used, required — without delay."

"What did you do about it?" Rosy asked.

"I went over and asked Page what I should do."

"What did he say?"

"He said — and this is incredible — he said to go ahead and place the order, and he'd find the money to pay for it! I couldn't believe what I was hearing. He seemed embarrassed. Can you imagine that? Page Carter *embarrassed*!"

Dolf Strongheart's complaint was of a different order. "McCracken circulated a memo calling for the division of sciences to meet at ten tomorrow morning, in order to discuss changes in the curriculum. Meaning, of course, his psychology course. Mike Donahoe is chairman of the division; it's up to him to call meetings, not the dean. I asked Mike whether McCracken had checked with him, and he said the first he'd heard of it was when he read the memo!"

"Protocol doesn't appear to be McCracken's strong point," Tom Lowndes remarked.

"No, and it's even worse than that. I saw him a little while ago, and he addressed me as Professor Rosenbaum. He thinks I'm *you*," Dolf said, turning to Rosy. "How's that for adding insult to injury?"

Rosy laughed. "He did the same thing with me. He called me Professor Strongheart. I think his problem is that he can't distinguish between Jews."

"He probably has the same trouble with Chinese laundrymen," Sara Jane said.

They laughed. "Here we are, joking," Rosy said, "when a hurricane's only a couple of days away from striking."

"Which do you suppose," Tom Lowndes said, "that Page would rather miss: the hurricane, or the faculty meeting this afternoon?"

"Page looked tired, when I saw him a little while ago," Rosy said. "I asked him what I should do with my boat if the hurricane comes, and he said to bring it across to his place and tie it to the trees under the bluff."

"That sounds like a good idea," Sara Jane said. "Much better than taking it up some creek. When are you going to do that?"

"As soon as we know for sure that it's coming. Right now it's just north of the Bahamas. Tomorrow afternoon, maybe, or the next morning."

"Well, that's one thing about keeping turtles instead of a boat," Dolf said. "If a hurricane comes, they can fend for themselves."

ooooo

THE MEETING WAS scheduled for four o'clock. After lunch Rosy drove back to Luden's Marine Supplies and bought a spare anchor and chain. Page Carter had spoken of setting out two anchors from the stern, and he didn't like the idea of removing the bow anchor. "Are you still selling lots of line?" he asked the clerk.

"We're down to our last spool of three-quarter inch. One thousand six hundred feet gone since eight o'clock this morning." The hurricane, he said, was reported moving northeast of the Bahamas. "That's only about six hundred miles away, you know."

"Better give me another hundred feet while you're at it," Rosy told him, "and ten feet of chain and a couple of shackles, too."

He took his purchases down to the wharf and brought them aboard the boat. The sky was blanketed with clouds, with the wind off the ocean. Some of the boats normally berthed at the wharf were gone. He looked out over the harbor. A tug and barge were headed down the Ashley River channel, across from the James Island shore, toward Sullivans Island and the Waterway. Several destroyers were moving along the Rebellion Reach channel, bound for the ocean. Things appeared to be about as usual. The run over to Page Carter's creek, if he had to make it, would be about two miles. He would see how things looked tomorrow morning. He set the new anchor and another spare in the stern cockpit, attached chains and lines to them, got out another line from a locker, and placed it and another hundred-foot line in the forward cabin near the hatch. He located some rags and tore them into strips, for wrapping the lines if needed. There was nothing more he could do. It had begun to drizzle. He drove back to the campus.

When Horace Hewitt had been going on about the dean being without culture and the like, Rosy had felt a certain amount of sympathy for McCracken. Not only Hewitt but certain others of his colleagues sometimes acted as if the faculty were supposed to be a gentlemen's club. That the dean was awkward and gauche — he *looked* awkward, too; gangly and with the tooth-displaying grin — was true, but scarcely a crime. But what Sara Jane and Dolf had reported was something else again — not awkwardness, but arrogance and insensitivity. That was another matter. And Sara Jane's comment about Turner Muray being behind the dean's coming was disturbing.

There was trouble ahead. The campus had seemed so peaceful that summer, as peaceful and without complication as the ocean had appeared, that night out on the beach with Sara Jane. Now a hurricane was possibly in the offing, while the campus was caught up in a little tempest of its own. If the meeting weren't handled properly, things could get highly unpleasant — just as, if the hurricane began moving in a certain direction, the ocean off Dewees Island, and the harbor and the city as well, would likewise turn very stormy very quickly.

THE DEAN HIMSELF was not present at the faculty meeting — which, since he would be the subject of the discussion, was only proper. Page Carter opened the proceedings by explaining that Dean McCracken wished to offer an introductory course in experimental psychology. The opportunity to acquire Dean McCracken's services had arisen only after the spring term had ended, during the summer vacation, he said, and it seemed appropriate for the dean to offer a course in his field. He himself taught a class in physics whenever he could, and he believed it important that college administrators continue to maintain contact with the classroom, even though it was not always feasible.

When he finished speaking, there was a pause. Copies of the course description for the subject the dean proposed to teach were circulated and scrutinized. Somebody asked whether the library collection was adequate to allow students to do the necessary research in the subject. To which the president replied that it was not, but that funds had been made available to order certain basic materials at once, and Dean McCracken had assured him that an introductory course in experimental psychology required only a minimum of library work.

Made available by whom? Rosy wondered.

"What about laboratory facilities?" someone asked. "Don't they conduct experiments with rats in mazes?"

There was no problem about that, the president replied. The ground floor of one of the buildings across Greene Street was serving as a laboratory for now.

At that point Horace Hewitt rose to his feet. Here it comes, Rosy thought.

"The question is not whether facilities are available to teach a course in experimental psychology," Hewitt declared. "The question is whether as a faculty we desire to have a course in experimental psychology taught. Speaking for myself, I don't feel that I am prepared at this stage to vote on such a matter. I should have to be told a great deal more about the field in question before I could form an opinion about its desirability. This is not anything about which one can make a snap judgment. It requires careful consideration.

"Is it a subject matter that that we *wish* to offer our students? How does it fit into the curriculum as a whole? How will it affect the scientific fields that we now offer courses in? Who will take it? How will they make use of it in their overall programs? Even assuming that this chap is competent to teach it, given our limited facilities and budget is it the best use we can make of them? These are not questions that can be settled in cavalier fashion like this!"

The meeting quickly developed into a verbal free-for-all, with various faculty members striving to gain the floor. Rosy watched Page Carter. The president was saying nothing, merely recognizing in turn those who wished to speak. Hewitt's remarks about "in cavalier fashion," and questioning the dean's competence, must have riled Page, but he gave no sign of it.

No more than a half-dozen persons were doing almost all the talking, while the majority were listening and saying nothing. There was a group, more or less led by Horace Hewitt, who were adamantly opposed to the dean. What they really objected to, of course, was not the appropriateness, or lack of it, of a psychology course in the curriculum, but the presence of McCracken on the campus. Since they couldn't legally question that, they used what objections they could muster.

Some of the arguments, however, were proving effective in quite the opposite way intended. When one of the science teachers made a remark about psychology being only a pseudo-discipline, Dolf Strongheart entered the fray. Academic exclusivity and snobbishness were always quick to arouse Dolf's ire. He despised professorial smugness, and he knew that what the biology teacher who made the remark really objected to was the possibility of losing students. The "pseudo-discipline," Dolf said, was being currently taught at Harvard, Yale, Columbia, Princeton, Chicago, Duke, Chapel Hill, and fifty or sixty other universities, he declared, so that he supposed that made them only pseudo-universities.

Did Page Carter really *want* the proposal approved, or did he want it rejected? Like Sara Jane, Rosy's impulse was to trust the president. Rosy thought about it, and decided that if Page believed the College's best interests lay in not having the dean teach the course, he would most certainly have found some way to keep the matter from coming before the faculty. As it was, the president was being placed in an impossible position. How could he go back to the board of trustees and admit that even though he had appointed McCracken as dean of the College, his faculty wouldn't permit the man to teach a course?

Rosy had the sense that what a majority of those present at the meeting wanted was a way of allowing the course to be taught, without abdicating the faculty's right to decide.

He raised his hand. Page Carter recognized him at once.

"By whose authority," Rosy asked, "was Dr. McCracken made dean of the College?"

"By the authority of the Board of Trustees," the president replied.

"In that case, I move that the Dean be authorized to offer a course in experimental psychology for the 1940-1941 school year, and that the question of whether it should be a permanent part of the curriculum be referred to a committee to be appointed by the president."

That ought to do it, Rosy thought as he sat down.

"I second the motion," Tom Lowndes declared, "provided that Rosy means that letting him do it this year doesn't commit us beyond that. That's got to be understood very clearly."

"That is exactly what I meant," Rosy said. "This year only, and it's not to be used as a precedent."

"Hear, hear!" someone said.

"Is there any discussion?" Page asked.

There was a pause. Nobody said anything.

"I call for the question," Mike Donahoe said after a moment.

The motion passed, with approximately two-thirds of those present voting "aye."

"THINK OF ME voting in favor of that rat-running son of a bitch!" Dolf said as they walked out. "I'm going to have to play the B minor twice tonight to get the taste out of my mouth!" Dolf's recourse in time of stress was to listen to the Bach B Minor mass on his phonograph.

"You got us off the hook, Rosy," Tom Lowndes said.

"You got Page off the hook," Dolf said.

They walked out onto Greene Street. It was raining steadily. Fortunately, all four of them had brought umbrellas.

"Can I give you a ride?" Rosy asked Sara Jane. "I'm parked right down the block."

"Thanks," Sara Jane replied, "but I have a ride."

She walked off with Tom Lowndes.

"COMRADE, YOU DONE good," Dolf declared as he prepared to cross the street to where his car was parked behind his laboratory. "I'm proud of you. But all the same, I have the sneaking feeling that the day may come when both you and I are going to regret the way we voted this afternoon."

Rosy didn't respond. He was watching Sara Jane getting into Tom's car.

"Did you hear what I said?"

"Oh? Sorry. What did you say?"

"I said that the day may come when we're going to wish we hadn't voted the way we did."

"I hope not," Rosy said.

"See you tomorrow," Dolf told him.

Rosy walked down Greene Street toward his automobile in the rain. The wind was tugging at his open umbrella, but he scarcely noticed. Across the street Dolf was watching him, and smiling wryly.

ROSY ATE DINNER in the St. John's Hotel restaurant and read the *Evening Post*. The direction of the hurricane had shifted to north northwest, and hurricane warnings were flying from Savannah to Norfolk. The Weather Bureau was predicting that it would turn northward, come ashore in eastern North Carolina, and move up the edge of the coast. But so far it had not done so, and if it continued on its present course Charleston lay squarely in its path.

After dinner he went up to his rooms, mixed himself a drink, and settled in to read *Robinson Crusoe*, which was the first novel he would be teaching in his course on the British novel. It opened with a lengthy description of a fierce storm, which did not make him feel any easier. But he found it difficult to keep his mind on what he was reading. He kept thinking about what had happened. Today Sara Jane had gone off with Tom Lowndes. On Sunday she had been busy and couldn't go to supper with him. Of themselves the two turndowns signified nothing. After all, there had been no formal understanding that they would dine together after the harbor expedition, even though they usually did, and certainly she had every right to ride home with Tom, or go to dinner with him if that was what was planned.

The thought that Tom Lowndes might be interested romantically in Sara Jane, and vice versa, had never crossed his mind. Now that he thought about it, however, certainly Tom had been much in her company in recent months. And why not? They were old friends, had grown up together in the same neighborhood, been students at the College together.

It had simply not occurred to him that Sara Jane might *have* such interests. He had grown comfortable with her company, had come to assume that her company would be available. Now, abruptly, without warning, it was denied to him. *I'm sorry, but I'm doing something. Thanks, but I've got a ride.*

Certainly she had every right to have made other arrangements. Yet the fact was that he had assumed she would not have done so, and until now that assumption had always been correct.

THE TELEPHONE RANG. It was Page Carter. "If it's still raining in the morning," he told Rosy, "I think you ought to go ahead and bring your boat over." It was still too early to know whether the hurricane was headed for Charleston, he said, but the fact that it was raining steadily indicated that it had not begun veering due northward, and since it was known to be moving steadily ahead, the surmise had to be that it was on its way to the city. If so, by late tomorrow afternoon it might become difficult to cross the harbor in a small boat.

"Incidentally," Page said, "your motion at the meeting was very welcome. I was hoping that I wouldn't be placed in the position of having to propose it myself."

Afterward Rosy stood at the window for a while, watching the falling rain. His rooms faced north, away from the direction from which the storm would come, if it came. It didn't seem to be blowing a great deal, but with his window in the center of the building as it was, it was difficult to tell. He set his alarm clock for 6:30. That would give him time enough to decide what to do in the morning, and to do it..

He resumed his reading of *Robinson Crusoe*. "Poor old Robinson Crusoe. How could you possibly do so?" To have lived alone all those years, on a deserted island, until finally there was his Man Friday available for company. Well, he had lived alone, too, except that he had Sara Jane for company. Until now — But wasn't that the trouble? That he had treated her as if she were his Man Friday, which is to say, sexless, requiring no emotional commitment on his part, existing entirely for his convenience. What justification had he in feeling resentment because Tom Lowndes was interested in her? None whatever. He had in effect invited it.

"Don't take her for granted," Dolf Strongheart had once told him. Hadn't he been doing just that? Dolf — and Linda, too, no doubt — must have thought so; why otherwise would he have said that? Was Dolf warning him, perhaps? If so, he had been too dense to perceive it.

But then, he wasn't in love with Sara Jane, was he? He thought of that moment when he had looked up to see Sara Jane rowing the boat back, working at the oars, her back to Dewees Island, facing him as she rowed off, and how he had waved to her and she smiled. The remembered image went through him like a knife.

THE ELEVEN O'CLOCK radio news reported that the hurricane was still moving north-northwest, and very likely picking up some force as it crossed the warm water of the Gulf Stream. If it continued on its present course and did not veer northward or due westward, it would reach land near the mouth of the Cape Fear River in North Carolina. Rosy looked at a map; that was less than two hundred miles away. The winds of a hurricane were supposed to extend out to the east and west about one hundred fifty miles. That was cutting it close.

By tomorrow morning he would know whether to move the boat. He hoped it wouldn't be necessary. Meanwhile, outside the window the winds blew, silently, invisibly.

10

MIKE QUINN WAS delighted with the outing aboard the *Gilmore Simms*. He liked Dr. Rosenbaum, and he liked Miss Sara Jane Jahnz. It was too bad that Betsy hadn't found the occasion very enthralling. What they were doing with charting the Civil War harbor defenses didn't interest her. She had been concerned solely with seeing which of her friends were sailing in the regatta or out cruising. He was afraid her obvious boredom might have communicated itself to Dr. Rosenbaum and Miss Jahnz. When Billy Hugenin and Annie Holmes had come by with the others in the speedboat, he had been worried that if they had invited her to join them, she might well have done it.

What a brainless bunch that crowd was! He managed to refrain from saying anything to Betsy about it afterward. If she had insisted that he go along to a riding event, he would probably have been equally bored, he thought, although if they were guests of some older people he hoped that he could have hidden it better. Still, Dr. Rosenbaum and Miss Jahnz were not mindless and vapid, the way Betsy's riding friends were. They could and did talk about other things besides the particular subjects they happened to be most interested in, while if he'd ever heard Betsy's riding friends in an extended discussion of anything other than horses, the movies, or college football, he couldn't recall what it was.

Betsy's lack of interest in what was happening aboard the boat might have been in part because she wasn't feeling especially well. She had a headache, and later that afternoon, after they returned to her house, she was feeling so bad that she went off to bed. Mike tried to remember exactly when was it last month that she'd had her period. He recalled the occasion quite well, because it was the time when because she couldn't make love herself, she had done the wonderful thing to him. He wasn't sure just when that had been, but it was something like four weeks or so ago, so perhaps that was what was wrong now.

He drove back to his room and read for a while, then went out to eat by himself. After dinner he stopped in at the news room and wrote a piece about Dr. Rosenbaum and his harbor project.

Later that evening he called Betsy to see how she was feeling. "She isn't here now," her mother said. Her headache or period or whatever it was must have gotten better. She might have called him at his home, and he hadn't been there to answer.

He didn't see Betsy again until Wednesday evening. Monday night she had to go to a riding club meeting, and Tuesday she went with her parents to a reception for the new commandant of the Naval Base in North Charleston. Wednesday evening he was able to get off work earlier than usual, and they went to see Walt Disney's *Fantasia* at the Riviera Theater. Betsy liked it even though it was classical music, which ordinarily was not to her taste at all.

On the way home, however, they had a fight. It started when Betsy said that her father was worried about the possibility of a hurricane hitting the city, because of the damage it might do to the buildings he had under construction out on Sullivans Island. "It's a good thing I'm not writing the weather stories," Mike remarked, "because he'd blame me for the hurricane."

He meant it as a joke, but Betsy didn't take it that way. "Oh, you're so very smart. You don't have to worry about little things like storm damage to houses that you're building. You're superior to all that."

"I didn't say that. All I meant was that since he blames me for writing those stories about Franklin Poinsett when I was just reporting the news, he'd probably feel the same way about the hurricane."

"You talk about him like he was a fool!"

"That's not so. But I don't think he's tried very hard to understand why I have to write what I'm told to write. You know very well that he doesn't care for me and never has."

"You haven't made much of an effort to get along with him, either."

"What am I supposed to do, give up my newspaper job?"

"No, but you don't have to take pleasure in being on the outs with him," Betsy said.

"Take pleasure? For goodness sakes, do you think I enjoy having your father dislike me? Do you think it's fun knowing that my future father-in-law hates my guts and wishes I'd disappear out of your life?"

"He doesn't wish any such thing. And if you'd just be patient and try to realize how much it hurts him when people print lies about one of his closest friends, and not argue with him, maybe you'd get along with him better."

"Now just wait a minute." Mike pulled the car to a stop next to the sidewalk on Murray Boulevard, a block away from Betsy's home. She was blaming *him* for the rift with her father; he couldn't accept that. "Look, sweetheart," he began, "you don't like it because your father doesn't approve of what I write. That's understandable. But can you honestly say that he and your mother wouldn't be delighted if you were to announce that we weren't going to get married at all?"

Betsy said nothing.

"You know that's true, isn't it?"

"Maybe they might feel a little like that right now, but they'd change their minds after a while if you'd just try to get along with them."

"I'll do my best," Mike said. There was no point in arguing

about it with her. She simply didn't want to accept the obvious fact that her father didn't approve of her choice of a husband-to-be, and Mr. Murray, accustomed as he was to having his own way, didn't mind letting everybody concerned know it. And it *was* hard on her. He drew her to him. "I'm sorry if my attempt at a joke didn't work. And I know it's rough on you, too."

"Just *try*. Try not to argue with him," Betsy said.

"I'll do my best."

He started the engine again, and they drove on to her house.

SHE WAS UP against something that she couldn't make conform to her wishes. That was the problem. She wanted him, and she also wanted her father and everything that went along with being Turner Murray's daughter, and she thought that, as was always true in the past, she could get her way if she played her cards correctly and kept working at it. But she was going to have to make a choice, because her father was also accustomed to having things go his way, and was at least as shrewd and as strong-willed as she was. The only chance she would have of getting her father to come around would be to go ahead and make the break, show him she was going to live her own life, and force him to come to terms with that.

But was she determined enough to do it? Enough to give up, for a while at least, what her father could provide, and make him understand that he couldn't control her life? Going to work for her father, doing the things her father approved of — obviously her parents liked the social status involved in riding — and accepting her father's largesse was no way to muster up the resolve that doing it would require. On the contrary.

Mike's one hope, he reminded himself once again, was to avoid any further occasions to let the rift between himself and Mr. Murray be widened, and to get Betsy married to him and out from under her parents' roof. He would do his best to carry through with that plan. But what of Betsy? Would she stay the course? Already she seemed to be wavering. The remark about his getting a "decent job" the other night, and blaming him tonight for not getting along with her father when from the start Mr. Murray had made it obvious that he didn't care for him, were not very encouraging. It was not a comforting thought to entertain as he drove home to his room in what was now a steady drizzle.

He had intended to ask her, just out of curiosity, where she had gone when he had telephoned her last Sunday evening to see how she was feeling. But the quarrel had caused him to forget about it until too late. It was probably just as well. She was given to doing things on the spur of the moment, and didn't like the idea of being accountable. You would have to say, he told himself, that if it weren't for that spontaneity, they might not now be engaged to be married. For certainly it hadn't been any kind of cold-blooded calculation that had led her to give herself to a newspaper reporter earning thirty dollars a week, from a third generation Irish Catholic family and without the social status and connections that her parents coveted and hoped she would help them secure. Falling in love for both of them had been swift and unrehearsed, free of premeditation. The question was, would that spontaneity survive the months ahead? It was going to be touch and go, he was afraid.

"THE SON OF a bitch is going to broadside us," Frank Blades informed his colleagues in executive session at the Porthole Thursday evening. "I got a feeling in my bones."

"I don't know about your bones," said Jim Igoe, "but if this baby shows up at high tide, your butt is going to be in a sling, along with everybody else's. Particularly where you're living." The Blades family resided on Rutledge Avenue facing Colonial Lake. "If you got any valuables you better move them upstairs, because Colonial Lake is going to become part of the Ashley River."

"Is it likely to flood where I live, on Montagu Street?" Mike Quinn asked.

"I don't think so," Igoe told him. "You live this side of Pitt, don't you? The areas that get the high water are the ones that are filled-in land. Every time there's a spring tide, they get flooded."

"Why is the tide higher in the spring?" Mike asked.

"Spring doesn't mean the season; it means a coil, or a trap — it has to do with the way the moon and the sun exert gravitational pull on the water. But it's strongest at the equinoxes, so you do get very high spring tides at the spring and fall equinox. Just imagine what would happen if a hurricane came ashore at the autumn equinox — which, I might remind you, is ten days from now!"

Mike had noticed, as the possibility grew that the tropical hurricane might descend upon the South Carolina coast, that his colleagues, without saying so, were to a man hoping that it would happen. They would never have admitted it. If called to account they would have denied it, and in all sincerity. They recognized the havoc that such a blow could wreak; they would never be so unfeeling as to hope, in any conscious way, for disaster to occur. Yet deep down, as newsmen they craved the excitement that catastrophe could offer. They were like those generals and admirals who know very well that war is hell, who as human beings would do or say anything they could to prevent its outbreak, yet in their heart of hearts cannot help but hope that they will be able to practice their profession.

The fact was, as Mike was swiftly coming to recognize, that however it might be widely said and believed that No News Is Good News, for newspaper staffs Good News is No News, while Bad News Is Big News. If the hurricane arrived, there would be widespread inconvenience, property damage, even loss of life, but there would be lots of News. His companions of the Fourth Estate, Mike realized, were observing the progress of the hurricane much as a house cat, installed in the shrubbery, observes the activities of a robin on the front lawn.

Meanwhile they diagnosed its operations. Jim Igoe, who being in his mid-thirties and having grown up in Charleston remembered the oft-cited Hurricane of 1911, had much to say about the subject. "It's the tidal surge that you got to watch out for," he declared. "A hurricane's like a magnet. It draws up the surface of the ocean into a hump, and brings it ashore when it comes. That's why you hope the hurricane won't arrive at high tide. Add the tidal surge to the already high tide, and there'll be bluefish swimming around in half the living rooms in town."

"Well, I'll tell you one thing," said Frank Blades, who was not a native of Charleston, "if this one does hit, it won't be like the Hurricane of 1911. That's because nothing could possibly be as bad as the Hurricane of 1911. It could put the city thirty feet under water and float the Francis Marion Hotel out to sea, and it still wouldn't be that bad. That's what I've been hearing all week long. I get the feeling that the only thing that could possibly be as destructive as the Hurricane of 1911 was the flood that did in the Tower of Babel."

"You should have seen the Hurricane of 1893," Jim Igoe told him. "Now *that* was a hurricane."

HE CALLED BETSY Friday morning. If the hurricane came ashore tomorrow, he told her, the chances were that he'd be working around the clock.

"Oh, no!" She had arranged for them to go dancing with two other couples tomorrow night at a club called the Cat's Cradle. She was appalled at the prospect that she might be forced to accommodate her plans to the vagaries of a hurricane. She had made her arrangements, and for a hurricane to come along and interrupt them would be so unfair that she hadn't conceded that it could really happen.

"Betsy, if the hurricane hits here, you can bet there won't be any nightclubs open," he told her. "The electric power lines will be down, and there'll be flooding, and everything will be closed up for a few days."

"Maybe it won't hit," she insisted. "The paper says it might go north."

"They've been saying that for two days, but it keeps right on coming."

"You sound like you want it to come."

"Sweetheart, what you or I want has nothing whatever to do with what's going to happen."

She was just like her father, he thought; when she couldn't have her way, it was somebody's fault.

What recurrently puzzled him, when he considered it, was why Betsy had been attracted to him in the first place. (There was no doubt why he was attracted to her. If he had ever wondered about that, what had taken place that night after they had gone to hear the combo on the Folly Beach highway, and ever since then, had removed it. She was, simply, the most alluring, most desirable girl he had ever known.) He hadn't been interested in riding, he wasn't good at dancing, he didn't share the kind of interests that her friends seemed to have. He hadn't even belonged to a social fraternity at W&L. His own interests — books, journalism, writing — were not hers.

Then what had caused her to respond so powerfully to him, so that almost from the time they had met at the party in Lexington last winter, there had been the sense almost of a magnet that was drawing the two of them together? It couldn't have been because he was so sexy. Might it have been because he stood for so much that wasn't and hadn't been part of her life in Charleston and at home, and so represented the chance to escape from it? If so, if escape had ever been part of his attraction for her, he had the uncomfortable and helpless feeling that it was losing its lure. Because she certainly showed every sign of getting back into the local swim, and of enjoying it.

Or was this all the product of his imagination, and Betsy was really as much committed to him as ever, and the difficulties with her father were no more than an annoyance that would disappear once they were married and once he began to achieve success in his chosen field of work? Wasn't the fact that he and Betsy were lovers, just as if they were already married, proof of her commitment? Wasn't it?

IF THE HURRICANE hit the city, the Weather Bureau estimated, it would probably do so sometime Saturday afternoon or evening. On Friday the managing editor and city editor called the staff together and went over plans for coverage. Quite possibly there would be a loss of electric power, in which case the mechanical plant would be unable to operate. 'We'll keep right on covering the news, however," the managing editor said, "and have everything ready to go as soon as they can set type again." It would be a good idea, the managing editor said, to bring not only raingear but a change of clothes to work. It would also be wise to bring flashlights.

That evening after work, Mike and Jim Igoe drove over to the Porthole in Jim's car for a beer. The rain was falling steadily. "I think it's on its way," Igoe said. "Tomorrow's going to be an interesting day." They divested themselves of their raincoats, took seats at the center of the bar, and ordered beers.

Two men were seated at opposite ends of the bar, and were arguing about of all things, the authorship of a line of poetry, "Sweet Helen! Make me immortal with a kiss!" Neither seemed to be exactly the literary type. One man declared it to be Shakespeare, the other insisted it was Poe. They listened, as the bartender winked at them.

The discussion was getting nowhere, when one of the disputants, the man seated at the end of the bar nearest him and who had championed the cause of Shakespeare, asked Mike which of the two authors had written the lines. "Neither one," he said. "It's by Christopher Marlowe." He had studied *Dr. Faustus* that spring in college.

The information was received in silence. Presently, after five minutes or so had passed in which the two men drank their beer and he and Igoe talked, the man who had queried him called to him.

"Who asked you to butt in on our conversation?" he demanded.

"You asked me."

The man said nothing for a minute. "You smart-ass son of a bitch, what gives you the right to come butting in like that?"

"All right, fellow, that'll be enough," the bartender said. "None of that kind of talk. Watch your language."

The man got off the bar stool. "Come on, Charlie," he said to his friend. "Let's get out of here and leave these smart-asses alone." The two of them left the bar and went on out to Market Street.

The bartender laughed. "Let the rain cool them off. They've been sitting here for an hour, drinking beer and arguing about it," he said. "Arguing about a goddamn poem!"

"You shouldn't have said anything," Jim Igoe told Mike. "You spoiled their evening. When two drunks are having an argument, and you get invited to express an opinion, there's only one safe answer: 'I don't know.' Isn't that right, Joey?" he asked the bartender.

"I don't know," the bartender said, and laughed.

"What are you going to do if this storm hits?" Igoe asked.

"Close up," the bartender said. "This is one of the lowest spots in town along here, you know."

"Think what it must have been like in the old days," Igoe said, "when they didn't have any warning, and all they had to go on was the way the wind was blowing and so on."

"My grandpa used to work for the Clyde Line," the bartender said. "He always said he could tell one was coming from his wound. He got shot in the shoulder in the Spanish-American War, and he said it always started to tingle whenever there was a bad storm coming. He said in 1911 it felt like a hornet's nest the evening before."

The door to the street opened and a man came in, wearing a yellow rubber raincoat and hat. He was of medium height and his eyeglasses were fogged over. He removed the raingear and cleared his glasses with his handkerchief.

"Now we'll find out the straight goods," the bartender said. "What'll it be, Frank?"

"Draw me one."

The new arrival and Igoe exchanged greetings. "Are we going to get it?" Igoe asked. He introduced Mike to him. "This is Frank Cox," he told Mike. "He's over at the Weather Bureau."

"It's headed straight for us, about 180 miles away. Miami keeps saying it's going to veer north, but I don't see any sign of it, and I don't think the cold front that's over the Great Lakes is going to arrive in time to shove it northward before it comes ashore."

"So you figure we're right in the line of fire?"

Frank Cox nodded. "I'd lay in a supply of flashlight batteries and candles, if I were you," he said.

They talked for a little while. "I guess we'd better be going on," Jim Igoe said. They paid for the beers they had consumed, climbed into their raingear, and left. Outside it was pouring down. Igoe had parked across Market Street alongside the arches of the open market.

Mike walked around to the far side of the car, stepped under the arch, and was removing his raincoat. Suddenly a tremendous blow against his shoulder sent him sprawling onto the pavement. He looked up. The two men who had been arguing about the line of poetry stood there. "You lousy son of a bitch!" one of them said. "I ought to kick the shit out of you!"

Mike was trying to regain his feet and to remove his raincoat from where it was bunched across his arms. Before anything more could happen, Jim Igoe ran around the car, shoved one of the men down, and landed a solid right onto the other's cheek. The man staggered back, Igoe hit him again in the stomach, and he collapsed. The man on the ground rose and started toward Igoe, who promptly hit him twice, once in the stomach, then on the chin. The man went sprawling again. By then, Mike had gotten his raincoat all the way off and was back on his feet.

"Come on," Jim said, "let's get out of here." Leaving the two men seated on the ground, they got into Jim's car and drove off in the rain. "The sons of bitches," Igoe said, "they've been hanging around out there all the time waiting for us."

"It's a good thing for me you were along," Mike said. He felt his shoulder. It was sore to the touch. It would be black and blue tomorrow.

"Like I said, don't ever get involved when two drunks are arguing with each other," Igoe told him. "Not even when they're arguing about a poem. 'Sweet Helen, make me immortal with a kiss!'" He laughed.

BACK IN HIS room, Mike climbed out of his damp clothes, took a hot shower, and got into bed. The rain was drumming steadily outside. His shoulder was sore. If Igoe hadn't been along, he would have been in considerable trouble, the more so because with the raincoat encumbering his arms he couldn't even have defended himself. And all because of the authorship of a line of verse! Igoe was right; he should have stayed out of it.

This is a strange city, he thought. He had never known a place where there was so much sheer talking for the joy of it; people were gregarious, loved to gather together and chew the fat. At the same time, there was a current of violence to the city, lying beneath the amiability and the pleasure-seeking — a kind of primitive streak. The advent of a hurricane, which he gathered was now quite probable, seemed almost appropriate, as if the pent-up city required a periodic purge.

Tomorrow, in any event, it was due to get shaken up. A lethal force, a tropical hurricane, was bearing down on it. There could well be destruction, casualties, disaster in store. Yet he realized, as he began to drift into sleep, that Betsy had been right; he was indeed hoping the storm would stay on its present path.

11

ROSY SLEPT UNEASILY, awaking several times to get up and look out of the window. All he could see was more rain. Shortly before six the telephone rang. It was Page Carter again. "You'd better come as soon as you can," he said, "before it gets too rough. The hurricane's headed this way."

It was dark outside, more night than day, and the rain was coming down steadily. How rough would the harbor be? He should have gone ahead and moved the boat yesterday. Perhaps he would just double the lines and leave her to fare for herself at the dock. If she sank — well, he was getting a little bored with the harbor project anyway. Would Sara Jane —

As if in response, the telephone rang again. It was Sara Jane. The radio reported that the hurricane was headed directly for the city, she said. When was he going to move his boat over to the Carters'?

He was about to leave, he told her.

"Come by for me," Sara Jane said.

"No, I can get over there by myself. It's only two miles across."

"You'll need help. I'm dressed and ready to go. Now you just come and get me."

"I can't let you go out on that boat. What would people say if there was any problem?"

"What would they say if you got out there by yourself and

drowned because you didn't have somebody else along? Don't be bullheaded."

"I'll call Dolf, then."

"Dolf's got to stay with his family. Now, goddamn it, Rosy, don't be bullheaded. Come by here and get me! I mean what I say!"

Never before had he heard Sara Jane so worked up. "Well, all right."

Whatever else might be going on, she still wanted to help with the boat. Storm or no storm, he felt better.

HE WALKED THROUGH the downpour to his car, drove up Queen Street, turned into Logan, and over to get Sara Jane. She was waiting on the porch. The rain and wind were tossing the oak trees along Logan Street.

"This is insane," he said. "I can't take you out on the boat. What you could do is drop me off at the dock and drive the car over to James Island and pick me up at the Carters."

"I'm coming along. Let's not discuss it further. Did you have any breakfast?"

"No."

"I thought not. I brought a thermos of coffee and some rolls."

They drove down Tradd Street toward the waterfront. The windshield kept fogging up, and Sara Jane cleared it off with a handkerchief. The rain was falling without stint.

"Don't you think," Sara Jane asked, "that you'd better leave your car up here, and we can walk down to the wharf? The water might come up over the waterfront, you know."

"We'll be back in plenty of time. If the storm hits it won't be until tonight."

"How do you know? There's no point in taking a chance."

She was right. "Okay, I'll let you out at the wharf and then come back and park it."

They crossed East Bay and bounced along the cobblestones.

The palmetto trees were swaying in the wind. The harbor was gray, visibility was limited, and the rain was coming down. More than half the boats at the wharf were gone from their slips. The White Stack tugboats were still there, rocking vigorously at their moorings. Tide was very high. That meant that if the hurricane came ashore that evening, the tide would again be up. The hope had been that if it hit the city, it would arrive at low tide.

Sara Jane got out of the car, and he turned around and drove back toward East Bay Street.

RELIEVED THOUGH ROSY was to learn that Sara Jane was concerned about him and the boat, his feelings were mixed. She did not realize how little he knew about operating a boat. If anything went wrong with the engine while they were crossing the harbor, he would not be able to fix it. They would be at the mercy of the wind and the current.

By insisting upon coming along, she had made it all but impossible for him to leave the boat at the wharf to ride out the storm as best it could. Why had he gotten himself into a situation like this? There was no reason why he had to do it. It wasn't worth taking a chance out on the harbor. If the boat sank, that would be it. He was not a professional waterman. He had nothing to prove.

He parked the car on East Bay outside Walker, Evans, and Cogswell, and walked back toward the wharf in the rain. As he drew near he looked out at the harbor. The surface of the water was bumpy, but there were no breaking wave crests. The James Island shoreline could not be seen through the rain. It was two miles across. Once there and they would be safe in the creek. He had told Page Carter that he was coming, and told Sara Jane he was going to do it. What would they think if he backed out now?

Sara Jane was waiting in the cockpit, standing under the roof.

He stepped aboard. The wind was blowing and the boat was straining beneath them. They went into the cabin, where he had several sets of black rubber raingear. He handed a set to Sara Jane, removed his fabric raincoat, and put on one set himself.

He lifted the top off the engine box and let it stand open. There was very little water in the bilge. He had checked the oil dipstick and the engine water yesterday, so that was all right.

If he was going to call it off, now was the time to do it. The further he went with his preparations, the harder it would be to reverse course and say that he was not going to make the trip.

He turned the switch. The engine cut on at once. He lowered the top back onto the engine box.

With the wind gusting out of the east toward the land and the tide running strongly, getting out of the slip and into the open water was the first problem. The best way would be to free all the lines except the starboard bow line, pull the bow out to the piling, then free that line. Sara Jane could stay at the controls and put the gear into forward before the bow was blown back across the slip.

Rosy started out toward the cockpit, then he halted, reached up, and removed two life jackets from the overhead rack. He handed one to Sara Jane, and put the other on, pulling the drawstrings around his back and tying them in front.

Sara Jane did the same. Rosy looked at her, in the heavy raingear and with the bulky orange life jacket tied around her. She looked back.

"What in the hell are we doing here?" he asked. They laughed.

She looked so pretty that he had an impulse to kiss her, but he didn't.

He went outside, disconnected the shore power, freed the stern and spring lines, then went up onto the bow. He freed the bow line from the bit, and began to pull the boat toward the outside piling. It came only slowly. The stern quarter of the *Gilmore Simms* was soon bumping against the pilings, but that could not be helped. With one arm around the piling, he draped the loose line around and over it and tied a clove hitch.

Holding onto the piling, with the rain coming down all about him, Rosy peered through the space between the wharves out at the harbor beyond. It was rolling and rough, with a strong, surging current.

He released the piling, turned and grasped the rub rail atop the forward cabin. Holding on with one hand, he waved to Sara Jane to come ahead.

As the boat began to edge forward he crawled up onto the cabin top, opened the hatch, and swung his legs into it. With the life jacket on he could barely fit into the opening, but he squeezed through down into the cabin. He pulled the hatch cover shut after him, and hurried to the wheel. Sara Jane had turned the bow harborward, but the wind and current were carrying the boat toward the north wharf. He spun the wheel all the way to starboard, gave the engine a burst of power, straightened the *Gilmore Simms* out, and headed for the harbor. They cleared the wharves and turned down the channel. His heart was beating a mile a minute.

IT WAS LIKE riding a roller coaster. Instead of heading due south he angled toward the southeast, steering about 190 degrees, on the assumption that the wind and incoming tide would be setting them off strongly toward the Ashley River. He could see nothing ahead but the driving rain. The *Gilmore Simms* moved through the water, the bow raising and lowering as she cut through waves, knifed into them, was shoved to one side, was lifted and then dropped, slid down the sides of waves, rode upon their crests. What had to be done was to keep the boat pointed into the waves and prevent her from broaching. Waves were slamming into the sea wall at the Yacht Club, sending spray high above it. He aimed across the harbor.

When they cleared the lee of Shutes Folly the going got very rough — rougher than he had bargained for. The waves were being rolled across the wide harbor by the east wind and incoming tide, and thrust into the narrower funnel of the entrance to the Ashley River channel. The route to Page Carter's creek lay across the mouth of that channel, perpendicular to the direction of the flow. Soon the current was hitting the *Gilmore Simms* almost completely abeam. Each successive wave lifted the hull up, rolled under it, and left it in the trough between the waves, while Rosy spun the wheel to keep the bow headed into the seas. Meanwhile the wind was blowing the pouring rain almost parallel with the surface of the water.

What he had hoped to do was to gain the south side of the harbor, then move up along the edge of the marsh to the creek channel. But the course could not be maintained without serious danger of broaching, and he was forced to point the bow still further eastward to quarter the oncoming waves. He decided to steer about 150 degrees. They headed into one crest, down the other side, across the trough, into another. The tops of the waves were almost as steep as the top of the cabin. Each time the bow drove into a wave, the spray was flung upward to shatter against the windows. The windshield wiper pushed water aside momentarily, swung back, shoved water aside again. The compass card swung so wildly that it was difficult to hold to the course.

He would dearly love to turn back, but there could be no turning back. Pointed almost downstream, the boat was struggling to keep from being moved upstream. The engine churned away as the propeller blades bit into the oncoming water. It was wave after wave, without letup, and nothing to do but keep heading into them.

Then, through the rain and the misted windshield, Rosy saw the edge of the marsh, no more than fifty yards away. What he didn't know was whether they were above or below the entrance to the creek. Whichever it was, they could only move into the seas; to attempt to turn and run upstream would be impossible. "Look for the creek marker," he told Sara Jane, who was standing alongside him. He turned directly downstream, wrestling the steering wheel to keep headed into the waves. If they were east of and beyond the creek, maybe he could get into the sheltered dock at the Quarantine Station. Otherwise he would have to steer for the Mount Pleasant shoreline several miles away, right across the open harbor. Either that, or run right up into the marsh. That would probably be safest.

"There it is!" Sara Jane said. Through the spray and rain a marker was in view off to starboard.

He kept the bow pointed beyond it, letting the wind and wave action move them into the creek mouth. Up one wave, over and down it they moved, the spray dashing against the cabin windows, the wooden hull quivering beneath them. Another wave, another . . .

Abruptly, they were inside the creek, the wave action slacked off some, and they could steer directly toward the land.

Moving by estimated compass bearing across almost two miles of water, unable to see more than a hundred feet or so ahead as they went, they had missed putting the boat squarely in the entrance to the creek by less than a hundred yards.

DURING ALL THIS time, Sara Jane had been standing across from him, holding onto the bulkhead, watching the oncoming waves. He looked at her. "I thought we were going to have to take our chances in the marsh," he said.

"So did I."

He realized that he was trembling all over. His arms ached from wrestling the wheel.

The water in the creek was bumpy, but by comparison with what the waves had been out in the harbor, it seemed like a millpond. The wind was still blowing strongly, though; he had to keep the boat from drifting toward the reed grass. He looked down at his watch. The crystal was beaded over, but he could make out the time: 7:59. The run across the harbor could have taken no more than thirty minutes or so. It had seemed like hours.

"Would you like some coffee?" Sara Jane asked.

"Very much."

She poured coffee from the thermos into a cup as the boat rocked, taking care not to spill it. Steam rose from the dark liquid. In his throat it felt pleasantly warm. He was quite hungry now. "How about one of those rolls?" he asked. She held the coffee cup for him while he ate the roll.

"I shouldn't have done that," Rosy said. "It was idiotic."

"We made it," Sara Jane said.

UP AHEAD THE creek widened and made a turn, and through the rain he could see the green hull of the Carters' ketch. She lay upstream from a dock, at the end of the marsh, her bow pointed toward the marsh. The proper place for his boat, he thought, would be to the left of the dock, offshore from the boathouse.

He cut the speed down, asked Sara Jane to take the wheel, and went up into the forward cabin. He unfastened the hatch cover, lifted it, picked up the line he had placed on the vee-berth and set it outside on the cabin top. He took a pair of pliers from the tool box, boosted himself up through the hatch onto the cabin top, and began unfastening the anchor line from the chain, to use as a second mooring line.

Page and Tennie Carter, clad in yellow oilskins and wide-brimmed seaman's hats, were walking down to the dock. They stepped down into a skiff, and rowed toward them. Rosy called to Sara Jane to take the engine out of gear.

The rowboat drew alongside. Rosy went back onto the stern and held onto the gunwale of the rowboat, while Page climbed aboard the *Gilmore Simms*. He would help Rosy set the anchors off the stern, he said, then take the bow lines ashore. "Stay nearby," he told Tennie. She nodded and backed the rowboat away expertly, as if it were all in the day's work. Both the Carters, Rosy thought, had doubtless handled boats in deep-sea conditions far rougher than the harbor had been.

Page looked into the cabin. "My gracious goodness, what a pleasant surprise!" he said when he recognized Sara Jane.

"What's a young lady like you doing out in this kind of weather?"

"Taking risks," Sara Jane said.

Page chuckled.

The stern anchors were lowered into place in turn and set. Then Page got back into the rowboat and took the anchor line ashore. He carried it up the bank, pulled the bow of *Gilmore Simms* close to the edge of the marsh, and tied the line around an oak tree trunk. Returning in the rowboat for the other line, he told Rosy to wrap the lines where they went through the bow eyes, and brought the second line ashore. While Rosy tied strips of cloth around the lines where they led through the chocks, he fastened the second line to another tree trunk.

He got back into the rowboat, Tennie stepped out onto the dock, and Page rowed back to the *Gilmore Simms*. He climbed into the cockpit, cleated the rowboat alongside, and adjusted the stern lines. He went into the cabin and looked around. "Have you closed the seacock to the head?" he asked. Rosy closed it.

"How about the raw water intake?"

Rosy closed that, too. He would not have thought of doing either.

"I think you'd better lash that hatch cover down," he said. "I don't trust those hook-and-eye fasteners. Have you got a piece of cord?" Rosy handed him a length of cord, and he wrapped it around the fastener and tied it.

The mooring operation had been done with no wasted motion, while the rain fell steadily and the wind gusted in powerfully off the harbor.

Page regained the rowboat, Rosy and Sara Jane climbed down into it, and they rowed back to the dock. Rosy helped Page drag the rowboat ashore and up the bank.

As they walked up to the house. Rosy looked back through the driving rain. The harbor beyond the marsh was not visible. The *Gilmore Simms* was rocking in the tide and current, downstream from the dock, ready for whatever came.

ooooo

ON NO ACCOUNT would Tennie hear of Page driving them back to Charleston. They would be imperiled by falling limbs and downed electric wires, and portions of the road were certain to be deep in water. "You stay right here," she declared emphatically. "We've got plenty of room. We'll lend you some dry clothes to put on."

Afterwards, wearing clothes borrowed from the Carters, they listened to the news over the radio. The hurricane had picked up speed, was headed straight for the city, and the center was expected to reach the area at about six P.M., about two hours before high tide. The tide was likely to rise more than six feet above normal. Top wind speeds of eighty to ninety miles an hour were predicted. The beaches were being evacuated. The barometric reading at the Custom House was reported at 28.91 and falling.

Page Carter had a recording barometer on the mantelpiece in the library, the cylindrical chart on which showed a steadily dropping line and a present measurement of 28.85. Atop a cabinet in the study was the receiver of an anemometer, indicating winds from the northeast gusting up to forty miles an hour.

Rosy described the trip over. The Carters had probably experienced much worse at sea, he said. They had been caught in far steeper seas, Page agreed, although in the shallow water of a harbor the waves came much more closely upon each other. "I should have insisted that you come yesterday afternoon. I didn't think it would arrive so suddenly," he said. "It's a good thing you came when you did. Another couple of hours and you wouldn't have been able to get across."

He should not have permitted Sara Jane to come along, Rosy said. Nonsense, Tennie said; she had been out in boats with Page in numerous storms.

Yes, Rosy said, but Page knew what exactly he was doing at such times, while he had had only the vaguest idea.

"Oh, pooh!" Tennie said.

ooooo

A LITTLE LATER in the afternoon he and Sara Jane were sitting out on the glassed-in porch, with the rain and wind flying against the windows and drumming upon the tin roof overhead. His arms seemed still to be vibrating from the strain of wrestling with the wheel. "I thought of leaving the boat at the dock this morning," Rosy said, "but I was afraid to do it, because I'd said I was going to bring it across. In order not to look cowardly I did something very stupid and dangerous. I risked your life."

"I didn't get drafted," Sara Jane said. "I volunteered."

"You didn't realize how little I knew about handling a boat in rough water."

"You put the boat right at the mouth of the creek, through all that wind and water and without being able to see. What more can you expect of yourself?"

"Just reasonable common sense, that's what."

"For heaven's sakes, Rosy," Sara Jane said, "stop second-guessing yourself! We did it, and there's nothing more we can do about it now, is there?"

What happened then was as if he had been playing a slot machine at a casino, putting coins into it and not paying a great deal of attention, then all of a sudden seeing three bells click into place, one after the other, for the jackpot. Out on the Carters' porch with Sara Jane, the lights flashed, and everything fell into focus for him. It took place in the form of a succession of images. Sara Jane in the raincoat and life jacket. Sara Jane waiting for him under the cockpit roof, Sara Jane on the morning when she was taking the skiff back from the Isle of Palms to Dewees, her back to the bow of the boat as she worked the oars, facing him, smiling.

"Yes, there is," he said. He got up from his chair, walked over to her, took her by the shoulders, and kissed her.

"You're wonderful," he told her, and kissed her again. He held her close.

"I'm glad you think so," Sara Jane told him. She stayed in place.

12

HIS SHOULDER SORE from having been knocked down the previous evening, Mike Quinn drove to work Saturday morning through the downpour. It was when he turned off George Street and into Meeting that it occurred to him that this was just about as thoroughly drenched a place as he had ever seen. It wasn't only that it was raining, or that the water was swirling along the curbs toward the drains, but that the very firmament itself seemed to be wet. From the sky overhead, with clouds so dark and fast-moving that they were visible even through the downpour, to the way the damp wind was blowing the signboards over the stores into swinging arcs, to the pools of water all along the sidewalks and in the driveways, the city of Charleston, South Carolina, seemed given over to falling and running and blowing water. Wetness was All.

There was in addition a curious kind of excitement in the air, so palpable that Mike wondered whether it was physically present, or only the projection of his anticipation about the approaching hurricane.

When he parked his car behind the newspaper building, the lot was several inches deep in water, so he removed his shoes and socks, rolled up his trousers, and walked barefooted out to Queen Street. With him he brought a canvas bag containing a change of clothes, several pairs of socks, a pair of sneakers, and a flashlight.

In the newsroom there was much activity. He was at once told to begin telephoning the airlines and railroads to see whether service to and from the city was likely to be disrupted. Throughout the early afternoon it was one lead after another that needed to be followed up. He was on the telephone constantly. Outside the windows the rain was driving down and the wind blowing.

Shortly after three o'clock the city editor told him to go over to the Weather Bureau office in the Custom House. Frank Blades, who was stationed there, reported that so many things were going on nearby that he couldn't get away to look into them. "Give him a hand," the city editor said, "and on your way, stop by and get a sandwich and a bottle of pop for him if you can find a store that's open. He says he hasn't had anything to eat since early this morning. In fact, it wouldn't be a bad idea to pick up some extra chow while you're at it. You don't know how long you might be over there."

"What time is the hurricane supposed to arrive?" he asked.

"Arrive? What the hell, this *is* the hurricane!" the city editor said. "The eye's only about sixty miles offshore. It's going to get worse, but the wind's already gusting to fifty. Don't try to drive over there. Walk up to the City Market, and cross over to East Bay under cover. Keep your eyes open, and stay away from any loose wires. And didn't you bring some old clothes along, like I told you to?"

"Yes, sir."

"Then change into them, for Christ's sake! You don't want to go out into that thing with a coat and tie! And you better take an extra pair of socks along if you've got any; you're bound to get your feet soaked."

He put on his old clothes and sneakers, climbed into his already-well-dampened mackintosh, and headed out. It was too bad he didn't have one of those heavy rubber raincoats like policemen and firemen wore. The rain was slanting down and the wind was blowing strongly. Even though it was the middle of the afternoon, what few automobiles were out were burning their headlights, and many of the stores had shutters lowered over their display windows.

So this was a tropical hurricane. He had expected something more dramatic.

The intersection of Market Street and Meeting was six inches deep in water. He slogged through it, entered the market. The little lunch stand just inside was open as always. He bought a half-dozen packaged ham-and-cheese sandwiches and bottles of fruit juice. Then he walked eastward underneath the covered sections of the market. The rain was blowing in through the open sides. At the street intersections he sprinted through the swirling water between the covered sheds. No tables loaded with produce from the islands were on display today, and no vendors were hawking their wares; the market was deserted. He glanced over at the Porthole. The neon sign was unlit, the windows were shuttered, and it appeared to be closed up.

He reached the end of the last covered section of the Market, at East Bay Street. Across the street was the columned Greek Revival façade of the Custom House, but he could see it only dimly through the heavy rain. The waterfront was just beyond it, and behind the noise of the rain he could hear a low, drumming rumble, which he supposed was the waves beating up against the land and the docks. At the foot of Market Street the water was well up to the hubcaps of several parked automobiles left there. Next to Carroll's Seafood, a telephone pole was bent far over, its wires dangling down almost to the sidewalk. He crossed over in water up to his ankles, entered the iron gateway, and waded along the walk over to the base of the stone stairs leading to the portico.

Inside the Weather Bureau office, Frank Blades was seated at a desk, talking over the telephone. A reporter for the *Evening Post* named Harper was at work at a typewriter. The rain was beating against the windows of the room. A teletype machine clicked away in one corner. Through the doorway to the next room Mike could see various weather instruments, and two men working at desks.

Frank put down the receiver, and Mike gave him a sandwich and a bottle of fruit juice. "Good man!" Frank said. "Welcome to the front line." Mike offered a sandwich and drink to the *Evening Post* reporter, who accepted gratefully. He had been there, he said, since six A.M.

While Mike was removing his soaked-through socks and putting on the dry pair, one of the men in the adjacent office came in. It was Frank Cox, the man that Jim Igoe had introduced him to at the Porthole the day before. "I hear you and Igoe had a little trouble after you left yesterday," he said.

Mike nodded. "Igoe took care of it," he said. He offered Cox a sandwich and drink, but he declined. "I came prepared," he said. "Save it; you and Frank may need it before you're done."

"How's it stand now, Frank?" Frank Blades asked.

"The barometer was down to 29.81 at four o'clock, and the wind's at 53 miles an hour."

"Anything more from Folly Beach?"

"They're still worried about the pier. The wave crests are only a few feet from the deck, and the tide's just beginning to turn."

"What time do you figure we'll get the center of the storm?" Frank asked him.

"I'd say around 8:30." Cox looked at the clock on the wall. "That's four and a half hours from now."

"In other words, just about the time of high tide?"

Cox nodded. "The low didn't drop more than a couple of feet," he said. "No telling what the high's going to be, the way it's going."

Frank wanted to go up to the Union Pier and see what was going on with a freighter tied at the dock there, and which was reported to be having trouble with its pumps. So he left Mike to keep abreast of developments and set out. The *Evening Post* reporter also departed; there was no reason for him to stay on, now that the afternoon paper had gone to press.

Mike watched the Weather Bureau men as they worked, then walked down to the end of the hall in his stocking feet for a look at the harbor. He could see nothing through the rain; it was coming in almost horizontally, and the afternoon was so dark that it seemed like dusk outside. As he walked back to the office, Frank came back up the steps, thoroughly drenched. He had given up the attempt to get to the Union Pier after proceeding no more than a block. "It's wild out there," he said. "The water's a foot high on the sidewalk, and the wind's blowing everything around. I couldn't see fifteen feet in front of me. Wires down all over the place. I almost got hit across the head by a piece of tin roof just this side of Leland Moore, so I figured I'd better get back while I could."

They went back into the office. "It's gusting over sixty now," Cox told them as they entered. "The barometer's at 29.79. That's a real drop since four o'clock."

For the next several hours there was nothing to do but to sit tight, take down information as it became available, and keep the city desk posted. The Weather Bureau personnel reported that the long-distance telephone lines must be out of commission, because they could no longer get through to anywhere except on local calls. The teletype giving out-of-town readings was no longer transmitting; the electric power was on, but no signal was coming through.

Mike called the city editor to ask whether he wanted him to come back. "No, just stay where you are," he was told. "If it slackens up and you can get over to the Power Company station on Charlotte Street, go on over there, but call me before you do. Don't try to make it over there now. Stay inside the building."

The roar of the wind grew in intensity; the rain was hurtling down. Outside the windows it was quite dark. Recurrent flashes of lightning illuminated the surrounding area. Mike walked back to the hall window overlooking the harbor and watched. Several times through the downpour, during momentary flares of lightning, he caught sight of wharves, and boats pitching and tossing. The far end of one wharf seemed to be dangling down, its pilings gone. Several rowboats were lying up against the iron railing of the Custom House, on what must ordinarily have been the side-walk. But there was no sidewalk or street in sight; water covered everything.

He dialed Betsy's number, but no one answered. The phone lines might be down, he thought.

A little after six o'clock the electric lights in the office flickered, went out, then after a moment came back on. "Oh oh!" one of the Weather Bureau men said. The barometer was now down to a reading of 29.68. The wind was hitting sixty miles an hour.

The city desk called to say that press time for the first edition was being advanced to ten o'clock, because they were afraid that the electric power might go out and make it impossible to run the presses. When Frank reported the news to the Weather Bureau people, they laughed. "By ten o'clock it'll either be long since out, or it won't go out at all," Frank Cox said. "The next two hours are going to be the worst."

As if in answer, all the lights in the room went out. This time they didn't come back on.

"Well, that's that," Frank said. "If they're out here, they're probably out over there, too."

The Weather Bureau personnel groped around in the dark, found flashlights, then retrieved several kerosene lamps from a closet. They lit them, and flickering yellow light illuminated the office. "They're left over from the tornado," Cox said. A tornado had ripped up the area two years before, and the building had been without power for several days.

The telephones were still working. The city desk called to say that operations there were at a standstill. Power was out all over the city. There was no telling when it would be restored. Until the worst of the hurricane had passed through and the winds decreased, the repair crews would be unable to do anything about it. Because of the downed wires throughout the city the Power Company had said it would leave the electric current off until daylight, but that it would try to get a temporary cable over to the newspaper plant as soon as the high winds slacked off. No guarantees had been made, however.

"What do you want us to do?" Frank asked.

There was nothing anybody could do now, he was told. They might as well wait until the worst was over, then come on back to the office and see where matters stood. Mike was not to try to get over to the Power Company station.

THROUGHOUT THE STORM, the Weather Bureau personnel had been taking turns going out onto the U. S. Corps of Engineers wharf behind the Custom House to make hourly checks of the harbor tide level. Each time they emerged drenched, with accounts of the ferocity of the wind and rain. This time, as Frank Cox prepared to leave, he asked them whether they cared to come along. They accepted at once. He lent Mike a heavy raincoat.

They went down the back stairs and out into the storm. Debris was strewn about — upturned rowboats, boards, clumps of oyster shells and uprooted reed grass, pilings, signs, wires. They moved from point to point in the dark, stepping over obstacles, leaning into the wind, keeping low, flashlights trained on the path ahead. The wind was whipping spume off the water in sheets. When they made their way across the street to the wharf, there were planks uprooted, splintered boards with nails exposed, and all manner of objects scattered about.

The instrument hut was located at the end of the dock, out over the water. The door was jammed shut. While Cox tugged at it, Mike shone the flashlight about. The scene of devastation was astounding. Several docks had collapsed, a large barge had been thrown all the way up onto another dock, huge oil drums were tumbled everywhere. Fishing boats were pitching and jerking at their moorings; several had sunk. Mike wondered how Dr. Rosenbaum's boat was faring at Adger's Wharf.

What fascinated him most was the harbor water itself, boiling and churning as it crashed into pilings and boats and against the shore, sending plumes of spray flying, the waves whipping in all directions, the wind raking the crests, the opaque surface punctured into masses of pocks by the driving rain. No matter how far out he trained the flashlight beam, the sight was the same: angry waves and spray, and wind and rain tearing at them. But he could not see very far; the murky downpour was too thick to be penetrated by the beam of light. All the while the floor of the wharf vibrated beneath his feet, and the clamor of the wind and water was close to deafening. The sheer force of the onslaught was what impressed him; he had never seen or heard anything like it. "'Howl, howl, howl, howl! O, you are men of stones. . . .'"

Cox finally pried open the door to the hut. Inside, the flashlights revealed chaos. Instruments were strewn about over the floor; there was broken glass everywhere. The clock gauge measuring the height of the tide was shattered. Moreover, the hut itself was rocking and swaying. Cox slammed the door shut. "We better get back," he said. "This thing's not resting on pilings; it's just hanging out off the edge of the wharf."

"Jesus Christ!" Frank Blades declared. "Let's get out of here!"

They made their way back along the wharf, bodies low, the rain and wind thrusting them forward as they went. They regained the street, waded across, stepped around several overturned rowboats and over a downed telephone pole, and reached the back door. Inside, the relative quiet, after the din of the raging storm, seemed almost eerie.

Back in the office, there was nothing to do but wait for the hurricane to do its worst and then move on. At nine o'clock the wind indicator was showing gusts as high as seventy-five miles an hour. The barometer had fallen to 29.64. Beyond the windows little was to be seen other than darkness and the rain. The telephone rang occasionally. Frank Blades telephoned the city desk but the line kept ringing busy; the wires were probably down.

There was a sudden lull a few minutes before 9:30. The wind died down, sand they could now hear the roar of the waves against the docks and shoreline. "We're in the eye," Frank Cox announced. They went to the windows overlooking the harbor and peered out. Flashes of lightning spasmodically illuminated the darkness, and they could see debris, downed trees, overturned rowboats, oil drums, powerlines draped over the sidewalk, sunken boats, and, out at the end of the Engineers wharf, the instrument hut, still intact but rising and falling as the waves struck the pier. Then the wind picked up and the rain resumed, this time blowing from the southeast. Soon it was as wild, and as noisy, as ever.

They had run out of topics of conversation; there was nothing to read. The storm outside seemed to be the only fact worth knowing. Sheltered from it by the walls and roof of the Custom House, he felt a kind of estrangement, as if sealed off from the entire world and helpless to make an impact upon anything whatever. He couldn't get over how the harbor water had looked, and how the wind and rain had beat against him out on the wharf.

He picked up a telephone and dialed the Murrays' number again. The phone rang for a while, but as before there was no answer. Whether that meant that lines were down, or that the Murrays had fled to another place less exposed to the water, there was no telling. Mike wasn't really worried about Betsy's safety. Whatever else might be said about Mr. Murray, he could be depended upon to do what needed to be done.

AS THE EVENING wore on, gradually the force of the storm began to slacken. By eleven o'clock the wind speed had dropped to thirty-five miles an hour, and the barometer had begun to rise. They decided to try to make their way back. The Weather Bureau personnel had been told earlier to stand by their posts until further notice, and even though there was no way that a countermanding order could get through to them from Washington, they were staying on the job.

Mike and Frank Blades waded across East Bay Street — the

water had receded to ankle depth — and stepped westward beneath the covered market. Debris and wreckage lay along the streets. Telephone wires were down everywhere. Signs were twisted and fallen along the store fronts on Meeting Street. A police car, its siren wailing, splashed its way past, bound south. The rain was still coming down, though no longer at an acute angle. In the distance there was the sound of other sirens.

They reached the newspaper building, made their way up the stairs in the dark and back to the *News & Courier* city room. The editors and several reporters were there, sitting around in the semi-darkness, with kerosene lamps glowing. Until the electric power was restored and the linotype machines could go back into action, there was nothing that could be done.

Frank Blades told about the trip out to the instrument hut, then took a kerosene lamp over to his desk to write a story about it. Mike wrote a brief story about the Weather Bureau personnel staying on duty. If and when power was restored, the various stories that had been prepared could be set into type and a truncated edition of the paper would be published.

A little before midnight the foreman of the composing room came up to the news room. The power company was hooking up a temporary line, he said, enough for partial operations. One bank of linotype machines would probably be ready to set copy about 12:30. Some telegraph news and feature copy had been set before the power went off, and with some advertising copy already in type, it would be possible to get out a four-page paper.

The managing editor gathered up the copy and headlines written during the evening and went down to the composing room. Jim Igoe arrived from police headquarters, and began writing an overall story about the damage done to various churches and other buildings. The city editor, who had been compiling a general running account of the hurricane, went to work inserting additional items and rounding out the story. The assistant city editor worked on headlines for some of the stories.

The managing editor returned with page diagrams. "We've

already got more copy than they can set. Keep your story down to the bare bones, Jim," he told Igoe. "I can't use more than ten inches of type. The rest of you might as well go on home," he said.

Now that it was established that there would be a morning paper, there was general relief. Even if only in four pages, the *News & Courier* would be able to tell the story first.

THROUGH DARKNESS AND intermittent rain Mike walked to his car. There was no water inside on the floor; apparently the water had not risen that high in the parking lot. The starter turned over, but the motor would not catch. He found a dry rag in the trunk, opened the hood and wiped off the spark plugs. He tried again; this time the plugs sputtered, then fired, and the engine caught. He drove home along darkened streets, through pools of water, around downed wires and twisted signposts, several times skirting fallen tree limbs. A sizeable oak tree lay across George Street, blocking the way, and he made a detour of several blocks to get to Montague. He made his way up to his room in the dark, removed his damp garments, and got into bed. He wondered how Betsy was doing. Doubtless there had been water damage, if not more, to the houses along Murray Boulevard. There was nothing to be done about anything now, however. The excitement of the long day and evening was receding, and he was very tired. Soon he was asleep.

13

"SOMETHING WONDERFUL HAS happened," Dolf Strongheart announced upon his return home the Monday evening following the hurricane.

"What? Did somebody poison the dean?" Linda asked.

"Better than that, even. I think the turtledoves have finally arrived."

"Really? In what way?"

"You should have seen him at lunch today. He couldn't take his eyes off her. He hung on her every word," Dolf said. " I swear to God, at one point I think they were holding hands under the table!"

"Marvelous! Do you think Tom's intervention did it?"

"I don't think it hurt. But going over there on the boat together during the storm must have been the decisive act."

Linda laughed. "So it took a tropical hurricane to wake Rosy up. It's a good thing an earthquake wasn't necessary; somebody might have been hurt."

THE AFTERNOON AND evening that Rosy and Sara Jane spent at the Carters' on James Island during the hurricane proved to be extremely interesting. For one thing, all of Rosy's and Sara Jane's hunches about what was going on at the College were abundantly borne out. Page Carter himself was discreet on the matter, but his wife Tennie was, as always, not hesitant to speak her mind when in the company of persons she trusted — and she trusted Rosy and Sara Jane.

"The man is a barbarian," she declared, referring to the dean. "He's quite impossible, and she" — meaning the dean's wife — "has all the personality and intelligence of a milch cow."

"Now, now, Tennie," Page said.

"Do you know," she told Rosy and Sara Jane, "that he actually wanted to attend that faculty meeting, and Page had to forbid him to come? Can you imagine that kind of insensitivity? "

"It would have been awkward," Rosy agreed.

"Awkward's hardly the word for it. It would have been gauche!"

"Now, now, Tennie," Page cautioned again.

"Don't you 'Now, now, Tennie' me! We've got to stand next to both of them and present them to people at the reception next Sunday, and I'm going to feel like I'm introducing the bubonic plague!"

It also became evident that, as Sara Jane had suspected, it was the chairman of the College's board of trustees, H. Turner Murray, who was behind the advent of the dean. In some way or another, apparently he had been able to persuade the president to accept the dean's appointment. Just how he was able to do so was unclear. But Tennie obviously ascribed the dean's presence to Murray's agency.

"Wasn't that the Murray girl who was aboard your boat when we saw you in the harbor?" Tennie asked.

Rosy explained how she came to be there, and how she was engaged to the young newspaperman, Mike Quinn.

"Lord help him, then," Tennie declared, "because she's a spoiled little brat. But I thought she went with Elliott Mikell. I've heard it said that they were as good as wedded and bedded. They must have broken up."

"Elliott Mikell?" Sara Jane asked. "You mean the boy who was involved in the cheating scandal at Carolina two years ago?"

"That's the one."

"And you say," Sara Jane continued, "that he and Betsy Murray used to date each other?"

"Date is scarcely the word for what they did, from all I understand, but that's what everyone said," Tennie Carter declared. "I remember it quite distinctly, because Page and I were chaperones for a dance at the New England Society, and there was some trouble with some of the boys bringing in whiskey through a side entrance, and Elliott Mikell and the Murray girl were supposed to be the ones who drove the whiskey over in a station wagon. It was strictly against the rules. Isn't that what happened, Page?"

Page nodded. "Something like that."

Sara Jane turned to Rosy. "Do you remember when that mahogany speedboat came up alongside us that afternoon? And that I told you I thought she really wanted to go off with them? Well, that was Elliott Mikell at the wheel."

"I'm not surprised," Tennie said, "that he'd have a speedboat. He seems just the type. The noisier and more foul-smelling the better. I'm surprised," she added, "that Turner doesn't have one, too!"

Rosy and Sara Jane laughed. Page raised his eyes, as if to say, "What next?"

The Carters were not notably inconvenienced when the electric power went off that evening. It was evidently a fairly common occurrence out there on the Island, because Page merely put on his raincoat, went outside to a utility building, and moments later the lights came on again. They kept a gasoline-powered generator for just such occasions. "It can handle about 1500 watts," Page said. "That's enough to provide a few lights and keep the refrigerators going. We take it along when we cruise the Caribbean."

Sara Jane and Rosy stayed in guest rooms at opposite ends of the hall upstairs. It took Rosy a long while to get to sleep, even though he had been up since dawn and had slept only fitfully the night before. He kept thinking of how he had held Sara Jane and kissed her, not once but again and again, and how she had stayed right there in his arms, as if it were the most natural place for both of them to be. He hadn't wanted to release her, and it was only when they heard their hosts coming down the stairs that they drew apart.

It had been a long, long day, beginning in anxiety and ordeal and ending in — ending in sheer wonder. Here he was, forty-one years old. To think of the years that had been wasted! But better late than never. Now he knew exactly what he had to do. Sara Jane was asleep in the room down the hallway. He must see to it that in the not very distant future neither she nor he would any longer sleep alone.

WHEN PAGE DROVE them back to the city the following morning, Sunday, it was along roads and highways filled with debris, and requiring several detours around felled trees. The city of Charleston itself looked like it had been taken in hand and given a vigorous shake. Trees were down along the streets, and limbs, palmetto fronds, and Spanish moss were spread in various places. Power lines sagged, several utility poles were bent at angles, there were pools of standing water everywhere. Here and there a tin roof was rolled back, while shingled roofs displayed unsightly gaps. The electric power was apparently still out, for no traffic lights were working. At several places entire trees lay in the street, and police were directing traffic around them.

Sara Jane was anxious to get to her aunts' home on Bull Street; she had two elderly aunts, one widowed, who lived together. Her sister and brother-in-law, who also lived in the city, would have seen to their welfare, but she wanted to find out how they had fared. "I'll go down and pick up my car," Rosy told her, "and I'll call you later."

Sara Jane got out at her aunts' house, and Page drove Rosy down to where he had left his car on Broad Street. From the outside it looked none the worse for wear, and when he stepped on the accelerator the motor started right up. He had Sara Jane to thank for that. He drove back to the hotel, stopped in at the chili parlor across Meeting Street for a cup of coffee, and went up to his rooms. The hotel lobby was dark and the elevator wasn't running; it was a six-story climb.

He was absolutely sure what he wanted now. He wanted Sara Jane.

HE CALLED HER later that afternoon and asked her to have dinner with him.

"I've already had dinner with my aunts."

"Then have supper with me. Let's go to Henry's."

"Will they be open?" Sara Jane asked.

"I'm sure they will. But if not we'll find somewhere else."

Henry's was open. The dining room was illuminated by candles. There was no ice for drinks; the ice-making machine was electric-powered. Rosy ordered red wine. They chose a dish called Seafood Wando. They talked about what the Carters, in particular Tennie, had said about the dean and the chairman of the board of trustees.

"Wasn't that interesting about Turner Murray being the person behind the appointment of McCracken?" Rosy asked. "It was just as you suspected."

"I'm not surprised," Sara Jane said. "They're both quite crude, and completely self-serving. It's just that Turner has learned how to conceal it better."

"But why would he want McCracken? That's what puzzles me."

"There must be something that we don't know about," Sara Jane said.

Rosy thought of what Tennie had said about Betsy Murray. "That's too bad about young Quinn," he said. "Do you really think he's in trouble with his girl friend?"

"I thought so when they were out with us on the boat," Sara Jane said, "but I didn't know why. Now I think I'm beginning to see why."

"What do you mean?"

"My guess is that she took up with Mike on the rebound, up there in Virginia at school after a fight or something with Elliott Mikell. She decided that she was tired of being used by her parents as a wedge to break into Charleston society. So she was going to marry this nice young newspaperman and live somewhere else and not have to worry about whether Daddy can ever get into the Saint Cecilia or the Yacht Club, or whether Mama can be elected president of the Garden Club. But now that she's back home, she decided that maybe she doesn't want to give up being Turner Murray's daughter, and what Daddy's money can buy. So she's holding on to him for the present, but she's looking over the field."

"Meaning this Elliott Mikell?" Rosy was fascinated.

"Or his equivalent — someone with a Below Broad name, and with parents that the Murrays would like to have for in-laws. Do you see what I mean?"

"You're marvelous," Rosy told her. "You figured the whole thing out, while I missed it entirely. What do you think Mike should do? I had a cup of coffee with him this morning, by the way, but we didn't talk about that, of course." He had seen Mike Quinn when he had gone into the chili parlor for coffee after bringing his car back to the hotel.

"If it's the way I think it is, I don't think there's anything that he can do," Sara Jane said.

"Maybe," Rosy suggested, "the best thing would be for him to precipitate the inevitable crisis, and get over being in love with her."

"That's quite true. But also quite impossible."

"Why do you say that?"

"Because people can't act rationally like that, particularly twenty-two-year-old innocents who are infatuated with the Body

Beautiful." She laughed. "She can lead him around like a lapdog on a chain. And I suspect that's exactly what she's doing."

Rosy was thinking to himself that as far as he was concerned, Sara Jane Jahnz could lead him around in similar fashion. He looked at her by candlelight, in her dark blue dress with white lace trimming, and the little plum-red hat with pale-yellow veil pinned on her long, light-brown hair, and thought of what he wanted to say, and how to say it. It would be best to wait until after supper, when they were alone in his automobile, not here where there were people seated within earshot all around them.

She was centrally important to his existence. He had been wandering, blindly, in a fog, without recognizing it.

He remembered the evening on Dewees Island with the turtles. In his insensitivity — more properly his protective emotional numbness — he had certainly botched that one, he thought. In order to redeem himself, they couldn't very well go back out there, but perhaps, despite the damage from the hurricane, they could still drive over to the beach on Sullivans Island.

So when dinner was over, Rosy proposed that they go for a ride. They drove across the Cooper River Bridge, through Mount Pleasant, and on out to Sullivans Island. There were trees and wires down, but the main highway had been cleared and was open. By now it was dark. They drove through Fort Moultrie, then turned onto a sand road leading toward the beach. He had the idea of driving down to where the dunes lay and the beach beyond them, and parking there, but there was thick white sand everywhere, making it impossible to tell where road ended and soft sand began. So he turned into the street in front of the second row of houses, and drove along that. The beachhouses were all shut tightly up and deserted. He pulled over to the side of the road and turned off the headlights.

"Like I said, it's not until you get away from the city that you begin to realize how much you're missing in your life," Rosy began. They laughed. "Now, let's have a talk."

"All right. What shall we talk about?"

"About us. I have a proposal I wish to make."

"What I propose," Sara Jane said, "is that we roll up the windows." It was beginning to drizzle.

They rolled up the windows. "Now as I was saying, I have a proposal to make. You are absolutely essential to my life. I love you. I want you to marry me."

Sara Jane did not reply.

"What I propose is the announcement of an engagement at once, followed by a wedding ceremony as soon afterward as feasible." Rosy was trying to sound lighthearted, but his insides were shaking.

Sara Jane still said nothing.

"Well, will you?"

"I'm thinking."

"You have to marry me, you know. You have no choice in the matter."

"Why?"

"Because I'm madly in love with you. To be precise, I can't go on without you. You know, like in the movies."

"Oh?"

"Shall I get down on my knees? 'Sara Jane Jahnz, tell me you will be mine'?"

"There isn't room for you to do that, is there? And I think we'd better open the windows a little now or we'll suffocate."

"All right," Rosy said. They rolled the windows partially down. "But what's a little heat, when I'm already dwindling away of love unrequited?"

"You sound healthy enough."

"Oh, come on now," Rosy said. "Stop being difficult. This is awkward enough as it is. I love you! Don't you love me?"

"I'm still thinking."

"This is no time for thinking. Tell me that you enjoy my company as much as I enjoy yours, that you wish it to continue, only more so!"

"What do you think I've been doing for the past several years, studying for a harbor pilot's license?"

Rosy laughed. "And you are willing to consider permanent arrangements?"

"Well, if you put it that way—"

"That's exactly the way I put it. In that case—" He took her in his arms and kissed her. The kiss became a full-fledged embrace, and continued for some moments. Then Sara Jane pulled her face away. "It's raining in on me," she said.

"Just so long as it doesn't quench your ardor, let it pour!"

"I'm not concerned about my ardor," Sara Jane said, "but this dress cost thirty-five dollars, and I'd just as soon wear it a few more times." She rolled up the window.

Rosy resumed kissing her.

After a minute Rosy lifted his head. Sara Jane began giggling. "How can I kiss you when you laugh?" he asked. "What's so funny?"

"You are. You've got lipstick all over your nose and chin."

"Goddamn it, who cares about looks at a time like this?" Rosy held out his hand. "See, you've got me shaking all over! You're absolutely indispensable to my life. How in the world could it have taken me this long to realize it?"

"I'd wondered about that myself."

"Well, to tell you the damn truth, I think I was afraid to think about it, for fear you'd go away. You do love me, don't you?"

"Yes, Rosy, of course I do." She held out her hand. "See? I'm shaking, too."

14

SUNDAY MORNING, AFTER the hurricane had gone its way, Mike again telephoned Betsy. Again there was no answer. The electric power was still out in his neighborhood. The rain had ceased, but the sky overhead was a blanket of gray clouds. He drove over to her house on Murray Boulevard, but no one was home. Her convertible was missing from its accustomed place under the overhang next to the sun porch. He walked around to the back of the house and looked through the side door to the double garage; her father's and mother's cars were gone as well.

In the yard next door a man was removing sections of palmetto frond off the driveway, and Mike asked him whether he knew the whereabouts of the Murrays. They had gone to Greenville, he was told. Early Friday afternoon they had closed up the house and departed. They took all three cars, and were going to leave two of them up at Mr. Murray's warehouse in North Charleston. The storm tide had covered the Boulevard and come well up the front steps of the houses along the block, the man said, but except for some loose shingles and the like he had suffered no damages, and as far as he could tell, the same was true for the Murrays. The salt water would probably play hell with the lawns.

Betsy had said that she had relatives in Greenville. It was to Greenville that her parents had gone that evening when they first made love. It was odd that she hadn't called Friday to tell him that they were going — but probably she had tried to reach him, and the switchboard at the newspaper had been so busy with incoming calls that she hadn't been able to get through before they left.

It was drizzling again. The downtown streets, sidewalks, and yards were spotted with fallen limbs and debris. Here and there were houses with sections of roof missing. Not a few automobiles parked in driveways had films of grime halfway up the doors, indicating that they had been partly covered by the tide. At White Point Gardens and Washington Park, tree branches were scattered everywhere. Telephone linemen and Power Company trucks, at work on downed wires and utility poles, faced a massive task.

The city editor had asked him to come in for a few hours that afternoon, even though it was Sunday. Tomorrow's would be the first full-sized paper to be published since the hurricane, and there would be a good deal of telephoning around and checking on the extent of the storm damage. He went by the office, where even though it was barely 10:00 A.M. the city editor was already at work, and told him he would report for duty after he got breakfast at the chili parlor on the corner.

"Bring me a cup of coffee when you come back, will you?" the city editor asked.

He picked up a copy of the truncated, four-page paper produced last evening, and took it with him. The restaurant was without electric lights, but the gas grill was working. He ordered coffee, orange juice, hotcakes, and sausage, and sat down in the booth nearest the plate glass window. "WIND, TIDE CAUSE HAVOC," the streamer headline across the front page read, and under it, "75-Mile Storm Piles Sea Over City's Streets." He read through the four-page newspaper. Frank Blades's story was bylined under a two-column headline, "Trip to Wharf's Tide Gauge Perilous Adventure in Storm."

Considering the circumstances under which the paper had

been assembled, it was a very creditable job. Almost every aspect of what had happened was chronicled. Frank Blades's story accurately described the trip they had made out onto the wharf. It seemed amazing that so many different developments could have been covered by the newspaper staff during such a hectic afternoon and evening.

Even so, having read the various stories about the hurricane, he felt disappointed. The important news was all there; no doubt of that. What was not in the paper, not even in Frank Blade's piece, was what he had seen and felt. The sense of being caught up in a huge event, of waiting for the blow to strike, and the enormous strength of the rain and wind and tide when the hurricane engulfed the city — these were missing from the factual news accounts.

He remembered the way that the harbor beyond the Custom House wharf had looked when he had shone his flashlight on it while waiting for Frank Cox to pry open the door to the instrument shack — the boiling and surging violence of the water, the spray being ripped off the crests of the wave in sheets, the rain slicing horizontally against the dock and pilings and boats. Nor was there anything in the newspaper that captured the feeling of being cut off and isolated that he had known as they waited in the Weather Bureau office, with the electricity out and only the flickering kerosene lamps to fend off the darkness, while beyond the windows the wind howled and the rain drove against the panes, and chaos raged.

He was thinking about this when the front door of the restaurant opened, and Dr. Rosenbaum came in. "May I join you?" he asked, and sat down opposite him in the darkened booth. Dr. Rosenbaum ordered a cup of coffee. He seemed in good spirits. He had just come back from James Island, he said, where he had spent the night with friends after taking his boat over there early yesterday.

Mike told him about what he had done during the hurricane, including the trip out to the instrument hut. Dr. Rosenbaum glanced through the four-page issue of the paper they had gotten out. He was impressed that they had been able to publish any kind of paper at all, so soon after the event. When Mike remarked the newspaper didn't really describe the sense of force and menace he had felt during the storm, Dr. Rosenbaum nodded. "That's probably true," he said, "but you can't expect to see that in a news story. That's not what newspapers are supposed to do."

"It seems to me that there ought to be a way to do it."

"Perhaps, but I doubt it. Not in a newspaper. For one thing, you'd need more room than you have. But remember this, too. If you're going to try to get into the way you feel about a storm, and not just report factually on what happened, you'd have to create a personality to experience the feelings, wouldn't you? Emotions are felt by somebody; they aren't just external phenomena. Either you do it with a fictional character, or you do it by dramatizing your own self — not just what you see and hear, but what it means to you. That would be hard to bring off in a newspaper article. Have you ever read a really good description of being in a hurricane?"

"I can't think of any," Mike said.

"Well, try it sometime. The best one I know is Joseph Conrad's *Typhoon*. Did you study Conrad in college?"

"No, sir."

"I'm not surprised. He usually gets overlooked. But try *Typhoon*. Then tell me whether you still think that kind of experience could possibly be conveyed in a newspaper story."

MIKE PICKED UP a container of coffee for the city editor and returned to the news room. He spent the next several hours making various telephone calls to check on reports of storm damage. The temporary electric power cable to the newspaper plant office was sufficient to keep most of the Linotypes in operation, and by press time that evening full resumption of power throughout the lower city was expected. Mike went out with the staff photographer to get pictures of the St. Matthews Lutheran Church spire and the Argyle Hotel, both of which had sustained considerable damage.

By midafternoon he had done all he could do and was free to leave. Several times during the day he had telephoned the Murrays' residence, but got no answer. He called a little before four, and got a busy signal, then called again five minutes later and Betsy answered. They had walked into the house only that very minute, Betsy said. She had been just about to call him. Wouldn't he like to come over?

He drove to her house. Mr. Murray had gone off to check on the damage to his construction sites across the Cooper River on the islands. Mrs. Murray was upset because much of the food in the refrigerator had spoiled while the electric power was shut off.

He told Betsy about his adventures. He had been there for a half-hour or so when Mr. Murray's black Packard rolled into the driveway. "How was everything?" Betsy asked him when he came into the living room. Mr. Murray reported that one of the houses on the Isle of Palms had had its roofing blown off, and another had taken considerable water when the surf had broken through the dunes. The other houses under construction were unharmed, except for a great deal of lumber and material being scattered about. He scarcely acknowledged Mike's presence; he was obviously still annoyed about the Franklin Poinsett business.

While Betsy and her father were talking, Mike made an estimate. It would have taken Mr. Murray at least a half-hour to drive out to Sullivans Island and the Isle of Palms, and as long to drive back. From what he said, he had inspected all the houses he was building out there; that would have required another hour's time at the very least. So Betsy's statement that they had only just walked into the house when Mike had telephoned could hardly have been literally true.

Still, there was no point in making an issue of it — not even in his own mind. When the Murrays had returned, there had been windows to be opened, suitcases to be unpacked, clothes to be put away, this or that to do. That she had not rushed to the telephone and called him at once, before doing anything else, was of no significance.

All of which was true. Yet it also remained true that, however logical and plausible the explanation, she had left town without telling him that she was going, and two days later had returned, and had waited for him to call her.

SHE WANTED TO drive across the Ashley River and out to Middleton Place Gardens, where she did her riding, to see how her horse had fared and whether the hurricane had done any damage. They went in her convertible. The newspaper had reported a number of downed trees on the Ashley River Road, and some were still blocking portions of the highway, forcing motorists to thread around them, with the result that at several places traffic was backed up, so that it was close to 5:00 P.M. when they reached the entrance to Middleton Place.

There was a "Closed" sign at the gateway, but Betsy told him to drive on in. The guard at the gatehouse stepped out as they approached, then recognized Betsy and waved them through. Mike had not been there before. They drove down a lane topped with crushed oyster shells, circled around the plantation house and a formal garden, and followed along to the stables, the car's tires making a crunching sound as they went. The impact of the hurricane was evident: there were oak tree branches and festoons of Spanish moss strewn over the lawn. Beyond the stables was a wide field with a white-painted rail fence, and in the field bars and jumps of various kinds; a number of the fence rails were down, and the jumps lay on their sides.

A pickup truck was outside the stables, and a half-dozen horse vans were parked across the way. As they got out of the car and Betsy was about to unlock the stable door so that they could go inside, it swung open from the inside and a small, swarthy-looking man emerged. Betsy introduced Mike to him; he was the manager of the stables, she said. He told Betsy that the horses were in good shape; there had been no damage to the stables. He had stayed there all Saturday night, and this morning he had replaced the hay in several stalls where the roof had leaked a little. Everything was all right, and tomorrow he would begin righting the fences and jumps that had been knocked down and removing debris from the riding paths.

"See you tomorrow afternoon," the man said, and drove off. They could hear the truck's tires crunching along the shell roadway in the late afternoon light. They entered the stables. There was a long passage down the center of the building, with a dirt floor covered with straw, and with horse stalls on both sides. They walked past a number of horses until they came to a stall at which Betsy halted. Inside was a large brown horse with black legs and a white blaze on its forehead. It was the horse that her father had given her in advance for her birthday present, she said.

He watched Betsy stroke the horse, apply a brush to its sides, and comb its mane, and move various things around in the stall. She obviously knew exactly what she was doing, and did it with a sureness that could only come from much experience. He knew nothing about horses. He had the sense that what was being shown to him was an aspect of her life in which he played no part at all. It involved money, it involved society, and an entire realm of activity that lay outside his experience and his interest as well.

When she was finished with the horse, she came out of the stall. "Let's go down here," she said. They walked along the stable past the stalls, and came to a crib, separated from the rest of the stable, in which there were saddles hung on the walls, folded blankets on shelves, and hay piled everywhere. Just beyond was a set of large double-doors, barred from the inside.

"What's this?" he asked.

"It's the tack room," she said. She wanted to make love, she told him.

"You mean right here? Won't somebody come along?"

She shook her head. "Nobody else will be out here today. Besides, we can hear them if they drive up."

She stepped up against him, and she touched him lightly and expertly. "I've been wanting you all weekend," she said.

They made love on a blanket thrown over the hay; it was done very quickly. When it was over they brushed off their clothes and walked back up the row of stalls and outside to the car. Less than a half hour after she had finished currying her horse and said, "Let's go down here," they were back in her car departing along the crushed-shell roadway, then out of the front gate and onto the highway.

AT FIRST HE thought that what happened was another example of Betsy's spontaneity. She decided that she wanted to make love, so then and there they made it. But later that evening he was not so sure. Wouldn't be it closer to the truth to say that she had taken him out there with the deliberate intention both of checking on how her horse was faring, and making love?

Which was the more important to her? Were they, he wondered, of approximately equal importance?

But that was unfair. How could she have known ahead of time that no one else would be in the stables? Of course she couldn't. Yet the way she had led him out to the room with the saddles and blankets. . . . There had been no hesitation; she was sure that if anyone were to come by, they would hear them coming well in advance. It was as if it had not been the first time she had gone to that place for just that purpose. *Gone there with whom?*

"I've been wanting you all weekend."

Had she indeed been wanting to make love with him all weekend? Or was it that what she had wanted was the lovemaking itself, and he was no more than a means, and — the thought was appalling — not necessarily the only such, or even the first choice, for providing it? When the telephone had rung busy five minutes

before he had gotten through to her, had she been calling someone else? And been unable to reach that person, perhaps?

In whose stead had she taken him over there?

He remembered what somebody on the news staff had said
about her father. "Turner Murray usually gets what he wants."
Like father, like daughter. She knew exactly what she wanted.
There had not even been the pretense of leading him on to ask
her. Not that he was averse to it; no indeed. It was simply that it
hadn't remotely occurred to him, there where they were.

What had seemed unplanned and spontaneous was instead
the result of calculation. Planned in advance, all the way.

The whole business was devastating to think about. He told
himself that he was becoming paranoid, that he was, literally,
seeing things under the bed. Betsy was wearing his ring. She
loved him. She loved making love with him. And wasn't that,
after all, what he *wanted* her to do?

Yet he couldn't rid himself of the ugly thought, couldn't dismiss the suspicion, try though he might. Just when he thought
he was viewing things sanely again, and no longer at the mercy
of his obsession, he would remember this or that small thing, this
or that incident. That first time they had made love, for example,
with her parents away in Greenville and after they had gone out
to hear the combo. Did she customarily lounge about her house
with a gown so transparent that anyone could see right through
it, see the dark nipples of her breast, the pubic hair itself? Hardly.
She had worn it for his benefit — and, since she certainly would-
n't have left it around where her mother might see it, must have
set it out ahead of time, after her parents had left for Greenville,
to be worn that evening. So the episode wasn't, as he had
thought, unplanned, after all.

There was another time when they were making love, one
night several weeks ago, on her sun porch, and she had whispered, "Do what you did last time again."

"What do you mean?" he had asked. "Kiss me," she had said at
once — but for an instant he had had the sense that there had

been something else meant that she hadn't intended to say, because there had already been kissing. Suppose there were someone else, who knew some act of lovemaking not known to him, and she had momentarily forgotten who was there making love to her —?

The thought was anguishing. They were going to be married! It couldn't be!

BY MORNING, HOWEVER, after he had finally fallen asleep and slept almost until time to report for work, things looked less desperate. No doubt he had greatly exaggerated his suspicions, given in to his fears. There was no point in that.

Before he went to work he stopped by the library and checked out a copy of the book that Dr. Rosenbaum had suggested he read, *Typhoon*, by Joseph Conrad. He ate breakfast at the chili parlor and read the morning paper, saving the book for that evening after work. His days had gotten so that his breakfast came when most people were considering lunch, and whether or not he went by Betsy's after work he seldom fell asleep before two in the morning or even later.

There was much in the paper about the hurricane, and yet it was already old news. Why was it, he wondered, that the aftermath of the storm had put him off so? It wasn't just the state of his mind after the business with Betsy; he had felt that way when he was reading the four-page edition yesterday.

The war news continued to be ominous. The Nazis were bombing London regularly. The Italians were invading Egypt. The Japanese were menacing French Indochina. The military draft had been signed by President Roosevelt, and he would have to register early next month, along with everyone else, males that is, between twenty-one and thirty-five. What would happen if he were drafted? For he well might be, being twenty-two, unmarried, and in good health. When he had thought of the possibility of having to serve in the military for a year, he had assumed that it would come after he was married. Now, depending upon the luck of the draw, it could be as early as November or December.

If that happened, what of Betsy? Would they get married, once he had finished his basic training and been assigned to duty somewhere, and would she go to live wherever he was stationed? Or would the wedding be postponed until after his year of military service was over? *Would Betsy wait for him?* It was one more worry to add to what was already a good-sized cloud of doubt that had been lowering itself over his consciousness, like the low-ceilinged sky after the hurricane.

THIS COULD NOT go on. They would have to have it out. But what if she declined absolutely to concede any need for changing anything about her ways, told him to take her as she was or not at all — to take it or leave it? Or even handed him back the ring he had given her, and told him to drop out of her life?

15

WHAT DOLF STRONGHEART had speculated to his wife concerning the significance of the behavior of their friends Rosy and Sara Jane at lunch was in fact confirmed within two hours of their conversation. The telephone rang, and Dolf answered it. He listened for a moment. "Sure," he said. "Come right on."

He replaced the telephone on the bracket. "That was Rosy. They're coming over," he told Linda. "Get out the champagne."

"Did he say ——"

"Why else would they be coming over?"

"Good point," Linda went into the kitchen. "Pick up the living room a little, will you?" she called.

"Okay, but I don't think they'll be paying close attention to the decor."

Twenty minutes later the bell rang, and Dolf went to the door. "Well!" he declared. "The noted Rebel blockade runner and his first mate. Come in!"

"We have news," Rosy declared as they sat down on the sofa.

"Oh?"

"The third finger of this hand," Rosy said, reaching over, grasping Sara Jane's right hand by the wrist, and raising it, "will soon be wearing an engagement ring!"

"Marvelous!" Linda shrieked, springing to her feet and rushing over to embrace Sara Jane.

"Hurrah for Karamazoff!" Dolf declared. "Only you got the wrong hand. It's third finger left hand."

"Is that so?" Rosy said. "Well, she can wear it in her ear, or on her nose, so far as I'm concerned, just so she wears it."

"That would look rather odd at the circulation desk," Sara Jane said. She held up her left hand. "There's room for a small diamond right here, don't you think?"

"Just a minute," Linda said, and departed for the kitchen. "Don't say a word until I get back. I want to hear everything!" She returned almost immediately with a tray containing a bottle of champagne, four glasses, and a towel.

"That was quick," Rosy said. "Do you always keep champagne and glasses available?"

"We had a hunch," Linda told him. "Dolf, you'd better let Rosy open the bottle. You'll blow up the house."

"Don't be silly," Dolf replied. He placed the towel over the bottle and began turning it.

"You have to unwind the little wires first, I believe," Rosy said.

"To be sure." Dolf removed the towel and twisted open the wires on the cork. "Now," he said, "I'll just—"

"FWOP!" The cork shot off the bottle, and champagne sprayed everywhere. Dolf grabbed the towel and covered it. "Noisy little contraption!" he declared. "Why is it, I wonder, that in order to celebrate an engagement to be married, you always have to extract a goddamn cork from the goddamn neck of a goddamn bottle?"

"Let's not go into the symbolism, dear," Linda suggested. "It's all over the rug. I'd better get another towel." She went into the kitchen and returned with one, and began mopping the rug.

A child's voice called from upstairs. "Mommy, what was that? Did somebody shoot off a firecracker?"

"No, sweetheart," Linda called back. "Daddy just opened a bottle."

"What's in the bottle?"

"Some rug cleaning fluid. Now go to sleep!"

Dolf poured champagne into the glasses and distributed them.

He held up a glass. "A toast! To our dear friends, who have come to their senses at last!"

"I'll drink to that," Rosy said.

They clinked glasses and drank.

"Now, the details," Linda said. "When did you decide? When will the wedding be?"

"We decided," Rosy said, "last night. Or rather, Sara Jane decided last night. I'd already decided."

"So now I won't have to go out on the boat any more," Sara Jane said. The Stronghearts laughed.

"What do you mean?" Rosy demanded. "You've never *had* to go out on the boat! I thought you enjoyed it."

"Of course I enjoy it. In my opinion," she said, "it's the very nicest boat that ever was afloat. Even in a hurricane."

"Particularly in a hurricane. In retrospect, that is."

"True."

"That's better. We thought we'd get married during the Thanksgiving break," he told the Stronghearts. "We haven't worked out any of the details yet."

"We'll be needing all sorts of advice from you," Sara Jane said. "I'm not exactly experienced at this sort of thing."

"Will it be a small or a large wedding?" Linda asked.

"I'd like a very small wedding, but before my aunts get done it's likely to be all too large. I haven't told them yet," she added. "They'll be thrilled, of course. It'll give them something to worry about for weeks to come."

"We likewise planned to have a small wedding," Linda said, "and then my mother and Dolf's got to work, and we wound up with a hundred and fifty people. But you'd better get hold of a book and read it, because you'd be surprised at just how much is involved in a wedding."

They sat and talked for a while. At one point, when Rosy was out of the room, Sara Jane looked at Dolf. "Dolf Stronghreart, I want you to give me an honest answer," she said. "Did you have a conversation with Tom Lowndes?"

Dolf blushed. "I converse with Tom almost daily. Why?"

"You know what I mean."

Linda began giggling. "I thought so," Sara Jane said.

"I regret to say," Dolf said, "that sometimes I get so concerned for my friends' well-being that I feel an uncontrollable urge to stick my big nose in."

"And you've got just the nose for it," Linda declared. "Did it work?" she asked Sara Jane.

Sara Jane laughed. "I think it helped. Something did. I think mainly it was the hurricane."

"He's been in love with you for years," Linda said. "You know that, don't you?"

Sara Jane nodded. "When you come down to it, we're both rather on the shy side."

"No fooling?" Dolf declared. "Is that so? Who'd have ever thought it!" They laughed.

As they did, Rosy came back into the room. "What's so funny?" he asked.

"Nothing," Sara Jane said. "The fumes from the cleaning fluid have gone to our heads. "

AFTER ROSY AND Sara Jane had departed, Linda collected the champagne glasses, took them into the kitchen, and began rinsing them in the sink. Dolf came up behind her, put his arms around her. "Thank goodness," he said, "I wasn't shy."

"No, you certainly weren't."

"I'm very happy for them, but we've had nine years," Dolf said. "Nine years they can never get back, no matter how happy their marriage is."

"It will be very happy," Linda said. "Now open the closet there and get the wash pail, and run some hot water into it. If we don't get that champagne off the carpet, it'll be sticky for months to come."

"You're so romantic," Dolf told her. "Well, the goddamn rug can just wait."

ooooo

THE NEWS SPREAD quickly. Tom Lowndes affected to be brokenhearted. "How could you do this to me, Rosy?" he asked at lunch the next day. "To me, your friend and colleague, who always seconds your motions at faculty meetings? And you, Sara Jane, whom I have adored ever since you let me carry your books to school in the second grade?"

"Never once did you offer to carry my books," Sara Jane told him.

"I would have if asked."

"All's fair," Rosy said, "in love and war."

"And faculty politics," Dolf added.

"I know, I know," Tom said. "But my life is blighted nonetheless. As a consolation prize, you can let me give the bride away."

"I don't trust you," Rosy said. "At the last minute you might change your mind."

The Carters telephoned their felicitations. "We must have a dinner party to celebrate this!" Tennie declared. "We'll talk about it on Sunday." The reception for Dean and Mrs. McCracken was set for Sunday at the Fort Sumter Hotel.

Sara Jane's aunts were, as predicted, enthralled. Both of them knew and liked Rosy. The question immediately arose of the nature and location of the wedding. Sara Jane's aunts would have been mortified by a civil ceremony alone, so to split the difference between a Lutheran and a Jewish ceremony, Rosy arranged with the local Unitarian minister to officiate. It would be held in the chapel of the College of Charleston on the Wednesday afternoon before Thanksgiving, when classes would have been suspended for the vacation.

MEANWHILE, CLASSES WERE under way. The faculty taught five classes apiece, meeting three times each week, so that they were kept busy preparing lectures and grading papers. Rosy had a friend who had gone to graduate school at Yale with him, and now taught at Duke University. He kept urging Rosy to complete his half-written manuscript on the role of the narrator in the American novel. "You ought to be someplace where you don't have to teach so many courses," his friend wrote, "so that you have enough time to write the books and articles you're capable of doing. You could write circles around the rest of us at grad school. Really, Rosy, it's a disgrace for you not to be using your talent."

Rosy showed the letter to Sara Jane. "He's absolutely right," she declared.

"You mean, leave the College?" Rosy was astounded.

"Why not? It's been done, you know."

Charleston was his home and hers. The thought of leaving was startling. He was amazed that Sara Jane would consider it.

In any event, he certainly wasn't going to get anything written this fall. It wasn't just the teaching. He would have to look for an apartment, or a flat, for them to live. His parents' furniture had been in storage since he had sold the house and moved into the hotel after his father's death. Some of it would do, some wouldn't. Sara Jane would have her own ideas. The thought of moving out of his two rooms at the hotel was formidable enough. They were loaded down with possessions accumulated over the course of nine years. And there were the parties. Already it was becoming obvious that he and Sara Jane were going to be invited out to dinner by at least half the faculty. Also there was the Poetry Society, which had been revived several years earlier after a period of suspended animation, and of which Rosy had allowed himself to be elected vice-president. And so on, and so on.

Yet it wasn't just a matter of classes to be taught, preparations to be made, meetings to be attended; the truth was that Rosy was in a condition of tremendous excitement. He had never been so keyed up in his life, or at least not since he had first left home and gone off to graduate school. It was as if he had been existing until now in a state of torpor, or if not that, then of emotional quiescence, with his feelings carefully sequestered and allowed to find an outlet only in certain narrow, restricted forms, upon which he had expended energy out of proportion to the occasions themselves. The involvement with the boat and the harbor defenses was, he now sensed, so intense and all-devouring because it carried with it all manner of significance that bore no inherent relationship to the activity, but only drew upon that as a way of expression.

He had, moreover, been incomplete, and without even recognizing that he was. He had friends and colleagues, of course, with whom he spent time. But there had been almost nothing of genuine emotional importance that he had been able or willing — able was the more accurate term — to share with anyone else. So much of what mattered most to him was kept sealed off, protected from violation from the outside, at the expense of remaining inert and unacknowledged. "Never seek to tell thy love." It had required, literally, a hurricane to allow it to be told, and now, in the first excitement and tumult of its being expressed, he was almost giddy with excitement.

ON SATURDAY AFTERNOON Dolf Strongheart drove Sara Jane and Rosy out to James Island and the Carters', so that the *Gilmore Simms* could be returned to Adger's Wharf. Observing her moored out in the creek, rocking lightly in the current as they drove up to the house, Rosy was struck by the fact that, in the eight days since the boat had been taken across the harbor and tethered there, he had thought about her so little — indeed, almost not at all. He had transferred his concerns from the boat to — to Sara Jane, of course. No, that wasn't precisely it; Sara Jane had been part of it all the time. He simply hadn't realized it.

They sat out on the porch with the Carters and talked. Tennie was not looking forward to tomorrow's reception with any great joy. She didn't liken it again to introducing bubonic plague to the community, but she made her feelings known. Page merely smiled; he was not going to say anything that overtly revealed what he thought. Rosy couldn't ever recall the president making an outright criticism of anyone on his faculty, although it was often evident what he was thinking.

"Next spring," Tennie declared, "you'll have to change to a sailboat. There's really nothing like it. You don't realize what you're missing."

"This seems to be my season for discovering what I've been missing, all right," Rosy said.

"The difference," Page said, "between sailing and operating a powerboat is something like the difference between chess and checkers. There's so much more to it."

"You too, Dolf," Tennie said. "Living in Charleston and not enjoying the water is like living on the Cape and not eating seafood."

"Being a landlubber from the Bronx," Dolf said, "I'll have to take your word for it. But if I wanted to go boating, it seems to me that I'd get a powerboat, for the same reason that nobody rides horses to work anymore."

"Oh pooh!" Tennie said.

"You wait," Page declared. "We'll convert you yet."

"Just so it's not an enforced conversion," Dolf replied. "In my family we've got a long history of resisting those."

"Oh, it'll be entirely voluntary. You'll see."

DOLF LEFT FOR the city, and Rosy and Sara Jane prepared to run the boat back. "There might not be much juice left in your batteries," Page said. "They pumped a lot of water out during the hurricane." He went over to the long, low closed shed at the edge of the creek and emerged with a spare battery and a set of jump cables. Then he rowed Rosy and Sara Jane out to the boat. Other than what appeared to have been some leaking around one of the windows in the main cabin, there did not appear to be much storm damage. "You better locate that leak and get it sealed, or you'll have some dry rot," Page said. The cabin ports were open. "I came out and opened them up a couple of days ago," Page said, "to get some air moving in the cabin. It was beginning to smell musty."

Rosy turned the ignition key. The engine chugged for a few seconds, then caught. He gave it full throttle, and soon it was roaring satisfyingly.

They retrieved the lines and the anchors, waved goodbye to Page, and set off down the creek, Rosy steering, Sara Jane standing alongside. The wind was light, the creek water only gently rippled. They looked at each other and laughed. "Conditions are very different today," Rosy said. He pulled her to him and steered with one arm on the steering wheel and the other around Sara Jane.

They had emerged from the mouth of the creek and were in the process of turning up the south channel when Sara Jane pointed out the window to the east.

"Rosy, what's that boat?"

Rosy looked. Over along the Rebellion Reach channel a warship of some kind, not gray but with camouflage colors, was moving upstream. Sara Jane took the wheel while he watched it through his binoculars. "It's got a big patch on the side," he said. Then, after a minute, "That's a British warship, and it's been shot up or something." One of the funnels was askew, part of the forecastle was torn off, and there was a sizeable gash in the hull near the stern. He handed the glasses to Sara Jane to look.

"She's probably going up to the Navy Yard to be repaired," Rosy said. A gray-hulled U. S. Navy tug preceded her upstream, and another trailed after her. "She looks like a destroyer."

It was a sobering, a grisly sight. Nothing he had seen in the newspapers indicated that British ships were being repaired in American yards, but doubtless it was happening regularly. The war was drawing nearer. The battle-ravaged cruiser was an index to the fact that even while Americans were going about with their own business as usual, deadly warfare was taking place out on the high seas and in European waters. Sooner or later the United States would be drawn in. Last time, in 1917-1918, he had been too young for it; when the Armistice came he was several weeks shy of being eighteen. This time he would very likely be deemed too old, especially with 20/200 uncorrected eyesight in one eye. War, unless you were a professional soldier, was a young man's business.

Along the waterfront channel, just off the High Battery, the Clyde-Mallory passenger liner *Cherokee* was coming toward them, in festive attire, black-hulled with gleaming white cabins and trim, large red star between two stripes on a field of white on her single black funnel, a string of colorful pennants suspended between her two masts. The contrast between the departing coastal liner on one side of the harbor, and the grim appearance of the battered warship on the other, was striking.

They reached the entrance to the waterfront channel at about the time when the *Cherokee* was turning eastward into the south channel to head for the mouth of the harbor and the ocean. They passed within a hundred yards of the liner; passengers on the upper deck waved at them as they went by. The bow waves of the ship sent them rolling and dipping. Up ahead the *Robert H. Lockwood*, one of the White Stack tugs, having helped get the *Cherokee* clear of the wharf and pointed downstream, was nosing into her customary place at the tip of the south wharf.

Rosy gave her a wide berth as he steered between the two wharves and on to the *Gilmore Simms's* slip. Two of the dock lines were gone from the pilings. He backed in, Sara Jane caught hold of a piling with the boat hook, and they edged the *Gilmore Simms* into the slip. "Home is the sailor, home from the sea, / And the hunter home from the hills," he thought. They cleated the lines, set out bumpers, strung replacement lines for those carried off in the storm, and he climbed up onto the dock with the power cable and hooked it up.

They went into the forward cabin, stowed the extra line under a berth, closed the ports, and fastened the ports and the hatch cover. Next summer, he thought, if they went on another expedition like the one to Dewees, not one but both vee-berths would be slept in.

He remembered what Linda had said when she first entered inside the cabin, about the boat being just perfect for a couple to take a trip, but that he would definitely need a mate. She had been trying to tell him something, only he had been too dense to get the message.

"Next spring or summer," Sara Jane remarked as they were leaving the boat, "it would be fun to take a trip on the Waterway to Beaufort or Georgetown, wouldn't it?"

THE RECEPTION FOR Dean McCracken was scheduled for four o'clock Sunday afternoon. In the *News & Courier* which appeared that morning, there was a news story:

COLLEGE OF CHARLESTON
TO GET SCIENCE BUILDING

the headline read, and beneath it a story announcing that the College of Charleston had been awarded a $252,713 grant from the Works Progress Administration and a $50,000 donation from the Murray Construction Company to construct a new building to house its physical science classrooms and laboratories.

The W.P.A. grant was cited as having been announced by Congressman Franklin Poinsett. The $50,000 from Turner Murray was announced by President Page Carter, who praised "the generosity of the chairman of the College's board of trustees in supplementing the Federal grant with funds to make it possible to purchase and install the most modern and up-to-date laboratory equipment." The building would be erected on the site of a residence located behind the College's present laboratory buildings on Greene Street. Construction would begin in the fall.

Rosy and Sara Jane talked about it when he called for her to go to the reception at the Fort Sumter Hotel. She was dressed, and most attractively, in a light green gown, pinned at the neck, and her hat russet with a veil. She wore white gloves and over her shoulders a white shawl. "I spoke with Dolf on the phone this morning," Rosy told her. "He said that about two years ago they'd been asked to submit plans for what they'd need if a science building was built."

"What I wonder," Sara Jane said, "is what it has to do with the dean?"

"You think there's a connection?"

"I think there must be," Sara Jane said. "I don't necessarily mean with the federal grant. But don't you think that the fact that Turner Murray had something to do with the appointment of the dean, and the fact that he's donating fifty thousand dollars for the equipment, have a relationship of some kind with each other?"

"But why would it be worth fifty thousand dollars to him to have McCracken appointed dean?"

"I have no idea," Sara Jane said.

"In your assessment of motives, aren't you leaving out the possibility of generosity?" Rosy asked. "Mightn't sheer benevolence be involved?"

"With Turner Murray? That's a contradiction in terms."

"You know, you really ought to be in politics," Rosy said as they pulled into the parking lot next to the hotel. "Why don't you run for higher office? I'll happily hold your coat."

"You might hold my purse while I get out of the car," Sara Jane said.

"You'd get my vote on appearance alone," Rosy told her as he opened the car door for her to step out. "You look absolutely ravishing."

"You're very nattily got up yourself today. Where did you get that lovely tie pin? I haven't seen it before."

Rosy's maroon and white tie — the College colors — was held in place with a gold pin. "It was my father's," he said. "I'd forgotten I had it until I came across it the other day."

The late September afternoon was hot and humid. There was little breeze off the Ashley River. They entered the hotel lobby and crossed the marble floor to the entrance to the ballroom. Several couples were ahead of them in the reception line. Beyond the opened double doors they could hear the sound of instrumental music and a hubbub of conversation. The Turner Murrays headed the reception line, with the Carters next, and then Dean and Mrs. McCracken. When they came to Tennie Carter, she managed a roll of her eyes as she greeted them. Rosy grinned. "This is Sara Jane Jahnz and Dr. Lancelot Rosenbaum," she said as she presented them to the dean and his wife.

"Ah, yes!" McCracken said as he placed both his large ungloved hands over Sara Jane's small gloved hand. "It is so good to see you! Miss Jahnz," he said to his wife, "is our librarian, and the very embodiment of charm and efficiency!"

Sara Jane withdrew her hand. "Thank you," she said.

The dean's wife was wearing an elaborate red-and-purple print gown, with a large orchid pinned to her sizeable bosom. "It must be so interesting to be a librarian!" she told Sara Jane. "But you must keep awfully busy, keeping track of where all the books are."

"I have some help with them," Sara Jane said. "You must come by some time and borrow some. Faculty wives are eligible to withdraw books, you know."

"Oh, I get my books at the lending library when I feel like reading," Mrs. McCracken explained. "But I know Joe will be your steady customer. He reads books almost every night!"

The long, rectangular ballroom was decked with wicker baskets of flowers. There were tables with food and drink, with an enormous bowl of iced shrimp at the center. The windows were open, and several large floor fans were droning. In the far corner a violinist and cellist worked away. Tom Lowndes and the Stronghearts were standing nearby, listening. Rosy got drinks for Sara Jane and himself and they joined them.

"What did you do to your hand?" Sara Jane asked Dolf. The fingers of his left hand were bandaged up.

"There was a slight misunderstanding with *Sternotherus odoratus* when I was rearranging the cage this morning."

"You mean you were bitten by a snapping turtle?" Rosy asked.

"Technically, not a snapping turtle; a stinkpot. But that didn't keep the little fellow from trying to bite the living hell out of me."

"I didn't realize your profession was so dangerous," Tom Lowndes said.

"Oh, this is nothing," Dolf said. "When we get this new science building I hope to have room for an alligator pen."

"What about that?" Tom asked. "Are you pleased?"

"Certainly I'm pleased. It'll be nice to have a decent-sized lab."

"And wasn't that generous of the chairman of the board of trustees to provide new equipment?"

"Ha! You know what a goodly chunk of that extra $50,000 will be used for, don't you?" Dolf asked.

"No. What?"

"The plan we'd drawn up didn't include a psych lab."

"Oho!" Rosy and Sara Jane exchanged glances.

"It must be ninety degrees in here!" Linda Strongheart declared. The ballroom was filling up with guests, and the several large electric floor fans were insufficient to moderate the rising temperature.

"Why don't we go outside for a little while?" Sara Jane suggested. "They'll never miss us."

"Let's go see how the kids are doing," Linda said. "We left them to play in the park." They walked out of the ballroom, across the lobby, and out onto King Street. Across the street was White Point Gardens. They crossed over and walked along a pathway paved with crushed oyster shells.

A little girl came running toward them from the direction of the bandstand. "There's Joyce," Linda said. "I wonder where Benjy is?"

"Mommy, Benjy's stuck inside the cannon!" the girl called out as she drew near.

"Inside the what?" Dolf asked.

"Benjy climbed inside a cannon, and he can't get out because his foot's stuck!" Joyce declared.

"Where?" Linda asked, putting her arms around the little girl, who was panting from the exertion of her run.

Joyce pointed toward the far end of the park.

Dolf ran along the path. Rosy and Tom Lowndes followed him. They rounded the bandstand in the center of the park. At the eastern end, across from the High Battery, were several large black-barreled Civil War siege guns, mounted on grey-painted iron gun carriages.

"Which one?" Dolf called back to Joyce. She indicated a gun near the corner of East Bay and South Battery.

Dolf and Rosy hurried across the grass toward the gun, with Linda and Tom Lowndes behind them. Sara Jane, holding Joyce by the hand, followed.

They went up to the gun. Underneath the long, heavy cannon was a space, several feet high and wide and three feet off the ground, within the iron gun carriage. Inside it was Benjy Strongheart, age seven. At the back of the gun carriage was an aperture, several feet wide and slightly less than a foot in height, through which Benjy had apparently crawled.

Dolf peered through the aperture. "I can't get my foot loose!" Benjy told him. "It's stuck." He was crouched inside, with one of his shoes wedged between two strips of iron.

Dolf handed his hat to Rosy, then reached in and tried to get at the shoe, but it was just beyond his fingertips. "Reach down and untie your shoe, and step out of it," Dolf said.

"I can't!"

"Yes, you can. Now just reach down there and pull the shoe-string, and your foot will come right out."

"No it won't!"

There was a pause, with Dolf and Linda looking through the aperture. "Sweetie," Linda said to Benjy, "just reach down with your hand and take hold of the little string. Now do what

Mommy says." Another pause. "That's right. Now just pull on it. All right, it's loose now. Now just slip your foot right out of it."

In another moment Benjy's head appeared in the aperture, and Dolf lifted the little boy out. Linda took him in her arms. Benjy began to cry. "There, there! Everything's all right, sweetheart," she told him. "Don't worry about your shoe. We'll get you another one."

Dolf again tried to reach the shoe, without success.

"See if you can get to it from below," Rosy suggested.

Dolf handed his coat to Tom Lowndes, then crawled under the gun carriage. After a moment he reappeared. "I can't reach it," he said. "There's a steel plate underneath."

"Don't bother with it, Dolf," Linda said. "Just let it stay there."

"Those shoes cost $3.98 a pair," Dolf declared. "I'm going to get it out of there one way or the other!" He looked through the aperture again. "If I can just reach my hand a little further in, I can get hold of it."

"Dolf, I said not to bother!" Linda said.

Dolf boosted himself up onto the base of the carriage. He reached far in, without success. He thrust his head and shoulders into the space, and leaned forward. "I almost had it that time!" he declared.

He pushed further into the space. As he did, his body slid forward, his feet lost their purchase on the gun carriage, and in a moment his shoulders and upper body were out of sight under the cannon, with his buttocks wedged into the aperture and his legs and feet waving in the air.

"Pull me out!" he yelled, his voice partly muffled by the surrounding metal.

"O my God," Linda said, "here we go again."

Rosy handed Dolf's straw hat to Sara Jane, and he and Tom Lowndes stepped up and, each grasping a leg, began tugging.

"Stop!" Dolf shouted. "My belt buckle's caught on the rim! Let me loosen it first!"

"Okay, pull," Dolf said. "Easy, now." Then, "Hey, hold onto my legs, not just my pants!" But he spoke too late, for his trousers slipped back from his waist, almost causing Rosy and Tom to lose their balance, and exposing his shirttail and a pair of B.V.D.'s.

By now several passersby had gathered to watch what was going on. "Mommy, why is daddy taking off his clothes?" Joyce asked.

"Because he's hot under the collar. But not as hot as I am."

"Dammit, you jerks, watch what you're doing!" Dolf called out, his voice still muffled. "Just ease me out. Don't pull the goddamn cannon down on me!"

"Oh, I can't stand this!" Linda wailed. "I'm going home to Mother!"

The rescue operation resumed. After some determined tugging, Dolf's upper body, head, and arms emerged from beneath the cannon, the missing shoe clutched in one hand. They lowered him to the ground, and quickly he pulled up his trousers, spilling a quantity of small change in the process. He tucked in his shirttail and rebuckled his belt. "My hat, please?"

"Act like you don't know who he is," Linda told Sara Jane.

Sara Jane handed him his hat.

"Thank you!" he declared. "Life does have its little côntretemps!" He straightened out his necktie, which was considerably the worse for wear. Then he stooped down and collected the coins that had fallen from his pockets. "Benjy, next time, before you crawl inside a Confederate cannon, watch it, because it might be a trap. By the way," he asked Rosy, "what kind of cannon is this?"

"A ten-inch Columbiad. Why?"

"We'll need to order some ammunition. It may have to be used on McCracken."

THE STRONGHEARTS DECIDED to call it a day and go home. Rosy, Sara Jane, and Tom Lowndes returned to the reception. The receiving line had been disbanded, and the Carters were standing just inside the doorway talking with guests. When

Tennie Carter saw them, she turned away and beckoned to them. "Look at that oaf," she whispered when they walked up.

The dean was standing next to the bowl of iced shrimp, talking away and grinning. Every fifteen seconds or so he reached over, lifted out a shrimp, and popped it into his mouth. "He hasn't strayed five feet from the shrimp in the last half-hour," Tennie said. "What have you been doing?"

"You'd never guess," Sara Jane said. "I'll tell you later."

The dean continued eating shrimp and talking. Rosy and Sara Jane walked over to the window and chatted for awhile with the Hewitts and the Donahoes. A little later they passed by Tennie Carter again.

"Twenty-seven," she said.

"Twenty-seven what?" Rosy asked.

"Twenty-seven shrimp. I've been counting."

"Meow, meow!" Rosy said.

"I know it," Tennie said. "But he's so horrible! There goes twenty-eight." Sara Jane laughed.

ROSY AND SARA Jane went into the Brewton Inn, on Tradd Street, for supper, and were shown to a table by a window. They ordered drinks.

"Are you going to have shrimp cocktail, in honor of the dean?" Rosy asked.

"No, I don't think so." Sara Jane laughed. "Wasn't he awful?"

"He's pretty gauche. But I wonder whether we're not being a little hard on him. I mean, just because he's naive and socially awkward doesn't mean he's wicked."

For answer, Sara Jane reached across the table and placed her hands over and under Rosy's hand. "It's so good to see you!" she repeated, in imitation of McCracken. With one finger she stroked the palm of his hand suggestively. "Miss Jahnz is the very embodiment of charm and efficiency!" She withdrew her hands. "Naive, is it?"

"Wow! I didn't see that."

"Let me tell you something, " Sara Jane said, "He may be socially awkward, as you say, but I wouldn't let myself be alone in a room with him for thirty seconds!"

"You think he's a ladies' man, do you?"

"Ladies' man? A shark is more like it. He's predatory — and he's also dangerous. Don't underestimate him, Rosy."

She was speaking in dead seriousness. Rosy was impressed. "You think he could cause trouble?"

"He's already done so, hasn't he? I'll tell you this. Page Carter isn't underestimating him one bit, and neither is Tennie. She can joke about how many shrimp he's eaten, but she doesn't think he's anything to laugh about."

"You make it all sound quite sinister," Rosy said. "Do you think there's some kind of a plot afoot?"

"I wouldn't go as far as that," Sara Jane said. "It's rather that we've got someone on the premises who's capable of causing trouble, and we'd all best keep our eyes open."

"It's amazing, the way that Page keeps his aplomb, never showing any stress or anxiety, never losing his temper," Rosy said, "when you know that he must be furious with McCracken."

"Yes, and if Turner Murray's responsible for him being here, if I were Page I'd be furious with Turner, too," Sara Jane said. "Yet he seems to handle everything that comes along, without displaying the slightest impatience."

"Who knows what vexation lurks in the heart of Page Carter?" Rosy said, paraphrasing a radio program. "The Shadow knows!"

The drinks arrived. Rosy held up his whiskey sour. "To the forces of Good!" he proposed. "May they emerge victorious!" They touched glasses.

"I hope Dolf didn't hurt himself with all that pulling and tugging," Sara Jane said after a minute.

"Think of it. Bitten by a turtle and trapped inside a cannon on the same day."

"A Confederate cannon at that," Sara Jane said. "Incidentally, do you remember what Tennie and Page were telling him about converting him into a sailor?"

"Yes. Fat chance of that!"

"I'll lay you odds that within five years Dolf owns a sailboat."

"Really? Why do you say that?"

"I just know," Sara Jane said. "For all his talk, Dolf is potentially the consummate Charlestonian. Much more so than you or I."

"I'm amazed," Rosy said.

"Just you wait and see."

16

MONDAY MORNING AFTER the hurricane when Mike arrived for work, the city editor called him over to his desk to inform him that he was being given a regular beat. Al Myers, the reporter who covered the three towns across the harbor from the city, was leaving the staff for a government job, and Mike was to take over his assignment. He would continue to work out of the news room, but instead of handling spot coverage and whatever was needed he would be responsible for all the news — government, police, business, whatever — from Mount Pleasant, Sullivans Island, and the Isle of Palms. The job carried with it a five-dollar-a-week raise, a book of bridge passes, and the use of a company car to get to and from his new assignment over the Cooper River Bridge. A beginning reporter would be hired to take his place in the news room.

Being assigned the beat and given the raise meant that in effect he had passed his tryout period, and was being accepted as a permanent member of the staff. The extra money would come in handy, and being able to use the staff car instead of his old Ford coupe to drive across the bridge was definitely an advantage. The new assignment had the additional virtue that he would be going to work in the late morning instead of the early afternoon, and ordinarily be finished by six or seven P.M., which meant that he could spend entire evenings with Betsy instead of having to wait until nine or ten P.M. to go to her house. All that was to the good.

What he didn't like was having to relinquish the activity and excitement of the news room in favor of spending his days moving about three small communities across the bridge. Being given a regular beat and a raise might be intended as a promotion, but he could not escape the feeling that he was being exiled to the provinces. His beat was on the periphery of events. He was also a little apprehensive. It would be up to him to come up with his own news now, instead of being given assignments. There would also be competition, too — the *Evening Post* had a reporter covering the same beat, although Mike's understanding was that the reporter had other responsibilities as well, since the afternoon newspaper generally concentrated on news within the city itself rather than the outlying communities.

The reporter he was replacing, Al Myers, was an older man, in his forties. Of the members of the news staff, Mike knew him least well. He came into the office, wrote his stories, then departed; he never went out with the others for meals, or over to the Porthole after work. Myers seldom wrote features; his stories were factual, routine, and, perhaps unless one lived across the bridge, for the most part of limited interest.

Mike arranged to go on his rounds with him the next day, so that he could be introduced to the news sources on the beat. He had never before been placed in a situation in which his success as a newspaperman would depend upon his ability to make friends with public officials, police, and the like. He was uneasy about it.

He called Betsy with the news; she was at work at her father's office. She did not seem notably impressed, but of course she understood nothing about the workings of newspaper staffs, and a raise of five dollars, even though it constituted a sizeable augmentation of his thirty dollars-a-week salary, was scarcely her idea of lots of money. He suggested that he might come over after he got off work that evening, but she reported that she wasn't

feeling well and was going to bed early. She had set up the postponed dancing date at the Cat's Cradle for Saturday evening, she
said. They would be going with Billy Hugenin and Sally Holmes
and another couple.

AT THE PORTHOLE that night Mike talked with the others
about the new assignment. The general opinion seemed to be
that he would find no great difficulty in covering it. "Just get in
good with the cops," Jim Igoe told him. "Spend some time with
them. They always know what's going on." There were in fact
only a couple of officers on the Mount Pleasant and Isle of Palms
police forces, and four on Sullivans Island, and except during the
summer when the beaches were crowded with summer residents
and the beach parties sometimes got out of hand, almost nothing
ever happened. Now that the Eighth Infantry Regiment had
departed from Fort Moultrie and only a caretaker force remained
at the post, there was almost no military news.

The biggest doings, Jim Igoe said, were about real estate
development. "What you got to be sure to do is to keep a lookout
for property transfers. Drop by the County Courthouse a couple
of times a week and check the deed books." Most of the disputes
at the town council meetings, he said, had to do with zoning regulations. The year-round residents, particularly the merchants,
were eager to attract new development. The summer residents,
who owned most of the property but who lived in the city, were
considerably less eager.

It was Igoe's impression that the Isle of Palms was the place to
keep under scrutiny. Sullivans Island had fairly strict zoning laws,
and there were specific regulations about what could be done and
what couldn't, in particular when it came to disturbing the sand
dunes along the ocean. Activities on the Isle of Palms were less
prescribed, and real estate developers and builders were constantly seeking easements and waivers.

"What you got to remember about most developers," Igoe

said, "is that they're ready to tear up everything and anything if they can make some money. As long as the place was just a summer resort for people living in the city, there wasn't any great problem. But now you got more and more people starting to live out there all year long — new people, come to work at the Navy Yard or the Ordnance Depot or the Air Base. They're knocking down good money, more money than a lot of them have ever seen in their lives, and they don't mind paying the bridge tolls. And most of them are from upstate or the Midwest, and they don't know a goddamn thing about the Atlantic Ocean and what can happen in a hurricane.

"What they want is to be close to the beach, where they can see the ocean from the front porch. So if some developer can level the goddamn sand dunes and build a couple of houses with the ocean right out there in view, they think they're moving into hog heaven."

Mike asked whether his future father-in-law was likely to be involved. "Not so far as I know," Jim Igoe said. "Murray doesn't mess with that kind of chickenfeed. He builds individual houses, but when he gets involved in any kind of development business, you can bet it's going to be something really big, not just scraping away a sand dune or two."

Mike confessed that he wasn't enraptured at the prospect of working across the river. "Oh, I don't think you'll be over there forever," Frank Blades told him. "I expect that once they get the new man broken in they'll stick him over there and use you on spot news and features. They're not going to waste your writing on the Sullivans Island town council."

"No question of that," Jim Igoe agreed. "Just keep them reminded how well you can handle features. Do what you can to scout out some good pieces. There must be plenty of possibilities over there. Myers never lifted a finger to turn up stories; all he did was cover the straight stuff."

Frank Blades looked at his watch. "My God, it's half past eleven! I told Eleanor I was going to have a beer after work, but if I don't get home quick she'll be waiting inside the door with the rolling pin!"

Blades had come to work without a car, so Mike offered to give him a ride home. He lived on Rutledge Avenue across from the Colonial Lake. Mike drove across to Beaufain and then westward on it. When he reached Rutledge, he stopped before making the left turn. As he did, a southbound automobile sped across the intersection in front of him. The car was going fast, and he caught only a glimpse as it went by in the dark, but he was sure that a girl was at the wheel of the car, which looked exactly like Betsy's Buick convertible.

He turned into Rutledge and watched its taillight as it receded down the street ahead of him. He stopped to let Frank out, and was tempted to continue along Rutledge and over to Murray Boulevard to see whether it was indeed Betsy, who if so would still be getting out of the car. But instead he turned right at Broad Street.

What was Betsy doing out well after eleven o'clock at night? She was not feeling well, she had said, and was going to bed early.

He continued around the Lake and up Ashley Avenue. The city was quiet; there was little automobile traffic. He drove home, parked behind the house, and went up the stairs to his room.

He laid down to his bed and stared at the ceiling. He felt nauseated. He had had too many beers. If he closed his eyes he would be sick.

If he asked her about it tomorrow, she would deny it. And she would be angry because he asked.

Perhaps she had loaned her car to someone else.

He should have driven on to Murray Boulevard, and seen whether the convertible turned into her driveway. That way, if it hadn't been Betsy's convertible he would know it.

But he had turned into Broad Street — because he was afraid of what he would have found out.

He half-closed his eyes, as if in pain, then opened them again.

He was losing her. Had already lost her. She didn't want him. Who did she want? Where had she been returning from, in the convertible?

If it had been Betsy.

HE SPENT MOST of Wednesday driving around his new assignment with Al Myers. He would take over the beat the following Monday. He was introduced to the municipal officials of the three communities he would be covering, and to certain local business people who were useful news sources. None of the communities had full-time mayors. A good deal of what Myers had to tell him about the area, he had already picked up. The town of Mount Pleasant almost never produced any news other than the routine civic doings; unlike the two beach communities its population was made up largely of permanent residents. Many of the families had lived there for generations.

Sullivans Island also had numerous year-round inhabitants, most of them living on the northern side of the island away from the beach, but in the summer months the population was quadrupled in size by Charleston families who owned or rented beach homes. The Isle of Palms was by far the newest of the three communities. Except for a half-dozen or so homes, for the most part it had been opened up in the early 1900s when a pavilion and hotel were built and a trolley line installed between them and the ferry wharf at Mount Pleasant. The trolley line was gone, and the opening of the Cooper River Bridge had brought an end to the ferry service, but the various streets along Sullivans Island and the Isle of Palms were still known as stations.

Much of the Isle of Palms was still undeveloped; the eastern portion of the island, beyond the pavilion, was a jungle. How long it would remain so was anyone's guess; there had been reports, Myers said, of surveying activity out there, and he had heard that somebody had built a cottage of some kind, but he had not gotten around to going out for a look. There had been a stir when a group of investors from Charleston had secured an option to purchase a sizeable tract of property to the west of the pavilion, with the idea of putting in streets and lots and building houses, but they had been unable to raise the necessary capital to do it, and nothing more had been heard from them for over a year. Mike made notes on all the names of the various people involved.

Myers introduced him to the Sullivans Island police and fire chiefs. The fire station was located near the bridge across the Inland Waterway from Mount Pleasant, while police headquarters was in part of a store building next to Wurthmann's Drug Store. There were only four full-time policemen, though in the summer several part-time officers were added. The police and fire chiefs, Myers said, didn't get along very well. The fire chief claimed that the police tended to respond to calls that should have been referred to the fire department at once. "The real trouble," Myers said, "is that except during the summer there isn't enough work for either of them."

The new job didn't sound very exciting. What did he care about what went on out on the islands and in Mount Pleasant? Still, he reminded himself, he was not in the best frame of mind to appreciate such matters. He had been a long time getting to sleep last night, and he was tired. The business of seeing Betsy and the convertible — if it was Betsy he had seen — left him feeling anxious and gloomy. It was as if a line had been drawn underneath all that had happened since he had first met her last winter — the falling in love, the engagement, the new job, the move to Charleston, the lovemaking — and below the line a question mark had been placed, with the value of everything above the line subject to the divisor.

HE WENT OVER to Betsy's after work Wednesday evening. Her parents were still up and listening to the Kraft Music Hall on the radio; they scarcely acknowledged his greeting. He and Betsy went out onto the sun porch, Betsy put some records on the phonograph, and they listened to them. He asked her how she felt, and she said she felt fine now. "Did you go to bed early?" he asked. Not too early, Betsy said, but she had gotten a good night's sleep, and was much better. When she said it, her expression changed slightly; she turned her head away and frowned for an instant. She's lying, Mike thought.

Mike asked how the horseback riding was going. Her mare was doing very well, she said, and was learning to take the jumps nicely. Yesterday she had shied away only once.

"Yesterday? I thought you weren't feeling well."

"Did I say yesterday? I meant the day before." Mike watched her out of the corner of his eye. There was the same turning away for a moment and the slight frown. "I wish you'd let me teach you how to ride. I just know you'd love it."

They listened to music, and Betsy wanted to dance, so they did. "You're a good dancer when you put your mind to it," she said. "But you're such an old stick-in-the-mud that you won't try."

"I'm trying."

"Not very hard. If you'd only concentrate on it, you'd enjoy it."

She was lying about not having gone riding yesterday. And also about having stayed home last night. He remembered once, back in the spring, when she had told several of her friends at college that she would go with a group to attend a play in Charlottesville, but then the two of them had decided to drive out to the Peaks of Otter for dinner. She had run into one of the girls shortly thereafter and told a lie about how she was expecting a long-distance call from home and so couldn't go with them to the play. There had been the same expression, the same gesture — turning her head away and frowning. She made it, a reflex action, when she was telling a lie.

Her parents turned out the overhead lights in the living room and went up to bed. Were they aware that things were not going well between Betsy and himself? If so they would beyond doubt be delighted. What would please them most would be for him to remove himself from the scene entirely.

He had no idea of how much Betsy told them; in general he had the sense that the Murrays knew very little of their daughter's activities. Doubtless they made a point of not inquiring very closely. Certainly they could have no notion of what regularly took place there on the sun porch after they went to bed.

They sat on the sofa and listened to a mystery show over the radio. Outside a thunderstorm was brewing. Mike followed the story only vaguely; he kept thinking about what was happening. If Betsy was seeing somebody else, or even if she wasn't but was leaving him out of activities because she didn't want him around, then it was an impossible situation, and could only get worse.

There was really no point in hanging on, pretending that nothing was worrying him. What he should do was to bring it out into the open. So he told himself, and resolved to have it out with her that very evening. "If she be not kind to me, What care I how kind she be?"

But when the mystery program was over he did not announce that the time had come for the differences between them to be faced, and that he would not go on being lied to and misled, and that she would have to make a choice between marrying a newspaper reporter and being his wife or continuing to enjoy the life of a wealthy building contractor's pampered daughter. Instead, Betsy drew close to him and called him her lover, and turned off the lamp, and what she wanted became what he wanted, too.

Afterward, as he drove back to his room in the rain, he rationalized to himself that Betsy must love him, or else why would she continue to make love with him as she had done? So from now on he would fret no more about it. And, for a brief while — say, the space of a quarter-hour — he did not.

THE CITY EDITOR asked him whether he thought he had gotten a sufficiently good idea of who he would be calling on for news on his new assignment. If so, then instead of Mike going back across the Cooper River with Al Myers that afternoon, there was a story that needed looking into down on the water-front. Captain Henry Magwood, who operated the White Stack Towboat Company at Adger's Wharf, had mentioned that last night about ten o'clock there had been another appearance of a mysterious boat in the harbor. His night watchman and several other people had reported seeing it on two previous occasions. Each appearance had come immediately after a thunderstorm. Supposedly the boat always traveled at great speed. If there was anything to it, it might make a good story.

Captain Magwood's office was on the top floor of the People's Building on Broad Street. He was a burly man with a thick Charleston accent. His night watchman at the wharf, he said, had first reported seeing the boat sometime in late July or early August, immediately after a thunderstorm and while it was still raining. His initial reaction was that the watchman might have been drunk, even though he was not known to do much drinking, but it soon turned out that people at the Union Pier and at the United Fruit wharf had apparently seen it, too. All of them told the same story: the boat was long and black, with a sharp bow, and it traveled at great speed.

He took Mike over to the window, from which there was a view of the entire harbor, and pointed out the route that the mystery boat had followed. It had come from the direction of the Ashley River, moved along the waterfront as far as the Port Utilities wharf at the foot of Columbus Street, circled around the northern end of Shutes Folly and toward the far side of the harbor, and then continued down the Rebellion Reach channel, and after that had disappeared.

The mystery boat had made a second appearance in the harbor, again immediately after a thunderstorm, about a week before the hurricane. That time it was seen by two members of the crew of one of his tugs which had been coming back down Town Creek after docking a coastal tanker at the Esso refinery. On that occasion the boat had apparently continued up Town Creek and turned into Drum Island Reach up beyond the Cooper River

Bridge, then come back down the Cooper River, because the sound had been reported as having died out to the north of Town Creek, then heard again about five minutes later across the harbor behind Shutes Folly and the Rebellion Reach channel, before again disappearing somewhere out in the center of the harbor. It was agreed, too, that the sound of the boat's engine was a high-pitched whine, rather than the roar of a conventional gasoline engine.

He had thought first that someone locally must have acquired one of the high-speed boats that were used in the Gold Cup competitions up North, like the kind that the speedboat racer Gar Wood used to set records, and that it was being kept at the municipal yacht basin on the Ashley River. But no one there knew anything about it.

Magwood had become curious. He had checked with the Coast Guard, but they knew nothing about it. Perhaps the boat was some kind of special high-speed craft being tested up at the Navy Yard; but he had spoken with the dockmaster there, who was a longtime friend, and was assured that no such naval craft existed.

Last night the mystery boat had been seen a third time, once again during a thunderstorm. Frank Thompson, who operated the Gray Line harbor tour boat from the wharf at the foot of King Street across from the Fort Sumter Hotel, had been aboard his boat at the time, and saw it. So, again, did his own night watchman, as also did Otto Thelning, who ran a marine repair service just to the north of Adger's Wharf.

Magwood had no clues as to the nature or identity of the boat. No one knew where it came from or where it went. On each reported occasion it was described as having disappeared out of earshot somewhere out in the eastern area of the harbor, in the direction of Fort Sumter — no one had actually seen it out there.

Mike was able to find and interview several of the witnesses. He also drove over to Coast Guard headquarters at the Lighthouse Depot, at the foot of Tradd Street at Murray Boulevard, and talked to the commandant, who said that while he was convinced that those who reported seeing the mystery boat were telling the truth, he had no idea whatsoever as to what the boat might be or what it was doing in the area. No one had ever reported seeing such a boat during daylight hours. No boatyard or repair shop had ever serviced such a boat. The boat fitted no known descriptions of either commercial or pleasure craft seen in Charleston harbor at any time. He too had checked with Sixth Naval District headquarters, and he felt quite sure that it was not a naval craft.

The commandant opened out a harbor chart on a table. On it he had penciled in the places where the mystery boat had supposedly been sighted. There were eight Xs along the waterfront from Adger's Wharf to the Port Utilities docks at Town Creek, one X in the Ashley River off the Gray Line pier, and question marks along the Rebellion Reach channel and the outer harbor. "The obvious place for it to come from would be from behind Sullivans Island, out the Waterway into the harbor," he said, and indicated on the chart the Waterway entrance and the bridge from Mount Pleasant and Sullivans Island. "But the bridge tender swears that on no occasion did he either hear or see anything like it pass under the bridge."

"Couldn't it be coming from out in the ocean?" Mike asked.

"It could, but in order to do that it would have had to pass Fort Sumter going and coming, and the caretaker out there says it didn't. He says he thinks he heard the boat, not last night but the time before, but the whining sound was from inside the harbor, and he's absolutely certain it didn't enter or leave the ship channel."

"How about from up the Ashley River?"

The commandant shook his head. He showed Mike where the Lighthouse Depot dock was located on the chart. "We're not much more than a quarter-mile across from the shoal where Wappoo Creek comes in. Somebody's always on duty on the dock here. They would have been certain to hear it. But nobody did."

Seemingly, then, the mystery speedboat appeared each time on the western side of the harbor near the waterfront, circled Shutes Folly and on one occasion Drum Island as well, came back down the eastern side of the harbor, then disappeared. Without warning, clue, or explanation, and always during and immediately after a thunderstorm moved across the harbor. None of its appearances had lasted longer than about fifteen minutes. And each, the commandant pointed out, seemed to have occurred at a time when tide was high.

"If it wasn't so fast and didn't leave a wake behind it, you'd almost believe it was an apparition," the commandant said.

"A ghost boat, maybe?"

The commandant laughed. "They do go in for ghosts around this town. Maybe so. A ghost boat that goes forty miles an hour, and whines."

MIKE REPORTED WHAT the commandant had said to the city editor, who was intrigued. "A ghost boat! That's just what we need," he said. "Be sure to get that well up in your story."

A good deal of what he knew about the mystery craft was second hand testimony, however reliable. Neither the Coast Guard commandant nor Captain Magwood had actually seen the boat. He had talked with several persons who had, but before writing his story Mike thought he had better interview the White Stack Towboat night-watchman at Adger's Wharf, who was the only person to have seen it on two separate occasions. It was fortunate that he did, for he discovered that no less than his friend Dr. Rosenbaum had been an eyewitness.

When he went down to the wharf about 6:30 P.M. and passed the *Gilmore Simms*'s slip en route to the tugboat office, Dr. Rosenbaum and Miss Jahnz were seated in the cockpit of the boat. They invited him aboard and fixed him a drink. It turned out that Dr. Rosenbaum had been aboard his boat on the evening of the mystery boat's first appearance back during the summer, and had seen it about as well as anyone else had. He told Mike how after the worst of the thunderstorm had passed he had heard the whining sound, how he had watched it go past, and had heard it last across the harbor.

Mike described his conversation with the Coast Guard commandant, and the fanciful suggestion that the boat was an apparition. The idea of a ghost boat delighted Miss Jahnz. "Just think! We could even give it a name. Maybe it's the ghost of the pirate Stede Bonnet. Wasn't he hanged just off the tip of the Battery, where the ghost boat always appears first?"

"Stede Bonnet never traveled forty miles an hour in a boat in his life," Dr. Rosenbaum objected. "Besides, he'd want a sailing ship for his ghostly craft, don't you think? Something along the order of the Flying Dutchman?"

"Why don't we just call it the Cooper River Ghost?" Miss Jahnz said. "That has a nice ring to it."

He chatted with them for a few minutes, then went out to see the night watchman, who told him about both his sightings. Last night he had been reading the evening paper in the hut, he said, when he heard the whining noise in the distance. He had grabbed a flashlight and gone out onto the wharf. This time, unfortunately, instead of passing close by, the boat was on the far side of the channel, and the flashlight was not of much help. But he had distinctly seen a person, dressed in white, standing about two-thirds of the way back in the boat. The boat had a deep hull for a craft of its size; he could tell that because it was planing. "It must have one hell of a power plant to move out like that," the night watchman declared. "If it ever comes by here again while I'm up in the wheelhouse of one of the tugs, I'll flip on the searchlight and see what it's all about!"

THE WAY TO handle the story was to give it the once-over-lightly treatment. He wrote an opening paragraph asking whether there was a ghost boat plying the waters of Charleston

Harbor on stormy nights, and although most of his story was
factual and it was clear that all the spectral references were made
facetiously, he referred several times to "the Cooper River
Ghost."

The assistant city editor was on the desk when Mike turned
the story in. He didn't like it. He wanted the story handled factually. Mike was irked. "I'm not going to rewrite it," he declared.
"Mr. Cutts told me to play up the ghost, and that's what I did.
Just hold it till he comes back. If he says to rewrite it, I will."

The assistant city editor scowled, placed the story in the news
basket, and went back to his copy-editing. Mike realized he had
called the man's bluff. The way to handle him was, on all but the
most routinely factual stories, to pay no heed to his objections,
and to ignore his opinions about what was and was not important. He would back down; he specialized in intimidation of the
easily-intimidated, which was to say, newcomers to the staff,
beginning reporters. It was the only opportunity that a man like
that got to feel himself important and powerful.

THE STORY CAME out on Friday morning. That afternoon
and evening there were more than a dozen telephone calls from
persons claiming also to have seen the mystery boat in action.
Many of the callers referred to the boat as "the Cooper River
Ghost," as if that were an established name for it. One old-timer
declared that the ghost in question had been observed for many
years, and that he personally had seen it once, moving just outside Shem Creek at Mount Pleasant, less than a week before the
Hurricane of 1893. Another caller said that the ghost was that of
the captain of the Confederate submarine *Hunley*, which had
foundered, drowning all aboard, after sinking the Union frigate
Housatonic off Sullivans Island with a towed torpedo during the
Civil War. Still another insisted that it was the ghost of her own
grandfather; she was certain of it, she said, because her grandfather, who had worked on the ferryboat *Sappho* in the 1900s and

1910s, always wore white shirts and white duck trousers, and before he died had several times vowed that he would come back to haunt the waterfront as a punishment for the city's allowing the Cooper River Bridge to be built and thereby doing in the ferryboats.

The telephone rang all afternoon and evening long. Everybody in the news room was amused. "Another ghost report on line three, Mike!" the city desk would call. While he was out to dinner, someone — Mike suspected Frank Blades — went down to the composing room and got somebody to pull a proof of the words GHOST EDITOR in large display type, which Mike found pasted above his desk.

FRIDAY EVENING, AFTER he got off work and returned to his room, he began reading the book by Joseph Conrad that Dr. Rosenbaum had recommended, *Typhoon*. It was the story of a ship captain who took his steamship straight through the heart of a typhoon in the China Sea. The description of the ship fighting its way in the storm was enthralling; he had never traveled on a ship at sea, much less during a typhoon, yet when he was reading the story, it was almost as if he were aboard the freighter — so much so several times when he looked out of the window he half-expected to see the sea and the storm. The feeling was uncanny, as if, while reading in his room, he were shut off from the world. It was too bad, he thought, that he had not read the story before the hurricane had struck the city; he would have appreciated his own experience better. The next day before he went to work he stopped by the library and checked out several more books by Conrad.

He could not get the situation with Betsy off his mind. There would have to be a confrontation. It could not go on as it was doing. They were to go dancing at the Cat's Cradle on Saturday night. Perhaps early the following week would be the time to have it out.

He looked forward with no pleasure whatever either to the dancing engagement or to the commencement of his new beat across the harbor on Monday. He could almost wish that he had been given a high number in the military draft. He wasn't very eager to go into the Army, but at least that would have settled a few things for a while.

17

THEY HAD GONE down to Adger's Wharf on a warm late afternoon in October to take the *Gilmore Simms* for a brief outing. The boat had seen little use since her return from Page Carter's creek. She performed satisfactorily, but her speed had decreased. A visit to the marine railway for a new application of bottom paint was clearly indicated.

It was after they had returned to the wharf and were seated in the cockpit enjoying a drink that Mike Quinn had come by and talked with Rosy about the mysterious motorboat he had seen that night during the summer. Sara Jane asked for Betsy, and although Mike said that she was fine and was now working in her father's office, the tone of his voice, as Sara Jane remarked after he left, had been less than buoyant.

"It sounds to me," she said, "like he's not at all happy about her. I think he's deeply worried. You know, with all due respect for the lure of the body beautiful and all that, I have to wonder sometimes how an intelligent kid like Mike can become so totally enraptured with a spoiled little tramp like Betsy Murray. I mean, Mike has brains, and taste, and he's decently good looking. I can think of several girls his age — and I mean attractive, popular girls — who'd have the good sense to appreciate how much he has to offer. Yet there he is, squirming miserably under Betsy Murray's thumb."

"What you don't take into consideration," Rosy said, "is that when women are involved, kids like Mike can be completely without confidence. I was that way myself when I was his age. They don't realize they've *got* anything much to offer — not anything that a good-looking girl would want, anyway. So when someone like the Murray girl comes along, beautiful, sophisticated, sure of herself, radiating sex appeal you could say, and aggressive, and she goes after Mike, he's so astonished, and so overwhelmed, that he's putty in her hands. Do you see what I mean?"

"I suppose so. I just hope he doesn't get hurt too badly."

PLANS MEANWHILE WENT ahead for the wedding. Sara Jane's aunts were active. Invitations were being engraved and posted. Rings were selected, fitted. Rosy went looking for apartments, and they found a second story flat on Gadsden Street several doors from Beaufain, overlooking the Ashley River. Rosy liked it because the old hulk of the ferryboat *Sappho* was moored — embedded would be more accurate; its seams had long since spread and let in the water and mud — in the tidal flat just beyond the marsh. They worked in the apartment in the evenings, fixing things up, with the Stronghearts frequently helping.

The preparations for his newly-achieved domesticity, at the age of forty-one, delighted Rosy. Such things as choosing rugs, installing brackets for curtains and shades, buying prints and having them framed, and purchasing electric appliances, lamp shades, bookcases, and the like, were largely without precedent in his experience. It reminded him, he told Sara Jane, of the opening scene of the *Marriage of Figaro*, in which Figaro and Susanna are measuring the floor in their room-to-be in the castle of Count Almaviva. He hummed the opening lines: "Trentasei . . . quarantatre."

"Yes, but who's the count?" Sara Jane asked, referring to the operatic Count Almaviva who threatens to dispatch Figaro on a mission and assail his bride's virtue.

"I don't know. Can you suggest someone? How about the dean?"

They laughed.

"He would if he could," Sara Jane said, "but he can't."

MEANWHILE, BACK AT the campus, a new element having been introduced into the workings of the educational process, it was not long in manifesting itself. It arrived in the shape of a memorandum, three pages long and single spaced, which turned up in the faculty mailboxes on a morning in early October. It was directed "To: Members of the Faculty," and entitled "Curricular Self-Study."

The faculty of the College were informed that they were to undertake an evaluation of the college curriculum, to examine what was being taught and why, and how the program of study might be improved. The document was listed as "From: N. Joseph McCracken, Ph.D., Dean of the College."

"Gee! A real Ph.D.!" Dolf Strongheart declared in the hall outside the mailroom. "Think of that!" The dean's listing of his professional degree was a bit much, since ordinarily only doctors of medicine feel it necessary to recite their credentials to each other.

It would be a time-consuming process, involving numerous meetings, reports, and discussions. "We went through this three years ago," Tom Lowndes said. "What's the point in doing it all over again? Nothing important's changed since then."

"Because, Tom Lowndes, Ph.D.," Dolf Strongheart said, "the dean wasn't here then. What kind of a dean would it be who didn't immediately make the faculty get involved in a lot of activity and paperwork, in order to let them know he's in charge? Isn't that right, Rosy Rosenbaum, Ph.D.?"

"I'm afraid so."

"What does Sara Jane Jahnz, M.L.S., soon to be Sara Jane Rosenbaum, think of it?"

"I don't know," Rosy said. "I haven't talked to her since the mail was posted. But remembering how much sheer drudgery and wasted energy the last one caused her, I've got a pretty good idea."

"Well, I think it's a crock of shit," Dolf declared. "And what amazes me is that Page Carter, Ph.D., is letting him do it. He knows how much work the last one was to do."

"What makes you think," Rosy asked, "that he did approve it?"

"You mean you think McCracken did this without asking Page?"

"I think it's quite possible. You know what a waste of time Page thought the last one was. Besides, Page would have caught the spelling errors before he let him send it out."

There were indeed a number of misspelled words in the dean's memo: "advisery," "volumnous," "pedogogical," "inter-dicipli-nary," and — this one caused raised eyebrows — "fellatious" for "fallacious." But it wasn't the presence of misspellings as such, in a document signed by the dean of the College, that was disturbing. It was what the document said, and, even more, what it forecast. The memorandum spoke of the need to "reevaluate the instructional effectiveness of our mutual pedogogical undertaking" and to "reexamine the curricular assumptions under which degree requirements are presently formulated." It made use of all kinds of polysyllabic words, as modified and expanded by education specialists, which when translated into English boiled down to the following: "let us have lots of meetings."

What was wrong was that it had already been done only three years before, and there was little point in going through the arduous and time-consuming process all over again so soon, merely in order to gratify the dean's self-esteem. As Sara Jane pointed out when they ate lunch together at Raley's that day, "It's a power play. He's announcing that he's now in charge of the academic program, not Page Carter."

"Do you think Page will let him get away with it?" Rosy asked. "It's awfully crude."

"The dean *is* crude," Sara Jane said. "But suppose Page simply countermands it. He's then caught in a public dispute over whether he or the dean is in charge of the curriculum. Does that sound like the kind of confrontation that Page Carter would welcome? I think not. It's not his way of doing things."

"With the result," Dolf said, "that instead of paying attention to what my turtles are up to, I'll have to spend half my afternoons this fall and winter going to meetings. To hell with Page's feelings. I'd say that he's knuckling under."

"Maybe he's working on the theory that if he gives the dean enough rope, he'll hang himself," Rosy said.

"Maybe so, but if he doesn't watch out he's going to have us all on the ropes before that happens," Dolf declared.

PAGE CARTER *WAS* apparently knuckling under. The question, as Rosy saw it, was, Why? For it was inconceivable that Page could have given his approval to the plan. But why hadn't the president, upon reading McCracken's memorandum, forthwith called him into his office, read him the riot act, and made it clear that no such program was to be undertaken without his specific authorization? Rosy worked in his office that afternoon, grading freshman themes, trying to figure out the answer to that question, and thinking about what to do.

Unless headed in, the dean was about to cause everybody a tremendous lot of trouble, when he hadn't even been on the campus long enough to gain a decent idea of what, if anything, might be in need of curricular revision. He had no idea of what the strengths and weaknesses of his faculty and departments were. Nor did he have any way yet of knowing which members of the faculty generally knew whereof they spoke, and which ones were hot air specialists. He also knew next to nothing about the student body. How, then, could he possibly do a decent job of guiding a curricular self-study, even if one were in order, which it wasn't?

Horace Hewitt came into the office. As might be expected, Rosy's colleague in English was outraged. What the dean proposed to do was outrageously presumptuous, an insult to the intelligence of the faculty; the faculty should draw up a petition demanding that the project be canceled and the dean dismissed, and present it to the president and/or the board of trustees.

Rosy didn't like the idea of a petition, because while a majority of the faculty would undoubtedly sign it, to draw it up and present it would be in effect to acknowledge that the dean possessed the authority to order the self-study undertaken. Instead, the thing to do would be for the faculty, individually and as a group, simply to vote to table the project indefinitely, the assumption thus being that it was the faculty's decision to make. The dispute would then become one of the faculty versus Dean McCracken, not of the faculty versus the College administration's right to order that a self-study be conducted. Maybe that was what Page Carter, in whatever unknown balancing act he was caught up in, was hoping for.

"BUT SUPPOSE," SARA Jane asked when they were eating supper at her aunts' house that evening, "the dean says that his project is *not* subject to a vote by the faculty? What then?"

"Then we'll walk out of the meeting, and leave it to Page to settle it. But I don't think it would come to that. Page would simply say that the matter would be taken under advisement, and that's the last anybody would hear of it for a couple of years."

"Well, if you're going to do that, you'd better get your votes lined up ahead of time," Sara Jane said. "I think almost everyone would support you, but I'd make sure that everything is well prepared."

WHAT WAS HE doing, Rosy thought, planning moves to block the dean of the College, and talking about faculty walkouts? He was becoming awfully bold these days. But after what had happened with the boat in the hurricane, and Sara Jane,

Rosy was getting into the habit of making audacious moves. At the poker game last Saturday night he had even bluffed Dolf and Herbert Simons out of a sizeable pot when each was obviously holding three of a kind and all he had were kings and eights. It had worked perfectly, because the two of them were convinced that Rosy never bluffed.

SARA JANE'S AUNTS were agog over the wedding preparations. The forthcoming nuptials were providing them with a field of operations such as they had not enjoyed for years. They talked of little else. Rosy much enjoyed watching them in action. They were the sort who could make a half-hour's conversation between themselves out of the request of a delivery man to leave a package with them for the next-door neighbors. The widowed aunt, Esther, was especially concerned over the music to be played at the ceremony. There was much consultation with a family friend, Mrs. Morrison, who was to play the piano in company with violin and cello. The other aunt, Ruth, thought that a harpist would be more appropriate. Sara Jane, who disliked harp music, sided with Aunt Esther. Aunt Ruth appealed to Rosy, who however declined to intervene. Privately he agreed with Sara Jane.

The pre-ceremony music would consist of compositions by Bach, Haydn, and Beethoven. Since the wedding was to be held in the College chapel, which contained neither an organ nor a choir loft, there would be no hymn-singing.

This rather perturbed Ruth. "What kind of a wedding can it be," she remarked several times, "without something from Isaac Watts?" It was finally agreed that Mrs. Morrison and the other two musicians would work out an arrangement of "O God, Our Help in Ages Past" to be performed at some point in the proceedings.

Esther, who when music was concerned tended to be somewhat more adventurous, proposed that the recessional consist of "See, the Conqu'ring Hero Comes!" from *Judas Maccabeus*, instead of the customary March from *A Midsummer Night's*

Dream, but Ruth was appalled. "Why, they might as well play the Bolero!" she declared.

Sara Jane, having voted with Esther in the matter of piano trio-vs.-harp, thought it appropriate to allow her other aunt's opinion to prevail this time, so she opted for Mendelssohn over Handel. "I'm only glad," she said to Rosy later that evening, "that Aunt Ruth didn't insist on 'O Promise Me That Someday You'll Be Mine.'"

"It must be a little disappointing for them not to have the wedding taking place in your church," Rosy suggested.

"I think they're so relieved that it's taking place at all that they aren't disposed to quibble over details," Sara Jane said. "Incidentally, they aren't particularly happy with our working in the apartment at night. They keep asking whether your furniture has arrived yet."

"Why does the furniture worry them?"

"Think about it for a minute."

"The beds?"

"Exactly."

"Don't they trust you?"

"Oh, it's not me they're worried about. It's what the neighbors will say."

"Well, it's time they started worrying about *me*," Rosy said, taking her in his arms. They were seated on the sofa in Sara Jane's apartment.

"Oh, they trust both of us completely. Besides, they're not prudes. All they're concerned with is what people might say."

There was a long pause. "When you kiss me like that," Sara Jane said after a minute, "my virtue is in your hands."

"If there's anything I can't abide," Rosy said, "it's a pun."

ROSY'S UNCLE AND AUNT from Atlanta and his uncle from Philadelphia were planning to come for the wedding. He had not seen them in several years. The aunt in Atlanta was his father's sister, and the Philadelphia uncle his mother's brother.

When his mother died he was eight years old. He remembered his Philadelphia relatives coming down to Charleston for the funeral. Thereafter his father had continued to maintain contact with them, and one summer, when he was twelve, he had been sent on the train to spend a week with them.

His father. When Rosy had come back to Charleston after finishing his work at Yale, and begun teaching at the College, it had been, in part at least, because of his father. His major professor, Dr. Williams, wanted him to apply for a position that was open at Cornell University, and was surprised and even chagrined when he opted instead to return to the small municipal college where he had taken his undergraduate degree, scarcely known outside the state of South Carolina, with heavy teaching responsibilities and no graduate program. It was if he were deliberately turning his back upon a career as a scholar. And there was some truth to that — as he had known even then. He had published his dissertation, a study of William Gilmore Simms, and except for a little poetry that had been all. But he had wanted to come home, back to his father and the house on Pitt Street where he had grown up. Now, more than a decade later, he was still there, and his book on the American novel was still only half-written.

SATURDAY MORNING, AFTER his American literature class, on an impulse he got into his car and drove up to the cemetery. He parked on the road outside the stone wall, opened and walked through the iron gate, and past the rows of tombstones, many bearing names of persons whom he remembered very well indeed, over to where his parents lay buried. "Abraham Louis Rosenbaum, born Baltimore, Md., May 31, 1869, died Charleston, So. Car., August 1, 1932," a granite marker read, and next to it another, "Frances Hoffman Rosenbaum, born Philadelphia, Pa., March 7, 1873, died Charleston, So. Car., June 6, 1907." The eight years since his father's death had weathered the stone so that it was beginning to take on the mottled cast that more than three decades of rain and wind, shadow and sun had brought to his mother's gravestone. He remembered some lines from a poem he liked, Allen Tate's "Ode to the Confederate Dead": "Ambitious November with the humours of the year, / With a particular zeal for each slab" — there were a few Confederate dead in this cemetery, but not many. Most of the Jewish Confederate veterans were buried downtown in the old cemetery on Coming Street.

HIS FATHER HAD come to Charleston as a tailor in the 1880s, had opened a wholesale dry goods business on Meeting Street, and had operated it until his death in 1932. Not an innovative businessman, he had earned a decent livelihood, enough to marry, to own his home, to educate a child, and when he died to leave a sufficient estate to make it possible for Rosy not to be completely dependent upon his teaching salary. He had worked steadily at his business, going down to his office six days a week and on Sunday mornings as well; his work was a habit, a trade — he did not even particularly enjoy it, Rosy thought, but it was his way of life, and the more so after his wife died and he had plunged himself into it.

If only his father could know about Sara Jane! He would have been so pleased. They would have liked each other enormously. His father was by no means an intellectual, but he was well read, and he loved music. They had an old crank-up Victrola phonograph, and his father used to sit by it some evenings and listen to the Beethoven and Brahms symphonies. When the first electric-powered phonographs came on the market, he had bought one, and had been replacing the old acoustical recordings with electrically recorded versions. Yet his father never attended concerts; music was a private, solitary occupation for him.

Why had his father never remarried? Never, so far as Rosy knew, so much as gone out with another woman? When his mother had died, he had been only thirty-nine — two years younger than he himself was, and he was only now about to get married. Wasn't that odd? For since being married had been so much to his father's liking, it seemed strange that once the immediate grief and pain of his wife's loss had worn off, he had not felt impelled to seek to resume it. Was it that the losing of that shared life was so rending, so terrible, that he could not risk its ever happening a second time?

Whichever it was, it seemed to Rosy that when his mother had died his father had withdrawn into a sheltered harbor, in which he had closed himself off from almost all the possibilities inherent in the life around him and settled for a diminished existence, protected against further grief and disappointment at the price of relinquishing the potential for new joy. And — without at all meaning to — his father had drawn *him* into a similar isolation, a similar shut-offness, so that he had, in his own way, replicated it, assumed that nothing more than that was possible for himself as well. It had taken him twenty years, half an adult lifehood, to break out of it, to recognize what he was doing to himself, how much he was missing. It was like the duet he so liked in the *Magic Flute*, between Tamina and Papageno:

Mann und Weib, und Weib und Mann,
Reichen an die Gottheit an.

Still, if the condition of man and wife could come close to what only the gods could know, it could also be a living hell on earth if the pairing worked out wrong. Even Mozart had his difficulties with Constanzia. At least, by waiting as long as he had, Rosy thought, he had avoided any chance of that happening. Of that, he was sure.

HE WALKED OVER toward the edge of the salt marsh which stretched for a quarter-mile between the shore and the Cooper River. This time of year, late October, the marsh was only just beginning to turn gray-yellow. By the end of the year the green would be totally gone; there would be a wide expanse of sallowness. And when in the spring new growth began, the green would rise from the base of the reed grass, so that eventually the tips only would be gray, with green beneath.

There was no one else at the cemetery. In Jewish tradition, still observed in orthodox congregations, one never went near a cemetery on Saturday; the graveyard was taboo on the Sabbath. There was an orthodox cemetery down the way, over toward Magnolia Crossing. He had gone there once to look. Numerous of the graves had a hand carved upon the markers, with the fingers spread into two groups of two fingers each. Supposedly that was the sign of the priests, the Cohens; the story was that only the descendents of the Cohens could spread their fingers that way. It wasn't any such thing, of course; it was a representation of the cloven hoof of the ram, the Hebrew tribal totem.

Judaism — even Reform Judaism — was filled with primitive survivals like that, going back far into pre-history. Like the glass that was stepped upon and crushed at weddings, and that supposedly commemorated the destruction of the Temple in Jerusalem by the Romans. Surely it had nothing to do with that. It was a symbolic breaking of the maidenhead, a shattering of the vessel.

Compared to his friend Dolf Strongheart, very little of that sort of thing — the ritual and community lore, the vast body of custom that Jews bore with them through several thousand years of survival — was his own personal heritage. As a Reform Jew he had grown up outside of it. He had never been made to learn Hebrew. Neither his mother nor his father spoke Yiddish at home. His parents — and doubtless *their* parents; he had never known his father's parents, and his mother's were now long since dead — had, for whatever reason, sought to put aside all but the strictly theological elements of Judaism. After his mother's death his father had virtually ceased attending services at the Temple, though he had maintained his membership.

As for himself, well, he could believe in nothing *except* the social identity. He was a Jew; he could not imagine being any-thing else. But the theology itself — like any and all theologies — was beyond his ability to credit.

Thus here he was, here in this little Hebrew burial place, located along the edge of the marsh overlooking a river and beyond that a harbor, 3,000 miles and more across the Atlantic Ocean from where his grandparents had come — and which was now locked in war and, wherever the Nazis were triumphant, engaged in persecuting and very likely in annihilating all Jews still there who had not the foresight, ambition, means, or sheer luck that had prompted his own forebears to get out.

Yet the salt marsh spread out in front of him, of reed grass and pluff mud and tidal creeks, and here and there a small island with a few shrubs, yellow and gray and green and gold and black, the occasional widened stretches along the creeks reflecting the pale blue and cloud-gray sky overhead, was like a gigantic tapestry, or perhaps a carpet. And, as if a figure in that carpet, he was, as a third generation American Jew—bereft of his heritage by history, engaged in being woven into the fabric of the place, the land — raveled by the turning of the tide along its edges and throughout its network of creeks, transformed into something else again, he was not sure what.

Enough! It was not up to him to reconcile or compensate for the behavior of forebears he did not know. He walked through the cemetery, got into his car, and drove off toward the land of the living. He was meeting Sara Jane for lunch.

18

THERE WAS A late-breaking accident story Saturday, so it wasn't until almost ten that Mike got off from work. He called Betsy to tell her that he would be late in picking her up. She wasn't happy about it. In what was now five months since he had begun working on the paper, she had not conceded that such things weren't to be helped. When he took over the new beat next week, at least his working day would end earlier and except in unusual circumstances he wouldn't be as vulnerable to last-minute assignments. That was one good thing, at least, to be said for the new beat.

He hurried to his room and changed his clothes, then called for Betsy shortly after ten. She was dressed very attractively in a dark red gown and a white fur wrap. As always, she was excited about going dancing — so much so that she soon forgot that she was angry with him. He made a vow to try his best to enter into the spirit of the occasion, and not allow himself to become glum or morose. They drove up to Calhoun Street and turned into an alleyway across from the statue of John C. Calhoun on Citadel Square. The Cat's Cradle was located behind an armory building, with a parking lot across another alley.

The lot was crowded, but there were two empty places at one end. As they were leaving the car, a tan-colored Lincoln Zephyr pulled into the space next to them, and a couple got out. Betsy knew them. The man was named Elliott Mikell; he was tall, athletic in build, with a round face, florid complexion, and a breezy way of talking. Mike was certain he had seen him before. Then he recognized him as the driver of the runabout that had pulled alongside Dr. Rosenbaum's boat out in the harbor when they were near the site of the Confederate fort. Billy Hugenin and Annie Holmes had been in the boat, and he had been afraid that Betsy might go off with them. He did not know the girl with him now, who had little to say.

They entered the Cat's Cradle together. There was something about Mikell that put him off, and he was relieved to find that they were not in their party. It was intermission, and Billy Hugenin and Annie Holmes were at a table in the far corner of the lounge, along with another couple. A half-filled pitcher of beer was on the table. A pianist was playing. Billy and Annie welcomed Betsy effusively, and were reasonably friendly to him; as always, they accepted his presence because he was Betsy's fiancé, not because they had much in common with him, or vice versa. That was his fault as much as theirs; they couldn't help it if he knew and cared nothing about horses, which was always their chief topic of conversation, and was only mildly interested in movies, which came second on their agenda. The other couple he did not know; he had met the boy once, at a party, and the girl, tall, dark-haired and quite attractive, seemed familiar, but he could not recall where he had seen her.

He made a special effort to converse, asking Betsy's friends what they had done during the hurricane, and telling about his trip out to the wharf behind the Custom House. In almost no time, however, the conversation moved from the hurricane to what little damage it had done to the riding facilities at Middleton Place, and on to riding again. He finished his beer, ordered another pitcher, and tried to stay interested in what they were saying. He resolved that he was not going to sit by himself and brood tonight.

The band returned; it was a seven-piece combo — piano, bass, drums, trombone, trumpet, tenor sax, and alto sax-clarinet. As musicians they played together reasonably well, but the music they chose was insipid. He tried to interest himself in it, but there was little or none of the feeling he got when a combo like the one they had heard out on the Folly Beach Road was engaged in doing things. Still, what they played was preferable to the reedy, syrupy bubbling of the Idol of the Airwaves he had heard out at the Pier. At least the musicians were working together, and extemporizing rather than reading from arrangements, although it was so thoroughly rehearsed that it could almost have been written down. They repeated what they obviously already knew, with no interest, seemingly, in exploring what further could be done with it. It was decent dance music, however, and that was what they had come there to do. He danced with Betsy and they traded off some, and all in all, he thought, it was adequate.

The other girl they were with, not Annie Holmes but the one he hadn't met, had a sly sense of humor. Her name was Polly Morrison, and when she said that she had seen him at St. Mary's, he realized that was why her face had seemed familiar. She was a senior at the College of Charleston, she said. He asked whether she knew Dr. Rosenbaum. She was currently taking a course with him, she told him. She even volunteered the fact that she was a history major. It was the first time, so far as he could remember, that any of Betsy's friends had ever so much as mentioned a subject taken at college.

During the next intermission, Elliott Mikell came over to their table, drink in hand, and talked with Betsy and the others. They joked about riding quite a bit. Apparently Mikell was known for his prowess on jumps. There was a good deal said about Betsy's new horse. Mikell had evidently ridden the horse himself, and was telling how best to handle her. The thing to do, he said several times, was not to give in to her. "You got to remember she's a mare, and she needs to know who's the boss. If she starts to shy, give her a good whack or two across the rump.

Treat her rough, and she'll come around. That's what you got to do with females. Isn't that right, Billy?" he asked Billy Hugenin.

"You ought to know," Billy told him. Everybody laughed.

Mike poured another glass of beer for himself. He didn't like Elliott Mikell at all.

"What's this I read about you cruising around the harbor at night, dressed up like a ghost?" Billy asked Mikell.

"Don't know anything about it. What you talking about?"

"Didn't you read the paper? There's a ghost boat been terrorizing the waterfront on stormy nights. They can't tell what it is, it goes by so fast. The minute I read about it, I told myself that's got to be Elliott Mikell."

"Not me, man! I'm sticking to terra firma these days. My boat's been hauled for the winter."

Mike said nothing about his having written the story. Neither did Betsy. She never mentioned his work. It was as if she didn't want it known that he was a newspaper reporter. As if she were ashamed of it. Then he thought, I'm starting to brood. I'm not going to do it.

The combo returned to the stand. This time they opened with a fast number, "Twelfth Street Rag." Billy Hugenin asked Betsy for the dance, and Polly Morrison's escort danced with Sally Holmes. Mike explained to Polly that the music was beyond his dancing competence. She didn't seem to mind. She asked him how he liked newspaper work. He liked it pretty well, he told her. Did he know Jim Igoe? she asked. He was a friend of her father's.

She had known Betsy, she said, most of her life, though they weren't really close friends. She had been a year behind her in school. They had both attended Crafts School, but then Betsy had enrolled at Ashley Hall while she had gone to Memminger High School.

"How come you didn't go to parochial school?" Mike asked.

"My father is principal of Courtenay School, and he thought that since he taught in the public schools my brother and I ought to go to them. Did you go to a parochial school?"

Mike shook his head. "Not high school. I went to parochial grade school."

"Why not high school?"

"We don't have one in Roanoke."

While they were talking, Mike was watching Betsy dance with Billy Hugenin. Annie Holmes and Polly's date were dancing. The number ended and Betsy and Billy waited on the floor for the next. It was another fast piece. As the music resumed and he and Polly Morrison looked on, Elliott Mikell came walking across the floor and cut in on Billy Hugenin. Billy returned to the table and asked Polly to dance.

"I think I'd rather sit this one out," she told him. Billy picked up his drink from the table and downed it. "I got to see a man about a dog," he said, and walked off.

Watching Betsy and Elliott Mikell on the dance floor, Mike felt a surge of resentment. There was something about the way they were dancing together that made him uncomfortable. He finished his beer and ordered another pitcher. They were jitterbugging — spinning, turning, whirling, moving out and around and in. Each seemed to know exactly what the other would do, as if they had danced together many times before.

A familiarity was on display. He could sense that at once. They were old, and close, partners. *How close?*

Mike had the feeling that what was happening to him was like one of those electric quiz board games that had been given to him for Christmas when he was a child. There were a number of little steel pins, over which a printed cardboard with questions and answers was fitted, and two probes, attached to wires, one for the question, one for the answer. When the correct pins were touched by the probes, there was a buzzing noise, and an array of light bulbs was illuminated. Watching Betsy and Elliott Mikell dancing, Mike felt that what he was seeing was in effect the answer he had, without realizing it, been seeking.

He poured himself another glass of beer. "'Lady Clara Vere de

Vere, from me you shall not win renown,'" he recited.

"I hope you're not referring to me," Polly said.

"Oh, not at all. I had someone else in mind." He paused a moment. "Betsy and Elliott Mikell certainly dance well together," he said, trying to make it sound like a casual comment.

"Yes, they do."

Polly Morrison's date and Annie Holmes came back to the table. The date, whose name was Charlie — Mike didn't catch the last name — was shorter than Polly, and was also well oiled. He began discoursing on the merits of the Clemson College football team. Billy Hugenin returned, and began arguing with him, citing what he considered the superior merits of the University of South Carolina Gamecocks. Then Elliott Mikell brought Betsy back and walked off, presumably to look after his much-neglected date. The combo was taking another break, and the intermission pianist was performing some songs from *Porgy and Bess*.

"That ought to be the band's theme song," Mike said. "I got plenty of nothing." Polly Morrison laughed.

"Well, *I* think they're *quite* good!" Betsy said. "Wonderful, in fact."

Mike started to make a retort, then said nothing. He was not going to sulk. But he thought of Betsy dancing with Elliott Mikell; he felt a tightness in his chest. He poured himself another glass of beer and took a deep swallow. "They ought to be wearing Confederate grey," he declared. "They're a Lost Cause." And what about me? he thought.

"You know everything about everything," Betsy said. "Your taste is so superior."

He wasn't going to have a fight. He drank another swallow of beer.

"The Tiger marching band," Polly's date declared, "can march rings around the Gamecock band."

"It ain't necessarily so," Annie Holmes began singing, along with the piano music. "It ain't necessarily so."

"There is nothing either good or bad," Mike said, "but thinking makes it so."

"Have another beer," Billy Hugenin said. He poured some beer into Mike's glass, and some into his own, then lifted his glass. "A toast! To the Garnet and the Black, and Coach Rex Enright!" He looked around. "Well, if nobody else's drinking, I'll toast 'em by myself!" He took a long drink from his glass.

"Who are you for?" Polly Morrison's date asked Mike. "Clemson or Carolina?"

"Neither one."

"You a Citadel man, then?"

Mike shook his head. "No. I believe in peace on earth, goodwill to men. And women."

"You've had too much beer, Mike," Betsy said. "You're drunk."

"Not I. I'm only drunk north-north-west."

"What?"

"When the wind is southerly I know a hawk from a handsaw."

Polly Morrison began laughing. "Don't laugh at him," Betsy told her. "It only encourages him."

"I don't get it," Polly's date declared. "What's a handsaw got to do with the Clemson-Carolina game?" Polly's date asked.

"Everything," Mike said. "Or just about everything."

The band music recommenced. Everybody but Mike and Polly Morrison got up. "Comrades, leave me here a little, while as yet 'tis early morn," Mike declared.

"Don't drink too much," Betsy told Mike.

"Me? 'Inebriate of air am I, and debauchee of dew'! Just a little tippler, that's me. Too bad the sun's not out tonight, or I'd go lean against it."

"Don't let him have any more beer," Betsy said to Polly Morrison as she walked off.

Polly smiled. "You don't look like Emily Dickinson to me."

"You spotted it, did you? You're the only one in this crowd who could."

"I recognized the *Hamlet* you were quoting, too."

"I'm not drunk," Mike said, "but they think anybody who doesn't have an opinion on the Clemson-Carolina game must be mentally deficient. Are you studying Emily Dickinson in Dr. Rosenbaum's course?"

"Not this year. Last year. This year I'm taking Victorian poetry."

"Do you know Miss Sara Jane Jahnz?"

"Yes. She's a friend of my mother's. My mother's going to play at the wedding."

"What wedding?"

"Dr. Rosenbaum and Miss Jahnz's."

"You mean they're getting married?"

"Yes. Didn't you know that? The day before Thanksgiving."

"No, I didn't know it." Mike poured another glass of beer. "Is your mother a musician?"

Polly nodded. "She teaches piano."

"So does mine."

"Really?"

"Yes."

Mike looked across the room and saw Betsy. She was dancing with Elliott Mikell again. They danced very well. He took a long swallow of beer.

"Did Betsy and Elliott Mikell used to go together?" he asked.

Polly Morrison did not reply.

"Don't you know?" he asked. He watched her out of the corner of his eye.

"I think they did. Yes." She was looking intently and determinedly out at the dance floor, rather than at him, obviously embarrassed at having to answer the question.

THE FIRST TIME he had heard Elliott Mikell's name mentioned had been early in the summer, when they were out dancing at the Folly Pier. Someone — Billy Hugenin perhaps — had told a story about how Mikell had taken the jumps in a race, and had said something about always rising to the occasion and not needing to practice. Everybody had laughed except Betsy, who had appeared not to think it was funny. Her reaction had struck him then as being somewhat strange.

"That must have been scary when you went out on the dock during the hurricane," Polly Morrison said. "I'd have been frightened to death."

She was changing the subject. "I was," Mike said. "Especially when we found out that the instrument hut wasn't on pilings, and just hanging out over the water."

She was a very nice person, who had in effect been forced by him to confirm what doubtless everyone present in their party knew, that his girlfriend and Elliott Mikell had been lovers. *Were* once again lovers — for everything began adding up now. Many things were falling into place — remarks, allusions, references, thought associations, apparent coincidences.

Betsy came back to the table, along with Billy Hugenin and Sally Holmes. Her face was flushed with exertion and pleasure. "I wish you'd learn how to dance!" she told him, running her hand through his hair. "You don't know what's good for you."

"Oh yes I do. At least I'm beginning to figure it out."

HE SPENT THE remainder of the evening going through the motions — dancing a little, pretending to be enjoying himself. The truth was that he was having a good time now, in a zany sort of way. He danced with Betsy, and also several times with Polly Morrison, whom he liked very much. He had had too many beers to drink, but they made him neither drunk nor ill — only more talkative. The odd part of it was that he could hear himself talking, as if it were someone else's voice. Everyone except Betsy was amused at what he was saying. He told about how he was the *News & Courier*'s ghost editor. "I could a tale unfold / Whose lightest word would harrow up thy soul," he declared. "Like quills on the fretful porpentine," he added.

"What's a porpentine?" Polly's date asked. "You mean a porcupine?"

"Nope, porpentine. First cousin to a turpentine."

"You're not making any sense, Mike," Betsy said. Polly Morrison laughed.

At one point he was dancing with Polly, and Betsy and Elliott Mikell were dancing together again, and Polly's date was dancing with the girl who came with Mikell. *It's been going on at least since she started riding again, if not before,* he thought. *Maybe that's why she took it up again.*

"I know I'm talking too much," he told Polly Morrison as they sat down. "I really don't usually have this much to drink."

"I don't think you're talking too much," she said.

"I am, though. Besides, nobody wants to hear about my newspaper work."

"It's much better than hearing about horses."

"Don't you ride?" Mike asked.

"No. It's far too expensive."

Betsy came back to the table. "Let's dance," she told him.

Mike shook his head. "The world is too much with me, late and soon," he told her. Then he heard the band begin another number. He recognized it. "Somebody else is taking my place." Has already taken. "On second thought, let's do," he said, climbing to his feet. "They're playing our song."

They danced for a few minutes. It seemed to Mike that Betsy was in a state of willed excitement, as if being on the dance floor and dancing were like taking an opiate that induced a condition of euphoria. In a sense it didn't matter who she was dancing with; it was simply necessary to have a partner, provided he was reasonably competent. Like fucking, he thought, only more drawn out and endlessly sustained, even if not as intense. She has to have someone around to do it with. Her whole life revolves around pleasure — physical pleasure. What am I going to do? he asked.

Then Elliott Mikell broke in, and as he handed Betsy over to him he thought that the question had just been answered. For what he was, figuratively, — and for that matter literally, too — was a stopgap, a temporary expedient who had come into her life while for reasons unknown to him she was at odds with Mikell, and now that relations had been restored, was no longer needed.

He went back to the table. Billy Hugenin and Annie Holmes were there, laughing about something. "Have some beer," Billy said, and poured some into his glass.

"Coals to Fincastle," he replied, but he drank some of the beer.

"You mean Newcastle, don't you?" Billy asked.

"No, I mean Fincastle. It's a town right outside of Roanoke."

Polly and her date sat down. "Let's drink a toast," the date said, "to Coach Frank Howard!"

"I don't know who he is, but I'm willing," Mike said. In actuality he did know.

"This beer's too warm," Polly's date said after taking a sip. "It's been sitting too long. We need another pitcher."

"'O, for a draft of vintage that hath been cooled a long age in the deep-delvéd earth,'" Mike said. "The English like their beer warm, though maybe that only goes for ale, not beer."

"There'll always be an England," Polly's date said.

"'The English were too drunk to know, the Irish didn't care,'" Mike said.

"Are you Irish?"

"Just call me Pat and Mike."

"So am I, on my mother's side," Polly's date said. "Have some more beer."

"No, Mike!" said Betsy, who had come back to the table.

"'Lady Clara Vere de Vere, / From me you shall not win renown,'" Mike recited. "'You thought to break a country heart / For pastime, ere you went to town.'"

Betsy shook her head. "Don't talk nonsense," she said. "It's time to go home."

"You mean, to town," Mike said.

"Don't cut out so early," Billy Hugenin told Betsy. "It's just a little after twelve."

"I don't feel well," Betsy replied, "and I've got to get up very early tomorrow. Come on, Mike."

He climbed to his feet. "Good night, sweet prince! Also sweet princess," he added, and bowed.

"Flights of angels sing thee to thy rest," Polly Morrison replied.

"You know it!" Mike followed Betsy to the coatroom. "Polly Morrison," he told Betsy, "is the only one of your friends who knows a hawk from a handsaw. Or is it a hacksaw? I never can remember."

They collected Betsy's wrap, Mike tipped the attendant, and they went outside. The air was cold and dry. It felt good. They walked across the alley to the parking lot.

The tan Lincoln Zephyr was gone from the space next to them.

"I'll drive," Betsy said.

"The hell you will! Sit your ass in that seat and shut up!"

He opened the car door, Betsy got in, then he walked around, climbed in behind the steering wheel, and started the engine.

"You're drunk, Mike." Betsy said. "Let me drive."

"No. I'm fine." And he was — in the sense of not being drunk. He had been pretending to himself that he was drunk. That was all. He backed the car out into the alley, drove out to King Street, turned left, and headed down King.

"Where are you going early tomorrow morning, Lady Clara?" Mike asked.

"Riding. And I'm not named Clara."

At Broad Street they waited for a bus to turn left, then proceeded through the intersection.

In front of the Fort Sumter Hotel the brisk wind was billowing the green awning. Across the street in the park there was no Spanish moss left on the trees after the hurricane.

He shouldn't let his anger show, he thought. "I wonder why they don't get some more moss from James Island?" he asked. Betsy did not reply.

She's acting like she's miffed because I drank so much beer, he thought to himself. Only that's only an excuse. If I were cold sober it wouldn't be any different.

"Do you still feel bad?"

"Yes. Just let me out at the front of the house. You needn't get out."

But he saw her to her front door anyway. Nothing was said about doing anything tomorrow. Today, he corrected himself.

He started the engine of the old Ford and drove off, not at all tired, feeling free and easy at the wheel, up the Boulevard and up Ashley Avenue and up Cannon Street, and across the bridge and through Windemere on the Folly Beach Road, and across the bridge over Wappoo Creek. He was fine. He thought he would just head out to Folly Beach and drive along the beach in the moonlight if tide was low. "Somebody else is taking my place," he sang to himself. "Debauchee of dew." But he still wasn't drunk. "Goodnight, sweet princess." He liked that girl.

Then all of a sudden he began to feel queasy. After a minute he turned on the high beam to see where he was going, pulled over to the side of the road, and sat behind the wheel. He reached out and turned the headlights off. He shut his eyes, but that made him feel dizzy, so he opened them, and then he stepped out of the car and walked around it. He stood there in the darkness, listening to the cicadas chirping, his arm against the car to steady himself. "You are inebriated," he told himself. "Here in a sea-side house to the farther south, where the baked cicala dies of drouth, you, Michael Redmond Quinn, have had too much to drink." Were a cicada and a cicala one and the same? Probably.

He began heaving up everything he had had to drink and eat, his stomach retching, his face on fire, his chest and sides feeling as if a million little needles were pricking his skin. He had made a fool of himself, he thought, with all that talking. That's why they were so amused. Even Polly Morrison. Everyone but Betsy. She's been getting it from Elliott Mikell, probably all summer and fall long, certainly for the last month or so. *She's been putting out for both of us, at home on the sunporch and out at the riding stables and probably other places I don't even know about. That was where she was the other night — with him. That's how she knew exactly where to go out at the stable — because she'd gone there with him, not just once or twice but often. All this time I thought she was in love and we were going to be married, when she was only dallying with me because she'd broken up with him, and the only reason she's been holding on to me, now that she's got him on the string again, is that she hasn't been sure she can keep him.* He knew this now for a certainty. So did Polly Morrison, and the others too. Polly Morrison felt sorry for him. The others just thought it was funny.

He got back into the car, started the engine, and sat there for a minute, with the motor running. If only he could just lie down somewhere. But he pulled on the headlight switch, flipped off the high beam with his foot, and drove off. He turned around at the next intersection, and drove back across the bridge to Charleston. He turned right in to Ashley Avenue and drove all the way to the end, at Murray Boulevard, and then turned left and eastward. He knew what he would find. A tan Lincoln Zephyr was parked a little ways up from the house, and the light was out on the sun porch. *You thought to break a country heart / For pastime, ere you went to town.* From Roanoke. Up in the hills.

He drove on home, and went up to his room. He had a splitting headache and his chest muscles ached from throwing up. He took a couple of aspirin tablets, which made him sick again. He went to the bathroom, retched a few times, then returned to his room. He was worn out. Hear me, Mother Ida, ere I die. Slowly, carefully, deliberately — he realized that he was still a little Under The Influence Of Alcoholic Beverages, as they wrote on the police reports — he removed his shoes and his clothes, got into bed, flopped over onto the pillow. Oh Jesus! What a fool I've made of myself, he thought. She's bound to think I'm a drunk. Too bad. Oh, too, too bad.

ooooo

ON SUNDAY HE did not call Betsy or go over to her house, but wrote four drafts of a letter to her, each of which began in various degrees of calmness and ended in rancor, and none of which he mailed.

On Monday when he left the house for work there was an envelope with his name on it lying on the hall table where the landlady put the mail. It bore no stamp; it must have been left by the house that morning. Inside was a letter. She had come to realize, etc., etc. The little bitch had beaten him to it.

He walked down the front steps and around the house to his car, an envelope with a letter and a diamond engagement ring in his inside coat pocket, and drove off to work.

19

THE PRESIDENT OF the Poetry Society of Charleston, of which Rosy was vice-president, was his friend Allen Faucheraud Grimball. Allen did not, so far as anyone knew, write poems himself, but the Poetry Society's role was cultural and appreciative, not creative. Founded in the early 1920s by ambitious local poets, several of whom later became extremely successful popular novelists, the Society achieved national prominence for its prize contests before it folded during the Depression. It was resurrected in the mid-1930s, though without its former renown. Mainly it brought authors in to give readings, and awarded some prizes to local bards. The Society held four meetings each year, of which two were given over to visiting virtuosi.

The November meeting was set for the first Monday evening in the month. The visitor was the noted British poet Alastair Wystan, now a resident of New York City. Allen Grimball, who loved all things British, was ecstatic in expectation. It was Allen's idea to arrange for Alastair Wystan to arrive in Charleston a full day before the reading was scheduled. If the weather was good, Rosy would take them on a ride up the Cooper River and about the harbor in his boat. In the event of inclement weather, the trip would be made by automobile.

"I'm for inclement weather," Sara Jane said.

"You don't have to come," Rosy said. "I can handle it all right."

"Oh, I wouldn't think of deserting you. If anything went wrong you'd need help, and what good would Allen be on a boat?"

"Maybe Alastair Wystan would know what to do. After all, there's the British maritime tradition."

"I wouldn't count on it."

They went down to Adger's Wharf Saturday and swept out and tidied up the *Gilmore Simms*. That night there was some rain, but Sunday dawned clear and mild, with the temperature in the low 60s and a light breeze. Rosy picked up Sara Jane and drove down to the wharf. Rosy had laid in a supply of potables the day before, and Sara Jane brought sandwiches. They were ready and waiting when Allen and the visiting poet arrived shortly before midday.

Alastair Wystan was a ruddy-complexioned man of medium height who had the look of a poet — which is to say, he was clad in a tweed jacket, a pair of corduroy trousers, and a tan trench coat, was tieless, wore steel-rimmed glasses and a black beret, and was in need of a haircut. Under his arm he bore a brown paper bag. "He brought along his own thermos," Allen whispered to Rosy as they stepped aboard. "He says on Sundays he always drinks Bloody Marys."

Sara Jane cast off the lines and they headed out into the channel. Rosy stayed at the wheel, while Allen, Sara Jane and the visiting poet sat outside in the cockpit. It was a pleasant day. Rosy steered upstream along the waterfront. Several freighters were tied up at the Port Utilities docks, and a dredge was operating off the northern edge of Shute's Folly. Several destroyers were tied to mooring dolphins just off the ship channel, and launches were moving back and forth between them and the government wharf at the foot of Market Street.

The sailors coming to town for shore leave, in their Navy blue uniforms and round white caps, had yet to undergo what the crew of that British destroyer they had recently seen being escorted into port had experienced — combat at sea, excitement and danger and death. Their turn would come soon enough, Rosy thought. Alastair Wystan, as an Englishman, had been criticized for deserting his country and emigrating to the United States in the face of the imminent outbreak of war. It was easy enough to make that kind of criticism; but how could those who made it know what might lie behind such a move? Certainly the poet had demonstrated his courage during the Spanish Civil War when he went to Spain as a volunteer ambulance driver.

After a while Sara Jane came into the cabin.

"How are we doing?" Rosy asked.

"We're getting a steady diet of history and ancestry. Allen's already dropped the names of every signer of the Declaration of Independence and the Constitution he's descended from, and now he's working on Confederate generals."

"How is our guest taking it?"

"Mostly what he says is 'Aoh?', 'Ah yes,' and 'how interesting,' and sips his Bloody Mary. He's already on his third. I don't blame him."

"Do you think he likes being out on the water?"

"I think he'd like it all right if it weren't for Allen's ancestors. But he's very interested in sailors," Sara Jane said.

"What do you mean?"

"When we passed the wharf at the foot of Market Street there was a Navy launch unloading sailors, and he wanted to know all about where they were going and what they did when they were in town. Don't you want me to take the wheel for a while, so you can sit outside?"

"Not yet," Rosy said. "I'm going to go up past the Ordnance Depot and then come back around Drum Island and down the far side of the harbor. You can take it then, if you will."

Two of the White Stack tugboats, the *Robert* and the *Cecilia*, were engaged in extricating a tanker from the Esso docks downstream from Shipyard Creek. As they passed, one of the tugs gave a brief hoot of her klaxon, and a man came out on the cabin top behind the wheelhouse and waved. Even without binoculars

Rosy recognized the burly frame of Captain Magwood. He gave an answering salutation on the *Gilmore Simms'* horn.

There was a little more breeze, and Sara Jane, Allen and Alastair Wystan came into the cabin. Allen was discoursing on Marshlands Plantation house, which he explained was still situated within the Charleston Navy Yard, and had been owned by Gabriel Manigault, "who was my mother's second cousin," and then by Wallace Lawton. "Do you know," he asked Rosy, "that your hotel is so named because Cecilia Lawton's people were St. Johnses? She owned the hotel."

"Actually it's pronounced Sinjin, old chap," Alastair Wystan said. "'Awake, my St. John! leave all meaner things' —"

"'To low ambition, and the pride of kings,'" Rosy responded.

"That sounds like Tennyson," Allen said.

"The 'Essay on Man,'" Alastair Wystan said.

"Oh, Coleridge! I should have known."

"Sorry, old boy. Pope."

"To be sure." Allen was momentarily discomfited, but soon recovered. "Do you know that Arthur Hugh Clough grew up in Charleston?" he asked.

"Did he? You don't say. 'For while the tired waves, vainly breaking, / Seem here no painful inch to gain, / Far back, through creeks and inlets making, / Comes silent, flooding in, the main.'"

"As a matter of fact, the tide's coming in quite strong," Rosy said. "'Say not the struggle naught availeth.'"

Close to Marshlands Plantation, Allen Grimball resumed, was a plantation known as the Retreat. "It was in the Robert Turnbull family, and one of the granddaughters, Mrs. Leonidas Walker, was my father's great-aunt. Just up the river was the Palmettoes, where Archer Smith shot an English officer at the landing during the Revolution. There was also an Englishman shot at the Parker residence a bit farther up the river. This was just before the British evacuated."

"I trust they don't still continue that practice," Alastair Wystan said. "If so I'd better keep out of sight." He walked over and stood next to Rosy at the wheel, and whispered, "I say, what does one do when one must repeat history, so to speak?"

For a moment Rosy was puzzled, then he understood. He grinned. "Just a minute." He called to Sara Jane and asked her to take the wheel, then led the visitor into the forward cabin, pulled the curtain across the companionway, and opened the door to the head. "When you're done, just pump that lever on the side a few times," he told him.

He returned to the wheel. "Keep it for a little while, will you?" he asked Sara Jane.

"Right you are."

He went outside and stood at the stern. Alastair Wystan did have a sense of humor. And he must be finding Allen terribly boring.

It was a lovely afternoon, all right; a little too late and too brisk for Indian summer, perhaps, but as balmy as might be asked for in early November.

In less than three weeks he would be married. Who would have thought it? The plans were all set, the invitations had been mailed, and the apartment on Gadsden Street was just about ready. Next week he would have his parents' furniture taken out of storage and delivered there, or the pieces that they would be using. The rest would either be sold or go to the Salvation Army. Sara Jane's furniture would wait until a couple of days before the wedding, since she was using it in her present apartment.

He heard the cabin door open and looked around to see Alastair Wystan stepping outside. "Is it always so warm as this in mid-autumn?" he asked.

"Oh, no," Rosy told him. "We have good days like this, but we get our share of rain and cold in November and December."

"Tell me, old boy, your colleague's awfully well posted on the local history and ancestry, but is that *all* he ever talks about?"

Rosy laughed. "That, and Charleston society. I'm afraid so."

"I don't wish to seem ungrateful, you understand, but there's only so much that one can absorb. I'm told that in the morning he's to take me on a tour of the downtown city. I'm sure it's very historic and all that, but the prospect of hearing about ancestors for two entire days is a bit much."

"Call him in the morning from your hotel and tell him you're not feeling well," Rosy suggested.

The cabin door opened and Allen came out. "Over there beyond the bridge," he announced to Alastair Wystan, pointing ahead to starboard, "is Haddrell's Point, where in 1705 a raiding party landed by the French was driven off, with considerable loss of life, by a force of Carolina militia led by Captain John Fenwick, who is by the way a collateral forebear of my own, his wife's brother Benjamin having married Eliza Rhett, whose daughter Henrietta was my great-great-great-grandmother on my mother's side."

Rosy went back inside the cabin to replace Sara Jane at the wheel. "Allen's driving him to distraction with all his history and genealogy," he told her.

"I was afraid of that."

"He says he can't face the prospect of listening to him all day tomorrow, too."

"It's too bad we can't think of some way to get him off the subject this afternoon," Sara Jane said.

Rosy thought about it for a few minutes. Then he had an idea. He remembered about Dolf and the drive over to Sullivans Island to play poker. "We're going to have an emergency," he told Sara Jane. There was somewhat more water in the bilge than normally, because of last night's rain, and he hadn't remembered to pump it out. He reached under the console and removed a fuse. "Take the wheel again for a minute, will you?" he asked Sara Jane.

He went up into the forward cabin and removed a small panel from the deck, located just above the bilge pump and designed to provide access to the pump. There was an inch or so of water in the bilge. Then he went outside into the stern cockpit, where

Allen Grimball was telling Alastair Wystan about the colonial proprietorship of Hobcaw Barony up the Wando River. He lifted a panel from the deck above the stuffing box. There was some water lying below the stuffing box. "Oh oh!" he declared.

"Is something the matter?" Allen asked.

"We're taking on water, and the bilge pump's not working. See?"

Allen peered into the opening. "You mean that water's not supposed to be there?"

"It certainly isn't. If it gets much worse we'll have to make a run for the waterfront and try to beach her before we sink. See?"

Alastair Wystan looked at him quizzically. Rosy winked at him.

"What can we do?" Allen asked.

"I'll have to ask both of you to help us," Rosy said. "If you'll stay here," he told Alastair Wystan, "and keep your eye on this water to make sure it doesn't rise any more, and Allen, if you'll do the same thing in the forward cabin, I'll try to get us back to the dock."

He led Allen up into the forward cabin, showed him the open panel. "What you've got to do," he said, "is to watch the water level closely. If it rises to where it's above that board" — he pointed to a piece of cross planking —"let me know immediately, and I'll try to beach the boat in shallow water."

"Do you think we can make it back?" Allen was obviously quite concerned. "This is embarrassing," he added.

"It'll be touch and go. Incidentally, are you a good swimmer?"

"Not too good," Allen said.

Rosy bent down and removed a canvas-and-cork life jacket from a locker underneath a vee-berth. "You'd better keep this handy, then, because if we have to abandon ship there won't be much time. You don't want to be trapped in the cabin while you're trying to locate a life jacket."

"Should I put it on?"

"It wouldn't hurt. Might as well stay on the safe side."

Allen climbed into the bulky life jacket, all the while keeping his eyes on the bilge. "I do hope we don't have to abandon ship," he said. "Think how embarrassing that would be."

"Yes, and the harbor water's cold, too. But maybe we'll be lucky. Remember, let me know if there's any change." He returned to the main cabin. Sara Jane, who had heard the entire exchange, was steering with one hand, her other held over her mouth to keep from laughing aloud.

Rosy went back out onto the stern. "Just have a seat and enjoy the ride," he told Alastair Wystan. "I think there'll be a little less genealogy from now on."

"Is the boat really taking on water?"

"There's nothing whatever wrong with the boat. That's rain-water."

Wystan chuckled. "I rather thought so. Many thanks. I didn't realize that one harbor could produce so many ancestors."

Rosy went back into the cabin. Before he took over the controls he called into the forward cabin. "How's it looking, Allen?"

"I — I think it's all right," Allen replied. "I don't see any change."

"Maybe we'll be lucky and make it back safely. We're not too far from the waterfront now."

Rosy turned the *Gilmore Simms* homeward. The engine thrummed steadily and the boat pushed nicely through the waters. Across the way and a half-mile or so up the Ashley River he saw the green hull and white sails of the Carters' sloop coming along. He didn't want them to come close, so he kept well in toward Castle Pinckney; tide was sufficiently in so that there was no danger of grounding.

He tore a sheet of paper from a pad, looked up Allen's telephone number in his notebook, and wrote it down on the paper, then added his own name and number as well. When they were off the High Battery, no more than five minutes from the wharf, he decided to give Allen an additional thrill. He cut speed sharply, which sent all the water in the bilge surging forward.

"It's coming up over the board!" Allen cried.

"Keep your eyes on it. The next few minutes will be crucial!"

"Are we going to have to abandon ship?"

"I'm going to try to get us in. Keep your fingers crossed!" He resumed speed, and replaced the fuse in the box under the console.

"Now it's gone down again," Allen called.

"Good. That means we've got a chance." The float switch would work now. He heard the pump cut on.

"The pump's working again!" he called out. "We're safe!"

"Are you sure?"

"Yes. You can stop watching now."

Allen, still wearing the life jacket, came into the main cabin. "What happened?" he asked.

"The pump decided to cut on again. We're almost to the wharf, anyway. After we're done I'll try to find the leak and plug it until tomorrow. I couldn't do that while we were moving."

"Should I take off the life jacket?"

"Yes. We're safe enough now."

"Thank goodness! What a scare!" Allen divested himself of the life jacket. "This is terribly embarrassing. I hope Alastair Wystan hasn't been too upset. And I didn't even get to point out all the historical sites in the lower harbor!"

"Oh, I'm sure he understands that accidents happen sometimes," Rosy told him.

"THAT WAS WICKED," Sara Jane said after Allen Grimball had gone out onto the cockpit to express his apologies to Alastair Wystan. "You know how he idolizes English poets. "

"He thinks that English poets are by definition country gentlemen," Rosy said, "and therefore interested in hearing about ancestors."

They backed into the slip, and secured the lines. After Allen had stepped up onto the pier, Rosy handed a slip of paper to

Alastair Wystan as the poet prepared to follow. "If you want to call Allen tomorrow morning, here's his phone number," he said. "I put my name and number down, too, if anything comes up that you need help with."

"Quite. Thanks, old chap. I do appreciate it," Alastair Wystan told him. "See you tomorrow evening, if not before."

"WHAT DID YOU think of him?" Rosy asked Sara Jane as they drove back to close up the boat.

"I don't think he's a nature poet. I had the feeling that he's the indoors type. He took no interest that I could see in the wildlife, except for the sailors. *They* interested him a great deal."

"I told him to call Allen tomorrow morning and say he wasn't feeling well."

THAT NIGHT ROSY was sleeping soundly away when the telephone rang. "Yes?" He looked at his watch; it was 1:30 A.M.

"Dr. Rosenbaum, this is Marjenhoff, down at police headquarters. Do you know somebody named Winston or something? Talks kind of funny?"

"You mean an Englishman? Alastair Wystan?"

"Yeah, that sounds like what he said."

"Yes, I know him. Is something wrong?"

"We got him down here. He was stumbling around down by the waterfront at the foot of Market Street, trying to pick up sailors. We figured we'd better bring him in before he got hurt. Can you come get him?"

"Yes. I'll be right over."

Sara Jane certainly called that one, he thought as he dressed. He hoped that Wystan hadn't been booked, whether for loitering or disorderly conduct or whatever. If he had, then despite the hour he'd better call Page Carter to ask what to do.

When he arrived at police headquarters on St. Phillips Street, the desk sergeant told him that Wystan was being detained in the next room. Rosy told them who it was that they were holding, and explained how embarrassing it would be for everyone concerned if charges were recorded and the incident found its way into the news.

"Oh, we didn't book him, Dr. Rosenbaum," the sergeant said. "We figured there was something peculiar about him. You know that little clip joint right across from the Custom House at the foot of Market? He was stumbling around out in front of it, trying to make connections with the sailors off those destroyers. That's a rough part of town, you know. He could have gotten in some real trouble. We brought him over here, and he gave us your name. You can just take him on back to where he's staying."

"Thanks."

He escorted Rosy into an adjoining room. Alastair Wystan was seated at a desk, a bit the worse for wear but seemingly unharmed. The expression on his face resembled that of a pouting child. Rosy wondered how many Bloody Marys he had consumed that day and evening.

On the way back to the Fort Sumter Hotel the poet had nothing to say, and Rosy did not attempt to make conversation. They pulled up in front of the hotel. Rosy helped the visiting poet out of the car, then escorted him into the lobby. The poet was wobbling as they walked across the deserted lobby, with its marble floor and wicker furniture. A clerk was working behind the desk, and a Negro bellman was asleep in a chair by the elevator. "I think you'd better give Mr. Wystan's key to the bellman and have him escort him to his room," Rosy told the clerk. "He'll need assistance, I'm afraid."

The clerk retrieved the room key from a pigeonhole behind the desk. He rang a bell. "Front!" he called. The bellman roused himself and came over.

"Take Mr. Wystan up to 614," the clerk told the bellman, handing him the key.

"This way, sir." The bellman took the visiting poet's arm.

"See you tomorrow," Rosy said. He slipped the bellman a dollar bill.

"Quite." Steered by the bellman, Alastair Wystan half-staggered off toward the elevator, and Rosy departed for his own rooms at the St. John's Hotel — pronounced Sinjin.

When the visiting poet telephoned Allen in the morning to say that he wasn't feeling well and wouldn't go touring, he thought, there would no need for him to fake it.

THE READING ITSELF, held at the New England Society Monday evening, went well. Alastair Wystan was in splendid form, and put on a glittering exhibition. If the previous night's activities had discomfited him, he showed no signs of it. He was witty, droll, even genial. "So natural," as Rosy heard a local matron remark afterward. After the reading, Rosy, Sara Jane, and Allen Grimball drove him out to the North Charleston station in Rosy's car, where he boarded the West Coast Champion for Washington shortly before midnight. From there he was bound for the West Coast, where he was to give several readings. The poet shook hands with them as he prepared to step up into the pullman vestibule. "'Say not the struggle naught availeth,'" Rosy told him.

"'But westward, look, the land is bright,'" Alastair Wystan retorted.

THEY DROVE BACK home along the highway into the city. Rosy said nothing to Allen about the rescue mission to the police station. The poet, Allen reported, had been unable to tour the city that morning with him as planned. "The strain of worrying whether the boat was going to sink was obviously too much for him," he remarked from the back seat, where he was riding.

"You don't think the Bloody Marys might have had something to do with it, too?" Sara Jane asked.

"Perhaps," Allen conceded, "but I know he was awfully nervous about the boat almost sinking."

"How do you know that?" Rosy asked.

"He told me so this evening."

"Really? What did he say?"

"I asked him whether he'd like to leave for dinner a little early and stroll down along the waterfront. He told me that it wasn't necessary, because he'd already seen enough of the Charleston waterfront to last him for a long while to come."

20

MIKE CALLED HIS parents in Roanoke to tell them the news. He had the impression that they were not especially disappointed. In June, when Betsy was graduating from college and her parents had come up to Roanoke for the event, Mike's parents had met and entertained them. They hadn't said anything afterward, but in retrospect he could see that they had not been enthralled with Mr. and Mrs. Murray. And as for the Murrays, once they found out that his parents were neither wealthy nor in the Social Register, they had been no more than dutifully polite.

The humiliation was what was so painful. He had gotten himself engaged to be married, found a job in Charleston as a newspaper reporter — was on the way, as it were, to full-fledged self-sufficiency as an adult. Now, abruptly, it was all over. He still had the job, but the reason for his coming to that place was gone. He had been playing a role. The role had not merely involved how he might appear to others; it was also the way he thought of himself. Now he could no longer view himself as a Young Man Engaged To Be Married. He was what he had been before he met Betsy — a youth, twenty two years old and therefore by custom and statute an adult, but without full credentials, no longer a Man Among Men. It had come without warning — no, that wasn't right, there had been ample warning. He hadn't heeded it.

He hadn't realized how very much he had come to depend

upon being engaged and anticipating marriage as a way of avoiding self-doubts and indecisions. It wasn't so much the actuality of Betsy's company, as the assurance that had arisen from seemingly having her as part of his life, including the fact that they made love regularly. He had used that assurance to paper over the disparity between what he wished to be and what he actually was. Yet during all that time the supposed assurance had been false, phony, a delusion; and only his vanity, his sublimely egotistical innocence, had kept him from recognizing it as such.

In retrospect he could see so many things that he had misinterpreted. She hadn't really ever wanted him here in town, and all along she had been toying with him, probably even without fully realizing it herself. By the time he showed up and started in to work on the newspaper, she had already begun having second thoughts, and had probably realized that it would have been easier and more painless to drop him if he were living elsewhere. At most he had been a kind of diversion, a not-very-realistic alternative to be kept and strung along for a time, good for sex if nothing else. He had been used, dealt falsely with, taken advantage of; he had every reason to be bitterly resentful and angry, to hate and despise her.

Yet — and this was perhaps most humiliating of all — he was not angry, but disappointed and hurt. So much so that he found himself half-waiting for the telephone call or letter that would beg forgiveness, tell him how the realization of how much she was losing and how much she loved him had overwhelmed her, and ask to be given another chance.

It couldn't come, of course. There was no chance whatever of it. He knew that very well. There was a line from a poem by Carl Sandburg that expressed the situation all too aptly: "And I will sit watching the sky tear off gray and gray / And the letter I wait for won't come." He also knew that he was fortunate to be rid of her, and her parents, and the whole rotten business. He knew it rationally — but emotionally he was unable to accept what logically and intellectually was obvious.

ooooo

WEDNESDAY EVENING HE was at the Porthole with Jim
Igoe, and he mentioned that he and Betsy had broken up. "No
fooling?" Igoe said. "When did this happen?"

"The other day — though it's been brewing for a long while."

"I can't say that I'm surprised, kid," Igoe told him. "I had the
feeling that the bloom was off the rose. If you want my honest
opinion, I think you're well out of it."

"You think so?"

"I'm just going by her parents, and everything I know about
the family, and a few things I've heard here and there. I've never
met the young lady, but when you told me a while back that she
was going to work for her father I thought to myself, Oh oh!
Because the one chance that a daughter of Turner Murray's got
to turn out all right is to head off in the other direction as soon
as possible."

Everything Igoe was saying was true. But it didn't make him
feel any better.

"Listen, kid, let me tell you something," Igoe said. "You know
what they say, 'It's always darkest before the dawn'? Well, that's
so much horseshit. It's darkest right when it first turns pitch
black. After that you begin to get used to the dark and don't
mind it as much. And a long time before you can actually see the
sun come up, it starts getting lighter. So have another beer and
hang in there."

IT WAS GOOD that he was starting out on a new assignment
that week, because there was plenty that he could do to keep
himself busy. He talked with various town officials and business
people, explored each community he would be covering. Despite
the feeling that he had been exiled, he liked Mount Pleasant. It
was an old town, quite small, not a resort, and did not have a
beach. The streets were shaded over with immense oak trees,

with Spanish moss hanging down from long, crooked limbs. There was Shem Creek, through the middle of the town, with trawlers, crab and shrimp packing houses, and marine repair shops along it. From Haddrell Point, which was the western edge of town, fronting on the harbor, one could look across and see the city of Charleston, with its church steeples and buildings, a little more than two miles distant.

He had been on Sullivans Island and the Isle of Palms before, but now he drove along all the streets and lanes, parked his car and walked along the beach. The ship channel led just off the beach; one afternoon during his first week on the beat, the Clyde Line passenger liner *Algonquin* steamed past, bound for New York. Seeing it made his heart beat faster.

Now that the summer season was over, there was very little going on. Fishermen stood out in the surf casting offshore for channel bass; he watched them, and thought of acquiring a rod and reel and trying his luck sometime.

He heard much talk from old timers about the ferryboats that used to run between Mount Pleasant and Charleston, before the bridge was built. There was, he found, still one ferryboat plying the harbor. It was small and ran between Sullivans Island and a dock not far from the Custom House on the waterfront, taking an hour to get across as compared with ten minutes or so via bridge. Its clientele were an odd lot — pedestrians, bicyclists, cars with drivers who for some reason didn't like driving across the high spans of the Cooper River Bridge, old cars and trucks too decrepit to ascend the steep spans, a horse-drawn vegetable wagon or two. Where the bridge was no more than a way to get from Charleston to Mount Pleasant or back, to ride aboard the little ferry was an experience in itself, a pleasure. He decided to write a feature story about it. He rode across the harbor and back, interviewed the captain, whose name was Baitery, and prepared a piece for the Sunday paper.

He had been told to check the property deed register at the county courthouse each week and copy down all the transactions.

Looking through back pages of the register for the Isle of Palms, he found an interesting item. In early July the Murray Construction Company was listed as having acquired a sizeable tract of property on the Isle of Palms. That was not long after he had driven over to the Isle of Palms with Betsy and her parents, when he had first arrived in the city, and also several weeks before the time he had seen Mr. Murray and Franklin Poinsett over there.

He asked about it, and learned that this was the tract that Al Myers had told him about, located to the east of the pavilion in the undeveloped portion of the island, which had been bought by a group of Charleston investors with a view toward developing it. They had been unable to raise the capital investment to do so, and had sold it to Turner Murray.

Apparently nothing had ever been published about the transaction. It was necessary for him to telephone Mr. Murray and find out about plans for development. He did not want to, but there was no alternative. So he called Murray Construction Company. Betsy answered the phone.

"This is Mike," he told her.

"Yes?"

"I want to talk to your father."

"Just a minute." There was a wait. "He said to give me the message."

The son of a bitch, Mike thought. "Tell him I'm calling for the *News & Courier* and that I'd like to ask him about the property he bought on the Isle of Palms."

There was another pause. Then Mr. Murray answered. "What do you want?"

"I'm calling for the *News & Courier*," Mike told him, trying to make his voice sound as impersonal as possible. "I'd like to know what plans you have for developing the property you've acquired on the Isle of Palms."

"There are no plans."

"Can you tell me why you bought the property?"

"That's no affair of yours."

"May I quote you on that?" he asked.

"No! Just say that the property was purchased for purposes of investment, and there's no plan to develop it now. That's all I've got to say about it."

"Thank you, sir," Mike told him, and hung up. He seemed more than ordinarily rude, even for Mr. Murray. It was as if he was on the defensive about the property.

He called one of the previous owners, to see what he could find out. The man, whose name was J. M. Vanderhorst, could tell him little. His assumption was that Murray intended to do something with the property, but he had no idea what, or when. Mike wrote a two-paragraph story on the sale, quoting Turner Murray about having no present development plans.

HEARING BETSY ON the telephone, even briefly, had been chilling. It was hard to accept the fact that a voice that only a short time before had been so intimate a part of his life, belonging to someone he had made love with again and again, was now frigid and distant. It was annoying, too, that while he was the aggrieved party, implicit in the tone of her voice had been that, in thus calling, *he* was the intruder.

As for her father, what he felt was anger. While he thought he had made it quite plain that as a reporter he would take no guff, it riled him that Mr. Murray had thought he could brush him off like that. Betsy's father believed that being rich gave him the right to say and do anything he wanted. Mike wished there were some way that he could get back at him, hurt him, puncture that arrogance and smugness. If he ever got the chance, he would show him.

To hell with him, Mike told himself. And with her. He didn't need either one of them. As between the two of them, there wasn't much difference; they were both out for Number 1, and nobody else. What money was to the father, riding and sex were to the daughter. One was as bad as the other. Yet why was he angry at Mr. Murray, but not with Betsy?

ooooo

HE WAS SITTING around the office late one afternoon, his stories all written, when the city editor called him over. Would he mind going by the College of Charleston some day soon and doing a piece on a new dean there, who did laboratory experiments with rats? The city editor said he realized it wasn't his beat, but he thought it was the kind of story Mike could handle especially well. Mike called the man and made an appointment.

On Friday morning he went over to the campus to talk to him. He hoped he wouldn't run into Polly Morrison there, after the spectacle he had made of himself at the Cat's Cradle. If only he hadn't become so upset when he realized what was going on between Betsy and Elliott Mikell. She seemed like a nice person, too. But after the way he had behaved he didn't dare approach her now.

The dean was strange looking, used big words, and seemed to take himself very seriously. His field was behavioral psychology, and his laboratory contained a number of cages with white rats in them. What he did was to run them through mazes in which the white rats were rewarded with food pellets when they behaved properly by figuring out how to get to the food with the minimum amount of exploring.

One word that the dean kept using was "reinforcement." Almost every time he said it, he grinned, displaying his front teeth very prominently and hissing. Mike asked him what happened if a white rat refused to follow the proper procedures and be rewarded, and was told that a certain number of them were unable to learn, and so could not be used in experiments.

He asked the dean whether what was true of the rats' behavior was also true for people. "In the sense of a response to environmental stimuli, yes," the dean answered. "The human organism, of course, is far more complex, but in certain basic drives — food, sex — there is a similarity in response that can shed light upon the underlying patterns of human psychological behavior."

Mike took notes, and told him that the staff photographer would call him to make an appointment to get some pictures.

While he was on the campus, he decided to drop in on Dr. Rosenbaum. Polly Morrison had said that he and Miss Jahnz were going to be married. Dr. Rosenbaum was in his late thirties or early forties. Mike wondered whether he would have to wait that long.

Dr. Rosenbaum was talking with a student. "Come in!" he said when he was done. "What brings you to these parts?"

Mike told him about interviewing the dean. He had the sense that Dr. Rosenbaum was not very interested in what the dean said or did. When he congratulated him on his forthcoming marriage, Dr. Rosenbaum thanked him and asked for Betsy. He told him that the engagement had been broken.

"I'm sorry to hear that," Dr. Rosenbaum said. "When did this happen?

"This past weekend."

"Those things can be rough. You must feel like you've been run over by a truck," Dr. Rosenbaum said.

"I'm doing all right."

Dr. Rosenbaum looked at his watch. "I'm meeting Sara Jane for lunch in twenty minutes. Don't you want to join us?"

"Sure." He didn't have anything that couldn't be taken care of later in the afternoon. He arranged to meet them outside in front of the library steps.

Walking through the corridors of the building and looking around, he was almost overwhelmed with a sense of dislodgement. It was the first time he had been back on a college campus since his graduation last June. The College of Charleston was much smaller than Washington and Lee; there was little to it other than the single city block with the one administration and classroom building, the little library annex, and the lawn and its oak trees. Yet seeing the students standing around and talking, watching them come and go, books under their arms, he realized how much he missed being in school. Now that he had spent six months away from school, what he saw around him as he strolled about the small campus made him feel excluded and envious.

Miss Jahnz was coming down the steps of the library as he walked out of the main building and around the cistern. There were students everywhere about, standing and talking. "Hello, Mike! I hear you're going to have lunch with us?"

"Yes, ma'am."

Dr. Rosenbaum emerged from the main building, and they set off down the walkway, out onto the sidewalk, and along George Street. They entered a place called George's, and found a booth in an adjoining room. The restaurant was crowded with students, some of whom exchanged greetings with Dr. Rosenbaum and Miss Jahnz.

They talked about various things. Dr. Rosenbaum and Miss Jahnz were obviously very much excited about the forthcoming wedding, and several persons whom Mike took to be faculty members stopped by their table to talk briefly and to examine and admire the engagement ring that Miss Jahnz was wearing. He thought of the ring he had given Betsy, which was now in an envelope in his bureau, waiting to be taken to a jewelry store and sold.

He told Dr. Rosenbaum how much he had enjoyed reading the book by Joseph Conrad that he had recommended, *Typhoon*. He had since read several other Conrad novels, he said. They discussed various books. He asked whether there were any good novels written about newspaper reporting. Not really, Dr. Rosenbaum said. Did he know Theodore Dreiser's autobiography? That was the best book he had ever read about being a newspaperman, Dr. Rosenbaum said.

"What current novelists do you like, Mike?" Miss Jahnz asked.

He thought about it; he didn't really read much recent fiction. "I like Ernest Hemingway, and John Steinbeck, and Somerset Maugham."

"Have you ever read any Thomas Wolfe?" Dr. Rosenbaum asked.

"No, sir. Do you think I ought to?"

"Well, I'll tell you this," Dr. Rosenbaum said, "Unless I'm mistaken, you'll find that he's very interesting. Go by the Free Library and get *Look Homeward, Angel*, and when you finish it, if you like that one, then try *Of Time and the River*. If the Library copy is checked out, give me a call and I'll lend you mine."

Two men came into the restaurant and over to their table. Dr. Rosenbaum introduced them to him as Dr. Rudolf Strongheart and Dr. Tom Lowndes. "Come join us," Miss Jahnz told them. "We can make room."

Mike stood up. "I've got to get back to work," he said. "Thanks very much for asking me."

"Come over and have lunch with us again sometime," Miss Jahnz told him.

"And let me know what you think of Thomas Wolfe," Dr. Rosenbaum said.

He walked over to the parking lot behind the Gloria Theater, where he had left his car, and drove back to the newspaper office. He telephoned the police stations across the river to find out whether anything was doing. None of the three had anything to report. He wrote the story about the dean and the white rats and turned it in, then took several stories over the telephone.

Tomorrow would be Saturday. Ordinarily Betsy would have made plans for them to go to a party, or dancing, or something on Saturday night. Ironically, now that he could get off early in the evening, instead of having to wait until nine or ten o'clock, there was no longer any reason for him to take advantage of it. He would have to think of something else to do. He could go to a movie, of course, but except for Polly Morrison he knew no other girls in the city, and he didn't dare ask her, while going by himself would be too depressing.

Was there any point in staying in Charleston now? There was nothing to hold him here any longer. But the thought of returning home to Roanoke, jobless, no longer engaged to be married, defeated, and beginning a search for a job on another paper, was too overbearing. At least he was earning a salary and gaining experience. Besides, it wouldn't look good on his record to quit his first job within six months after beginning it. And more importantly, he wasn't going to let Betsy Murray drive him out of town.

SATURDAY MORNING BEFORE he went to work, Mike drove by the Free Library and checked out copies of both the books by Thomas Wolfe that Dr. Rosenbaum had recommended. He would get to them as soon as he was finished with *Lord Jim*. There was no reason for him to drive over across the bridge that day; he checked with the police stations in Mount Pleasant, Sullivans Island, and the Isle of Palms, and nothing was doing except for a minor traffic accident on U.S. 17. He got the information from the officer on duty, then called Roper Hospital and was told that the only person injured involved was in satisfactory condition. He had already written the feature he was expected to produce for each Sunday's paper, and the staff photographer had gone across the harbor on the ferry and made pictures.

SOMEWHAT TO his surprise, Saturday night, when he had thought he would be at loose ends, went by without incident. He returned to the news room after dinner and wrote some letters, then went home to his room, read some more in *Lord Jim*, and listened to a mystery on the radio.

It was Sunday that posed the problem. He went to Mass at St. Mary's and took communion. While there he looked around to see whether Polly Morrison was in the congregation, but she was not. Thank goodness, he told himself. Then he drove over to the restaurant near the office, ate breakfast, and read the Sunday *Courier*. His story about the little ferryboat was prominently featured. He was hoping that Jim Igoe or someone else that he knew would come in, but no one showed up.

Afterward he went back to his room and read some more. It was 12:35. What was he going to do all afternoon and evening long?

He decided to drive somewhere that he had not been before, and have dinner there. He looked at the map and selected the town of Georgetown, sixty miles up the coast on U.S. 17. He drove across the Cooper River Bridge, through Mount Pleasant, and on eastward. The highway ran through forest land and swamps; there were few towns. It crossed the Santee River on a long causeway and low bridge, then through more fields and woods and across another bridge into Georgetown. It was a pretty little town, though marred by a paper pulp mill which cast a sickening-sweet odor over everything. There were some fine old buildings and a somewhat rundown waterfront. He drove around for a while, got out and walked along the dock area, looked at an array of shrimp boats and cargo launches tied up to the wharves. There was a clock tower on a red brick building, which according to a sign used to be the slave market. The hands on the clock showed 2:17 P.M.

He parked outside a restaurant on Front Street and went inside, taking a magazine along to read. He was shown to a table against a wall. He studied the menu and decided on pan-broiled shrimp, hushpuppies, a green salad with blue-cheese dressing, and rice. He read part of an article in the magazine, and watched people come into the restaurant and be guided to tables. There were families having Sunday dinner at the restaurant, just as sometimes when he was a child they would go to eat at the Hotel Patrick Henry instead of having dinner at home.

The shrimp were served in a hot steel skillet, and were quite good. There was a girl seated in a booth across the way; she was dark-haired, intelligent looking, nicely dressed. After a minute a man came from the back of the restaurant and sat down opposite her.

He finished the shrimp and the hushpuppies, ate some of the salad and rice, read a little more of the magazine article. The waitress came, took away the dishes, and asked whether he wished to order dessert. No, just a cup of coffee, he told her. He let the coffee cool a little, then sipped it. The waitress brought the check. He left her a tip, took the check up to the counter and paid it, then went outside. It was 3:03 P.M. Dinner had taken 46 minutes.

He drove eastward up the highway and then over to a place called Pawley's Island. It was full of old beach cottages and summer homes, with high sand dunes. There were very few people about. He parked the car and walked out to the beach. Beyond the coamers the ocean was placid. Gulls were wheeling, turning, banking, and diving above one spot several hundred yards out, probably feeding on a school of fish. He looked up the beach. A couple were walking along, with an Irish setter romping ahead of them. He remembered the time, the day after he arrived in Charleston, when they had gone riding with the Murrays out to the Isle of Palms, and he and Betsy had walked up the beach together. He returned to his car and headed back to Georgetown. It was a little after 4:30.

He drove on through Georgetown and back to Charleston. By the time he reached Mount Pleasant it was twilight; the days were getting short. For some reason, he always felt anxious being somewhere without a definite place to go when day was ending. He paid the toll and drove across the Cooper River Bridge in the gathering dusk.

He decided to stop by the office. The assistant city editor was on the desk, so he did not offer to help edit the county news and write headlines, as he sometimes did when sitting around the newsroom. The less he had to do with Moore, the better. He read some of the incoming copy off the Associated Press A-wire. War news, mainly bad. Jim Igoe was working on a police story; he waited to see whether Jim was going out for supper, but he wasn't.

It was just after seven. He wasn't really hungry yet, but he went back down to the corner restaurant and ordered a bowl of chili, some apple pie, and coffee. When he was done he drove back to his room. It was 7:50. He turned on the radio. Someone was singing a song entitled "All or Nothing at All."

Where was Betsy tonight? he wondered. Doubtless with Elliott Mikell. All, or Nothing at All. Wherever she was, she would give her All; there was no doubt of that. She had given it to Mikell, and probably to others before that, and she would go right on Giving All. Not that he had objected to getting it. To think that, when he had first known her, he had thought she was a virgin!

I'm lying here torturing myself, he thought. What the hell. He went back out to his car. All, or Nothing at All. Maybe he ought to drive down to one of those houses and see what it was like. He drove over to Archdale Street, turned into West. This was where they were supposed to be. The street was dark, with a few cars parked along the curbs. There were red and blue lights in doors and windows. Should he? He felt his insides stir. No, he wasn't going to do it. He continued through to the end of the street, turned into Logan, and drove back to his room.

The clock on his bureau showed 9:32. In a couple of hours he might be tired enough to be able to go to sleep.

21

"HOW DO YOU think he's taking it?" Rosy asked as they walked back to the campus after lunch.

"Very hard," Sara Jane said. "Did you see the look on his face when Mike Donahoe was admiring my ring?"

"No, I didn't notice. It must have been a painful reminder."

"He doesn't realize how lucky he is to be free of that little tramp."

"No, and nobody can tell him that," Rosy said. "It just has to wear off."

"I wish there were something one could do. But I suppose we'd better let him work out his own problems," Sara Jane said. "It's a shame to see a nice kid like that so unhappy. By the way, why were you so insistent on his reading Thomas Wolfe?"

"Because," Rosy said, "it would be the perfect match. I've seen it work before, with bright kids who don't have their lives under control yet. They identify with Eugene Gant. He becomes their soulmate."

"Was he yours, when you were Mike's age?"

"Wolfe wasn't publishing books yet when I was Mike's age. I had to make do with Browning and *This Side of Paradise*. To get the full effect, you've got to be in your late teens or early twenties. But if Wolfe had been around when I was that age, I'd have probably carried *Look Homeward, Angel* around with me, the way I did the Oxford Classics edition of Browning."

"It would have been pretty bulky, wouldn't it?"
Rosy laughed. "That's true, but I'd have managed."

WRECKING CREWS HAD lost little time dismantling the old onetime residence that was located behind the little yellow masonry building that housed Dolf Strongheart's zoology laboratory and the somewhat larger ex-residence that constituted Dean McCracken's psychology lab. When all the debris was carted off, work on the new science building began. There was a groundbreaking ceremony, presided over by President Carter, in which assorted dignitaries including Harry Hopkins, director of the Works Progress Administration, Congressman Poinsett, Mayor Henry Lockwood, and Turner Murray, chairman of the board of trustees of the College, each sunk a ceremonial spade into the earth, scooped up a bit of dirt, flung it elsewhere, and saw that it was good.

Then the ordeal began. A large steam pile driver was installed on the site, and the work of driving pilings deep down into the Cooper River marl that underlay the topsoil of the peninsula of Charleston began. For those lecturing or listening to lectures, concentration on the subject at hand became difficult while waiting each second for the hiss of steam, the resounding thud of the weight upon the piling, followed by a lengthy interval during which the weight was being hoisted aloft again for another blow. Dolf Strongheart moved all his turtles to temporary quarters in his garage and study. "It's bad for their nerves," he explained.

Rosy taught a survey course in English literature that met at one o'clock each Monday, Wednesday, and Friday afternoon. He was into Shakespeare's sonnets:

Sweet love, renew thy force; be it not said
Thy edge should blunter be
                    (Hisssssss!
          WHAM!) than appetite,

Which but today by feeling is allayed,
Tomorrow sharpened in his former might.
So, love, be
>   (Hisssssss!
>   **WHAM!**) thou; although today thou fill
Thy hungry eyes even till they wink with
>   (Hisssssss!
>   **WHAM!**) fullness,
Tomorrow see again, and do not kill
The spirit of love with a perpetual dull
>   (Hisssssss!
>   **WHAM!**)ness.

"If only," Rosy said to Sara Jane that evening, "we were up to Milton. He'd synchronize better."

"Just be glad you're not teaching Emily Dickinson."

THEY WERE TO be entertained that evening at a dinner at Page and Tennie Carter's. Page was still attempting to put the best face upon things in his relationship with Dean McCracken. Whatever his private opinion of the man, or his wife Tennie's (which was scorching), the president of the College was trying to preserve the amenities, to act as if differences on professional matters did not negate social civilities. Thus when the Carters gave a dinner party in honor of the coming nuptials of the College librarian and an English professor, they invited not only the Stronghearts, the Donahoes, the Hewitts, and Tom Lowndes, but the dean and his wife. There were thirteen in all, with Sara Jane flanked on one side of the dinner table by the dean and on the other by Rosy.

By now Sara Jane's blue dress was thoroughly restored to its original splendor, and she wore it that evening. The conversation at dinner was lively, the more so because it was preceded by drinks and accompanied by frequent servings of red and white wine — in particular to the dean, who downed them with avidity. He soon grew most expansive, and held forth on educational philosophy and the truths of behavioral theory with great enthusiasm. His voice boomed over the room.

Several times Rosy glanced at Tennie Carter, who returned his look with a momentary narrowing of her eyes that almost caused him to laugh aloud. As for Sara Jane, who was seated next to the dean, she had little to say, and even seemed somewhat distracted. She appeared to be trying to sit as far away from the man as possible.

He is sure he's the cock of the walk, Rosy thought. He thinks that Page has been afraid to call his bluff, and that he's gotten away with his self-study operation, and that at the meeting tomorrow he's going to inform all of us about what we've got to do, and the faculty will spend the next three or four months doing busy work so that he can perform as Dean of the College. Well, he had a surprise in store for him. For Rosy had been informing his colleagues of his intentions, and was quite certain that they would support him. Even Horace Hewitt had been persuaded not to organize a petition to the board of trustees, but to go along with Rosy's plan.

Rosy felt a little guilty. Here was McCracken naively and innocently assuming that his leadership was unchallenged, and that in order to have things his way he needed only to issue a pronouncement — and all the while his fellow dinner guest, seemingly unconcerned with any such thing as curricular self-study, was plotting to upset his apple cart. Still, only someone as self-absorbed as McCracken would have placed himself in such a position.

DURING DESSERT THE dean was emoting at length about the wisdom of a recently published book. The author of this book, a man named Skinner, was, he declared, the seminal thinker on the American scene today. If he could have his way, he would make the man's book required reading for every educator and every politician in the land. As he rattled on, Sara Jane turned to Rosy with comment, reached out, and removed from his tie his father's gold stickpin. Rosy was puzzled. He had thought she admired the pin, but something about it must have seemed tacky to her. He glanced around to see if anyone else was wearing a tiepin. Page Carter was attired in a bow tie, but both Tom Lowndes and Mike Donahoe were wearing tiepins that, so far as Rosy could tell, were at least as conspicuous as his own.

Coffee was served. All the while the dean was expatiating, seemingly enthralled by his own eloquence and charm. Then suddenly, without warning, McCracken gave a yelp. "Aaaiiiee!" And he jumped up from his chair and grabbed his trousers leg.

Everyone stared. "What's wrong?" Page asked him.

The dean grimaced. "Just a cramp in my leg," he said after a moment. "It's all right now!" He resumed his seat.

Linda Strongheart, who was seated directly across the table from the dean, was giggling. It *was* funny, although for Linda to express her mirth openly was scarcely in the best form. He glanced at Sara Jane. She seemed unconcerned, and did not show even the trace of a smile. Meanwhile the leg cramp must have continued to give the dean trouble, because thereafter he had little to say, and repeatedly reached down to rub it.

They adjourned to the parlor and sun porch for brandy, and the dean, after absenting himself for a few minutes, remained thereafter much subdued. When time came to leave, the McCrackens were the first to depart for home.

As the other guests were preparing to leave, Tennie Carter whispered to Rosy and Sara Jane to stay on for a minute. Rosy nudged the Stronghearts, in whose car they had come, and they remained behind.

When the red taillights of the other cars had disappeared down the road and out the gate, Page closed the front door.

"Did you ever?" Tennie declared. "What a horrible person!"

Page shook his head.

"I'm glad he finally he had the leg cramp," Tennie said. "What he needed was a jaw cramp."

Linda Strongheart looked at Sara Jane, and began laughing again. "Shame on you," Dolf told Linda, "for laughing when the poor man was writhing in pain, despite how desirable it was!"

"You don't know why I was laughing," Linda told him. "You can give Rosy back his pin now," she said to Sara Jane.

"What's my tiepin got to do with it?" Rosy asked.

"Tell them," Linda said, laughing some more.

"Tell us what?" Dolf asked.

"It's nothing important," Sara Jane said.

"Oh, go ahead and tell them," Linda said again. "I knew what he was doing!"

"The dean," said Sara Jane, "kept rubbing his knee up against me all evening long."

"You mean intentionally?" Rosy asked.

"Yes. It became so annoying that finally I borrowed your tiepin, and the next time he tried it I reached down and—" She held up the tiepin and gave a little jab with it.

"You didn't!" Tennie Carter shrieked. "Marvelous!"

Sara Jane nodded.

Page Carter roared with delight. Linda and Tennie laughed until the tears came to their eyes. Rosy and Dolf were highly amused.

"That's the best thing that's happened since that imbecile arrived!" Tennie declared. "The colossal nerve of the man! Page, how can you tolerate him for another week?"

Page shook his head.

"Oh, it's *awful!*" Tennie said. "That man will never enter this house again!"

"I TOLD YOU," Linda said to Dolf a little later as they drove down the dirt road toward the highway, "that he was a lecherous old goat, didn't I?"

"Yes, you certainly did."

"Sara Jane said the same thing," Rosy said. "I guess women pick up these nuances more quickly."

"Nuances?" Linda asked. "You mean if somebody crowns you over the head with a baseball bat, it's a nuance?"

Sara Jane laughed. "It was obvious from the first time he was introduced around."

"If he tries it again, just tell me," Rosy said, "and I'll show him how to be obvious."

"You'll do nothing of the sort," Sara Jane told him. "I can fend for myself quite well."

"I'll say you can!" Dolf agreed. "Just lend her your tiepin when she needs it, Rosy."

Dolf turned into the Folly Beach Road. "Let's pretend we're kids out on a double date," he said, and put his arm around Linda. "Remember?"

"Yes, dear," Linda said. "Only we didn't have a car. The best we could do was the Staten Island Ferry. A nickel to ride over, and a nickel to ride back."

"That's true. Still, we managed."

They drove homeward along the highway, with Linda's head nestled against Dolf's shoulder and his arm around her. In similar fashion, but free of any need to steer the car, Rosy and Sara Jane also managed.

THE FACULTY MEETING to discuss the dean's proposal was set for 4:30 P.M. At lunch Rosy, Sara Jane, Dolf and Tom Lowndes speculated on how it might go. "Do you think Page will preside, or the dean?" Dolf asked.

"I hope Page," Rosy said. "If he doesn't, the dean can figure he can call faculty meetings any time he wants, without bothering to involve Page."

Tom Lowndes shook his head. "You know, I still can't understand how Page could possibly ever have agreed to appoint a man like McCracken as dean, even if Turner Murray did promise to kick in an extra fifty thousand dollars for the science building."

"If we knew why Turner wanted the dean taken on in the first place, we might be able to figure it out," Sara Jane said. "Somehow Turner got Page to agree to take the dean, perhaps only on a provisional basis — after all, we don't know what the terms were."

"And ever since then he's been kicking himself in the tail for agreeing to it," Rosy said.

"Exactly. And Tennie's been doing a little kicking of her own, too."

"How can Page stand it?" Tom Lowndes asked. "How can he go on day after day, with this man a constant presence, without blowing his stack?"

"I guess that's what makes a good college president," Rosy said. "The ability to keep cool no matter what the provocation, and not to display emotion."

"Still, you'd think he'd have to let off steam somehow. Maybe he does, but if so I've never seen it."

"What will happen this afternoon," Dolf asked, "if Rosy makes his motion to table the self-study project, and the dean says that the decision to conduct the project isn't up to the faculty but to the administration?"

"Then Page will have to make a ruling," Rosy said.

"Really? If so, certainly Page couldn't possibly *not* support the dean's position, no matter how he might dislike the whole business," Tom said. "If he didn't, he'd be undercutting the administration's, which is to say his own, authority, wouldn't he?"

"I don't believe Page is worried about protecting his own authority," Sara Jane said. "If he were, he'd have sent McCracken packing weeks ago."

"If that's true, " Dolf asked, "then why are we having to go through all this? Why are we having to say we won't take part?"

"Maybe because Page is sure we'll do it," Sara Jane told him.

ooooo

ROSY'S SOPHOMORE ENGLISH literature survey was enlivened that afternoon as always by the presence of José L. Lopez, Jr., the student poet. He had taken to handing out calling cards reading,

> José L. Lopez, Jr.
> POET

Except in very warm weather he wore a black cape over his shoulders and a wide-brimmed western hat, and cultivated a flowing moustache. What José L. Lopez, Jr., liked to do was to rewrite some of the poems being studied into class into colloquial English. Not only were his parodies often funny in their own right, but Rosy liked them because they were a way of making the other students in the class aware of the difference in language conventions, and letting them see the contemporaneity of the poems they were reading. So Rosy always asked José L. Lopez, Jr., to read his versions to the class.

For class that afternoon he produced his own version of Shakespeare's sonnet, "Let Me Not to the Marriage of True Minds":

Sweetie, when it comes to you and me
Nothing's gonna get in our way.
Our love don't adjust to the scenery,
Like the flats in a three-act play.
You see that cute little star up there
Beaming its light all around,
Strutting its stuff in the stratosphere
A million miles off the ground?
Well, that's us. They say when you're old
That your love life is all through,
But til' the day I turn stone cold
I'll be making out with you.
And if what I say ain't the True Gen
There never was a poet took up his pen.

"What's the 'True Gen'?" somebody asked.

"I don't know for sure, but it's what Ernest Hemingway says when he means the real stuff," José L. Lopez, Jr., replied. "Do you know, Dr. Rosenbaum?"

Rosy shook his head. "I don't know. It might be British."

Most of the students got the joke of the parody and enjoyed it, however much some of them razzed the poet. Some few registered looks of incomprehension. In any event, Rosy thought, it was a welcome relief from the imminent unpleasantness of the upcoming faculty meeting.

IT WAS OBVIOUS from the start of the meeting, which began at four o'clock, that the dean didn't consider his curricular self-study plan a proposal, but a decree. He set out to explain how it was to be carried out in the months ahead. So when Rosy got up and offered a motion to table the proposal indefinitely, he was clearly surprised.

"Is there a second to the motion?" the president asked.

"I second it," Mike Donahoe said.

"Is there any discussion?"

"Will Professor Rosenbaum give his reasons for making his motion?" somebody asked.

The reasons, Rosy said, were that the faculty had completed a curricular self-study only three years ago. There had been no changes made in the curriculum since then, and given the tremendous amount of time and labor involved, there was insufficient reason to to do the whole thing over again so soon.

This, as Rosy knew very well, was the Lie Direct. If Dean McCracken had any sense he wouldn't respond to his objections, but would stand on a point of authority. The decision whether to proceed or not was not up for discussion, he would say. This would force Page to make a ruling. Certainly the dean ought to be able to see that whatever his chances were, they would be better that way than by trying to get a majority of the faculty to vote in favor of another massive self-study project.

But McCracken, for all that he was supposedly a psychologist, obviously had no sense of what others might think of a project that was sure to require a great deal of work on their part, and no notion that the faculty might not be willing automatically to do his bidding. So, instead of asking the president to declare the motion out of order, he proceeded to give his reasons for undertaking the self-study. They consisted of the same platitudes he had already set forth.

When he was done, there was silence. Then Tom Lowndes called for the question. The vote was overwhelmingly in favor of tabling the dean's project. Only four faculty members voted the other way.

During all this time Page Carter had said nothing in the way of expressing an opinion on either the dean's project or the motion to table it. He recognized the discussants in turn, waited until the question was called, then surveyed the show of hands and announced that the motion to table had been carried. He then adjourned the meeting and left the room.

To say that the dean was chagrined would be a notable understatement. He must have perceived that Page Carter had wanted the project dropped. He was furious. He turned fiery in complexion, so much so that it became difficult to distinguish just where his forehead ended and his red hair began. He had been rejected by a vote of the faculty — and, it no doubt began to dawn upon him, outmaneuvered by the president, who could easily have blocked the opposition to the self-study project merely by ruling that the motion to table it was out of order.

"I COULDN'T HELP it. I felt sorry for him," Rosy told Sara Jane as they walked along Greene Street to Rosy's car. It was drizzling lightly. "I don't enjoy seeing anyone humiliated like that, no matter how awful he is."

"He *wasn't* humiliated, Rosy! You'd feel humiliated if it happened to you, but his mind doesn't function that way. He's been thwarted, and he's angry. He's furious at Page, and at you, and he'll do his best to figure out how to get back at everybody who voted against him. But he isn't humiliated. You can't humiliate a saber-toothed tiger."

"Especially one that hisses," Dolf said.

"I suppose you're right," Rosy said. "Anyway, I hope he's learned not to bypass or ignore Page when he wants to do something."

"I'm sure he sees that now. Next time he'll be more subtle. But he won't stop trying. You can be sure of that."

"'Archers, be on your guard!' You frighten me."

"Don't be afraid of him," Sara Jane said. "Just don't let yourself be taken in by him, that's all."

22

IN THE ONGOING experience of discovering that the world was not constructed for his pleasure, Mike Quinn had lost his fiancé. Now he was finding out that being a successful journalist was going to be a trifle more difficult than he had thought. During the first several weeks on his new beat, Mike was roundly scooped by the reporter for the *Evening Post*. He found himself in the uncomfortable and unenviable position of reading stories in the rival newspaper about important political developments in the communities he was covering, and of which he had no inkling and no warning.

The first time it happened, nothing was said to him. But when the front page of the afternoon newspaper featured a two-column story about a town councilman on Mount Pleasant being accused by a political rival of receiving a kickback on a street paving contract, the city editor expressed his displeasure. Writing interesting features about ferryboats and the like was fine, he told Mike, but he had also been sent out there to cover the news.

Mike felt sick. He had called at the Mount Pleasant town offices the day before and talked with the mayor, and nobody had breathed a word of any such development. Yet they must have known about it. How could he make himself into the kind of reporter who was given tips on stories, who enjoyed the confidence of the people who could be counted upon to know what was going on?

ooooo

MEANWHILE THE PRESIDENTIAL election was over. The editor of the *News & Courier* had given due warning of the destruction of American liberties if Franklin D. Roosevelt were elected to a third term and the New Deal allowed to continue to debauch the moral fibre of the republic. The voters of neither the city of Charleston, the state of South Carolina, or the nation as a whole had heeded the warning, however; Roosevelt had been reelected handily over the "Barefoot Boy from Wall Street," Wendell Willkie. The only solace that the editor had was that the downtown precincts had followed the editor's advice. Yet this was, after all, something, for there, mainly Below Broad, dwelt the Quality, the True Charlestonians.

Nothing more had been heard about the accusation that Franklin Poinsett and certain other southern congressmen had connived with the War Department to release the news of the new defense installation shortly before the date of the Democratic primary election in July. Supposedly it was up for investigation by the House Ethics Committee, but if so, nothing had been concluded.

Poinsett was a local hero; there could be no doubt of that. Defeated opponents might cavil, but he appeared to know how to use his position on the Military Affairs Committee to get money spent and jobs created in the Charleston area. It had long since become clear that the city's economy stood to benefit greatly from the approach of the war. The Navy Yard was being steadily expanded; the Army Air Force had a full-fledged transport operation going on at the local airport; the Ordnance Depot, the Port of Embarkation, the Remount Station were all booming. An Army general hospital was reputed to be in the works for North Charleston.

To what extent these were due to the congressman's influence, as distinguished from the natural advantages inherent in the area's location and the available shipping and transportation facilities, no one could say for sure. But certainly Poinsett's position and relative seniority on the Military Affairs Committee did not diminish the area's chances, the more so because the congressman knew how to stay on the good side of the president, who was known to call him by his first name. (The president called numerous congressmen by their first names; he was good at that.) And to that extent, the fortunes of Mike's ex-father-in-law-to-be, Turner Murray, could only be enhanced — insofar, that is, as it might be of advantage, in a time of military and naval build-up, for a building contractor and developer to number among his oldest and closest associates an influential member of the congressional committee charged with overseeing much of that build-up.

"Do you think Mr. Murray's got political ambitions?" Mike asked Jim Igoe one evening after work.

"It depends on what you mean by that," Igoe said. "I could see him running for mayor sometime in the future. But I doubt he'd try for anything beyond that. What he's interested in is local prestige — and money, of course. It's an old Charleston pattern. You work your way up and in, get elected or appointed to the governing boards of the right societies and civic groups, make the right kinds of donations to charities and cultural organizations and the like, get the right people obligated to you. Then, particularly if your children can make strategic marriages and set you up with the right in-laws, and you steer clear of scandal and notoriety — which is a different thing from being prominent — you might have a chance to make it all the way.

"Will the country boy from Greenville make it into the St. Ceci? Tune in next week's installment of 'How I Used My Pile to Climb to the Top of the Heap.'

"You see what you were up against, don't you, kid? You didn't fit in with the grand design."

THE WEATHER TURNED cold. Chilly winds came fanning down from off the Canadian shield. Dry cold was one thing.

Having grown up in the valley of Virginia, Mike was used to that. But when the winds reached the coast they combined with sea breeze and thereby acquired an additional infusion of moisture, which made them both icy and clammy. The frigid dampness came off the harbor and seeped into one's clothes, coated the skin, lay over everything. Mike thought he had never been so cold in his life one night when, having driven out to the Isle of Palms to cover a town council meeting, the staff car he was using had broken down out on the highway not far from Breach Inlet and, after he called a tow truck, he had had to wait a full hour for it to arrive. The sky was absolutely clear, the moon was bright, and the wind came knifing in off the ocean. He hadn't worn his overcoat. All he could do was to sit in the car, with newspapers stuffed under his coat, and shiver.

SEVERAL EVENINGS EACH week he made it a practice to spend an hour or two at the police department office on Sullivans Island, as Jim Igoe had advised. The night desk sergeant was a retired Army noncom who had been stationed on Fort Moultrie. The patrolman on night duty was from upstate South Carolina. When the patrolman was out on his rounds he called in on the police radio, but most of the time both he and the sergeant sat around headquarters and listened to commercial radio programs. A few local residents dropped by during the evening to sit for a while and exchange gossip. Very occasionally the telephone would ring and there might be something for the patrolman to investigate.

Mike sensed that the two policemen were uneasy at his presence. Even in a tiny outpost like that on Sullivans Island, there seemed to be an inevitable division between the Fourth Estate and the guardians of the law. Individuals like Jim Igoe, with his capacity for conversation and his joy in whatever was idiosyncratic, could have bridged it in short order, but otherwise the men in blue were inherently suspicious of the press. They couldn't keep

Mike from sitting around the station house, but it was obvious that they felt inhibited in their comments when he was around.

ON THE SATURDAY evening after he had been scooped on the political story, he lay in his room reading *Lord Jim* until ten o'clock or so, until he realized that he was thinking so much about his failure, and about the absence of a girl in his life, that he scarcely paying attention to the book. He slammed the book shut, put on a coat and tie, and left the house. There was a night-club around the corner from the Porthole where he had been told it was possible to pick up girls without too much difficulty. He drove over there, parked down the block, and went inside.

The room was smoky, with a trumpet, piano, and drum combo playing just offstage, and a girl on the stage singing and also thrusting her hips back and forth in time to the drum. He took a seat at the bar and ordered a beer. A girl was sitting at the bar. He watched her out of the corner of his eye for a few minutes. He was sure that she was aware of him. He was about to muster up the nerve to make his move, when somebody else came in, sat next to her, and in no time was conversing with her.

He looked at the floor show for a while — the girl on stage was now doing a full-fledged striptease, and was down to a fringed cloth over her breasts and a rhinestone G-string. She was swarthy, quite muscular, and after a time, with her back on the floor and her knees spread, she thrust her crotch in and out and around in circles while the drum pulsated. Several drunks seated at tables near the stage began tossing coins at her crotch. She ignored them and kept on, but when someone threw a balled-up bill onto the stage, without changing her posture she reached out, grabbed it, inserted it in her vagina, and resumed her gyrations. That got the crowd's full attention. More bills were thrown, and with each she repeated the performance. When the music was done she reached down, retrieved the bills, blew a kiss to the drunks with them, picked up the coins, and strutted offstage.

The performance was highly arousing. He wanted a woman. He paid for his beer and drove over to the street where he had seen the red and blue lights in the windows. He parked, went up to the door of one of the houses, and rang the bell. A black maid opened the door, and led him into a parlor. A woman wearing a green housecoat came in, sat next to him on a sofa, placed a hand on his thigh, and asked him whether he wanted to go upstairs. When he said yes, she left the room, and a few minutes later another girl came in, who obviously knew what to do. She led him upstairs.

Less than twenty minutes later he was back outside on the street returning to his car. It had been as impersonal an episode as he had ever known. Store-bought sex. He drove back to his room. He was disgusted with his life, his job, and everything about himself.

SUNDAY AFTER MASS he ate breakfast at the restaurant just down the street from the office and read the newspaper as usual, then drove back to his room. There he decided finally to try the book that Dr. Rosenbaum had recommended, and which he had been putting off. He began reading. By the time he was twenty pages into the story, he was conscious of nothing else. He had never read anything like it.

Look Homeward, Angel was about a family in a mountain city in North Carolina, the Gants, and particularly about Eugene Gant, the youngest son. What spoke to him was the way it was told. It caught him up. He couldn't ever remember a book speaking so directly to him before.

The town reminded him a great deal of Roanoke, which was also surrounded by mountains. So much of what it described were things he had seen himself, but hadn't recognized for what they were. It wasn't simply a matter of description, however, but the feelings that went with them. Nothing he had previously encountered had shown him how to feel about so many things that were part of his everyday experience. No, that wasn't it; he had already felt that way. What reading them in the novel did was to make him realize that he did.

Several chapters into the novel there was an episode about a man boarding a streetcar in the early morning. It gave his thoughts as he came home from a trip. "There was a warm electric smell and one of hot burnt steel." That was exactly the way that the trolley cars smelled when he used to ride out to Mill Mountain on Sunday afternoons, back before the buses had replaced the street cars. It was uncanny; he could smell it as if it were right there in his room. Never had he encountered a book, whether a novel or any other kind, that had bothered to describe how it felt to be stepping aboard a streetcar. He had not thought of so ordinary a thing as that as being worth trying to describe.

What also enthralled him with the novel was the feeling of being lonely. It was not only that Eugene Gant was a lonely young man, but that Thomas Wolfe understood *why* he was, and was even proud of him for being lonely. Clearly Wolfe believed that it was only extraordinary people, like Eugene Gant, who possessed the emotional force and sensibility to be lonely in that way. Reading about loneliness, his own loneliness diminished.

Mike read all morning long. When it was time to eat, he took the book along with him and read it in the restaurant.

THE WOLFE NOVEL made him think about trains. In Roanoke, surrounded as it was by mountains, there had been trains everywhere, day and night; the big articulated Mallet locomotives that hauled the Norfolk and Western coal trains through town, the passenger trains with their handsome red coaches, the electric box-cab coal train locomotives on the Virginian. Lying in bed at night, he could hear the whistles blowing from far off, and then the low, intensifying sound of the locomotives, and finally the rattle and clank of the rolling gondola cars as the trains came through the city. Sometimes he used to walk over to the N&W

tracks downtown, at the place just beyond the passenger station where the branch lines up the Valley and the "punkin-vine" run to Winston-Salem joined the main line, and sit for hours at a time watching the locomotives and the freight and passenger trains come and go.

There were trains in Charleston, of course, although nothing like in Roanoke. The coastal gradient was level, and there was no need for the huge Mallets and 4-8-4s of the mountains. At night he heard freight trains coming into Charleston from across the Ashley River on the Seaboard tracks up by Hampton Park. He had intended one evening to drive up there and watch one come through. The main line through Charleston, however, wasn't the Seaboard or the Southern, with its green passenger locomotives, but the Atlantic Coast Line, which didn't come down into the city but stopped at North Charleston en route to and from New York City and Florida. He had driven past the station there several times during the afternoon and seen cars and buses waiting there for a train to arrive.

Now that he had finished dinner, he decided to go up and have a look. He drove up Meeting Street and on out the highway, through the built-up area and out to the North Charleston station, which was located next to a viaduct just off the highway. There were a number of cars there, and several purple-colored ACL buses.

He parked his car, walked over to the station, and looked at the train board. The northbound Havana Special was due in shortly, and the southbound two hours later. People were spread out along the tracks, and the mail carts were in place up beyond the viaduct. After a little while he heard a locomotive whistle blowing off to the west, and then the rolling wheels of an approaching train, and several minutes later two locomotives came stroking around a bend and toward the station, with a string of coaches in tow.

He watched the activity along the tracks, the passengers going aboard, the mail sacks, express packages, and baggage being handed off the carts onto the coaches, and then after a few minutes came the "All aboard!" calls and the locomotives swung above and past him, followed by the baggage coaches, a half-dozen day coaches, twin dining cars, and a long string of pullmans. He walked down to the station and took a seat outside on a bench. He enjoyed sitting there by himself after the bedlam of the departing train, listening to the telegraph instruments clicking away inside the station, and thinking about nothing in particular. He felt at peace. A mainline freight train came slamming by after a while. It swung around the curve and out of sight, headed for Florida. A local freight came along, a single locomotive pulling a dozen boxcars and flatcars, and moved on toward the city. For a long while all was still except for the occasional chatter of the telegraph instruments. Then, after an hour or more, automobiles began to pull into the parking lot. A little later the southbound Havana Special came booming into the station. When the train moved out and the station again grew still, Mike drove back to town and to his room. There was more than half of *Look Homeward, Angel* still to be read, and another novel by Thomas Wolfe waiting after that.

23

GOING WITH SARA Jane to inspect his parents' furniture in the warehouse, where it had been stored for eight years, was something of a melancholy experience for Rosy. He left to Sara Jane the decision about what to keep and what to discard, specifying only that his father's reading chair and floor lamp be retained. It was a heavy, overstuffed chair, in dark leather and no thing of beauty, but having it there, with the floor lamp and its familiar dark-green lamp globe next to it, would provide a kind of continuity.

Each chair, each table, each bureau or chest seemed to call up an image, most often of things he had forgotten. There was a sewing cabinet which had stood by the window in his parents' bedroom; his father had left it undisturbed after his mother's death, and it had remained in place until his father died. What he remembered now was a day when he was about twelve or thirteen, and engaged in building a sailing ship model, and he needed some straight pins. He went looking in the sewing cabinet and found there, wrapped in tissue paper, a small pair of scissors, with elaborate but mottled and tarnished mother-of-pearl and silver handles. He took them down to the kitchen table where he was working on the model, and was using them for trimming cloth.

His father came home that evening and saw them. "Where'd you get these?" he asked. It turned out that the scissors had once belonged to his mother's mother, which she had brought over the ocean on a sailing ship from Germany when she was a young girl. "They were very poor, you know. She told your mother that they were the only valuable thing she owned." His father took them. "I'll keep these now, so they don't get damaged," he had said. "Some day you'll want them."

He told Sara Jane about it. "Where are they now?" she asked. The sewing cabinet was empty. "Probably packed in one of the boxes somewhere." There were a dozen large boxes and several barrels of china stored with the furniture. He would have to have them delivered to the new apartment, where he could go through them.

SARA JANE SENSED Rosy's mood. "You're thinking of your home, back when you were a child, aren't you?" she asked.

"I remember where each piece of furniture was located. It's like they're the flats and props from a stage set, left over after the play has closed out and the actors have dispersed."

"Wouldn't your parents have liked knowing that some of the things they had in their home will be in yours?"

"Yes, indeed. My father never got rid of anything in the house. He wanted everything to stay just as it was. For twenty-four years after my mother's death, we still had a treadle-operated sewing machine, a player piano that neither of us could play, an icebox —this was after we got a refrigerator — clocks that no longer ran, a wind-up gramophone with one of those big horns, even though we had a good electric phonograph. When I broke up housekeeping after he died, I gave away a truckload of things like that to the Salvation Army."

"It must have been a terrible blow to him, when your mother died."

"He left everything she touched in place. Even her clothes stayed in the closet and dresser in their bedroom, right where they were. When I think back on it, I sometimes feel that I grew up in a museum, not a house."

ooooo

THE FURNITURE THEY decided to keep was delivered to the apartment one week before the scheduled date of the wedding. Sara Jane's furniture would not be brought over until several days before, when she would move in with her aunts until the wedding. Rosy would move his possessions from the hotel on the Monday before the wedding, and stay in the apartment thereafter.

Sara Jane's Aunts Ruth and Esther professed to be delighted with the apartment, but even though Sara Jane kept pointing out to them that her own furniture, when installed, would more than fill the seeming bare spaces, they kept proposing to donate items of their own furniture. They did admire some of what was there, in particular an old clock with an iron frame, that had belonged to Rosy's parents. "It's lovely!" they agreed.

What amused Rosy most was their reaction when shown what was to be the master bedroom, in which the large double bed that had been his parents' was in place, without springs or mattress as yet. The associations taking place within their thoughts were obvious. Esther immediately asked Sara Jane whether her sister-in-law, Susan, had informed her that the family Dalmatian, Daisy, had had a litter of puppies. "Five of them," she said, "and they're pedigreed!"

Sara Jane winked at Rosy.

"Oh, by the way, Esther," Ruth said, "did you call Mr. Bicaise this morning and ask him to come and repair the lock? The front door key broke off in the lock yesterday."

"I'VE BEEN THINKING about Mike Quinn," Sara Jane told Rosy later that evening, after they had taken the aunts back to their home. "I believe I know just the girl for him."

"Really? Who?"

"Ethel Morrison's daughter."

"Polly? You might be right. She's taking my British poetry

course this term. Are you sure she's not booked up, though?"

"I don't think so," Sara Jane said. "And if so, she's not planning to get married any time soon, because she's going to graduate school next year."

"That's true. In history. She asked me to write recommendations for her. To Chapel Hill and Duke, I think."

"I've known her all her life. She's a very bright kid, and I'd think Mike might go for her, and vice versa."

TWO DAYS BEFORE the wedding, on Monday afternoon, and following an eight-year residency, Rosy moved out of the hotel. It proved to be a formidable task. His living quarters had for a decade been confined to two medium-sized hotel rooms. He had loaded them down with all manner of belongings, including six or seven hundred books.

Several hours passed before the movers had hauled everything up the stairs to the second floor of the apartment on Gadsden Street, and Rosy and Dolf Strongheart could sit down with a drink and contemplate the pile of boxes, suitcases, clothes bags, bookcases, phonograph, boxes of record albums, typewriter, and other articles now lying in the center of the living room floor.

"One thing you got to say about turtles," Dolf declared. "They travel light."

"Why is it," Rosy said, "that when you look at an empty apartment it seems so roomy, but when you move your belongings in it looks so tiny?"

"Now that, Dr. Rosenbaum, is what I call a profound question. It was to be able to propound questions like that that Yale University awarded you a Ph.D. But, comrade, if you think this is bad, try moving a laboratory sometime."

"Speaking of laboratories, how's McCracken's psychology course doing?"

"He's got about eight or nine students. I'm told he spends a good deal of his time in class proving that everything in the college curriculum except science and math is meaningless. That's the word he uses. The assumption is that if you can't count it or measure it, it's without meaning."

"So we've got a dean who tells his students that what most of the faculty teach is a waste of time."

"Right. He also believes in working late with his students. The other evening I stopped by about 11:30 to get something out of my office, and as I came up the sidewalk, the door to the psych lab opens and out step McCracken and a coed. It seemed like an odd time of the night to be running rats."

"Did he say anything?" Rosy asked.

"No. Just 'Good evening, Dr. Strongheart!' Didn't seem a bit fazed."

"Well, at least he's learned to distinguish one of the faculty Jews from the other."

"Hah! The son of a bitch knows exactly who you are now, my friend. Just don't turn your back to him in a dark alley any time soon."

THERE WERE FOOTSTEPS on the stairs, and Sara Jane and Linda entered. Sara Jane's furniture and possessions had been moved in, and were now mostly in place. She was living with her aunts until the wedding. She stared at the array of boxes and luggage. "Where's it all going to fit?" she asked.

"We'll find a place," Rosy said.

"Did you start off your marriage with as much junk as this?" Sara Jane asked Linda.

"No," Linda said. "But we were still in our early twenties. All we had were two straight chairs, a dinette set, an innerspring mattress, and four cages of turtles and snakes."

"Snakes? In your apartment?"

Linda nodded her head. "The Garden of Eden came fully equipped with a serpent."

Rosy fixed drinks for them.

"When I consider," Dolf Strongheart said, "the indignities I have undergone, the sarcasm that has been directed my way, all because of my selfless labors in the cause of science, it is enough to make the statue of Sherman's horse weep. That woman" — he pointed at Linda — "has even had the effrontery to inform me that I may not use our garage to maintain a small maternity colony of *Nycticeius humeralis* for purposes of detailed observation next summer."

"He's talking about bats!" Linda declared. "He wants to keep a bunch of bats in the garage. That's all I need, to go out to the car and find a bat fastened to the steering wheel. Ugh!"

"Actually they're very well-mannered creatures," Dolf said. "They never bother anyone, and they only come out at night. What I want to observe is the way they give birth. They are reputedly the only known mammal in the world to give birth to their young feet first."

"I don't care if they give birth while hanging upside down on the rafters with their toes, they're not going to do it in our garage! Can you imagine, keeping a bat colony?"

"Not to change the subject," Sara Jane said, "but do you happen to know a good clock repair shop in town? Rosy's got a lovely old table clock that doesn't work, and I'd like to see if we can get it fixed."

"Where is it?" Dolf asked. "I can fix it."

"No, Dolf," Linda said. "You don't dare let him touch that clock," she told Sara Jane.

"Don't be silly. It's an inherited racial instinct," Dolf said. "Where is it?"

"Over there on the sideboard," Sara Jane said.

"I give you fair warning," Linda told her.

Dolf went across the room and began to examine the clock, its dial mounted in a black iron frame which was decorated with faded painted flowers.

"It was my mother's," Rosy said. "I had it in storage. I don't think it's been in working order for many years."

"Do you have a screwdriver?" Dolf asked him.

"Yes, I'll get it." He went into the kitchen and returned with a tool kit. He handed a screwdriver to Dolf.

"Have you ever heard of Pandora's Box?" Linda asked. "Well, it is about to be opened."

Dolf opened a little glass door on the front of the clock and moved the pendulum. The clock gave a couple of ticks, then the pendulum stopped swinging. He turned the clock around, removed the screws, and took off the back plate. He observed the mechanism for a minute. "I think I see your trouble," he declared. "Let me see those needle-nosed pliers, will you?" Rosy handed him the pliers.

"Dolf," Linda said, "please don't!"

Dolf inserted the pliers in the works and gave them a turn. "Just as I thought," he said. "Now if I just move this a little to the right—"

Suddenly the clock made a whirring noise, causing Dolf to jump backwards, and began ringing. It rang very loudly. **Bong! Bong! Bong! Bong! Bong! Bong!** Nor did it stop at twelve, but kept right on ringing away. **Bong! Bong! Bong! Bong! Bong! Bong! Bong! Bong!**

"For heaven's sakes, Dolf, make it stop!" Linda said.

Bong! Bong! Bong! Bong! Bong! the clock continued.

Dolf poked frantically at the mechanism with the screwdriver. **Bong! Bong! Bong! Bong! Bong! Bong! Bong!** the clock rang on. Eventually, Dolf did something that caused the clock to whirr and stop.

"All right," Linda declared, getting to her feet. "That completes your virtuoso performance for this afternoon, Dolf. It's time to go home."

"I'll come over and get it running right some evening next week," Dolf promised.

"It's ticking now, anyway," Rosy said. "The pendulum's swinging. It'll keep time. It doesn't need to ring."

The Stronghearts departed down the stairs.

"Do you think Dolf really wanted to keep a colony of bats in their garage?" Sara Jane asked.

"Of course not. He just says those things to tease her. He knows she'll be horrified."

"It would horrify me, all right."

"I can assure you," said Rosy, "that never will I bring any bats, or snakes, or even turtles home to live with us. Never!"

"I don't think I'd mind turtles," Sara Jane said. "Little ones, that is. No *Caretta carettas.*"

"Please don't remind me of that evening. I'm lucky you even spoke to me afterward."

"What you forget is that I happened to be in love."

ON TUESDAY NIGHT, after he and Sara Jane had stocked the pantry and refrigerator that afternoon in preparation for their homecoming on Sunday, Rosy took a shower, put on his pajamas, and climbed into the large double bed. For the first time since his father had died and he had sold the house, he was no longer living in a hotel room. And after tonight he would no longer be living alone.

He was a very lucky man for Sara Jane to have put up with his obtuseness for so long. For she was attractive, intelligent, witty, popular. She was bound to have had offers. Yet she had turned everyone else down in favor of a clumsy mediocrity like himself.

Suppose she hadn't, as she might well have not? What would he have done? Go on the way he had been, pursuing his little projects, living solely within his own thoughts, the wellsprings of his affection kept corked up and unused, knowing no better than to settle for a partial existence. At forty-one, he had been getting perilously close to a lifetime of being only half-alive. The thought made him shiver.

He could hear the clock ticking away in the living room. Tomorrow that half-life would end — though it had already ended, ever since that day out at the Carters, when he had thought about how Sara Jane had looked as she set off to row the skiff back across the inlet to Dewees Island. That moment had transformed his life. The gray-black-and-white world in which he had been existing up until then had suddenly turned into full color.

SOMETIME DURING THE very early morning Rosy began dreaming that a fire alarm was sounding and the house was burning. Then he realized that the clock had commenced to ring again. He turned on the light, hurried into the living room. **Bong! Bong! Bong! Bong! Bong! Bong!** it was sounding. **Bong! Bong! Bong!**

If he didn't stop it, the noise would awaken the people who lived downstairs. But he didn't know how to shut it off.

He picked up the clock and carried it into the kitchen, even while it rang on, **Bong! Bong! Bong! Bong!** He opened the door to the refrigerator, placed the clock inside, and closed the door. (**Bonk. Bonk. Bonk. Bonk.**) The sound was much muffled. He went back to bed. For a minute longer he could still hear it ringing away inside the refrigerator. (**Bonk. Bonk. Bonk. Bonk.**) Then it ceased. The spring had finally run down.

Fire in a dream meant passion, Rosy thought. He was thirsty. He got out of bed again, returned to the kitchen and poured himself a glass of water. It would take more than water to dampen him down any time soon, he thought. His wristwatch showed that it was a little after 3 A.M. on his wedding day.

24

WINTER WAS DEFINITELY in the offing. A cold front had come in late Wednesday evening behind a vanguard of wind and rain, the temperature dropped into the twenties, and Thanksgiving morning Mike Quinn's car wouldn't start because of a dead battery. He walked to work. There was little in the way of breaking news that day. He ate dinner at the Francis Marion Hotel coffee shop; it was the only time he could remember that he hadn't been at home for Thanksgiving dinner.

The Murrays were doubtless having their dinner at home. He didn't think about Betsy all the time now. The whole business — meeting her, becoming engaged, the feeling that things were going badly, the realization that he was being two-timed, the final rupture — seemed like a nightmare, from which he was now slowly and painfully awakening. It was his devout hope that not ever again would he be made to have anything to do with Betsy, or her father, or anything involving them.

At late Mass Sunday he saw Polly Morrison, seated in a pew several rows across from and ahead of him with what appeared to be her family. No doubt she knew that he and Betsy had broken up, and about Elliott Mikell's role in it. If only he hadn't gotten so drunk that evening and made such a spectacle of himself. He hurried down the aisle and out of church immediately after the benediction.

There was a girl who worked downstairs at the classified ad desk that he stopped to talk with occasionally, and he made a date with her. They went to the movies, and afterwards stopped in at Bootle's Barbeque across the Ashley River Bridge for a snack. She was pleasant enough, and quite pretty, but not very bright. He had the feeling that if he picked a secluded place to park he might have gotten somewhere, but he didn't really want to go to the trouble.

A NEW REPORTER had joined the staff, in replacement of Al Myers. His name was White; previously he had worked for several years on the *Greenwood News*, a small daily upstate, so that in fact he had more professional experience than Mike. He was a graduate of the University of Georgia school of journalism. He was quiet, and so far as Mike could tell, quite competent at his work. He went out with them to the Porthole for beer after work several times, where he had little to say. It was Mike's hope, and Frank Blades's prediction, that after the new man had had a couple of months on the staff he would be moved out to the across-the-harbor beat and Mike returned to working on spot stories in the news room.

There was one story, however, that no matter what beat Mike was assigned to cover, was always his to write: the appearance in the harbor of the mystery speedboat, or the Cooper River Ghost as it had come to be known. He was still the Ghost Editor. The boat always showed up after a rainstorm, on a moonless night. Cold weather seemed not to deter it, for on Thanksgiving day there were reports that the Ghost had been seen on the harbor the night before. Mike called around. The watchman at the White Stack Towboat installation at Adger's Wharf had heard it go by, looked out, and caught a glimpse of it as it sped out of sight beyond the Clyde-Mallory wharf.

This time Frank Cox, the meteorologist at the U. S. Weather Bureau office at the Custom House, had gone out to the instrument hut at the end of the government wharf to check the tidal rise, and was on his way back when he heard a noise and turned to see the mystery boat go past. He confirmed the descriptions reported in the past by others. It was black, about thirty feet long, and piloted by a figure in white who stood in a cockpit about two-thirds back. The hull was very deep; it was planing, traveling at least forty miles an hour; and the sound it made was a howling whine. Cox said he watched the boat go upstream toward the Cooper River Bridge, and a few minutes later heard it, much more faintly, on the far side of the harbor, so that it had apparently rounded Shutes Folly and come back down the harbor along the Rebellion Reach channel.

Mike called the Coast Guard. Nobody at the wharf at the foot of Tradd Street on the Ashley River had reported hearing it. He also checked with the bridge tender at the drawbridge between Mount Pleasant and Sullivans Island and the night watchman out at Fort Sumter; neither had seen the boat, although the Fort Sumter watchman thought he may have heard it in the distance, but wasn't sure. So once again the Cooper River Ghost had repeated its previous course, being spotted first out in the channel in the lower harbor, then further up the waterfront, then crossing over to the eastern side of the harbor, coming along the channel there, and vanishing from sight and earshot shortly thereafter. The entire run had taken no more than twenty minutes, and the mystery craft had subsequently exited neither via the mouth of the harbor into the ocean, nor the Waterway eastward behind Sullivans Island, nor yet via the Ashley River beyond the Coast Guard wharf.

Mike wrote the story for Friday morning, once again employing a tongue-in-cheek approach. The news being light, the story ran on the front page, and predictably the telephone rang recurrently during the day, with callers reporting sightings of the Cooper River Ghost or advancing theories as to its nature. Most of the explanations proposed verged upon the supernatural, but one caller, a retired Navy officer, was quite sure that the craft must be powered by storage batteries such as those used to propel submarines when running submerged. Mike asked the Coast Guard commandant about that, and was told that the batteries needed to propel a boat as fast as the mystery boat was said to travel would make the boat so heavy that it could not possibly get up onto a planing configuration. It would have to move through the water, not atop it.

"It's very simple," the commandant explained. "You multiply the square root of the length of the waterline by the figure of 1.25. A displacement hull that's thirty feet or so long can attain a speed of a little over eight knots. In other words, it would be impossible." Mike wasn't sure what all that meant, but he wrote it down and put it in a follow-up story.

SUNDAY IT WAS bitterly cold and clear. That afternoon Mike went to the matinee of an eighteenth-century play, *The Beaux' Strategem*, by George Farquhar, at the Dock Street Theater. After supper he decided to drive across the Cooper River Bridge and stop in at the police headquarters of the communities he was covering.

When he arrived, there was an elderly man seated next to the kerosene stove in the station house, talking with the desk sergeant and the patrolmen about the Cooper River Ghost. It turned out that the old-timer had been a deckhand aboard the old harbor ferries before the bridge put them out of business. His theory about the mystery boat was that it was an ultra-secret government craft designed to hunt submarines, and that the Navy and Coast Guard authorities were all deliberately lying to cover up their knowledge of it. Mike talked with him about his days on the ferryboats. The old-timer left about ten o'clock, and Mike stayed for a little while longer.

He was sitting over against the wall, reading a baseball article in an old copy of *Collier's*, when the telephone rang. The sergeant answered it, listened for a moment, and wrote on a pad. "What color's the house?" he asked. He listened for another moment, then turned to the patrolman. "Man says he lives at forty-three Creek Street, and there's something funny about the house next door. He says it's a green house with a side porch. Better get over there."

The patrolman leaped to his feet and sprinted out the door. Mike followed. The patrolman sped off in his car, and Mike got into his car and trailed him.

Creek Street was a dirt thoroughfare that ran along the edge of the Mount Pleasant side of the island. When he pulled to a stop behind the parked police car the patrolman was standing in the yard, his flashlight trained on one of the windows, the panes of which seemed to be discolored. As he watched, the patrolman turned, ran back to the patrol car, and began talking into the microphone.

The patrolman went around to the side of the house. It was cold and clear. There was an acrid smell in the air. A man came out of the house next door and walked over to where the patrolman and Mike stood. Then Mike heard the sound of a siren in the distance. Shortly afterward a fire truck came around the corner, lights flashing, and pulled up in front of the house. A fireman climbed out and ran over to them. There were other sirens, and several automobiles, red lights blinking atop them, sped up.

Apparently there was a fire smouldering inside the tightly sealed house, which because of the absence of drafts had not burst into flame. The firemen ran to the truck, put on smoke masks and canisters, and, bearing axes, hurried around to the back. They found an unlocked window, pried it up, and climbed inside. Another fireman followed, carrying a fire extinguisher. The patrolman stood outside the window watching them.

By now several dozen people were gathered to observe. Mike talked to the man from next door, who said he had made the call to the police. The occupant of the house, he said, was a retired waterman who lived alone. He was something of a recluse and not very friendly. He drank a great deal, the man said, and several times had fallen when drunk and injured himself.

The neighbor had noticed that something seemed strange about the house, and had gone over to look. There were no lights on, and when he tried to peer through a window he had been unable to see anything within. "I could tell something was peculiar," he said. That was when he had returned to his home and called the police.

"Did you think there was a fire?" Mike asked.

"I didn't know what it was. I just thought there was something wrong."

A fireman reemerged from the rear window of the house, took off his smoke mask, went back to the truck, talked into a microphone, then took a pair of fire extinguishers back into the house, replacing his smoke mask before he did. The patrolman went back to his car and began talking to the sergeant over the radio. A few minutes later the front door opened from the inside. A fireman stepped out, hurried to the truck, and brought a stretcher into the house. After a little while the body of a man was brought outside on the stretcher, with a blanket draped over it.

A man arrived in another car, got out and came over to the body, carrying a black valise. He was obviously the coroner. He knelt down, examined the body, removed a stethoscope from the valise and placed it on the body. He listened, moved the stethoscope around, listened some more. While he was doing so an ambulance pulled up, and the crew came out and stood nearby. Then the man replaced the stethoscope in the valise and stood up. The ambulance crew transferred the body to another stretcher, placed it inside the ambulance, and drove off. They moved with no great urgency, and the ambulance drove off slowly. Mike talked to the coroner. The victim, he said, had apparently died of smoke inhalation. He could have been dead inside the house for several hours.

The surmise was that while seated in an easy chair he had fallen into a drunken stupor, and a cigarette he had been smoking had dropped into the upholstery and set the chair afire. There were charred marks on the man's body, but the likelihood was that he had died of smoke inhalation before being burned. Because the house was tightly shut, there was little draft, so that the fire had smoldered without bursting into flames. As the coroner was talking, the firemen brought the remains of the chair outside onto the lawn. The upholstery had been half eaten away, exposing the coils in the seat. Mike got all the names, secured statements from the fire chief, and went back to police headquarters, from where he called the news room with the story.

The fact that Mike had been at the scene of the incident appeared somehow to have changed his relationship for the better with both the patrolman and the sergeant. They now talked more freely with him. It was as if, having witnessed the affair from start to finish, he was no longer an outsider.

THE NEXT AFTERNOON Mike drove over to Sullivans Island, to find that a controversy had developed. The fire chief had issued a formal complaint to the mayor, charging that instead of sending the patrolman to the scene to investigate, the police department should have notified the fire department immediately upon receiving the telephone call. It was one more instance, he declared, of a failure on the part of the police to involve the fire department in situations in which the distinct possibility of fire existed.

He talked to the mayor, who gave him a copy of the fire chief's letter of complaint. The issue centered on what the caller from the house next door had actually told the police sergeant when he telephoned the alarm. The police sergeant was insisting that nothing in the telephone call he had received pointed to the likelihood of fire. "The man said there was something wrong about the house next door," he declared. "That's it. He didn't say nothing about a fire."

The story in the afternoon newspaper featured the chief's charges. For the next morning's newspaper, he wrote a story in which he recounted what he had seen and heard, including the statement by the man next door that while he had thought something was "wrong" about the house, he had not mentioned anything about the possibility of fire. The statement, Mike pointed out, had been made while the firemen were still inside the house and the patrolman was outside watching, so that there was no way for the man to have known that a dispute might be in the works.

In effect, the story was a vindication of the police department's contention. The sergeant declared that if the caller had said anything about an acrid odor, or even about being unable to see through the windows, it would have been logical to suspect the presence of fire. But since no such details had been given, all that the fire chief could now claim was that the police sergeant should have interpreted the statement that there was "something wrong" as meaning that the house might be on fire — which was dubious.

FROM THAT DAY onward, there was no more trouble getting police news from Sullivans Island. Not only that, but thereafter both the sergeant and the patrolman telephoned him on occasion to tip him off on non-police stories. Contrariwise, the only way he could find out anything about fire department activities on Sullivans Island was from the accompanying entries on the police blotter, and when he sought additional information he could elicit only the most literally factual answers. But since usually there was considerably more going on in the way of police news than reports of fires, and the police almost always knew when the fire department was involved in anything, from a news gathering standpoint it was by no means a bad trade-off.

HE DECIDED TO write a feature about the old-time ferry-boats. He read through the clippings in the newspaper library, talked with various people who had been involved in their operation, and went down to the Historical Society and found some more material, including some photos. Some of the old-timers also had photos. The hulk of one of the old ferries, the *Sappho*, was moored in a tidal flat near the foot of Beaufain Street off the Ashley River. He drove over to look at her. She was a forlorn sight, used as a dock and breakwater for small craft, and no longer afloat but imbedded solidly in the mud. In point of fact the *Sappho* had not been in service for some years before the discontinuance of cross-harbor operations, having been succeeded by more modern craft, but she seemed to be the boat the people remembered best. He located a man who had served as engineer on the *Sappho* and they took his photograph standing on the deck. The story was published in the Sunday paper and attracted much comment.

THE SAME ISSUE of the paper contained a story that Mr. Elliott Mikell and Miss Elizabeth Murray had been named co-managers for the New Year's Day hunt of the Ashley River Hunting Association. It also mentioned that a donation from the Murray Construction Company had enabled the Hunt to renovate all its jumps and to construct a series of new bridle paths on its property.

25

AT MIDDAY WEDNESDAY, classes at the College of Charleston ended for the Thanksgiving break, and at two o'clock that afternoon Miss Sara Jane Jahnz and Dr. Lancelot Augustus Rosenbaum were married in the College chapel. The Reverend Raymond Adams, minister of the First Unitarian Church, officiated at the ceremony. A reception followed at the home of Dr. and Mrs. Rudolf Strongheart.

The bride was given in marriage by her brother, Mr. John L. Jahnz. Her sister-in-law, Mrs. John L. Jahnz, was matron of honor. Dr. Rudolf Strongheart was best man. The Misses Margaret Jahnz and Joyce Strongheart were flower girls. Serving as ushers were Dr. Thomas Lowndes and Dr. Page Harrison Carter. The bride wore white.

Music for the occasion was furnished by Mrs. Henry C. Morrison, pianist, Miss Elizabeth Rutherford Seydel, violinist, and Miss Suzanne Victor, cellist.

Following the reception the couple left for a wedding trip to Savannah, Georgia.

"I NEVER EXPECTED to laugh at my own wedding," Sara Jane said as they drove across the Ashley River Bridge shortly after four that afternoon, bound for Savannah.

"Me, too. I tried my best not to, but when Page came back in with the coat hanger, I couldn't help it."

In the course of handing the wedding band to Rosy, Dolf Strongheart, who was extremely nervous, had dropped it. The ring rolled underneath a radiator and settled in a wide crack in the flooring. Not until Page Carter had hurried into his office and returned with a wire coat hanger was the ring extricated and the ceremony continued.

"What I liked best was when Benjy asked Linda whether Dolf was looking for turtle eggs under the radiator," Sara Jane said.

"I didn't hear that. What did she answer?"

"She said she hoped they were snapping turtles."

Meanwhile the car sped westward along Highway 17. "How do you like being a married woman?" Rosy asked. He was driving with an arm around her shoulder.

"I haven't decided yet."

"Let me know when you do."

The late afternoon sky was gray, and noticeably darker along the northwest horizon. "Looks like we'll have to drive through some rain before we get there," Rosy said.

"It's supposed to turn very cold tonight, isn't it?"

"Yes, but I've got my love to keep me warm."

"I hope you also brought your overcoat," Sara Jane said.

THEIR SUITE WAS on the fifth floor of the Hotel DeSoto in Savannah, overlooking the Savannah River. On the coffee table when they arrived was a bottle of champagne in an ice bucket and two glasses, with a card reading "Bon Voyage. Page and Tennie."

The meal in the restaurant downstairs was very good. Sara Jane was in rare form. One of the things Rosy always liked most about her was her sense of humor; she could always spot what was ridiculous. But he had never seen her quite so amusing as at dinner that night. She found something funny to remark about everything. Then, after dessert and coffee were served, she grew more subdued, and she had little to say when they rode back up on the elevator.

"Shall we have some champagne?" Rosy asked.

"Why not?"

He opened the bottle and poured champagne into the glasses. They touched glasses. "Here's to us," Rosy declared. "It might not be good form to brag, but right now I'm very proud of what I accomplished today."

They sipped the champagne.

Rosy watched out of the window of the hotel room. The rain, which had been coming down heavily when they arrived at the hotel, had eased off, and the slight drizzle was not enough to keep him from making out the lights of a ship, a freighter, moving up the Savannah River. He could also see the lights of a tugboat leading the way, her masthead light oscillating, indicating that there was considerable wind and wave action. Another tug's lights were visible alongside the hull of the ship, the dark shape of which could barely be perceived in the darkness. Unlike Charleston, there was no harbor, but instead a river front twenty-five miles from the ocean. Because of the wind and the river current, maneuvering a ship in and out of a dock here must be a ticklish job, he thought.

"I don't suppose there'll be any good French champagne available for a long while now," he said.

"Probably not." She stood alongside him looking out of the window.

"I guess that goes for wine and brandy, too."

"Uh huh."

"It'll be California and New York State wines, mostly."

"Yes."

"They say some of the California wine is very good now."

"I've heard that, too."

"Have you ever been to California?"

"No."

"I'd like to see San Francisco."

"So would I."

"But not Los Angeles, especially."

"No."

"It would make a nice train trip for us sometime."

"Yes, it would."

"It would be even nicer to go by boat, through the Panama Canal. I've always wanted to see the Panama Canal."

"I'd like to see it too."

"But I don't think I'd want to drive all that way."

"No."

It was their wedding night, Rosy realized, and Sara Jane Rosenbaum, until a few hours earlier Jahnz, was scared. Or embarrassed. Probably some of both. Humor, wit, sophistication could only go so far. He realized now that there had been a frenetic quality to her merriment at dinner. He was surprised, for while he was sometimes nervous and self-conscious, Sara Jane had always seemed to be completely self-possessed, in entire command of whatever situation confronted her. But now it was a complete turnabout. *She* was nervous, and he was not!

The source of the awkwardness, he decided, was probably not the imminence of the overt lovemaking itself — after all, there had been times when they had come pretty close to that —so much as the abrupt advent of complete intimacy, their being in the room with each other as man and wife, ready to undress and get into bed together. And this even though their every action and wish for several months had been directed toward just the situation in which they now found themselves.

It was his place to act to set the embarrassment to rest — a move that he could make, he knew, with absolute confidence of full collaboration.

"Who do you think's more nervous," Rosy asked, "you or me?"

"I don't know."

"I'd say you are."

She didn't even smile.

He gathered her to him. "Are you glad to be here?" he asked.
"Yes."
"With me?"
"With you."
"So am I."
She nodded.
"Then here we are."
"Here we are."
"A little more champagne?"
"Yes."
"Candy is dandy," he quoted, "but liquor is quicker."
This time she laughed.
Everything was all right after that.

FOR A LONG time to come Rosy could not get over marveling at the stored-up affection being married released for both of them. He had never known such affection in his life. His wife deluged him with it. He had to learn how to return it, for he wasn't accustomed to it. His parents had loved him, of course, but there had been a constraint about their ways, a reluctance to appear demonstrative, which he realized he had adopted. Now he and Sara Jane were married, and he discovered what affection could be. She was in no way constrained. It was not simply physical passion, though there was no shortage of that. It was joy in being so thoroughly together. The realization that his presence could be *wanted*, and that being wanted and needed was what he had always sought but never before known, came as a revelation. It was a surrender that involved no defeat, a conquest without opposition.

So that he understood now why it was that happily married couples like the Stronghearts were always so comically eager to encourage and facilitate romances among their yet-unmarried friends, as his and Sara Jane's had been. For they had discovered what those friends, being unmarried, could not imagine: what a fully shared life could offer.

Obviously it was not that way with all marriages, of course. But for this marriage, a powerful enhancement of their lives was taking place.

THEY RETURNED TO Charleston late Sunday evening, having stopped in Beaufort en route to have dinner at a restaurant that the Carters had recommended, the Golden Eagle. This time, driving eastbound instead of westbound across the Ashley River Bridge, Sara Jane said, "Do you remember what you asked me four days ago?"

"What was that?"

"How I liked being a married woman?"

"Oh. Yes. I was just teasing you, though."

"I didn't realize it was possible to like being something quite so much."

"Well, in that case we'll just keep right on being married, shall we?"

"Let's do."

MONDAY MORNING, WHEN Sara Jane set out to prepare some bacon and eggs for breakfast, she was surprised to find a large iron clock inside the refrigerator.

"Rosy, what is the clock doing in the refrigerator?" she called to him.

"The what?" Rosy had forgotten all about the clock. "Oh, that. I just thought it might keep better time that way."

"Are you out of your mind?"

He came into the kitchen, lifted the clock out, placed it on the table, sat down, and described what had happened with the clock the night before the wedding.

"I've been thinking about the clock," Sara Jane said. "It's got a very loud ring. I think maybe it's meant for a house, not an apartment — a quite large house."

"Now that you mention it, I believe that's why my father didn't get it fixed when it stopped running. It was so loud it used to wake him up when it rang." He drank some coffee. "Let's give it to Dolf. He'll enjoy trying to fix it."

"No, let's just keep it. It's very pretty, even if it doesn't work," Sara Jane said. "We can get it to run. We just don't have to wind the striking mechanism."

Rosy shook his head. "I don't trust it. It can be ornamental without keeping time."

"All right." She poured Rosy some more coffee. "We'll leave it on the sideboard. Here, have some bacon."

"I'm teaching the Metaphysical poets beginning on Wednesday," he said. "'But at my back I always hear / Time's wingèd chariot hurrying near.'"

"Well, eat your eggs and drink your coffee," Sara Jane said, "because Time's Wingèd Chariot has got exactly seventeen minutes to get your coy mistress to the library before opening time."

"You can take the car," Rosy said. "I'm in no hurry. I'll walk over later on."

Sara Jane looked at him. "Oh, you will, will you?"

"Sure. It's not far."

"In that case, you can just wash the dishes and scrub the skillet before you come."

"Never mind," said Rosy. "I'll leave when you do."

One thing about living at the St. Johns Hotel and eating in the coffee shop, he started to remark, was that you didn't have to worry about washing the dishes. Then he thought better of it, and did not remark it.

26

THERE WAS BIG news on the Isle of Palms. It was made public by a joint announcement from Congressman Franklin Poinsett's office and the Army that a 400-bed hospital was to be constructed on a hitherto-undeveloped 1500-acre tract on the island. Construction would begin in January, and when at full operating capacity the facility was expected to provide upwards of five hundred jobs.

The story had broken in the morning, so that there had been no way for the *News & Courier* to get it first. "Go out there with the photographer," the city editor told Mike Quinn, "and get some shots of the site. And get some quotes from people on the island. Find out what they think of it. And see if you can get someone at Poinsett's office or the War Department to comment on the danger from hurricanes. Seems like a damn strange place to put a hospital, out there on the edge of the ocean."

Mike called the congressman's office. The query must have been anticipated, because Poinsett already had a statement ready, which a secretary read to him. "The facility will be erected on the mainland side of the Isle of Palms, a half-mile distant from the ocean front, and well out of range of possible flooding. The area is dry and salubrious, and easily reached by an access road which will be constructed in December."

"Bullshit," declared the city editor. "You know damn well

they'd have to evacuate the patients if a hurricane came anywhere near. See what you can find out about the outfit the Army's buying the property from. And go out there with Tom Peck and get some pictures."

The property belonged to a company known as I. & M. Associates, Inc., of Greenville. Beyond that, no information was immediately available.

He arranged to meet the photographer outside the dance pavilion on the Isle of Palms at 3:00 P.M., then drove on over to Sullivans Island. At police headquarters the sergeant told him that the way to get to the property in question was not via the road through the woods, but by driving along the beach. "If you go about a mile past the pavilion, you'll see where there's a road through the dunes. Go through there and follow the trail for about half a mile. You'll come to a row of stakes. Everything past there's the land the Army bought."

What had crossed Mike's mind at once was the possible relationship of the Army hospital to the property that the Murray Construction Company had purchased last summer. Located as it was between the hospital tract and the built-up portion of the island, its value was bound to be enhanced. He asked the sergeant whether there had been any previous indication that the Army was interested in the tract. "That's what everybody's been wondering about. The property owners had some roads cut through there last summer," the sergeant said. "They wouldn't have had that done without some reason to believe that it was going to be of interest to somebody. But I don't think anybody knew who."

He drove on to the Isle of Palms. When he crossed the Breach Inlet bridge he remembered the incident, back in the early summer, when he had been sent out to ask about the impact on the area of the departure of the Eighth Infantry Regiment from Fort Moultrie to Georgia. He had been talking with the owner of the gas station and boat dock just across the bridge when Congressman Poinsett and Mr. Murray had driven into the station. Later that day Mr.

Murray had called him at the office and asked him not to say anything about him having been with Poinsett. He remembered that Jim Igoe had scoffed at Mr. Murray's statement that he didn't want to be identified with the congressman's campaign.

But what if that hadn't been the real reason why Mr. Murray hadn't wanted his name mentioned?

Then there had been the occasion, the Sunday after he had arrived in Charleston, when they had gone driving with the Murrays across the Cooper River Bridge, and over to the Isle of Palms. Betsy had proposed that they go for a walk on the beach, and Mr. Murray had said that he wanted to drive around, and would pick them up later. What had Mr. Murray wanted to look at that afternoon? It hadn't been the houses he was building on Sullivans Island, because they had already stopped at all of those.

Mike interviewed several business people on the Isle of Palms; they were the only ones available now, because there were very few year-round residents. As was to be expected, the response was favorable. As far as the island's merchants were concerned, the more people living and spending money on the Isle of Palms, the better for everyone.

HE AND THE photographer drove around the pavilion and onto the beach. It was a bright but chilly day and the ocean looked cold. There were a few shore birds running along the edge of the tide, but otherwise the winter beach was deserted. They found the place where a road led through two dunes; planks had been laid across it to keep automobile tires from miring in the soft sand. Beyond the dunes a road led through underbrush and thickets; it appeared to have been only recently cleared.

They reached the place where the stakes that the police sergeant had described were in view. At that point the road forked. There was nothing in particular to photograph. Trees had been felled, thickets cleared, and clearings cut throughout the area. There was one spot where the ruts of an older road appeared to come in from the west; a row of stakes lay along it. Further along, the road curved and skirted the bank of a lagoon, beyond which was salt marsh and, well across the marsh, the mainland shoreline. The Inland Waterway ran through the marsh; a tug and barge were in view to the east, and they waited until these drew opposite the lagoon so that the photographer could get a photograph.

They followed the road around, seeking to find something that might serve as the subject of a photograph, but there was really very little to differentiate one part of the tract from another. The photographer stopped at a clearing through which several roadways had been cut and a pile of felled trees and underbrush lay nearby. "Climb up there on top of that stuff and look off in the distance," the photographer told Mike. "Got to give this thing a little human interest." Mike did as instructed. The photographer climbed atop his car, and took several shots. They drove on, and eventually they reached the place where the roads had diverged. The photographer made shots of the row of stakes. Then they returned up the beach and to the pavilion. "I'll print what I got and leave them at the desk," the photographer said, "but there won't be much to see in them."

Back at the office, Mike called Murray Construction Company. "This is Mike Quinn on the *News & Courier*," he said, to make the status of his call clear, even though this time it wasn't Betsy who answered the phone. "May I speak to Mr. Murray?"

After a pause, Mr. Murray answered. "What is it?"

In view of the announcement about the Army hospital on the Isle of Palms, Mike asked him, was there any change in the Murray Construction Company's plans for the property it had recently purchased?

"Not at present."

"Does that mean that there may be something doing in the future?"

"Other than there is no change in plans at present, I have no comment to make."

"Thank you."

It was obviously galling to Mr. Murray to be queried on the subject, and by himself of all people. But no matter who was handling the story, Mr. Murray would have been less than pleased, for the very fact of the query posed a possible relationship between the announcement of the Army hospital and the purchase of his property.

Mike had no doubt that a connection existed. Everything he knew of Mr. Murray's way of doing things made it likely that he was aware of what was brewing with the property bought by the Army when he acquired his tract of land. If that could be proved, and also that the people who had sold the land to Mr. Murray last summer hadn't known about the Army's plans, it would make very interesting reading. Mike imagined for himself a front-page story, top right hand column, headlined something like "MURRAY TIPPED OFF ON ARMY'S PLANS BY POINSETT" with a byline, "By Michael Quinn," and a lead paragraph proclaiming that documents had turned up demonstrating conclusively that the Murray Construction Company's purchase of the property on the Isle of Palms was based on inside knowledge that the purchase of the hospital tract was imminent. That would be getting the son of a bitch back, all right.

HE WAS NOT the only person to suspect a connection. His friend and fellow reporter Jim Igoe brought it up on his own, at the Porthole that evening. "Keep your eye on construction permits," he told Mike. "I'll lay you dollars to doughnuts that it won't be long before Murray starts building houses. My guess is that the people he bought that property from are foaming at the mouth. They've been royally screwed, and they can't do a thing about it except bitch."

"You think Mr. Murray knew about the hospital last summer, then?"

"Knew about it? You can bet your bottom dollar he knew

about it! You don't think he put all that money in Franklin Poinsett's campaign just out of disinterested admiration, do you?"

MIKE WAS WORKING on an obit at his desk in the news room the next morning when the telephone rang. It was the desk sergeant at the Sullivans Island Police Department. "You coming over this way today?" he asked.

"Yes, I'll be leaving in a little while. What's up?"

"I'll tell you when I see you. Just stop by."

He drove across the Cooper River Bridge and through Mount Pleasant. When he arrived at police headquarters it was almost three o'clock.

"Do you know a man named Vanderhorst in Charleston?" the sergeant asked him.

"You mean one of the people who owned the property that Murray Construction Company bought? J. M. Vanderhorst?"

"That's the one. I think it'd be worth your while to talk to him."

"Okay, I'll do it. What about?"

He didn't want to get mixed up in anything, the sergeant said to Mike. But Mike ought to get hold of Vanderhorst.

"Does it have something to do with the Army hospital?"

"It might. Just do what I say. Talk to him."

Mike chatted with the sergeant for a while longer. When he returned to the office he called J. M. Vanderhorst, and was told by his secretary that he was in Cleveland, Ohio, on business, but was due back late Sunday and would be in the office Monday morning. Mike made an appointment to see him at eleven o'clock.

He got out the original story in the *Evening Post* announcing the Army hospital, and studied it carefully. There was one detail he had not picked up on earlier, but which now caught his eye. The corporation selling the land to the Army, I. & M. Associates, was listed as being located in Greenville, South Carolina.

Greenville?

He looked in the Greenville city directory, but found no listing for a corporation under that name. How, he asked Jim Igoe,
could he find out more about I. & M. Associates? Igoe said it
would be best to call the *News & Courier*'s capital correspondent
and ask him to have it checked out, because to get the information from the State Corporation Commission himself by telephone might take days.

The capital correspondent told Mike that he had a friend at
the S.C.C. who would look it up for him. Twenty minutes later
the telephone rang. I. & M. Associates had been incorporated in
1937. The address was 2087 Poinsett Street, Greenville. The
president was listed as J. Irby Inabinet, the vice-president as Walter L. Lawton, and the secretary-treasurer as N. O. McCracken.

He located the notes that he had made back in June, when he
had covered the story of the road being run through the Secessionville battlefield. The property had been owned by Island
Properties, Inc., also of Greenville. He read through the notes
until he found what he wanted, which was the address for Island
Properties, Inc. It was 2087 Poinsett Street.

Island Properties had also been the owners of the tract that
had been sold to the Army Air Force for the weapons repair
facility in North Charleston, the announcement of which on the
eve of the primary had caused Franklin Poinsett's opponent to
accuse him of using his position on the House Military Affairs
Committee for political advantage. He found the clip of that
story, but it gave no information about the seller.

Two defense installations, both being built on land owned by
corporations located at the same street address in Greenville.
Turner Murray had done construction work for one of the corporations, and had bought land close to the property sold to the
Army by the other. And Mr. Murray's close friend Franklin
Poinsett was a member of the congressional committee which
oversaw all defense spending, including the purchase of land for
the two military installations.

How recently had the corporations acquired the property that the government bought from them? That wouldn't be hard to find out. When they did so, had there been any inkling that the government might be interested? If so, how had they known that?

Very likely he was on to something big. As a newspaper reporter, he had every right to feel extremely excited.

Yet he didn't feel excited, but only a little sick to his stomach.

HE DECIDED FOR now not to tell anybody what he had found about the addresses in Greenville. He would wait until after his interview with the man who had been one of the owners of the property that Mr. Murray had bought. Was J. M. Vanderhorst, who was probably going to claim that Mr. Murray knew of the plans for the Army hospital when he purchased the adjacent property, aware of the similarity in addresses? If Vanderhorst did know about it and intended to make it public, that would be one thing. But if not, and he, Mike Quinn, was the only person who had picked up on the fact of the common address for both corporations selling land to the government, then it was his duty as a newspaperman to see that the matter was looked into.

It might mean nothing at all. It might very well be the product of his own imagination — not the fact itself, but its possible significance. And to what extent was that the result of his own dislike and resentment of Betsy's father? If it hadn't been for Betsy, and the broken engagement, and her father's obvious encouragement of her break with him, would he have noticed anything of the sort, or made anything of it if he had?

But he *had* noticed it. And if, as the police sergeant on Sullivans Island had intimated, the people who had sold the property adjacent to the hospital tract to Mr. Murray's company were prepared to claim that Mr. Murray had known about the Army hospital deal, then Franklin Poinsett's role, and Mr. Murray's ties with Poinsett, would certainly come under scrutiny — which meant that the two transactions with the Greenville corporations would be of considerable interest.

Here he was, still a beginning reporter, stuck with an otherwise tedious backwater beat, and the opportunity might now be his to ferret out and write a major front-page investigative story. If he reported his discovery to the city editor and the managing editor, he might very likely be told to drop everything else he was doing and follow it up. From a career standpoint, wouldn't it be a lucky break indeed? He could imagine what his journalism teacher at Washington and Lee, Professor Riegel, would say if he told him about it. *You didn't make the news, you're just reporting it. Your job's to keep the public informed and the politicians honest.*

When he finished work on Saturday, he helped out on the sports desk editing wire copy and writing heads, then he went back to his room. He lay down in his bed, and tried to continue reading *Of Time and the River*. But he couldn't keep his mind on it. The whole business kept going through his head.

Why was he so disturbed? He tried to figure that out, but couldn't. It stayed in his consciousness like an aching tooth, making it impossible for him to concentrate on anything else. What if this, what if that? He turned out the lights and tried to go to sleep, but kept thinking about it. If only he could just be left alone to write about things like ferryboats and the Cooper River Ghost.

ON SUNDAY MORNING he attended Mass, ate breakfast at the Francis Marion Coffee Shop, then went to the office and wrote an overdue letter to his parents. Jim Igoe came in; he wasn't on duty Sundays, either, but Jim covered his police beat seven days a week, morning, noon, and night. He knew every cop in town and in North Charleston, was friends with every desk sergeant. They called him at all hours, at the office or at home, whenever anything newsworthy was happening. He was a bachelor, in his late thirties, and lived with a married sister. He had worked on various newspapers large and small, could undoubtedly secure and handle with thorough professionalism a job on a metropolitan paper if he so wanted, but Charleston was his home. He liked living and working there, and he earned enough money for his own needs.

"Want to run up past North Charleston with me?" he asked. "The County Patrolmen's Benevolent Association's having a target shoot and I told them I'd stop by."

They drove out the Meeting Street Road on a bleak December day. "It's hard to realize," Igoe said, waving one hand at the mile or more of commercial buildings and housing projects north of the Army Yard turnoff, "that five or six years ago there was almost nothing out here except Pinehurst Sanitarium. A couple of more years, and there'll be more people living and working up in North Charleston than in the city. And every one of them's a vote for Franklin Poinsett."

Igoe had a radio in his car which picked up police calls. "Two-car accident on Meeting Street, nobody hurt bad," he said in interpretation of what seemed to Mike to be a puzzlingly opaque transmission. He also kept a radio tuned to the police band at his desk in the office, and one at home as well, he said.

"Where's the Weapons Depot located that touched off all the fuss last summer?" Mike asked.

"It's out the Remount Road. I'll drive by it; it's not far out of the way from where we're going."

They crossed the viaduct by the Atlantic Coast Line station, turned off Highway 52 onto a paved road, crossed another double set of tracks, and drove through mostly pine woods to a cleared-off area enclosed by a high chain-link fence, where warehouse buildings were under construction. There was much exposed soil, scraped clean of grass and foliage and looking raw and muddy, with railroad spur tracks throughout and a water tower in place. "This is it," Jim said. "You could almost say that it's a gigantic footprint on the countryside, made by Franklin Poinsett. And there'll be lots of others before he's done. Like the one that's going to be left on the Isle of Palms."

"You'd think," Mike said, "that some of the other congressmen would resent all these things being located in Charleston."

"Don't worry, there'll be plenty to go around for everyone before the war's over," Igoe said. "If you think this is a lot of activity, just wait till we actually get into the war. Then you'll really see something."

"You think we're going to get in?"

"There's not a chance in a million that we won't. It's a question of when, that's all."

They drove on. "You know," Igoe said after a minute, "I thought of something. Did you notice any signs giving the building contractor's name?"

"No."

"Well, the last time I drove by here, about three weeks back, there was a large Murray Construction Company sign in front. I guess they decided it was better not to brag about defense contracts."

Mike was tempted to tell Igoe what he'd found about the corporation that sold the Weapons Depot property having the same street address in Greenville as the one that was selling the Isle of Palms tract to the Army, but he didn't.

Igoe turned into another road, drove through several miles of farmland, thickets, and woods, and arrived at a place where more than a dozen automobiles and trucks, including several patrol cars, were drawn up next to a small multi windowed building with white asbestos siding and a green roof, and, several hundred feet beyond it, a long grassy bunker. Beyond the bunker was a broad stretch of marshland, now yellow and gray, fronting a stream, which Mike decided must be the upper Ashley River. Several men were standing behind a rope fifty feet or so in front of the bunker, shooting at targets. There was the steady noise of gunfire.

Inside the building several dozen people, some in police uniform, mostly males, were seated or standing around, talking, drinking, and eating. On a table was a plentiful array of cake, sandwiches, potato salad, baked beans, sliced ham, and other items, and next to it a washtub filled with bottles of beer and another with soft drinks. Jim Igoe was immediately greeted by a half-dozen people, to whom Mike was introduced. Igoe was obviously both quite popular and fully accepted among the gathering, all or most of whom Mike assumed were law officers of one sort or the other. They tended to be large, hefty men. At intervals people came in from outside to mark scores on sheets of paper posted on one wall, and others went out to take their turns at shooting.

Mike sipped a beer and watched Igoe in action, exchanging stories, listening, sharing jokes. It was a wonderful gift that Jim had, this capacity for genuine and open curiosity about what so many different kinds of people, with interests and concerns very different from his own, did and said and thought. It was a talent that he did not have, and could never really hope to acquire. By dint of luck he might come to know and gain the cooperation of an occasional person, such as the officers on Sullivans Island, but it wasn't the same. His curiosity, his concern for others, was narrow and limited, in a way that Igoe's wasn't.

They were invited out to the range to try their hand at the target shooting. Jim Igoe was good at it; obviously it was by no means the first time he had fired a handgun. Mike was handed a service revolver and told to aim at a target. He had never shot a pistol of other than .22 caliber before. When he pulled the trigger the revolver jerked his arm upward like a cracking whip. "Hold the handle tight, and squeeze off the trigger, don't pull it," somebody told him. He fired five more times. Afterwards a whistle was blown, and when his target was retrieved Mike found that he had hit it three times, though never close to the center of the bull's-eye. If he were drafted into the Army next year, he thought, as well he might be, he would no doubt gain ample experience with firing ranges.

"THAT WAS QUITE a spread of food," Mike remarked after they left.

Igoe laughed. "All they have to do is get the word out and the restaurants and food stores and drink distributors load them up. You'd be surprised how many people like to stay on the good side of the cops."

"I didn't see any hard stuff, though."

"No, they wouldn't have any of that out — not while they're using the range. You come out here with me next Saturday night for the Christmas party, though, and you'll see all the good Scotch and bourbon you want, courtesy Vincent Chicco and others."

Driving back along the King Street Road, Igoe pointed to some very black smoke off to the left, toward the Cooper River. "That's an oil fire," he said. "I didn't hear a call on it. Let's go see what it's all about."

They cut across the tracks at the next grade crossing, drove along the Meeting Street Road, then turned eastward, drove through several blocks of shabby, dilapidated houses, crossed some more tracks, and bumped along a dirt road next to a high chain fence. Beyond it were a number of oil tanks. At the gate they stopped for a watchman, who recognized Igoe and waved them through. They drove down toward the river. Some fire trucks, a red chief's car, and a police car were parked out in a field, and some firemen were hosing streams of chemical foam onto a fire. "Must be some kind of a drill," Igoe said. He pulled up next to the fire trucks, and they got out and walked over to where the firemen were at work.

The smoke was coming from several blazing oil drums, spaced over an area of a half-acre or so. Crews from one truck were engaged in hosing foam onto them, while the crews of the other fire trucks were standing by, hoses unlimbered, watching. Igoe talked with one of the firemen, who told him that they had recently acquired some new chemicals designed for use on gasoline and oil fires, and they were trying them out.

"How's it work?" Igoe asked.

"It does some good," the fireman said. "I wouldn't say it was letter perfect, though."

In the raw chill of the late afternoon the heat from the fire felt good. Mike looked around. There were several dozen huge oil tanks, spaced a hundred yards or so apart, and along the edge of the river a wharf, parallel to the bank, alongside which a large tanker, the *Esso Explorer,* was tied. Hoses led from the tanker to a network of pipes on the pier, and there was the sound of pumping engines.

"I wonder why they needed four trucks to do that?" Mike asked when they drove off. "Only one of them was pumping the chemical foam."

"Because," Igoe said, "this place is potentially one large torch. They didn't want to take any chance on the wind catching the flames and blowing some sparks. If one of those large tanks was to catch fire, and there was a strong wind to spread the flames, there'd be the goddamnest explosion you'd ever want to see or hear in your life. Hell, it'd shatter every window pane from here to Hampton Park.

"Think what would happen," he continued, "if a Nazi submarine was to sneak into the harbor one evening and lob a few rounds into these tanks. People just don't have any idea how vulnerable the whole damn seaboard is, the Atlantic and Pacific coast both."

They drove down a road past Magnolia Cemetery, and beyond it a junkyard heaped with rusty iron and steel. "Worn-out bodies, human and mechanical," Igoe said. "Funny thing, you drive by here at night and you'll see half-a-dozen cars parked along here. It's a favorite lover's lane. The cops don't bother them. Kids making out, with the dead all around them. In the midst of death we live. After all, it's the most natural thing in the world."

Mike remembered the time when he and Betsy had gone out to Folly Beach, driven along the beach, and made love on a blanket on the sand next to the car. No cramped car seat with the steering wheel in the way for Betsy Murray; she had come prepared. It had all been planned out in advance, long before they'd left her house. In retrospect, what was so amazing was that when he first knew her, it was her seeming spontaneity that he had so admired. Looking back, he could see that almost everything they did together had been by deliberate design on her part; even the "spontaneity" was planned.

"You getting on all right these days without your ex-ladyfriend?" Jim Igoe asked as they turned into Meeting Street. He must have made the same association in his mind, Mike thought.

"I'm doing okay."

"What you need," Igoe said, "is to meet some nice young Catholic girl whose old man isn't worth a couple of million and trying to make it into the Saint Cecilia Society. Not that there's anything wrong with money, you understand. But when it goes along with social ambitions, that's a mean combo to buck."

"I'll keep my eyes open."

"With the help of Franklin Poinsett, that son of a bitch Murray is going to own half this goddamn county before he's done," Igoe said.

Mike thought of his scheduled interview tomorrow morning with the aggrieved ex-property owner, Vanderhorst. Again he felt unhappy. He didn't want to get involved. It wasn't for him, not even though Mr. Murray was everything Jim Igoe had said, and more besides.

They arrived at the newspaper building. Instead of returning to the news room, Mike thanked Igoe for taking him along, got into his own car, and drove back to his room. He felt ever more disquieted at the prospect of the interview, and what he was sure would be the resulting enforced immersion in the whole business of Mr. Murray and Franklin Poinsett and defense installation sites and charges and counter charges and God knows what else.

He wished that he could talk to Jim Igoe about how he felt. But Jim was too good, and too dedicated, a newspaperman ever to be able to understand why he might not want to grab hold of what was beyond doubt a prime opportunity. For all Jim's friendship with the officers on the police beat, if one of them were to become involved in something illegal and shady he wouldn't hesitate for one minute to search out the facts and write the story. Jim would think he was out of his mind. And perhaps, if he really wanted to be a newspaperman, he was.

I don't want to do it, he thought. I don't want to have to write stories about Mr. Murray's connivings. I don't feel a damn bit sorry for him, and I don't feel sorry for Betsy, either. But if Betsy's father is going to get shown up in print for being not just a slick operator but a crook, I don't want to be the one to write about it.

Perhaps, he thought, he could call in sick and ask the city editor to assign someone else to the interview. Or maybe he should just tell the city editor how he felt, and ask to be taken off the story.

He couldn't get it off his mind, and he didn't know what to do.

27

THE ROSENBAUMS WERE settling into a routine. Their apartment had been put pretty much in the shape they wanted, and they were becoming accustomed to the new surroundings and to sharing each other's company all the time. The apartment, which consisted of the second floor of a house, was quite roomy enough for their needs. There was a living room, with a spinet piano and a desk in one corner where Sara Jane worked, a library where Rosy had his desk, a dining room, a bedroom, and a guest room. At the outset, Rosy's phonograph and collection of records were placed in the living room, but after he played music for several hours each evening for several days running, Sara Jane proposed that he move them into the library. The problem was that she liked to listen to music *or* read *or* do something else, while Rosy liked to listen to it *while* reading, writing, or doing something else. She played the piano a little, but despite Rosy's urging, not very often.

Sara Jane was busy writing thank-you letters. Rosy was grading papers and preparing for his classes. There were less than two weeks to go before the Christmas holidays. As always, Rosy was running behind schedule. In the English literature survey he was supposed to be well into the eighteenth century, so that he would be ready to take up the Romantic poets when the second term began in early February. But as it was, he had just completed

Milton and was launching into Andrew Marvell and John Dryden, with Pope, Swift, Gray, Johnson, Goldsmith, all the novelists, and William Blake still to go.

Rosy was always glad when he had finished Milton. However much he enjoyed the poetry, his class did not readily respond to it. The diction was too much for them; they could not translate it into their own concerns. This, even though José L. Lopez, Jr., had produced a contemporary version of "L'Allegro" beginning

> *Get moving, Melancholy Gal!*
> *Go find you a sanctuary*
> *Up by Magnolia Cemetery.*
> *Dig you a hole where it's damp and foul.*
> *Cuddle up with a hoot-owl*
> *Or maybe some old buzzard or crow.*
> *I don't care where you go;*
> *Just don't sit around here on your tail and*
> *howl.*

The class didn't even think it was funny, because they hadn't been able to take the original seriously enough to enjoy the undercutting. As for *Paradise Lost*, even José L. Lopez, Jr., let that work go by without an attempt at vernacular revision. In Rosy's experience the only thing harder than *Paradise Lost* to get most college undergraduates interested in was *The Faerie Queene*.

There was the usual round of faculty parties, involving almost everybody except the McCrackens, whom almost nobody wanted to have anything to do with after hours, and the Carters, who were out of town in New York where Page was attending meetings. They would be gone until just before the holiday recess began. Rosy and Sara Jane had thought of taking a trip over Christmas and New Year's; their wedding trip had been very brief. The season had been so hectic, however, that they decided just to stay home and enjoy their apartment.

For both of them, being married had the effect of relaxing

defenses that had been developed to cope with private existence. Sara Jane had always seemed to be so thoroughly in control of events, so completely mistress of her emotions. But what Rosy discovered was that the seeming calmness and even jauntiness masked an absence of self-confidence that, now that he was there to share her life, could be strikingly and even painfully revealed, and was. In the same way, Rosy had always been thought of by his friends as bemused, self-sufficient. It was Sara Jane's chosen role to be able to penetrate that façade, to identify the shyness that it concealed, and to encourage the expression of what lay behind it. She had been able to do this out of her own need.

The foundation of their marriage was not what an outsider, noting their backgrounds and the nature of their cultural interests, might have assumed: intellectual affinity. On the contrary, one could almost say that for both of them, it had been necessary to get beneath precisely that for the marriage to take place. Far more than either had recognized until it happened, and more so than either would have thought possible, they had both craved emotional intimacy.

THEY HAD FINISHED supper and were putting away the dishes on Sunday evening when the telephone rang. Rosy answered it. Sara Jane listened to what he was saying. "Sure. Of course. Come on over . . . Do you know where we live? . . . That's right. It's right across Gadsden Street from the *Sappho.* The third house from the corner, second floor . . . Don't worry about that, just come on . . . We'll be looking out for you."

"That was Mike Quinn," Rosy said. "He said he needed some advice, and could he come over for a little while."

"I wonder what's up. Do you suppose he's still carrying the torch for that little Murray girl? I'd hoped he was getting over that."

"I don't know. He sounded pretty distraught. He's probably at loose ends now."

"Well, let's see what he has to say."

ooooo

TEN MINUTES LATER the doorbell rang, and Mike Quinn arrived. Sara Jane offered him a drink, which he didn't want; he would take a cup of coffee, though, he said.

They settled down in the living room, Sara Jane and Rosy on the sofa, Mike in an easy chair. Mike apologized again for bothering them, and was told not to worry about it. "What's on your mind?" Rosy asked.

They listened as Mike told them what was happening — how Franklin Poinsett had been accused that summer of using his congressional status to influence the timing of the announcement of the weapons station, how he was now about to be accused of tipping off Murray Construction Company on the advent of the Army hospital, how Mike had encountered Poinsett and Mr. Murray on the Isle of Palms that summer before the sale of the property adjacent to the hospital to Mr. Murray, how he had then made the discovery that the weapons station and the Army hospital properties were both owned by corporations with the same street address in Greenville, and how he suspected that there might be a great deal more to the matter than was presently known. If the interview he had scheduled tomorrow went as he assumed it would go, he might find himself right in the middle of a very big story in which his ex-fiancé's father would be deeply implicated. He asked them to keep what he had said in strict confidence.

"We won't tell a soul," Rosy told him. "Do you *not* want to write the story?"

"No, sir. I mean, yes, sir. I don't want to write it."

"Why not?"

"I'm not sure."

"Is it because of Betsy Murray?" Sara Jane asked.

"In a way. I'm done with her, but I don't like the idea of making her father look like a crook, either."

"But you wouldn't be doing that, would you?" Rosy asked.

"You'd only be reporting the facts."

"I know, but I don't want to be the one who reports them."

"Do you feel guilty?" Sara Jane asked. "Is that it?"

Mike stared at her. "I don't understand what you mean."

"I mean, are you afraid that you'd be writing your stories for the wrong reasons — in order to get back at Betsy and her family?"

"Something like that, maybe," Mike said. He took a sip of coffee, then set the cup down in the saucer. "It's because I hate it!" he burst out. "I hate the whole business! The lying, and the crookedness, and the conniving, and the whole dirty mess! And I don't want to write about it, or have anything to do with it, and I wish I'd never laid eyes on Betsy Murray or her father, and never taken a job on the paper where they live!" There were tears in his eyes. "I know it's silly, and if I want to be a newspaperman it's a big break that I shouldn't pass up, but I don't care, I just want to be left alone and not have to interview anybody or expose anything or get anywhere close to any of it!" He wiped his eyes. "I'm sorry. I'm blubbering. I can't help it."

Rosy got up, walked over to where the young newspaperman was sitting, and put his hand on his shoulder. "Let me tell you something," he said. "You've got a lot of talent. But you've got something more important than talent. You've got a great deal of integrity. Do you realize that?"

"No, sir."

"Well, you do. Isn't that right?" he asked Sara Jane.

"Yes indeed," she declared. "And, Mike, you're worth a dozen Betsy Murrays. And Turner Murrays as well. They're crude, vulgar, selfish people."

Rosy sat down again alongside Sara Jane. "What do you think your editor would say if you told him you didn't want to do it, because of your involvement with Betsy?"

"I think he'd understand all right. He'd have somebody else do it."

"Then why don't you do that?"

"Maybe I will," Mike said.

"I think you probably ought to," Sara Jane said. "But I certainly wouldn't do it out of any feeling that otherwise you'd be taking advantage of your position to get back at the Murrays. There's no reason whatever for you to feel any guilt about it. But I do think that it might be better for your own peace of mind if you turned it over to someone else." She stood up. "How about some more coffee? I think it's gotten cold."

"Yes, ma'am. Thank you."

Sara Jane took up the cup and saucer and went into the kitchen.

"You're also worried," Rosy said to Mike, "because you think that you ought to want to write the story, aren't you? You believe that a true newspaperman wouldn't ever voluntarily pass up a chance like this. Isn't that part of it?"

"Yes, sir. I think that's so."

"So you're afraid that it means that therefore you're not a good journalist?"

"It's crossed my mind," Mike said.

Sara Jane came back into the room with a fresh cup of coffee for Mike.

"What's wrong with that kind of thinking," Rosy said, "is the idea that in order to be a successful journalist you have to write political exposés. That definition would rule out a number of pretty good newspaper writers, wouldn't it? Grantland Rice, for example, or Ring Lardner. I've never worked on a newspaper, but it stands to reason that different reporters are good at different kinds of news. Not many people could write pieces like you did about the ferryboats."

"That's true," Sara Jane told him. "I can't tell you how many people I ran into who mentioned reading that story and how much they enjoyed it."

"That's not what they want me to do at the paper, though. Writing features is all very well, but what they care about is politics."

"I can't accept that," Rosy said. "Of course politics is important, but I know the people at the *Courier* and the *Post*, and they know good writing when they see it. I don't for a moment believe that they haven't got sense enough to appreciate the kinds of stories you do. How long have you been on the staff?"

"Since June."

"June, July, August — a little over half a year. Good lord, Mike, they're still trying you out. They want to see what you can do best. I don't think you ought to jump to any conclusions about what they do or don't want in the way of writing just yet. Besides, you're not tied down forever to one newspaper. Try it for a while longer, and if you decide you don't like what you're doing, move on to another paper."

The young newspaperman stayed for a while longer, then left. He seemed to be reassured. They listened to his steps receding down the stairwell.

"What a fine kid," Sara Jane said.

"You were marvelous," Rosy told her. "You spotted just what was worrying him. When you said what you did about feeling guilty, it was like a revelation to him. He hadn't seen that. The whole thing began to clear up for him."

"I think we both helped him," Sara Jane said. "But aren't you glad you're not twenty-three years old any more?"

Rosy laughed. "Yes, now that you mention it."

"We need to find him a girlfriend. Someone who's right for him."

"You're probably right. Anyway, let's just hope that it doesn't take him as long as it took me to find his true love."

"Well, you did," Sara Jane said. "And here we are." She leaned over and kissed him on the cheek.

28

ON MONDAY MORNING Mike Quinn told the city and managing editors everything that he knew about Franklin Poinsett, Turner Murray, and the various defense property transactions, and asked to be taken off the story for reasons having to do with his former ties with Betsy Murray and her family. The upshot was that Jim Igoe was told to interview J. M. Vanderhorst at eleven that morning, and entrusted with doing whatever was necessary to track down every aspect of the story, devoting his entire time to it for as long as it took to do the job. Until he was done, Mike would take over the police beat. The new reporter on the staff, White, would be shifted across the harbor.

The project was to be kept strictly secret. The fewer people who knew that the story was being developed, the better. It was of crucial importance not to reveal that anything was known about the corporations having the same address in Greenville, or that Turner Murray had ties with them. Igoe was to go to Greenville and to the State Corporation Commission offices at Columbia and find out everything he could about the corporations owning the land, the pattern of other recent transfers of land for military use in the state. He was to trace the land records to find out when the properties had been acquired by the corporations selling or to the government. And he was to look into the relationship between Murray and Congressman Franklin Poinsett from their college days at Clemson onward.

So Jim Igoe now had Mike's big story, and, temporarily, Mike had Jim's police beat. He felt greatly relieved. What Dr. Rosenbaum and Miss Jahnz—Mrs. Rosenbaum, that was — had said was quite right; he was better off not handling this particular story. Nor had the newspaper's editors seemed to hold his reluctance to write the story against him. On the contrary, they praised him for having spotted the possible relationship between the two Greenville corporations. Chances were that they were glad of the chance to put an experienced reporter like Igoe at work on the story, he decided.

IGOE'S INTERVIEW WITH J. M. Vanderhorst produced not only what had been predicted, but went beyond it. The group of investors who had acquired the tract on the Isle of Palms with a view toward developing it, had been unable to raise the capital needed to do so, and had sold it to Murray Construction Company last summer, were filing a suit claiming that they had been bilked. They were prepared to demonstrate, they said, that Turner Murray and Congressman Franklin Poinsett had several times visited the future Army hospital site during the previous spring and early summer, well before Murray Construction Company had approached them about buying the adjacent property — a clear indication, they claimed, that the congressman had known that an Army hospital was to be built there and had communicated that knowledge to Murray.

They were also claiming that I. & M. Associates, which was selling the hospital tract to the Army, had hired Murray Construction Company to cut roads through it last summer, well before the announcement of the hospital purchase, which was additional evidence of a connection between the congressman, Turner Murray, and I. & M. Associates.

"Did they show any interest in the Island Properties deal?" Mike asked Jim Igoe.

"No. But once the lawyers start looking, it's bound to come out.

And you can bet that Howard Wade and his friends will notice it."

"What are you going to do next?"

"I'll have to call Murray, and also try to get through to the congressman," Igoe said. "I've got to start checking deed books at the Court House to see how long ago Island Properties and I. & M. acquired the land. Then I'm heading upstate. This could turn into one hell of a story, kid. You should have stayed with it."

Mike shook his head. "No, I'm glad you're doing it." And he was. Although the police beat wouldn't have been his ideal choice of assignments, he would happily take it on and do his best while Jim was occupied elsewhere.

Igoe typed out a list of names and telephone numbers for him to use in covering the beat. He also called several of the people he had listed, told them that Mike would be handling the news from them for a while, and asked them to help him. But even with such help, coming along behind Jim Igoe as a police reporter would be a hard act to follow.

"I'll be glad when you're done," he told Igoe. "I couldn't handle the cops the way you can."

"I wouldn't worry about it," Igoe told him. "Not with your luck."

"What do you mean?"

"Hell, you cover a routine political concession speech and you walk right into a big story about Franklin Poinsett and four other congressmen being given election help from the War Department. You get sent across the bridge to cover Sullivans Island and the Isle of Palms and you turn up a big story about hanky-panky on the Army hospital deal. I'll bet you a dollar to a doughnut that within two weeks there'll be a bank robbery downtown, or Japanese saboteurs will blow up the Navy Yard, or something."

WITHOUT WISHING TO in the slightest, Mike had also become the public relations outlet for the dean of the College of Charleston. Ever since he had written the story about McCracken and his experiments with rats and mazes, he had been getting telephone calls and letters from the man, informing him about his activities. He was a publicity fiend of the first magnitude. If he attended a meeting anywhere, or published an article, or gave a speech, or took part in a working committee of a professional society, he wanted it proclaimed in the newspaper.

Every reporter on the staff had certain regulars like the dean, who kept them posted on their exploits, and for whom publicity was a constant concern. There was, for example, an amateur weatherman in town, who made forecasts in advance. He had a reporter that he called almost daily, in this instance Frank Blades. The *News & Courier* carried a daily column of paragraphs about local doings, and which was perhaps the most widely read feature in the newspaper. Reporters were expected to turn in several items each day, and much of the material came from people like Dean McCracken.

It was ironic, because his friends on the College faculty, Dr. and Mrs. Rosenbaum, didn't like the dean at all. Although they had never said anything about him, he was quite sure of it. And for that matter, neither did Mike. He had the distinct sense that the dean's continuing pursuit of publicity was something more than the usual harmless desire for attention; there was a purpose behind it. Not that vanity wasn't also involved, for, as far as the dean was concerned, everything he did was important and warranted being proclaimed to a waiting world. But there was something very self-serving about the supposed news items that he wanted published; they were meant to accomplish something.

Whenever he published a summary of one of his experiments in a scientific journal, which apparently he was doing all the time, he wanted it noted in the paper. The first couple of times that he called with the details of an experiment showing that so many white rats out of so many solved certain obstacles set up in various forms of mazes to get food pellets, Mike dutifully transcribed the information and wrote stories. Thereafter the city editor had told him to confine the dean's experiments to single-paragraph items. McCracken made it obvious that he was not satisfied with such mention in a column, but there was nothing he could do about it.

On the afternoon when Mike turned over the Isle of Palms property story to Jim Igoe and took over the police beat, the dean called once again. He had an important story, he said, which was too complicated to be explained over the telephone. Would Mike come by his laboratory in the morning?

Mike agreed to stop by. The appointment was set for 11 A.M. The dean proposed that he bring a photographer along with him, but Mike explained that photographic assignments were made by the city editor on the basis of stories turned in, not in advance.

THE DEAN'S LABORATORY was located in what was once a private residence behind and across the street from the main building. When Mike arrived, there was a girl present, whom the dean introduced to him as Miss Lee Witt. She was, the dean said, one of his students, and he was gratified to announce that the American Institute for Behavioral Science had awarded a $1,250 grant to Miss Witt and himself to carry out a study in the response of white rats to rhythmic patterns in the selection of food sources during fatigue stress.

As a teacher of science, the dean explained, it was his conviction that students should be directly involved in the research projects of the faculty. He had applied for and been awarded the study grant, he said, not only as constituting valuable research in its own right, but as a kind of pilot program designed to demonstrate to the College of Charleston faculty the feasibility of encouraging student participation in their research. It was his hope, he said, that his example would serve to encourage other faculty members to undertake similar ventures with talented students.

Miss Lee Witt was a somewhat buxom, shapely young woman with straw-blond hair, whose lipstick, fingernail polish, and shoes were in matching lavender. She did not strike Mike as being the scholarly type. He also had the sense that she knew her way around.

The experiment that the dean and his student were performing consisted of placing a rat on a treadmill for a given period of time, and after that, recording how long it took for the rat to find its way to some food pellets at the end of a maze. While the rat was engaged in searching for the food, a musical metronome was made to produce a rhythmic beat. The experiment was being conducted with a series of white rats, which were placed on the treadmill for varying periods, and then set to look for food while varying rhythms were being sounded. The dean's part in the experiment was to prescribe the idea, the time periods, and the rhythmic beats to be used, while Miss Witt's contribution was to remove the rat from the cage and run it through the experiment, using a stopwatch to time how long it took to locate the food pellets.

"What do you see as the significance of this project?" Mike asked the dean.

"The primary significance," McCracken declared, "is the exploration of the hypothesized relationship between conditioned rhythmic stimuli and the capacity for problem solving, as modified by factors of fatigue as these impact upon muscle sense. The secondary significance is the hypothesized extent of correlation between dietary appetite and sensory rhythmic anticipation."

Mike took it all down, having several times to request the dean to repeat words and phrases. He asked the dean's co-investigator for her thoughts on the award. "I think it's neat!" she said. "It makes me feel like a real scientist!"

How did she enjoy doing experiments with white rats? "I just love them! I didn't think I would at first, you know, but they're real cute little things once you get used to them!"

Mike made notes on everything. If the city desk wanted a photograph, he told the dean, someone would call to set up a time. "I think they should," Dean McCracken said. "This is a monumentally significant development in the history of the College of Charleston."

ooooo

WHILE HE WAS on campus he stopped by Dr. Rosenbaum's office. Dr. Rosenbaum was talking with what appeared to be a student, who was dressed in a black cape and sported a luxuriant moustache. The student got up to leave, and Dr. Rosenbaum introduced him. His name was José L. Lopez, Jr.

"José is a poet," Dr. Rosenbaum explained after he left. "He's quite good. He writes parodies of the poems we take up in class. He just brought by this one on Marvell's 'To His Coy Mistress.'" He handed Mike a sheet of paper with a poem typed on it:

> *Honey, the way you keep holding out on me*
> *They ought to send you to the penitentiary —*
> *Now if we had a few billion years to spare*
> *You could take your good time and I wouldn't care.*
> *We could just keep right on going steady*
> *And not make out till you're good and ready.*
> *There's plenty of you to keep me occupied*
> *For years to come, just from the outside,*
> *So if I had time, and nothing else to do,*
> *I wouldn't mind the wait for the rest of you.*
> *But, baby, though history might be bunk,*
> *This year's Ford is next year's junk,*
> *And the used-car lots at the edge of town*
> *Line the highways for miles around.*
> *It's all very well to plan ahead,*
> *But the car won't start if the battery's dead,*
> *And the back seat of a worn-out Cadillac*
> *Ain't no place for balling the jack.*
> *So tell Father Time to stay away*
> *Because you and me have got games to play.*
> *It's no use his even bothering to knock;*
> *We're booked up all around the clock.*
> *The months may pass, the years may fly,*

The hearse will pull up by and by
At the front door — but me and you, honey,
Going to give the driver a run for his money.

Mike read it and laughed. "It's very clever," he said.

"Do you know the poem he's parodying?"

"Yes, sir. 'But at my back I always hear Time's wingèd chariot hurrying near.'"

"Well, how goes it with you now?" Dr. Rosenbaum asked.

Mike told him about turning the Isle of Palms property story over to Jim Igoe.

"I noticed his byline on the story this morning. What did they say when you told them you didn't want to work on it?"

"They were very decent about it. I've taken over Jim's police beat while he's on it. I feel a lot better now."

"I thought you would."

It was time to go by the police station and see what was doing. Mike rose to leave. "On your way out," Dr. Rosenbaum said, "why don't you drop over to the library and tell Sara Jane what you told me? She'll be interested to hear."

"Yes, sir, I will."

He went down the steps, through the corridor and out the front entrance, crossed over to the library, and found Mrs. Rosenbaum in her office. He told her about having had himself taken off the story, and she too seemed pleased. "Keep us posted," she said.

Dr. Rosenbaum was fortunate, he thought, to be married to someone like Miss Jahnz. As for himself, would he ever be lucky enough to meet a good-looking girl who didn't think that books were intended for decorating living rooms? He wondered what Polly Morrison was doing.

HE WENT BY police headquarters on St. Phillip's Street, then to the county sheriff's office, and checked the blotters. He also stopped by the fire chief's office. Everybody wanted to know whether Jim Igoe would be coming back, or whether the change was permanent. When he assured them that Jim's new assignment was temporary, and that he was sure to return when done, they were pleased. Everyone was reasonably cordial to him, but it was because he came recommended by Igoe and under his sponsorship.

Several of the people he had met out at the shooting match with Igoe were on hand. "You think he'll be back in time for our Christmas party Sunday a week?" he was asked. He told them that even if Igoe were still working on his special assignment, if he were in town he certainly would attend the party.

There was a certain amount of curiosity about what the special assignment might involve. The clerk at police headquarters, a man named Margenhoff, had noticed that Igoe had written the story about the property transaction on the Isle of Palms. "Is that what Jim's working on?" he asked.

"That's part of it," Mike told him. "It has something to do with politics." That was vague enough, he hoped.

"Well, you tell him," the sergeant said, "that if he's looking into how Turner Murray finds out what he does, to check with me, and I can tell him everybody who's on his payroll."

"I'll tell him. I'm sure he will."

Igoe's story in that morning's paper about his interview with Vanderhorst, he thought, in which a link between Murray, Poinsett, and I. & M. Associates was at least suggested, must have caused Betsy's father some unease — if, that is, there was indeed something there.

The thought did occur to him, after the managing and city editors had made arrangements for Igoe to get on the story, that it could still be no more than coincidence that both the corporations had the same address in Greenville. There might be no relationship whatever. It might simply be a large office building, with numerous tenants. In any event, he was glad that Jim Igoe, and not Mike Quinn, would be the one to find out.

29

HAVING SUCCESSFULLY GOTTEN themselves married, Sara Jane and Rosy now felt it obligatory to improve Mike Quinn's romantic prospects, or lack of them.

"Polly Morrison was in to check out some books today," Sara Jane remarked, the evening after Mike had stopped by to tell about his change of assignments. "She's writing a senior thesis on the impact of the Dred Scott decision in South Carolina. She's all excited about it. I still think she'd be just right for Mike, and vice versa."

"Well, she'd certainly be an improvement on the last one, anyway. How do you know she's not already committed?"

"Suppose we ask them to dinner Sunday — that's Mike's day off, isn't it? — and I'll tell her there's a young man we'd like her to meet. If she's not in the market, she'll say she can't come."

"Suppose she *is* in the market, but is already doing something Sunday?"

"For heaven's sake, Rosy, give me credit for a little finesse!"

"Sorry. I wasn't thinking."

"How about telephoning Mike at the newspaper, Rosy, and invite him to dinner Sunday? Tell him to come about 1:30. Don't say anything about anyone else coming."

"Okay." Rosy went out into the hallway and made a call. "He'll be here," he told Sara Jane.

"Good." Now it was Sara Jane's turn to call. "All right," she told Rosy. "She's coming."

"Not to display my obtuseness again, but why didn't you want me to tell Mike that somebody else was coming?"

"Because," Sara Jane said, "I didn't want Mike to think we're trying to run his love life for him. "

"But it's okay to let Polly think so?"

"Polly won't think so. It doesn't work that way with girls."

"Well, I'll take your word for it, but damned if I see the difference."

"The difference is that all unmarried females are supposed to be on the lookout for husbands, so it's okay to mention it openly. Unmarried males are supposed to have better things to do, so you musn't ever insult their masculine self-esteem by suggesting that they could possibly use some help."

"That's true," Rosy said. "I mean, it's true that's how it's supposed to be. I hadn't thought of it that way."

"No," Sara Jane said, "I'm sure you hadn't. That's part of the problem."

THE NEWS STORY about Dean McCracken's grant, together with photo of the Dean and Miss Lee Witt putting a white rat through its paces, annoyed not a few members of the College of Charleston faculty, but none more so than Dolf Strongheart. When the College's professor of zoology read the story, he was furious. To one who was notorious for involving his students in his research and encouraging them to undertake projects of their own, and upon graduation sending them off to graduate school, the assertion that the dean had applied for the award in order to demonstrate to the faculty the possibility of including their students in their research projects was anathema. "The schlemiel," Dolf declared, "not only doesn't know what he's talking about, but he's never made the slightest effort to find out what anyone else is doing."

His indignation was shared by numerous others on the faculty. "He comes down here and teaches one course for a couple of months," Tom Lowndes said, "and he announces to the public that he's here to lead us out of the desert and into the Promised Land."

Rosy's colleague in English, Horace Hewitt, made his usual response. He proposed that when Page Carter returned from his meetings in New York City, the faculty should present him with a petition demanding that the dean be formally rebuked for insulting the faculty of the College by implying that it did not work with individual students. He would draw up the petition himself, he said.

"If we do that, he'll simply claim that he was misquoted," Tom Lowndes said.

Mike Donahoe agreed. "Wait till Page gets back from New York, and see what he says. He doesn't like McCracken any more than we do."

"I STILL THINK," Rosy said to Sara Jane and Dolf at lunch, "that the man's at least as much naive as he is vicious. He thinks he's been put on earth to bring enlightenment to the heathen, among whom are included all of us."

"You think so, do you?" Dolf told him. "Well, I think he knows exactly what he's trying to do. He wants to make us all look as bad as possible, including Page. Then he can offer to step in and rectify the situation. Give that kind of bastard half a chance and he's off and running."

"But look, Dolf," Rosy said. "Except for trying to set up a self-study project that we didn't need or want, what has he actually done that's objectionable? Granted that he's a slob, without tact or judgment, and also that he's a womanizer, but has he actually done anything wrong as dean, except fail to fit into our group?"

"Goddamn it, Rosy," Dolf responded, "when you find a rattlesnake — *Crotalus adamanteus* — coiled in your tent, is it a good idea to wait until it sinks its fangs into you? No indeed. The minute you hear the rattling, you take steps to get rid of it. And that ought to go for you in particular. Don't think he's forgotten that motion you made at the faculty meeting."

"You may be right. But obnoxious as I find McCracken personally, I think it may be stupidity at least as much as malice."

"That's where you're wrong," Dolf declared. "He may be naive, like you say, but he's not stupid. At least, not in the way he operates. He may be stupid for thinking he can get away with it in the long run."

Tom Lowndes came in to the restaurant and joined them. "Well," he said, "I don't know how complex this project is that McCracken and the Witt girl are collaborating on, but it better not be too intellectually demanding, because the young lady was in my European history survey last year, and brain power is not her strong point. Has she been in any of your classes?"

"She's in my English literature survey," Rosy said. "Right now she's a borderline pass. Maybe she's better at math and science. Some kids are, you know."

"Bah!" Dolf Strongheart responded. "Don't try palming her off on us! Mike Donahoe had her in chemistry last year, and he says she barely scraped through. I'll tell you what I think she's really good at, though: biology. And I don't mean in class, either."

"Why do you say that?" Tom Lowndes asked.

"Remember me telling about seeing McCracken coming out of his lab building very late one evening with a coed? Well, that's the coed. And I've since heard other things about it. The students know what's going on."

"Well, maybe," Rosy said. "But just because we don't care for the dean is no reason to look for something wrong with the girl."

"The mere fact that the young lady is collaborating voluntarily with a lecherous bastard like that," Dolf declared, "would constitute prima facie grounds for both intellectual and moral suspicion, even if I and others hadn't seen them coming out of his lab at late hours. For God's sakes, Rosy, you ought to run for president of the Pollyanna Society. Brighten the corner where you are. Look on the sunny side."

Sara Jane laughed. "Rosy, he's right," she said. "You carry forbearance to the point of absurdity."

"Maybe. But I still think we can trust Page to head him in."

"Well, I hope so," Dolf said. "But he's sure as hell taking his good time about doing it."

ON FRIDAY AFTERNOON Rosy finished teaching Andrew Marvell in his sophomore survey of English literature, and prepared to move onto John Dryden. The student that the dean was working with, Lee Witt, was one of several who, habitually positioning themselves in the back of the classroom, sat through lectures with facial expressions registering neither comprehension nor interest. What did such a student get out of Marvell's compacted wit and imagination? He could not recall her ever once asking a question in class. To be sure, he had learned long since that what students wrote on exams and in assigned papers, not what they said in class, was what mattered most. Miss Witt's written work, however, was quite pedestrian.

His seminar in British poetry, by contrast, in which Polly Morrison was one of the students, contained no such uncomprehending segment, for the reason that it was an elective, not a college requirement for graduation. Nobody was enrolled in it who did not wish to be there. To be sure, there were some who possessed the interest without much in the way of insight, and toiled hard and long over their written work without ever achieving more than satisfactory competence. The correlation between earnestness and aptitude was always imperfect at best. There were very few students like Polly Morrison, who combined intelligence and imagination with determined effort. She was going to graduate school in history, but could as appropriately do so in literary study if she wished. Sara Jane was right; she and Mike Quinn would make a good pair.

ooooo

THE SATURDAY NIGHT poker game that Rosy and Dolf Strongheart played in continued without interruption. Rosy's tactics had turned somewhat more adventurous since the events of the late summer, but it was Dolf who remained the game's principal adventurer, managing sometimes to lose as much as ten dollars at nickel-ante poker, and at other times winning as much. One of the game's regulars who kept the records reported that although Dolf's win-lose performance fluctuated more widely from week to week, over a period of several months he came close to breaking even, with a slight advantage on the profit side. Whereas Rosy, who never bet to fill inside straights on the come, and regularly folded low pairs whenever there were high pairs on the board with a down card still to come, seldom lost or won more than three or four dollars at a sitting, yet ended up, though likewise close to breaking even, a trifle in the red.

Now that it was well into December, the *Gilmore Simms* was shut down for the season. Rosy went by Adger's Wharf to check on her, and make sure the batteries were being kept up by the trickle charger. He had done nothing on the Civil War harbor defenses project since early autumn. He didn't really feel any urge to get back on it. It seemed to him now that the whole business had been an excuse to enjoy Sara Jane's company. In lieu of simply asking the then-Miss Jahnz to go boating with him, he had been able to pretend that he and she were participating in a scholarly investigation. That way, had she at any time chosen not to keep company with him, he would be able to tell himself that there had been no rejection of him as such.

Sara Jane had not been fooled. She had gone along with the whole charade. Or had she, perhaps, not been entirely certain that it *was* only that — and anyway, charade or no charade, simply enjoyed doing it? Whichever it was, when spring came there would be better things to do with the boat than chart the trajectories of the wartime artillery batteries.

SUNDAY AFTERNOON, ONE week before the close of classes for the Christmas holiday, Rosy and Sara Jane set the table for four. It was the first dinner party they had given, although there had been spur-of-the-moment suppers thrown together with the Stronghearts and Tom Lowndes. Having previously prepared her own meals, Sara Jane was a good cook, and with a husband for clientele she was adventurously expanding her repertoire. As for Rosy, after doing almost all his dining in hotel coffee shops for years, to have his meals prepared at home, with special attention to how he liked things fixed, was a luxury indeed — so much so that, although having been married for what was still not quite a full month, he was beginning to find that, inexplicably, his clothes had begun shrinking a little.

The bell rang, Rosy activated the buzzer opening the door, and Polly Morrison came up the stairs. "It's almost like spring outside," she said. "It must be in the sixties." She seemed to be a little nervous, whether at having come to dine with one of her professors, even though she had known Sara Jane all her life, or because Sara Jane had told her there was someone they wanted her to meet. Rosy took her jacket and was hanging it in a closet when the bell rang again, and this time Mike Quinn arrived.

Rosy was about to introduce him to Polly, but when the young newspaperman caught sight of her, his eyes opened wide, his jaw dropped, and his face turned red. Polly also seemed a little taken aback.

"Uh — hi," Mike stammered.

"Oh, hey!"

"You know each other, then?" Rosy asked.

"Yes, sir. Sort of." Mike was obviously very embarrassed. Polly seemed less so.

Sara Jane came to the rescue. "We didn't realize you were

already acquainted," she said, "but we thought you ought to be."

"We met once before," Mike said. "Under very unfavorable circumstances. For me, that is. I'm afraid I had too much to drink," he explained.

"I thought you managed very well," Polly said.

"We were on a double date," Mike told the Rosenbaums. "I talked all over the place, and made a complete fool of myself. Not that that's hard to do."

"You did not!" Polly insisted. "You were the one person present who said anything worth listening to all evening long."

There was a pause.

"Well," said Sara Jane, "whatever it might have been, here you are. Now Rosy will get you something to drink."

"That's right," Rosy said. "What will you have? Tomato juice? A little white wine? Or how about some beer?"

"Beer's what did me in the last time," Mike said. He seemed to be a little less constrained now.

Polly laughed. "Some wine would be nice."

"That would be fine for me, too," Mike said.

Rosy went into the kitchen to fix the drinks, and Sara Jane followed. They exchanged glances, as if to say, what in the world have we stumbled into?

They heard Polly say, "I read the story you wrote about the old ferryboats. It was fascinating."

"Thanks."

"In fact, my father enjoyed it so much that we went for a drive that afternoon and rode across the harbor on the little ferry they've got now."

Rosy and Sara Jane came back into the room. "I liked what you wrote about the *Sappho*, too," Rosy said as he handed them glasses of wine. "You're too young to remember that," he said to Polly, "but my father used to take me across the harbor on the *Sappho*."

"I've heard about it all my life," Polly said. "Daddy's always talking about it."

The conversation began to move more easily. Rosy asked

Polly about her senior thesis, and they talked about that. Mike seemed impressed; he had taken a course on the causes of the Civil War at Washington and Lee, he said, and what Polly Morrison was writing about was of interest to him. Dinner was served, and the talk continued, with the topic shifting to literature, and in particular to Thomas Wolfe — Rosy saw to that. Rosy was to remark to Sara Jane later that he had the sense that he was sailing a boat in a fair breeze; all he had to do was to set the tack, and the conversation would fill the sails, and they were off in that direction.

It was Sara Jane, however, who set up the key situation. After they had eaten dessert and were back in the living room, and knowing that Polly was an accomplished pianist, she asked Mike whether he had ever studied music.

"Only for a couple of months one summer," he said. "Didn't you tell me that your mother taught piano?" he asked Polly.

"Yes. And you said yours did, too."

At which point Sara Jane asked Polly to play something for them.

Polly sat down at the piano. "Is there anything you'd like me to play?" she asked.

"Do you know *Für Elise*?" Mike asked.

For answer, Polly began playing. The music flowed smoothly and gently. The touch was sure. It was one of Rosy's favorite pieces. While Polly was playing, he happened to glance at Mike. He was listening intently, leaning forward, his eyes narrowed, his head nodding slightly to the tempo.

There was not a sound in the room except for the piano music. When she was finished, Rosy and Sara Jane applauded.

Mike didn't clap his hands at first, but continued gazing at Polly. Then, after several seconds, he shook his head. "That was — beautiful!" he said. "Marvelous!"

"Polly, didn't you play that at Gertrude Cappelman's class's recital, the year you graduated from Crafts School?" Sara Jane asked.

Polly nodded. "That's right. You were there, weren't you?"

"The reason I remember it so well," Sara Jane said, "is that it was on a Saturday morning and there was a thunderstorm going on outside when you were playing, but you didn't miss a note. You should have been there, Mike."

"I've heard it played lots of times, because my mother always taught it," Mike said. "But I've never heard it played like that before."

"Play something else," Sara Jane proposed.

"Some Mozart, maybe?" Rosy suggested.

Polly played the opening movement of Mozart's A major sonata.

LATER ON, WHEN Polly said it was time for her to go home, Mike offered to give her a ride. She accepted, and they left together.

"Well," said Rosy after they heard the front door close downstairs, "I don't know about her, but Mike Quinn has been roped and tied."

"You think so?"

"I don't think so, I know it. He was really taken with her — especially her playing."

"She does play very well. Ethel says she wanted to be a concert pianist, but then she decided she wasn't really good enough for that."

"He was already impressed by what she was saying about her honors thesis. But you should have seen the expression on his face while she was playing *Für Elise*. It was stout Cortez silent upon a peak in Darien."

"I think she went for Mike pretty well, too," Sara Jane said.

"I hope so," Rosy said. "It was difficult at first, wasn't it? I wonder what the occasion was that they were talking about? Mike obviously thought he'd disgraced himself."

"It must have happened when he was still engaged to Betsy

Murray. Did you notice how nicely she reassured him?"

"Well, he certainly must have found her a considerable contrast to the Murray girl."

"I think it worked both ways," Sara Jane said. "I believe she thought he was a decided improvement on the local supply."

30

MIKE WAS ENTHRALLED with Polly Morrison. Here was a young woman, who, if not stunningly beautiful, was quite attractive, tall with dark hair and a fresh, clear complexion, a body which though it did not flaunt its charms was nicely proportioned. More impressive even than the physical attributes was her intellect, which was accompanied by an unmistakable warmth and sense of humor. There was a naturalness about her, which he had recognized even that night when she and her date had gone dancing with Betsy and him, though he had been in no fit frame of mind to savor it then.

It was exactly that quality of genuineness that had caused him to be so careful afterwards to avoid running into her at church. Behaving as he had on the evening when the knowledge of Betsy's treachery had finally become inescapably apparent, he felt sure that he had disgraced himself in the eyes of someone of taste and discernment. It was fortunate that the Rosenbaums, who knew her, had not been aware of their previous acquaintanceship. When she talked about her thesis and her plans for graduate school he had been impressed, and then when she knew and played the one piece of music he most loved and had heard played all his life at home — well, he had simply never met anyone else like her.

He drove her home from the Rosenbaums' — she lived only a few blocks away, on Rutledge Avenue facing the Colonial

Lake, in the house next door to where Frank Blades lived —
and he should have asked her at once to go out with him one
evening soon. But he didn't; he was afraid he might seem to be
too importunate. He said only that he hoped they would see
each other again soon, to which she responded that she did,
too.

HE WENT BY the news room. In taking over Jim Igoe's beat
while he was at work on the defense property story, he had in
effect inherited Jim's seven-day-week coverage of the police and
fire departments. He called the police sergeant and the county
sheriff's office, was given the details on a few minor mishaps and
incidents, and wrote stories on them. Then he helped out the city
editor with some time copy; he always enjoyed editing copy and
writing headlines. But all the while he kept berating himself for
not having asked for a date, and resolving that he would call and
do so, and hoping that Polly Morrison's friendliness and seeming
interest in him weren't merely because they were fellow dinner
guests, but that she really liked him.

He was cautioning himself that it wouldn't be good tactics to
do that for another day or so at least. But, even while engaged in
supposedly composing a headline for a story about a blizzard
that was shutting down rail and highway traffic in Ohio and
Indiana, he recognized that such a rationale was no more than an
excuse to keep from running the risk of being turned down.
When he completed writing the headline he got up from the city
desk, went to his own desk, looked up the Morrisons' number in
the telephone book, and dialed.

THE MORRISONS WERE finishing supper when the telephone rang. Polly's father answered.

"It's for you," he told Polly, returning to the table.

Polly went out in the hall to the telephone. Mrs. Morrison

lifted a finger to her lips to signal to her husband and Polly's younger brother Jack to be quiet.

"Oh, hello! . . . I'd love to. . . Friday sounds good. . . That's fine. Goodbye."

She returned to the dining room.

"Did he?" Mrs. Morrison asked.

Polly nodded. "Friday." She grinned.

"Did who?" Mr. Morrison asked.

"A young man," Mrs. Morrison told him.

"What did he do?"

"Asked her to go out with him."

"That's scarcely news, is it? Which young man?"

"The right young man," Polly told him, and leaned over and kissed him on the forehead.

"No fooling!" her father said. "May I inquire who this prodigy is?"

"You'll find out in good time," Polly told him.

"I certainly hope so. You haven't acted so excited about a date since the time that Arthur Williams asked you to go to the high school senior prom with him."

Polly laughed. "That was different."

"It sounds very much the same to me," Mr. Morrison said.

JIM IGOE, WHO had been away in Columbia and Greenville for four days, arrived back in the office late Tuesday afternoon. He and the city editor immediately went into the managing editor's office for a conference.

"Let's go get some supper," Igoe said to Mike afterward. "I got things to tell you."

They walked over to the coffee shop at the Timrod Inn, and found a table in a corner.

"It's turning into an amazing story," Jim said after they ordered. "The more I dig, the more I discover. You wouldn't believe it."

"How deep is Mr. Murray involved?"

"Up to his goddamn ears. I don't want to go into all the details. In the last year and a half, the War Department has acquired ten tracts of property in North and South Carolina, including three of them around here, two in the Greenville-Spartanburg area, two near Charlotte, one in Sumter, and two in eastern North Carolina. Six of them were from corporations at Number 2087 Poinsett Street in Greenville. In all but one of the six, the property was acquired by the corporation less than a year before the government bought it. What does that suggest?"

"That somebody had a pretty good line on what the government was looking for in the way of defense installations."

"Right. Now guess what's at 2087 Poinsett Street?"

"An office building?"

"A law firm named Inabinet and Lawton," Igoe said. "Good Upcountry South Carolina names. Now guess who the senior partner, J. Irby Inabinet, is?"

"I don't know."

"Turner Murray's brother-in-law, that's who. His wife's brother. And that's not all. Walter Lawton, another partner, is Franklin Poinsett's brother-in-law."

The conversation ceased while the waiter served them, then resumed.

"You've heard the story about how Murray got his nest egg from building barracks at Camp Croft in Spartanburg during the last war?" Igoe asked.

"Yes. Is it true?"

"It's true, all right. But you know what the name of his construction firm was? Murray and Poinsett. The two of them were in partnership."

"Weren't they roommates at Clemson before that?" Mike asked.

"That's right. Class of 1911. Murray didn't graduate. Poinsett did, then went to law school at U.S.C. in Columbia. Got his degree in 1913, and began practicing with his brother-in-law,

Lawton, in Greenville. He moved down to Charleston in 1922, the year after Murray did."

On the way back to the news room after supper, Mike had a question. "Other than the fact that Mr. Murray's brother-in-law is senior partner of the law firm, there's no direct evidence that he has anything to do with all those corporations, is it?"

"Oh, yes, there is. To some of them. He's listed on the incorporation papers as an officer of two of the corporations."

"How about Poinsett?"

"He's not an officer for any of the corporations, but he's on record as having handled lots of legal work for several of them. Not the War Department property transactions, but others."

"What's this going to mean, Jim?" Mike asked.

"It's going to mean that there's got to be a congressional investigation into Poinsett's use of his committee connections for personal gain. I don't see how the hell they can avoid it. And when they investigate they'll subpoena all the corporation records, in order to find out who holds stock in the corporations, and who was paid how much and for what. My guess is that Poinsett and Turner Murray raked in their full share of the take."

JIM IGOE'S STORY appeared on the front page of the *News & Courier* on Wednesday morning. Igoe meanwhile had departed for Washington, to do more digging. Reading it, Mike Quinn felt renewed gratitude for having gotten off the story. All his suspicions were being confirmed. What he had feared might be the result of his imagination, fueled by his anger and resentment over his personal dealings with Betsy and her father, was clearly no such thing at all.

Moreover, what Igoe had been able to turn up made it apparent that he had been right to give up the story for another reason — which was that he would not have possessed the experience and the investigatorial skill to handle it properly. He would never have been able to turn up what Jim was finding out about the family relationships and the like. Indeed, his sense that the newspaper's editors might have been relieved to be able to assign a more experienced reporter to the story must surely have been correct. So the guilt that he had felt over his failure as a journalist to make the most of his opportunities was really irrelevant.

MEANWHILE, THERE WAS the police and fire department beat. On Monday he made the rounds, inspected the police blotters and sheriff's records, checked regularly with the fire chief's office, wrote the stories. He would be glad when the whole investigative story was done and Igoe could resume the beat. He didn't find crime news particularly interesting.

He kept thinking about his date with Polly Morrison Friday. The Footlight Players were producing Maxwell Anderson's *High Tor* at the Dock Street Theatre, and it might be nice to go to that instead of to a movie. The trouble was that he couldn't be sure of being finished with his work in time. With a movie, if you arrived after it was under way you could see whatever you'd missed the next time around, but if you were late for a play you had to wait until the next scene or act, and there was no rerun afterwards. He hoped that he wouldn't have to be late for the date; it would be getting off to a bad start. Throughout all the time he had been engaged to Betsy Murray, she had never really been able to accept the fact that it wasn't his fault when breaking news kept him from leaving at a prearranged time.

In Betsy's eyes there had been nothing to distinguish newspaper work from any other kind of job, except that the hours were unreliable and the pay low. Not once could he recall Betsy's ever having complimented him on a story he wrote, the way that Polly Morrison had done with the ferryboat piece. Polly had even said that her father had liked it so much he had taken the family for a ride across the harbor on the ferryboat! Her father was a school principal. He had the sense that his own parents would like Polly and her family; in retrospect he could see they hadn't cared for Betsy and the Murrays at all. And of course the Morrisons were Catholics, too. That was very good to know. There would be no trouble if . . . . The thought that in September she would be leaving to go to graduate school elsewhere was dismaying, even if it was nine full months away.

He was getting ahead of himself, as usual. Here he had been in the girl's company exactly twice, been alone with her for all of fifteen minutes or so on the way back from the Rosenbaums', and he was thinking about being married to her! It was a good thing she couldn't read his mind.

DOWNSTAIRS, BELOW THE news room in the basement of the building, the presses were running. The vibration could be felt through the floor. The Monday afternoon edition of the *Evening Post* would be along any minute. It would be interesting to read the follow-up to Jim Igoe's story. No doubt Howard Wade, the man that Franklin Poinsett had defeated for Congress and who had demanded a probe into the timing of the weapons depot announcement, would issue a renewed call for an investigation. The latest developments were built to order for him. It would be interesting, too, to see whether Mr. Murray had issued a statement.

A boy from the press room came into the news room with folded copies of the *Evening Post*. He handed one to Mike, who opened it and began to read. What his glance fell upon, however, was a story that was of considerably more concern to him than anything having to do with Turner Murray, Franklin Poinsett, or claims of corruption in the sale of War Department property.

31

EARLY ON WEDNESDAY afternoon, two days before classes were to end for the Christmas holidays, Rosy received a call from the dean's secretary, asking him to come to McCracken's office. He met his English literature survey class, then went down to see what the dean wanted. The dean announced that he had received a visitation that morning from the family pastor and the parents of a student in his English literature survey class, protesting the inclusion of immoral and lascivious material in the course.

"What are you talking about?" Rosy asked.

The dean read from a letter which he said had been addressed to him: "We object to our daughter, a pure and innocent Christian girl, having to be exposed to a foul and wicked poem about sex. In the poem a man tries to get his girlfriend to have sex with him. They are not married. The poem uses all kinds of arguments to get her to lose her virginity. We demand that the teacher of this poem, who is named Doctor Rosenbaum, be stopped from making our daughter and other students of good Christian rearing read dirty and immoral writing like this poem about a coy mistress."

Rosy laughed. "You know what they're referring to, don't you? That's Marvell's 'To His Coy Mistress.' It was written in the late seventeenth century. It's in all the textbooks."

"It doesn't matter how old it is," the dean declared. "There is no room for pornography in the college curriculum."

"Are you out of your mind? A work of pornography? Andrew Marvell's 'To His Coy Mistress'? That's ridiculous." He could scarcely believe that the dean was taking the complaint seriously.

"These good Christian people do not consider it ridiculous."

"What did you tell them?"

"I informed them that a full investigation would be conducted into the matter."

"An investigation? You told them that there'd be an investigation into teaching a poem by Andrew Marvell? Good God!"

"I told them that the College does not condone the use of sexually suggestive material in classes, and their complaint would be taken with the utmost seriousness," the dean declared. "I also told that to a reporter from the *Charleston Evening Post* who telephoned to inquire about the matter."

It was incredible. "You told that to a newspaper reporter? Do you realize that you'll make this school into the laughing stock of every college and university in this country?" Rosy asked. "Does Page Carter know about this?"

"The President is out of the city, and as the chief executive officer I am fully empowered to conduct the business of the college."

Rosy was flabbergasted. "May I ask the name of the student whose parents came to see you?"

"I am not at liberty to divulge that information," the dean said. "Quite naturally the student and her parents fear retaliation."

"Why, you dumb bastard!" Rosy said. "You're getting me and this college into a terribly embarrassing hassle over absolutely nothing!"

"Dr. Rosenbaum, watch your language!"

"I called you a dumb bastard. You're also a dishonest son of a bitch!"

"I decline to continue this discussion," the dean said. "Please leave this office at once."

"All right," Rosy said. "But first let me have a copy of that letter."

"I have summarized its contents. That is all that is necessary."

"If someone has made a complaint about me, I have a right to see the complaint. You're not operating a star chamber here."

"This is not a court of law. Now please leave."

IN NO TIME the news was all over the campus. Rosy's colleagues began coming by his office to confirm it. There was general astonishment and indignation. Horace Hewitt proposed that the faculty meet at once and draw up a resolution condemning the dean and supporting Rosy. Dolf Strongheart favored going en masse to the dean at once and demanding a retraction on the spot: "And if he gives us any guff, I'll punch him in the nose then and there." While they were talking, the telephone rang. It was a reporter on the *Evening Post*, who wanted a statement from Rosy.

"The whole thing is absurd," Rosy told him. "Marvell's poem is one of the classic lyrics in the English language."

"Do you consider it pornographic?" the reporter asked.

"If it is, then so is two-thirds of the literature being taught in American colleges and universities today."

"What do you think of the idea of an investigation?" the reporter asked.

"There's nothing to investigate. The poem's right there in the textbook to see. The textbook's used all over the country."

"Why do you think these people are making the complaint?"

"I don't have any idea. If they think this poem's pornographic, they obviously don't know anything about poetry."

The reporter thanked him.

"That stupid McCracken doesn't know what the hell he's doing," Rosy declared after he hung up the phone. "This thing's going to make him and the College look ridiculous."

"On the contrary, he knows exactly what he's doing," Dolf said. "What do you think about having no proof of malice now?"

Rosy shook his head. "It's so damned incredible."

"Does it strike you as odd," Dolf asked, "that the letter was written to McCracken instead of Page? How did the girl's parents know Page was out of town?"

"I don't know. They probably called and asked."

"And how come the newspaper got hold of it so quickly? You'd think that when McCracken told them he was going to investigate, they'd have waited a couple of days at least, to see what happened."

"You think McCracken told them to go to the newspaper?"

"You goddamn right I do."

Rosy was inclined to treat the matter as an annoying farce, which Page Carter would dismiss as soon as he got back in town and heard about it. Sara Jane wasn't. "A great many people who've never heard of Andrew Marvell are going to wonder what's going on," she said. "And some of them are quite willing to believe that this wicked college professor is corrupting the minds of his innocent students."

"You think people will take this seriously, then?"

"Some of them. I certainly do."

"And don't think the dean's remark about 'good Christian people' was just accidental," Dolf said.

Rosy was astounded; he hadn't thought of that. "You really think he's trying to make something out of my being a Jew?"

"Rosy, Rosy, where have you been living?" Dolf Strongheart asked. "In Cloud-cuckoo-land?"

"Sweetheart, that's exactly what he's doing," Sara Jane declared. "That man is evil! He'll use anything against you that he can think of."

Tom Lowndes came walking into Rosy's office with a copy of the *Evening Post*. The story appeared on the second page of the paper:

PARENTS CLAIM 'OBSCENE' POEM BEING TAUGHT

College To Investigate Professor's Use of 17th-Century Literary Work

A College of Charleston professor has been teaching an "obscene" poem in his English literature class, according to a complaint made to College authorities by the parents of a female student.

Contending that Professor Lancelot Rosenbaum's teaching of the poem "To His Coy Mistress," by the seventeenth-century English poet Andrew Marvell, exposes their daughter to "a foul and wicked poem about sex," a North Charleston couple and their family minister, the Rev. Bobby Simpson, have demanded that College authorities bar the use of the work in literature classes.

The College will undertake an investigation into the charges, Dean N. Joseph McCracken said. "We do not condone the use of sensational and pornographic material in class under the guise of so-called academic freedom," he declared.

The poem, written in 1681, appears in numerous literature textbooks and anthologies. Professor Rosenbaum has described it as "one of the classic lyrics in the English language." If it is pornographic, he said, then so is "two-thirds of the literature taught in American colleges and universities."

The Rev. Simpson, pastor of the North Charleston Heights Evangelical Church, said that he and the parents of the student, whose name was not made public, were "shocked" to discover that the reading of a "filthy and lewd" poem was required of "pure and innocent Christian students."

The poem, Simpson claims, consists of a plea to an unmarried girl to lose her virtue by engaging in immoral sexual activity. "It is the voice of the Devil speaking in this poem," he said. "If that is great literature, Christians are better off sticking to the Bible."

THAT EVENING THE telephone rang constantly. A reporter on the *News & Courier*, not Mike Quinn but one that Rosy didn't know, called to ask whether he intended to go on teaching the Marvell poem in his course, now that its use had been questioned. "I see no reason not to," Rosy told him. "It's a standard work. If I didn't teach it, I'd be shortchanging the students." Various people called to offer support. There were also a couple of crank calls, including one which began, "We'll get you, you dirty Commie Jew!" Rosy hung up on the caller. Another asked whether he was interested in buying some dirty photographs. Rosy hung up on him, too.

THE STRONGHEARTS CAME over after dinner. "I put in a call to Page in New York," Dolf said. "I couldn't reach him, but I talked to Tennie. She said to tell you not to worry, that Page would be back Friday and would squelch the whole thing."

"That's not enough," Sara Jane said. "Page ought to issue a statement from up there." Her patience with the president appeared to be at an end.

"I'll call him and tell him he should," Dolf said.

"No," Rosy said. "Let's see what happens. All this time we've trusted Page to handle things. Now I want to see whether he'll come through."

Sara Jane shook her head. "He'd better."

A little later the telephone rang. This time it was Page Carter, calling long distance. He had called the *News & Courier*, he told Rosy, and issued a statement denying that there would be an investigation and expressing his complete confidence in Rosy's judgment. He was cutting short his trip and he and Tennie would fly back tomorrow morning if weather permitted. Otherwise they would be back midday Friday on the train.

He asked whether anyone knew the identity of the student who had supposedly made the complaint to her parents. "Try to find out," he said when Rosy told him of the dean's refusal to divulge the identity of the complainants. "If you can't, I'll find out when I get back."

"I feel a little better about Page now," Sara Jane said after the conversation had ended. "But it's high time that he did something."

"I'll bet I know who the student was," Dolf said. "Didn't the story in the paper say she lived in North Charleston?"

"It said that the minister's church is in North Charleston," Linda Strongheart said. "Presumably that indicates the family lives there, too."

"Who do you think it is, Dolf?" Sara Jane asked.

"That babe who's doing the project with McCracken. What's her name, Witt? Didn't the story about the grant say she lived in North Charleston? And didn't you say she was in the class, Rosy?"

"Yes."

"Well, then. Doesn't it figure?"

"You think that the dean may have put her up to complaining to her parents?" Sara Jane asked.

"In view of what I've heard from several students about what's been going on between the girl and McCracken, that's exactly what I think."

"In other words, the whole thing was contrived by the dean?" Rosy asked.

"Right."

"But surely he must have realized that Page would countermand his statement, and make him look like a fool."

"Rosy, I told you, don't underestimate the son of a bitch's cleverness," Dolf said. "So what if Page countermands the investigation? McCracken comes across, in the eyes of a lot of people who don't know Andrew Marvell from Emily Dickinson and never heard of either one, as the defender of virtue and purity against this pornographic professor."

"I certainly wouldn't put it past the man," Sara Jane said. "He'll do anything he thinks he can get away with."

ROSY WAS A long while getting to sleep that night. He was angry and, even more than that, exasperated. What was frustrating was his helplessness. No matter what he did, no matter what Page Carter or anyone else did or said, there were some who would remain suspicious that there was something to the accusation. Even if Page were to fire the dean — and he'd better do it forthwith — it wouldn't change that; there would be those who would see McCracken as a victim who dared to stand up for virtue and goodness, and was therefore suppressed.

Was it that coed, Lee Witt, who had made the complaint? Dolf could very well be right. If so, surely she couldn't have thought of doing it all by herself, since at no time in any of her written work had she shown the slightest sign of comprehending the relationship of anything in any of the literary works they had studied to her own experience. She had only parroted back his own lectures.

No, someone else would have had to put her up to complaining to her parents, who wouldn't have known any better, and through them to the pastor of her church — who, to judge from his quoted comment, was ignorant and a bigot. Dolf was right; the dean was the odds-on candidate.

He had been relieved when Page Carter called. Page had sounded furious — as well he might have been. There could be no doubt that Page's heart was in the right place, that his intentions were of the best. But why hadn't he come down on McCracken long before this, the moment he had shown signs of causing trouble? He had not done so, and now it was Rosy who was paying the price.

THE MORNING PAPER featured Page Carter's statement prominently on the front page:

NO INVESTIGATION
OF POEM PLANNED,
CARTER DECLARES

College President Backs Professor's
Use of Marvell's "Coy Mistress"

The story quoted Page as saying that "Any suggestion that exception could be taken to the appropriateness of studying a centuries-old poem, one of the acknowledged classics of the English language, in a college literature course is totally unacceptable. No inquiry is needed or will be made." Page was also quoted as declaring that "Dr. Lancelot Rosenbaum is one of our most distinguished teachers, and I have every confidence in his taste and judgment." The story then continued to the effect that "Carter's statement is in direct contradiction to yesterday's announcement by Dean N. Joseph McCracken that the use of the poem in a class taught by Rosenbaum was under investigation because of the complaint by the parents of a student that it was immoral and pornographic. Asked to comment on the disagreement, Carter said only that the dean's action was 'unauthorized.'" The story went on to say that "Dean McCracken was unavailable for comment."

"Well," Rosy said to Sara Jane when he read the story, "Page certainly makes it clear to all what he thinks of McCracken."

"*Now* he does," Sara Jane said.

UPON ARRIVING ON the campus that morning, Rosy had scarcely settled in to his office when José L. Lopez, Jr., the class poet, showed up. Did Rosy know the identity of the student who had made the complaint to her parents? he asked.

"No, I can't say that I do," Rosy told him.

"Dr. Rosenbaum, I don't like to talk about anybody the way I'm going to, but this whole thing's got to be a put-up job. The only girl in the class who would have said that is Lee Witt. She lives in North Charleston and goes to that church. And," — he was clearly embarrassed —— "I happen to know firsthand that she's nobody to be complaining about her purity and innocence being violated."

"Really?"

"She's been putting out since she was halfway through high school, and everybody knows it."

"Then why do you think she made the complaint — if she's the one who made it?"

"Dr. Rosenbaum, you know about that psychology project she's doing with Dr. McCracken?"

Rosy nodded. "Yes, I've heard about it."

"Well — that's not all she's doing with him."

"You mean —?"

"Yes, sir. She's been seen going with him into his lab at night by quite a few people. Everybody knows about it, sir. I mean, all the students do."

"But that's not necessarily proof that anything wrong is taking place."

"It might not be," José L. Lopez, Jr., said, "but then why do the lights get turned out when they go inside?"

"You think, then, that Dr. McCracken may have put this girl up to making a complaint about the poem to her parents?"

"I'm sure of it. She's too dumb to think of it herself."

He thanked him for the information, and asked that he say nothing more about it to anyone. There was no reason to doubt anything that José L. Lopez, Jr., had told him. So — Dolf had been quite right. The question was, how to prove it?

He went over to the library to tell Sara Jane what he had found out. She closed the door to her office. Polly Morrison had come in to see her, she said, and had told her pretty much the same thing about the girl and her relationship with the dean, which apparently was common knowledge among the students. She also said that there was talk of the students holding a mass meeting tomorrow to protest the dean's actions and to express support for Rosy. The editor of the *Meteor*, the College newspaper, was preparing an editorial calling for a public apology by the dean, Polly had reported.

Polly also said that Mike Quinn had telephoned her last

evening to get her help on a story he was writing. He was calling a number of literary critics and professors in various colleges and universities and asking them whether they taught the Marvell poem to their students, and what they thought of the charge that it was pornographic.

It was time for Rosy to meet his 10:00 A.M. class, on the American novel. He went off to lecture on *The Rise of Silas Lapham*. Surely nobody could complain that William Dean Howells was a pornographic writer.

FROM THE SIDE window of the zoology laboratory, Dolf Strongheart pointed out to Rosy a little later that day, it was possible to observe anyone entering or leaving the onetime residential building that was now the psychology lab. "We're going to keep a lookout until the son of a bitch and that little floozie go in there and turn off the light," he declared, "and then we're going to catch them red-handed!"

"Who is 'we,' Dolf?" Rosy asked. "You and Tom and I?"

"I've got my majors lined up in one-hour shifts, from nine to midnight, until we spot them. My guess is it won't be more than a couple of days, from what I hear."

Rosy was uneasy about getting students directly involved. "Do you think it's proper for you to enlist them to help in this?" he asked.

"Me enlist them? Hell, they enlisted me!" His students were already upset over the newspaper story about the dean's project, he said, and when they heard about this, they were waiting outside his office door when he arrived this morning. "You don't realize," he told Rosy, "how much most of the students dislike the bastard, too. He's been meddling in their affairs, he tried several times to censor the College paper, he's been criticizing Page and all of us to his class, and he's about as popular as a skunk at a picnic — *Mephitis mephitis*, that is."

The students knew all too well what had been taking place

with McCracken and his protégé, Dolf said, and were ready to go in a body to the president, or, since he was out of town, the chairman of the board of trustees, and accuse the dean of misconduct and hypocrisy.

"Did you head them off?" Rosy asked. "I don't think that would be a good idea at all."

"I told them that there were better ways to do it. That's when we set up the patrol. The minute somebody spots McCracken and the girl going in there at night, they'll call me on the phone, and I'll be there in five minutes, with camera and flash attachment. I've got a key to the back door." He extracted a key from his coat pocket and showed it to Rosy.

"Suppose you break in on him and nothing's going on?"

"Something will be going on. Why the hell else would the lights be turned out and the doors locked? You can't run rats through mazes in pitch darkness, you know. Not even white rats."

IT WAS A degrading business, yet it had to be done. It couldn't be handled obliquely, couldn't be finessed. Rosy saw that now. Nuances, hints, implied rebukes, and censure were wasted. The man neither understood nor was daunted by them. He had to be combatted head-on, openly, bluntly, for that was the only response that got through to him. In short, fire had to be fought with fire. And Rosy was willing to do it. The blinders had been removed from his eyes. Dolf had been correct; he had been playing the part of Pollyanna. No more.

Should Page Carter be apprised of the plan? Sara Jane, when consulted, thought not. "If he knows about it in advance, and for any reason it backfires, that *will* make McCracken into a martyr," she told Rosy. "Keep it to yourself. And for goodness sakes, I hope Dolf has sworn those students to absolute secrecy. If the dean were to get the slightest hint that anything's going on, it would be disastrous. The trouble with fighting fire with fire is that you can get badly burnt in the process."

"He said he warned them specifically, and they understand why."

"I hope so."

"I told him," Rosy said, "that when he gets the phone call to come over, to call me and I'll join him. If it's got to be done this way, then I'm going to help do it."

IT OCCURRED TO Rosy that while Sara Jane was undoubtedly right about not telling Page what was being planned, once again it was being left to others — in this instance to Dolf and himself — to do the dirty work. Perhaps that was what being a good administrator involved.

Dolf had insisted, only a few days ago, that the dean wasn't stupid. And in a sense he was correct; McCracken was clever, dangerously so. Yet the whole business — not only the assault on Rosy as a teacher of pornography, but everything else he'd done — was the product of, if not stupidity, then a blind recklessness so thorough as to be oblivious to all possible consequences. The metaphor of the bull in the china shop did not cover it; the wildness, the frenzy of his behavior weren't properly conveyed.

In his ambition, his plotting, his malice, his deviousness, his goatish sexuality he was truly a wild man. The slightest degree of calculation would have let McCracken see that there was no possible way that he could succeed in wrestling control of the College from Page Carter's hands by main force, as obviously he had sought to do from the outset. But he did not consider consequences or plot long-range strategies, did not seek to divide and conquer, to create a faction, to isolate those persons who were obstacles to his plans. He only acted, savagely and instinctively.

He was like one of those horseflies that get into a house and go buzzing around from room to room, disrupting everything, until finally they alight somewhere long enough to be swatted. Introduced — inexplicably; how he had ever been appointed remained as moot as ever — into a situation, he had dropped onto the premises on his feet, running, and would not ever cease running until entirely squelched, totally suppressed. Until then, nothing, no one would be safe.

He would have to go. Page would have to fire him. The president would have to act. If he didn't — then he, Rosy, would leave. He would tell Page just that when he returned from New York tomorrow.

PAGE CARTER'S PLANE landed shortly before two o'clock. By three he was in his office, and shortly thereafter he summoned Rosy. "I feel," he said, "as if I left what I thought was a reasonably tranquil cove, only to find that it was the eye of a hurricane." He ran his hand through his hair. "Now tell me everything that's going on."

Rosy brought him up to date.

"Did you find out who the girl is?"

Rosy told him about Lee Witt. He didn't tell him about what he and Dolf were planning.

"Mike Donahoe warned me that something was going on, and I was planning to look into it as soon as I got back. Oh, my! Here we are, one day before the Christmas break. Isn't it all lovely?" He shook his head. "You can imagine how I felt, sitting in a meeting of college and university presidents, to have word reach me that an administrative officer of the College of Charleston had announced an investigation into the teaching of a poem by Andrew Marvell. And it was in all the New York papers this morning, too. The *Times* and the *Herald-Tribune* both featured it prominently."

"Imagine how I felt, Page."

"Of course," Page said. "You've had to bear the brunt. You and Sara Jane. I was indulging myself. I'm sorry." He held out a sheet of paper. "This is going in every faculty mailbox, and on every bulletin board, and will be mailed to every member of the board of trustees," he said.

It was a letter, on the College's letterhead. Rosy read it:

> *December 19, 1940*
> *A Letter to the College Community*
>
> *As President of the College, I wish to express my regret and chagrin at the totally unwarranted statement, by a member of the College administration, that an inquiry would be conducted into the study of a poem in a literature class taught by one of our most respected faculty members. Any such action would not only violate the principles of free speech and of academic freedom to which this College is dedicated, but would be personally obnoxious to me.*
>
> *Needless to say, the statement was neither authorized nor approved by myself.*
>
> (signed)
> Page Burwell Carter

"If it was anyone else but McCracken," Rosy said, "reading this letter would make him consider himself so compromised that he would resign forthwith. But it will mean next to nothing to him."

"I'm afraid you're right."

"He's got to go, Page. It's him or me."

"Yes, and it mustn't be you." The president shook his head sadly. "Rosy, I know that you, and numerous others, must find this man's presence on this campus, much less his appointment as dean, to be incredible, and doubtless you've been wondering about my sanity, not to speak of my judgment. I can't say that I blame you. I wish I could tell you the full story, but I can't — not just yet. All I can ask is that you try to bear with me a little longer, and wait and see what transpires."

Rosy got up. "That's fair enough," he told Page. "I'll be waiting."

THE *NEWS & COURIER* for Friday morning featured a lengthy story, under Mike Quinn's byline. "Prominent educators and literary figures the nation over," the story began, "have branded as ridiculous the charge that Andrew Marvell's seventeenth-century poem 'To His Coy Mistress' was pornographic and should not be taught to students at the College of Charleston."

Professor William Lyon Phelps of Yale University was quoted as saying that "Marvell's poem is one of the triumphs of the English language; not to teach it in a literature course would be to deprive one's students of a golden treasure."

Professor Mark Van Doren, of Columbia, declared that "one might with equal appropriateness outlaw the reading and teaching of 'Romeo and Juliet,' 'Anthony and Cleopatra,' 'The Canterbury Tales,' and 'Paradise Lost.' A good deal of the King James Bible would also be suspect."

Dr. Henry Seidel Canby of the *Saturday Review of Literature* said that "the freedom to teach without fear of censorship is a precious right, to be cherished and safeguarded from assault either by bigotry or, as seems likely in this instance, purblind ignorance."

The poet Alastair Wystan said that "any college administrator foolish enough to take such a complaint seriously ought to be teaching jackasses, not people, for clearly he can speak their language."

Archibald MacLeish, poet and Librarian of Congress, characterized the person who would make such a complaint as "worthy of enshrinement in the annals of idiocy along with the Greeks who accused Socrates of corrupting the young."

H.L. Mencken's comment was that "almost every college dean I have ever encountered has been either a fool or a hypocrite. This one obviously belongs in both categories. He probably votes the straight Prohibitionist ticket and reads *Naughty Tales* on the sly."

The poet Carl Sandburg said that "Andrew Marvell was a great poet. Banning his poem from being taught is the act of a fool."

Finally, Mike had been able to secure a comment from Robert Frost: "I thought all the idiots were working for the federal government in Washington now, but evidently there is still one at loose in coastal South Carolina."

"HOW IN THE world," Sara Jane asked after reading the story at breakfast, "do you suppose Mike was able to get through to all those people?"

"I suppose he just called them on the telephone, told them he was a newspaper reporter, and asked them for a comment," Rosy said. "Most of them had probably already read about it. What marvelous publicity for the College! Page is fit to be tied. It's been in every newspaper in the country, he says."

ROSY STOPPED BY the zoology lab on the way to his office that morning. "I take it that nothing happened last night?" he asked Dolf Strongheart.

"No, all was quiet. But we'll be watching him tonight and tomorrow night and Sunday, and we'll get him yet."

"You're not going to keep up the surveillance after the carol singing on Sunday night, are you?" On the Sunday night before Christmas the faculty and student body of the College traditionally strolled through the neighborhood around the college singing carols.

"If necessary, yes."

"Oh, boy. Joy to the world."

WHEN ROSY ENTERED the classroom to teach his English literature survey that afternoon, it was for the first time since the news of the complaint and the dean's promise of an investigation had become known. The entire class rose to its feet and gave him an ovation.

"Thank you," he said. He settled into his seat behind the desk and prepared to discourse on Dryden's "Alexander's Feast." Before he did, he took the roll. The day before the commencement of a holiday was by college regulation a no-cut day, with class attendance required. Miss Lee Witt was not there to answer to her name.

$$32$$

WHEN MIKE QUINN read the article about Dr. Rosenbaum and the poem in Wednesday afternoon's paper, he was astounded. "Did you see this crazy story?" he asked the city editor. "An Andrew Marvell poem, of all things!"

"I can understand the preacher being stupid enough to complain about something like that," the city editor said, "but what's amazing is that dean taking it seriously. I heard the guy was an oddball, but you think he'd have more sense than that. I suppose Shakespeare'll be next."

The city editor had already told the new reporter, White, to do a follow-up for the next morning. It was agreed that Mike would work on a story for Friday, calling various educators and writers long distance and asking them what they thought about investigating a poem by Andrew Marvell as pornographic.

Mike telephoned Polly Morrison, and from her he learned something about the dean and his role on the campus. Now he understood why Dr. and Mrs. Rosenbaum had disliked him. Polly didn't like him, either, and neither, she told him, did most of the students. He told her about the story he was going to write. The upshot was that he would come by her house after he got off work and she would help him think of some people to call.

In other words, he wouldn't have to wait until their scheduled date Friday night to see her again. So to his indignation at the wrong being perpetrated upon Dr. Rosenbaum was joined the prospect of collaborating with Polly Morrison in helping to combat it, thereby intensifying what was already a considerable zeal for the project.

HE MET POLLY'S father and mother. Her father was principal of Courtenay Elementary School, and he had a good sense of humor. Her mother was a friend of Mrs. Rosenbaum. "She speaks very highly of you," she told Mike — which made Polly blush, because it indicated that her mother had been inquiring about him. They talked about Mike's mother. He explained that one of the reasons he had enjoyed so much hearing Polly play *Für Elise* at the Rosenbaums was that he had heard it played at home so often, though never so well.

Mr. Morrison laughed. "Well, don't tell her that," he said, "because she'll play it on the drop of a hat as it is. Ever since Gertrude Cappelman had her learn it to play at her recital, in June of 1933 I think it was, she's been playing it twice a week. We call it the National Anthem around here."

"That will do, Henry," Mrs. Morrison said. "His idea of good music is 'Take Me Out to the Ball Game,'" she told Mike.

It turned out that Mr. Morrison had some suggestions about who Mike might ask for comments on the Andrew Marvell poem. "Why don't you try the editor of the *Saturday Review of Literature* — what's his name, Canby?" Mrs. Morrison found a copy of the magazine and they looked it up.

"I understand this man McCracken runs rats through mazes and supposedly proves things about behavior," Mr. Morrison remarked. "You know what's wrong with that, don't you?"

"No, sir."

"If a rat tries to do anything different, and decides it doesn't want to run through the maze, they get rid of it. In other words, they kill off all the genius rats!"

Mike laughed.

"How's Jim Igoe these days?" Mr. Morrison asked.

"He's fine. He's away working on a special assignment right now."

"He and I played together on the Standard Oil team that won the city championship in 1927. He did the pitching and the hitting, and I did the catching and the thinking."

Polly's parents excused themselves after a little while and went up to bed. Polly brought out some books and magazines and they began compiling a list. The Morrisons' living room reminded him of his own at home, although there were several bookcases filled with books instead of just one. There was a phonograph and a cabinet with several shelves of classical music albums. It was comfortable looking, and not at all ostentatious — very different, in fact, from the Murrays'. There were no English sporting prints, no green leather furniture and brass lamps with green shades, and the rug wasn't one of those thick pile affairs.

In an alcove was a baby grand piano and a bookcase filled with sheet music, mostly yellow-jacketed Schirmer editions just like his mother's. A metronome was in place atop the piano, there were little busts of Beethoven, Brahms, Mozart, and Wagner here and there in the living room, and on the wall of the alcove, above the piano, a painting of Brahms playing the piano and smoking a cigar.

"Does your father really not like music?" Mike asked.

"That's just Mama's joking," Polly said. "He likes some things quite a bit. What he really loves is good jazz. He's got dozens of old records from the twenties and early thirties — they call them race records — and he loves Louis Armstrong and Jelly Roll Morton and the Benny Goodman Sextet. Have you ever been over to the Alhambra?"

"You mean that colored pavilion over on Mount Pleasant?"

"They have marvelous jazz. Daddy's taken us over there several times to hear it."

"Does your mother like it, too?"

"Well, she's not crazy about jazz, but of course she's a trained musician and she admires anything that's really played well."

Mike tried to imagine his own mother in a nightclub listening to colored musicians playing jazz, but could not. His father taking her to such a place was an even more improbable thought. Yet on second thought, if his father had taken her, she might very well have enjoyed it.

They drew up a list of several dozen people from whom Mike could try to get comments. They talked for a while, with Polly telling him considerably more about the background of the incident at the College. She was convinced, and said that most of her friends were as well, that the student who had complained about the poem was the same girl that Mike had met when he had interviewed the dean about his grant, and she was sure that she had been put up to making the complaint by the dean. She also told how the dean had been known to make some anti-Catholic and anti-Semitic comments in his class. Nobody could understand why the president of the College had ever appointed such a man as dean in the first place, she said. The rumor was that the chairman of the board of trustees had had something to do with it.

"You mean Betsy's father?"

"Yes."

It suddenly occurred to Mike that the dean's name was the same as one of the names of the officers of the corporation that had bought the property on the Isle of Palms for the Army hospital: McCracken. He hadn't so much as thought about the similarity. That was certainly dumb of him, although at the time the dean hadn't been figuring importantly in his thinking. He could not, however, imagine the dean having anything much in common with Mr. Murray, other than both being obnoxious, if in very different ways.

"I saw Betsy the other day," Polly said. "At Mangel's."

He had the sense that she had made the statement with some awkwardness. "I haven't seen her since — since that awful evening at the Cat's Cradle," he said.

"You really were very funny that evening — the things you said."

"I was under the influence."

"Not really. You knew what you were saying. You were quoting lines from poems, and they were devastating, and none of them realized it. When Betsy accused you of being drunk, and you quoted Hamlet and said you were only drunk north-north-west — it was marvelous."

"*In vino, veritas*, I guess, but I don't like to remember it," Mike said. "I'm just lucky you were along."

"I wasn't of any help to you."

"Yes, you were," Mike said. "You gave me a standard of comparison."

THE NEXT MORNING Mike went right to work on his story. It took him all morning and afternoon, with an hour out to check by police headquarters and the sheriff's office, but one way or the other he was able to track down and talk with enough of the people on the list of names to make a good story. Almost every one of those he talked with had already read about the incident in a newspaper. In several instances he had to modify their language. What Carl Sandburg really said that was that barring Andrew Marvell's poem was the act of a shithead; Mike changed it to fool. Robert Frost said that he had thought that all the idiots and faggots were in Washington working for the government; Mike omitted the homosexual reference.

ON FRIDAY MIKE made all his rounds and got all his stories written early, so that he would be able to leave by eight o'clock for his movie date with Polly Morrison. Outside the windows of the building, the late afternoon grew dark even earlier than was usual only a few days before the winter solstice. The Associated Press wire had carried the report of a line of severe storms causing damage in western South Carolina and around Augusta, Georgia, in advance of a formidable cold front that was moving in from the north and west and ending what had been almost a full week of unseasonably warm temperatures. By suppertime the wind was blowing briskly and it was raining.

The police radio on Jim Igoe's desk was busy with reports of automobile collisions. Then about seven o'clock the alarm bell in the fire station tower just down Meeting Street began ringing. Mike counted the rings, looked on the map. It indicated that whatever it was was located up in the area just north of the city, toward the Cooper River. He dialed police headquarters. The report they had was that lightning had hit a tank up at the Standard Oil refinery. Then the alarm began ringing again.

"Hey, that's a five-alarm fire!" the city editor declared.

Moments later they heard the sirens of the fire trucks from the nearby station as they rolled northward up Meeting Street.

He telephoned Polly's home, told her that he would probably be late; she had heard the fire sirens, she said. Then he hurried out the building. As he sprinted through the rain to the parking lot he could hear, in the distance, what seemed like a chorus of sirens. He jumped in his car and drove out the driveway onto Queen Street and up to the corner of Meeting just in time to watch another fire truck roar past. He gunned his car, turned the corner, and took up a position in its wake as it sped along.

From all he had heard, the location of the fire was right in the area where he had stopped with Jim Igoe on the way back from the police shooting match, to watch the fire crews practicing the use of a chemical to fight oil fires. All that was needed, Jim Igoe had said, was for one of the oil tanks to catch fire while there was a strong wind blowing. Overhead rain was falling, though only lightly, and there was a brisk wind.

A block or so beyond Magnolia Crossing the fire truck turned off the highway and raced eastward toward the oil storage area, with Mike following close behind and several police cars following him. It had stopped raining. Up ahead was dense smoke. The fire truck sped through the entrance gate. He pulled to a stop, held out his press card, and was waved through. Police had cordoned off a wide area around the Standard Oil tank installations. With his press pass he was allowed inside.

A large tank was burning fiercely in the dark, with the wind blowing the flames, and a dozen fire trucks in action or setting up. He went into the Standard Oil headquarters building, called the news room, and told the city editor what was happening. He was told that the staff photographer had left and would be along soon.

The firemen and police were all wearing protective helmets. Jim Igoe had turned over to him a steel helmet and a heavy yellow raincoat to use while he was handling the police beat, so he got them out of the trunk of his car and put them on. He walked out to where a cluster of firemen were standing, directing operations. Among them he recognized the fire chief, and he asked him what was going on.

The chief pointed to the firemen who were ringed around the burning tank, training a dozen or more fire hoses on the sides of the tank. They were not worried so much about the burning gasoline inside the tank, he said, as that the heat might melt the steel sides of the tank, whereupon the burning gasoline would quickly spread to nearby tanks and touch off a blazing inferno. Even if this did not happen, there was danger that wind-borne sparks might touch off blazes elsewhere. The heat was intense; barely a week before Christmas, it was like a day in mid-July. The steel sides of the tanks nearest the one burning were being wet down by hoses.

He looked at his watch. It was almost eight o'clock. He hurried back into the building, called Polly and canceled the date. "I'm awfully sorry," he said, "really. But I can't help it."

"You don't have to apologize," she said. "I understand. It must be a big fire."

"It's very big."

"Please be careful."

"How about tomorrow evening?"

"That'll be fine."

Now he could devote his full attention to the fire, which in truth was something to behold. With the lights, the smoke, the heat, the wailing of distant sirens, the blazing cauldron of the incinerated tank, the firefighters sprinting here and there, the scene resembled the newsreel depictions of the German bomber raids on London. Every so often there would be a flare-up of fire atop the tank, and a trail of sparks. Each time there was a rush to extinguish them before anything could catch. Sometimes the fiery trail, caught up in the wind, would stream out a goodly distance, and reach close to other tanks before they burned out.

There was activity at the dock along the river. Giving the flaming tank a wide berth, Mike walked over there. Two tugboats were engaged in aiding a large Esso tanker to move away from the dock and out into the stream, while another was setting up alongside the far end of the dock. As Mike watched, the tugboat, which was equipped with fire hoses, began to train streams of water upon several nearby tanks and pipes. He thought about what Igoe had said, that a German sub could lob a few shells into the tanks and raise hell. This one was caused by lightning, however; we weren't at war yet.

He returned to the landward side of the burning tank, where the chief and others were located, looked on for a while as they gave orders and directed newly arriving fire trucks and crews from out in the county to take up various locations, and talked to the superintendent of the Standard Oil plant. The photographer arrived and began taking pictures.

Mike went back, called the city desk again. He would stay on the scene until eleven o'clock or so, he said, then either come back and write the story, or if things were still touch and go, call it in.

The firefighting effort continued. The Esso tanker was now anchored out across the channel, and several tugboats were alongside the dock with fire hoses shooting long streams of water out onto nearby tanks. He walked along the dock, under the streams of water, stepped aboard one of the tugboats, and found his way up into the wheelhouse. He talked to the tugboat captain, a man named Leon Ward, and looked on for a while. Then he went back ashore.

A little before eleven he telephoned the desk. There was no sign thus far of the fire slackening; no fire trucks had departed the area. He had better stay on, he thought. He dictated a story to John White.

Now this, he thought, is what newspaper reporting ought to be like all the time. The thought that Polly Morrison had told him to be careful was also pleasing.

NOT UNTIL WELL past two in the morning, after the final edition of the paper had gone to press, did he leave the scene and go home. By then the blaze appeared to have been tamped down, and some of the fire trucks were leaving. The whole occasion was very exciting. It was what he had imagined, when he was a kid, that being a member of the working press would be. His clothes were sweaty, and smelled of smoke and oil fumes. He remembered Igoe's prophecy. It had turned out very satisfactorily.

THE FRONT PAGE of the morning paper featured the fire story, with a quite dramatic photograph of the blazing tank and the fire-fighting crews silhouetted against the light. His byline was over the story. But it wasn't the only big story. On the top left-hand side of the page was a story by Jim Igoe, labeled "Special to the *News & Courier*" and datelined Washington, with a three-column headline:

HOUSE WILL INVESTIGATE POINSETT TIES TO MURRAY, GREENVILLE CORPORATIONS

The lead paragraph quoted the chairman of the Ethics Committee of the House of Representatives as saying that an investigation into Congressman Franklin Poinsett's personal relationships with building contractor W. Turner Murray and the Greenville corporations selling property to the government for military use would be an early order of business when Congress reassembled in January.

It also gave more particulars on the property transactions, citing instances in which, according to various individuals, sizeable sums of money were lent to the corporations involved, on little or no collateral, to enable them to purchase tracts that then became defense installations. There were also several claims by rival contractors that favoritism had been shown to the Murray Construction Company in bids to construct the weapons depot north of the city.

Igoe had found out more about the interlockings of the various corporations based at the same address in Greenville. Although detailed access to the stock holdings of individual investors remained unavailable, it was apparent that the corporate affairs were very much under the control of no more than four or five persons, including the brothers-in-law of both Franklin Poinsett and Turner Murray. Certain sources, described as "knowledgeable" but with their identities left unrevealed, insisted that both the congressman and Murray had to be deeply involved in the corporate operations.

MIKE CALLED POLLY, apologized for having to break their date, and arranged to take her to a movie that evening. She had a funny story to tell. Someone at school, she said, had made an enlargement of the quotation from Robert Frost in Mike's story of the day before, "I thought all the idiots were in Washington now working for the federal government, but evidently there is still one at loose in coastal South Carolina," mounted it on a poster board underneath a photograph of Dean McCracken, and posted it on the bulletin board in the ground-floor corridor of the College administration building. It remained there all morning, until finally someone must have told the dean about it, whereupon he emerged from the psychology lab, came striding into the building and down the corridor, ripped down the poster, thrust it under his arm, and started out the door — until he noticed that all the students sitting and standing around in the corridor were laughing. He turned to see that in view on the bulletin board now, previously concealed by the poster, was a large photo, in color, of the rear end of a horse, with "Guess Who?" lettered underneath it.

"What did he do then?" Mike asked.

"He came back and tore that one down, too."

What was the tie-in, he wondered, between the dean and the business with Franklin Poinsett and the Army contracts? If there was a tie-in at all, that is. Polly had said something about a rumor to the effect that Mr. Murray was involved in McCracken's appointment. He would have to ask Jim Igoe about it.

THERE WAS ANOTHER development, this time in what was universally assumed on the staff to be his personal bailiwick. While the fire at the Standard Oil tanks was raging Friday night, the Cooper River Ghost had put in another appearance. The next day the newspaper got two calls, and when Mike began checking he found that not only had it been observed by two night watchmen along the downtown waterfront but that one of the men aboard the tugboats fighting the fire had happened to glance back downstream and had seen it round the upper reach of Town Creek and turn eastward along Drum Island Reach toward Remley's Point. Partly illuminated by the flames of the oil tank fire and the batteries of searchlights trained upon the nearby tanks, it was in clear view for at least a half-minute. The description given by the tugboat crewman tallied with earlier views: a low hull, about thirty to thirty-five feet long, painted black, a figure in white standing behind a windshield of some sort, moving at a goodly clip. Because of the din of the firefighting operation and the tugboat's engine and pumps, the crewman had heard no sound, but the night watchman at the Clyde-Mallory Line dock had picked up the high-pitched wailing noise. The circumstances of its appearance had again held true: stormy, moonless night, high tide.

If nothing else, the advent this time of the Ghost confirmed that the mystery craft did not make its entry into the harbor from up the Cooper River, since it would then have had to pass close by the Standard Oil wharf both coming and going, and almost certainly would have been noticed. This meant that it was unlikely to be any kind of secret experimental naval craft based at the Navy Yard, as had earlier been thought possible. As always Mike checked with Coast Guard, the bridge tender at Sullivans Island, the night crew at Fort Sumter; the result was the same. The appearance of the Cooper River Ghost was confined to the lower harbor and downtown waterfront — and how it got there or where it went to after its customary circuit remained a mystery.

JIM IGOE ARRIVED back in the news room early Saturday afternoon, after a week in Washington, Greenville, and other points. "I'm about done," he said. "A couple of more things to run down the first of the week, and I'll have everything I can get until they start the hearings in Washington in the spring."

Mike asked him about the identity of the "knowledgeable sources" in his story. "I don't want to name names," Jim told him, "but let's say that not everyone holding stock in several of those corporations is entirely happy with some of the decisions made or the fees paid. By asking around Greenville long enough, I found a couple of people who were mad as hell about the deal. By the way," he added, "what did I say about you being lucky?"

"Who, me?" Mike grinned.

"A goddamn five-alarm fire! All these years I've been waiting for something like this to happen, and you take over the beat and within two weeks a lighting bolt hits an oil tank at Standard Oil, and you got yourself the biggest fire in Charleston in years. I'm just glad you're not in Washington covering the Navy Department, because if you were, the Jap fleet would probably invade San Francisco."

Mike laughed. "The police sergeant told me to tell you he hoped you'd be around for their Christmas party tomorrow afternoon."

"I'm planning on being there. You want to go with me?"

"I might. It depends."

"It depends on what?"

"Well, I might have to be somewhere else."

Igoe looked at him. "Anybody I know?"

"Do you know a man named Morrison, that you used to play baseball with?"

"Henry. Sure. Oho — so you're going out with Polly these days, is it?"

Mike nodded.

"Your taste in females, my young friend," Igoe said, "has improved wonderfully."

Mike told him about the rumor that Turner Murray was responsible for Dean McCracken's appointment at the College. "I wouldn't be surprised," Igoe said. "But if so, I daresay he's sorry as hell he had anything to do with that character. That's all Turner needs right now: more bad publicity. He'll never make it into the Yacht Club that way."

AFTER IGOE'S RETURN to the police beat next week, the managing editor said, Mike would henceforth handl certain spot news as needed, write features, and work on the desk editing copy on a regular basis. The assistant city editor, Moore, with whom Mike had experienced so much difficulty when he first joined the staff, was being taken off the city desk and given the job of editing the financial page, out-of-town obits, movie listings, weather data, and other material requiring precision rather than imagination. The city editor didn't say the last, but the intent was obvious.

SO HE HAD received a promotion, he told Polly Morrison that evening. He would be writing, not covering a beat, and also editing copy and writing headlines, which he liked doing. They had gone to a movie and then stopped in at the Rampart Room of the Fort Sumter Hotel. Yet it also meant, he declared after a couple of beers, that he had failed. "I wanted to be a reporter. I'm a decent writer, I think, and a competent editor, but I can't ferret out news from people. And that's what good reporters do."

"That seems kind of dubious to me," Polly said. "I mean, just because you can't do one particular kind of newspaper work doesn't mean that you're a failure, does it? — even if what you say is true," she added, "and you really can't."

"Failure's not exactly what I mean. But the important thing on a newspaper is getting the news."

"When I came down to breakfast this morning," Polly said, "Daddy was reading the paper. He showed me the front page, and he pointed to your name on the story on the top right-hand side of the page, and Jim Igoe's on the story on the top left-hand side. Daddy said that Jim had been writing for the paper for twelve years, and you'd been doing it only since last June, yet there were your names together, and your story was better written than Jim's."

"Yes, but if Jim hadn't been off on the special assignment, he'd have been covering that fire. It was his beat."

"Then you would have written about something else. Besides, Mama ran into Jim today at Mazo's, and he told her that you were considered the best writer they've had on the staff in a long time."

"That's very flattering, even if untrue." And it was flattering. "I'm glad," Mike said, "that your father likes what I write. Betsy's father certainly didn't."

Polly made a wry face. "Daddy says Mr. Murray's the worst thing that's happened to Charleston since the 1918 flu epidemic. To tell you the truth, he was delighted with that story this morning, because it bears out everything he's been saying about Mr. Murray and Franklin Poinsett all along."

"Your father," Mike said, "is obviously a man of taste and discernment. I just hope he approves of me."

Polly laughed. "He does."

Mike drained his glass of beer. "I believe I'll have just one more," he said. "Tell me if I start talking too much. How about you?"

"One more. Two's my limit, though."

Mike held up two fingers, then pointed to his empty glass. "'And the sin I impute to each frustrate ghost,'" he quoted, "'Is — the unlit lamp and the undrained beer container.'"

"We've just finished Browning in Dr. Rosenbaum's class," Polly said.

After a minute the waiter delivered two more glasses of beer. "As I've said before, *In vino, veritas*," Mike said, taking a sip. "Or whatever the Latin is for beer. *Birrus? Pabstum? Anheuser?* Do you happen to know?"

"No. But I know the Romans drank it."

"Well, then, it doesn't matter what the name is. The point is that having had a couple of brews, I tend to lose my inhibitions and say what I mean. Such as — there's one thing I don't appreciate about you."

Polly looked at him. "What?"

"You're going away to graduate school in September."

"September's a long time off."

"It doesn't seem so long to me. It's more like a sword of Damocles, suspended above my head by a thread."

Polly laughed. "Maybe what you need to get is a steel helmet."

"I expect the Army's going to arrange for that before so very long." Mike took a swallow of beer. "Seriously, though — *in*

Anheuser, veritas — I do hate to think of it. Not your going to graduate school, you understand, but leaving town."

She nodded.

"Where do you think you'll be going?"

"Chapel Hill or Duke, I hope."

"What would you think," he asked, "if I came along with you, and got a job on a paper in Durham or Raleigh?"

Polly sipped her beer. "I would be very much in favor of that." she said. "Also in *Anheuser, veritas.*"

ON MONDAY MORNING he took the wedding ring Betsy had returned to a jeweler on King Street, and asked whether it might be taken for credit on a new ring, to be chosen later.

Yes, the jeweler said. "If you want, though, we could just remount this stone on a new setting. It's a very nice diamond."

No, thanks, he replied. He did not want anything on this ring to be used on the new one.

"When will you be needing the new ring?"

"In about a week," he said. "I hope," he added.

The jeweler smiled. "Good luck," he told Mike.

33

THE SINGING OF Christmas carols at the College of Charleston took place each year on the Sunday evening after the last classes before the holidays. Students, faculty, employees, and their families assembled en masse outside the main building, candles were handed out, and the College glee club led the procession on a tour of nearby streets.

In character, if not in all the songs sung, the event was secular, enthusiastically participated in by almost everyone, whether Catholic, Protestant, or Jewish. It had taken Dolf Strongheart, being Bronx born, several years to accept the fact that no theological significance need be attached to the communal caroling of "*Gloria in Excelcis Deo*," "Silent Night" and the like. Now he and his family were among the most enthusiastic carollers. Rosy, who had been singing the likes of "Holy infant, so tender and mild" since childhood at school assemblies without so much as a second thought, had gone caroling when an undergraduate at the College, and resumed it when he returned as a faculty member. "When in Rome, do as the Charlestonians do," he told Dolf when his friend had expressed his misgivings. "Singing 'Rule, Britannia' doesn't make you a Limey, does it?"

"That's all very well, but what about singing 'Christ our Savior is born'? He's *their* Savior, not ours."

"What do you want them to sing, 'Where was Moses when

the lights went out'? Besides, you don't have to sing every line of every carol."

The evening was on the chilly side when the carollers assembled, at least two hundred strong, in front of the cistern. Friday night's cold front had ended the unseasonably warm weather, the temperature was in the mid-thirties, and breaths condensed in little clouds as the singing got under way.

Rosy, Sara Jane, Tom Lowndes, and the Stronghearts were standing together. Polly Morrison came over to say hello; Mike Quinn was with her. A little later, as the procession filed out of the front gate of the College and turned right on George Street, Sara Jane nudged Rosy.

"Look." She gestured in the direction of Polly and Mike, who were now walking a dozen yards ahead of them. They were holding hands. "They do belong together, don't they?"

Also among the carollers was Tennie Carter, with Becky Donahoe. Page and Mike were not in sight.

"Have you seen?" Tennie asked.

"Seen what?" Rosy asked.

"Over there. Isn't that the limit?" Dean McCracken was present, and with him neither wife nor children but his prize prodigy, Lee Witt. "Of all the nerve! How can he show his face at a gathering like this, after what's happened?"

"He doesn't embarrass easily," Sara Jane said. And it was true, for not only was the dean present, but his voice, off-key by a half-note, was conspicuous in the singing.

The procession grew in size as it moved along the sidewalks, with numerous stops for caroling, until by the time it had reached the intersection of Greene and College and stopped to sing "Joy to the World" at Mr. Albert Sottile's ornately illuminated Victorian house, fully three hundred carollers were taking part.

The final station in the processional was, as always, the Greene Street entrance to the College building, where they would sing a last round of several carols, ending by custom with

"Here We Come A-Wassailing," and then disband.

Arriving there shortly after nine o'clock the assembled multitude launched into a rendition of "It Came Upon the Midnight Clear." Scarcely had the number commenced, however, when Dolf Strongheart abruptly turned to Rosy and grasped his arm. "Let's go," he said. And, to the others, "We'll be back in a little while. Wait for us out here."

They crossed the street and went into the zoology lab. "McCracken and his girlfriend just went into his lab," Dolf declared. From his desk drawer he extracted a camera and flashgun. "Come, Watson! The game is afoot!"

They stepped out the back door onto the porch. The area was completely dark. The little building that housed the dean's laboratory lay across the walk, screened from Greene Street by the zoology building. A onetime private residence, the building had not only front and rear entrances but a side porch as well, from which French doors opened into the room being used as a laboratory. There were no lights to indicate that anyone was within.

"Are you sure they're there?" Rosy whispered.

"Positive."

Outside on the street, beyond the lab, the caroling continued. "It Came Upon the Midnight Clear" was followed by "Deck the Halls":

> *Follow me with merry measure*
> *Fa-la-la fa-la-la la-la-la*
> *While I tell of Yuletide treasure*
> *Fa-la-la-la-la la-la la-la*

With Dolf in the lead, the two of them tiptoed around to the rear entrance, until they stood silently in the darkness outside the closed door. From his pocket Dolf drew out a key, which he slipped into the lock, taking care not to make a noise. "We'll give them a couple of minutes," he whispered.

They waited.

Now it was "A-Wassailing" being sung:

> *Here we come a-wassailing*
> *Among the leaves so green*
> *Here we come a-wandering*
> *So fair to be seen*

"Okay. Here goes." Dolf turned the key in the lock, swung the door open, stepped inside, and held up his camera and flashgun. "Say cheese!" he declared, and fired.

To their astonishment, the flare of light was accompanied almost simultaneously by two additional flashes, one from the front door, another from the French doors on the side porch.

Someone flicked a light switch; the overhead lights came on. At the front entrance stood Page Carter and Mike Donahoe, with camera and flashgun. Inside the parted French doors at the side, similarly equipped, were José L. Lopez, Jr., and the editor of the College newspaper, Billy Mood. At a desk along the back wall of the lab were Dean McCracken and Lee Witt, the former seated in a large, high-backed upholstered chair, the latter seated in the lap of the former. Both were in considerable sartorial disarray.

Outside in the street beyond the zoology building the caroling continued:

> *We are not little beggars*
> *Who go from door to door*
> *But we are neighbor children*
> *Whom you have seen before*

"I'll expect you in my office by nine A.M." Page Carter told the dean. And, to José L. Lopez, Jr., and his associate, "Gentlemen, if you'll remove the roll of film from that camera and let Dr. Donahoe have it, I'll be obliged. I shall trust in your complete confidentiality. No one else must hear of this."

"Yes, sir!"

> *God bless the master of this house,*
> *The mistress bless also,*
> *And all the little children*
> *That round the table go.*

"Why don't you give me your film, too, Dolf?" Mike Donahoe said. "I'll print all three of them in my darkroom tonight."

"By all means."

> *Love and joy come to you*
> *And a right good Christmas too*
> *And God bless you and send you a Happy New Year*
> *And God send you a Ha-ap-py New Year*

Dolf removed the camera from its case and began to reverse the film preparatory to extracting it.

"This," Dean McCracken said, "is blackmail!"

"If it is, then you of all people would certainly know how to recognize it," Page told him. "In any instance, I should hate to have to exhibit these photographs at the next meeting of the board of trustees."

Miss Witt began to cry.

"As for you, young lady," the president said, "I think you had better have a talk, just as soon as possible, with your parents, and let them know that this man" — he pointed to the dean — "put you up to making the protest about the poem, in order to besmirch the reputation of a highly respected teacher."

"Yes, sir," she sniffled.

"I need hardly say," Page continued, "that any public repetition of the charge made by your pastor would make it necessary to inform the press of the circumstances under which the original accusation was made."

"Yes, sir."

"Gentlemen, an evening of degrading but regrettably necessary work is complete," Page said. "Let us depart."

TWO NIGHTS LATER there was convened, in the den of Page and Tennie Carter's house on James Island, a group of the president's colleagues and friends. The Lancelot Rosenbaums were on hand, as were the Rudolph Stronghearts, the Michael Donahoes, the Horace Hewitts, Tom Lowndes, and several other faculty members. They had come to hear Page Carter describe what in years to come those present were accustomed to refer to as:

34

'The Case
of the Concupiscent Dean'

"LET ME PREFACE the story that I am about to tell you by insisting that the man is insane," began Page Carter. "Mad. Loco. Off his rocker. Meshugga, I believe it is called.

"And let me admit, too, that I was taken in, utterly, completely. Pride goeth before a fall, and I had reached a point at which I fear I had come to think of myself as close to infallible. I assumed that I could handle any situation, any individual that might come along — a dangerous assumption, and for which I, and I regret to say others in this room as well, were to pay most dearly for my having made it.

"It was early last spring when I asked the chairman of our board of trustees to talk with Congressman Poinsett to see whether something might be done to speed the decision on our application to the Works Progress Admission for funds to build a new science building. Now as you may be aware, I am not especially enamoured of Mr. Murray...."

"He's a pompous ass, and he and his wife are blatant social climbers!" Tennie Carter put in.

". . . Yet his, shall we say ambition, has more than once turned out to be helpful to the College, in that we have been enabled to hit him up for several nice gifts. *Pecuniam non olet*, as the Romans put it. 'Money don't stink.'

"In any event, he promised to look into the matter. Within two weeks' time he informed me that Congressman Poinsett had reported that the prognosis was favorable. There was, however, another and related matter that he wished to discuss with me in complete privacy, and he asked whether he might come around to my office that afternoon.

"He appeared to be — well, nervous, although he sought to disguise it. It was the only time that I can recall ever seeing the chairman of our board less than fully assured in manner; he is not exactly what one would call the sensitive type. He had, he said, a nephew, his sister's son, who although still in his mid-thirties was already well launched upon career as a scientist and academic administrator. He was currently associate dean and professor of psychology at Iowa State College. There had been, however, a purely jurisdictional dispute with the dean, and he had determined to resign his position at once and seek another appointment elsewhere.

"I shan't go into all the details, but what Turner proposed was that his nephew be offered an interim appointment at the College. It would be for a maximum of two years, during which time he would personally be responsible for his nephew's salary, as well as for any expenses involved in his coming. His nephew wanted such an appointment only as a temporary expedient, to give him time to select and move into a permanent position elsewhere. Turner intended also, he said, to make a contribution of $50,000 to supplement the W.P.A. grant for the new science building.

"I replied at once that while we would welcome such a gift, it could in no way be made contingent upon an appointment for his nephew. Of course he insisted that he hadn't meant to imply any such thing, et cetera, et cetera. If the W.P.A. grant came through, the gift would be forthcoming, with no conditions attached."

"The stinker!" Tennie declared.

"I also pointed out," Page continued, "that we did not offer psychology as part of our curriculum, and that we were fully staffed in terms of faculty positions authorized by the board. Turner said he was aware of the unavailability of authorized faculty positions. He had studied the minutes of the board meetings for a number of years back, he said, and had learned that some time ago the board had authorized the position of dean of the college, which had never been filled. So what he proposed was that his nephew be given that title — with the clear understanding, of course, that it was *only* a title, and that he would exercise none of the customary functions of a dean, would teach no classes, but instead be in effect an administrative assistant.

"You may ask why I was willing even to consider such an arrangement. Well, we *do* need a science building, and badly. Our stipend from the City remains meager, and the extra $50,000 would go a long way toward properly equipping such a building if we were to secure it. Morever, if we were awarded the grant by the W.P.A., there would be a formidable burden of administrative correspondence and government paperwork while it was being constructed, and having an experienced administrative assistant, trained in science, would be most helpful. And I have to say, too, that without knowing why, I had the sense that the matter was of much importance to the chairman of our board — who had been very useful to the College in the past, and would be in the future.

"The upshot was that I agreed to interview the nephew, which I did. I have to confess that he took me in completely. It is true that he seemed a little, what shall I say, rough at the edges. . ."

"Crude," Tennie Carter broke in. "Loutish."

"No, my dear, not as he seemed then. Not on that initial occasion. He had been well rehearsed. No doubt I should have spotted it, but I did not. In any event, I checked out all his references. I made inquiries about his scholarship, which was reasonably respected in the field of experimental psychology — I'm afraid that I didn't then realize how self-aggrandizing that field can be.

"I also looked into the supposed jurisdictional dispute at Iowa

State. I called the president himself. He told me that it was a matter of divergent personalities. Now in light of what has happened, and what I later found out about what took place there, that was scarcely a candid reply. But surely I need not remind you that we academics can be very sinful creatures when it comes to offering honest appraisals of our colleagues. We tend to cover over all flaws outside of outright criminal conduct; and even then. . ."

"Yes, and you ought to be ashamed of yourselves!" Tennie Carter declared.

"*Sauve qui peut*," Page said. "But it was for two years only, it would cost nothing, it might help with the science building application, and if the grant came through I'd have some experienced administrative help and $50,000 for equipment. So over Tennie's objections I decided to go ahead. I have to give her credit. From the outset she smelled a rat."

"A white rat!" Tennie declared. "When Turner Murray was involved, nothing could be that simple. There simply had to be more to it. And once I laid eyes on the man and saw what a clod he was, I was positive that Turner would never in this world have voluntarily risked jeopardizing his social position in Charleston through association with such a creature!"

"You're getting ahead of the story, my dear," Page said. "Besides, no one was to know that McCracken was his nephew. The relationship was to be kept completely secret, so that there would be no talk of nepotism, and no reason to link McCracken to Turner.

"Well, you all know what happened once the chap arrived. He had no intention whatever of living up to the agreement we made — to exercise the rank of dean in name only. He insisted upon teaching a course. He set out to take charge of the curriculum, to supervise the faculty, oversee the student body — to assume command completely! I was appalled. I confronted him with our agreement; he denied having made it.

"I could have forced the issue. In retrospect God knows that I should have. But I did not, because — to speak candidly — I had compromised myself. To have to admit publicly that I had consented to give the man the rank of dean without the duties and the authority would have been extremely embarrassing. 'Ah, what a tangled web we weave / When first we practice to deceive.' Hubris. Pride. Call it what you will; I was guilty.

"When he came out with that self-study memorandum — semi-literate, jargon-crammed, distributed without so much as a word being spoken to me about it in advance — it was the last straw. I called Turner in at once. He persuaded me to let him deal with McCracken. There would be no more trouble, he pledged. I went along with it, but I also made it clear that if there was any further difficulty, McCracken would be terminated forthwith.

"And that is how things stood for several weeks. But meanwhile, Tennie and I became suspicious —"

"I was suspicious from the first moment I laid eyes on him," Tennie said.

"You were that," Page agreed. "What did Turner have personally to gain by McCracken's appointment as dean? I could think of nothing. Turner has never been really interested in the academic life of the College. His sole concern was for the prestige that being chairman of the board of trustees conferred upon him. Why, then, had he been so eager to get the position for his nephew?

"It was Tennie, as always, who came up with the probable answer. She reasoned that the impetus must be coming from the other direction. That is, that the nephew, McCracken, must have some hold on his uncle, some form of leverage as it were, that enabled him to persuade, or perhaps to cajole, Turner into arranging a place for him, at whatever expense. A form of blackmail, as it were. But if so, of what might the threat of exposure consist?

"It was at that point that the news stories began to appear linking Turner's construction firm to possible collusion with

Congressman Poinsett in obtaining preknowledge of the leasing of property on the Isle of Palms for an Army hospital. It occurred to me that perhaps McCracken had found out about it, and was using the threat of tipping off the press to blackmail Turner.

"I knew that McCracken and Turner, and Congressman Poinsett as well, were all from the Greenville area, and the newspaper story indicated that the corporation involved in the property transfer was located in Greenville. Moreover, I noted, in one of the stories, that one of the officers of the corporation was named McCracken. So I called an old fraternity brother of mine, who is an attorney in Greenville, and asked him to find out what he could for me about Turner, the family, and anything else.

"It turns out that Turner's brother-in-law, his wife's brother, a man named Inabinet, is a lawyer with a decidedly dubious reputation, and there was the suspicion among his colleagues at the bar that Congressman Poinsett has been associated with him and Turner, through a number of holding corporations, in some property transactions with the federal government. Until the story in the *News & Courier* the other day, however, it was all in the way of rumor, and nothing was definitely known.

"It also turns out that the McCracken who was involved in the corporation was yet another brother-in-law of Turner's, married to one of his wife's sisters, and that he was our man's father. Unlike almost everybody else, this one was said to be dissatisfied with the financial split, and was apparently threatening to blow the whistle on the whole thing — and our McCracken knew this very well.

"So there was every reason for Turner to want to keep McCracken conciliated, and every reason for McCracken to feel confident that his dear Uncle Turner would see to it that he wasn't given his walking papers.

"Then came this absurd business about the poem, and the protest by the Witt girl's family. As you know, rumors had been circulating that McCracken was engaged in an affair with the girl. It soon became apparent that the rumors were quite true, that it was taking place in the laboratory late in the evening, and that some of the students were well aware of it.

"So with Mike's cooperation I set up a surveillance operation. For two evenings, Mike and I took turns keeping a lookout from the window of the physics laboratory office. Several evenings went by without results. I feared that he had become suspicious and therefore cautious. In any event, with classes let out for the holidays, I had made up my mind to call him in on Monday morning and fire him, come what may. But then came the events of Sunday night.

"What was our surprise, of course, when we moved to unlock the door and enter, to find not only Rosy and Dolf, but the two students as well, all with the same objective in mind! It was an instance of what in science is called overdetermination.

"In any case, we had him dead to rights. He brought in a letter on Monday morning, to the effect that he was resigning his position because of personal considerations that made it impossible for him to perform his duties to his own professional satisfaction. I told him it wouldn't do. Would you believe that he wanted to argue about it? His hopes of future employment, he said, depended upon his being able to show that his resignation was voluntarily and due to factors beyond his control! I told him that his future prospects depended solely upon my willingness not to reveal the facts of his leaving to prospective employers. I also told him that if I received an inquiry involving a deanship, or any academic position other than that of a teacher of psychology, I would feel obliged to report the full circumstances. And that's where we now stand.

"Oh yes, after the business about the self-study, I decided that it might be wise to look further into why it was that he had left his position at Iowa State College. I found that I had gone to graduate school with someone on the faculty there. It turned out that McCracken had done much the same thing there as here.

"Needless to say, I regret the embarrassment and inconvenience you've all been made to undergo because of my poor judgment," Page said, "and in particular what Rosy has been made to go through. It has been as humiliating an experience as I have ever known, an educational, administrative, and personal nightmare, so to speak, such as I hope I shall not undergo again during my tenure. For your patience in bearing with me throughout the ordeal I am and shall ever be grateful beyond words." The president of the College bowed his head. His eyes were moist.

"ROSY," SARA JANE remarked later that evening, "if you so much as intimate that you're the slightest bit sorry for McCracken, I'm going to crown you over the head with that clock in the living room." She was already in bed; Rosy was en route.

"I don't feel sorry for him. I'd like to bust him in the snoot before he leaves town. On the other hand, think of the poor jackass, thinking he's having a secret liaison, only to have three flashguns go off and three cameras photographing him with a coed in his lap and her dress halfway up to her neck! It must be rough on his family, too. Think of having to live with that man!"

"Oh, you're incorrigible!"

"Now having to live with you," Rosy said as he got into bed, "is another matter entirely."

"I should hope so."

"We've been married exactly one month and one day now. Do you still enjoy being a married woman as much as you said you did when we were driving back from Savannah?"

"I certainly do," Sara Jane said. "Even if you do have cold feet."

35

SO THE DESPICABLE dean departed the premises, and when classes were resumed in January, life on the campus of the College of Charleston settled down to its accustomed pace, with nothing more heard about the teaching of pornographic seventeenth-century poems.

But for Rosy, thereafter it was not as it had been. What had taken place, however briefly its immediate impact had lasted, had intensified a process of dislodgement that in actuality was under way even before his marriage, though not before he had proposed to Sara Jane and been accepted. He had begun to perceive the extent to which he had been engaged in building around himself a kind of protective wall — a shield, or covering, or perhaps a cocoon designed to insulate against disappointment, confusion, and unpleasantness.

Some lines from a poem by Robert Frost imbedded themselves in his mind: "Before I built a wall I'd ask to know / What I was walling in or walling out . . ." To protect himself from trouble and grief he had been walling out too large a segment of life itself. Sara Jane had helped him see that, had made it possible for him to confront it. Now he began seeing that he had been settling for a too-easy, too-comfortable academic niche — quaint old eccentric, lovable Doctor Rosenbaum, teacher of the young — in a professional milieu that required little further intellectual growth or enhancement of understanding, but only continuing cleverness at what he already knew.

He had been leaving to others — to Page Carter, most of all — the task of justifying and protecting what he did and was, as if it were no responsibility of his own to make the most of his capabilities, to engage himself thoroughly and imaginatively in his chosen vocation so that what might be said and thought about his professional work by others outside that vocation would carry little weight or importance. And Page had, after a delay, proved able to do it.

But what if Page Carter had been unable to protect him? He remembered that infuriating interview with the Dean, in which McCracken had declared himself chief executive officer and fully empowered to carry on the affairs of the College. Suppose the president had suddenly been removed from the scene — had been run over by a taxicab while in New York, or fallen off his boat in a storm and drowned, or something else catastrophic and unpredictable had happened. Wouldn't he and his colleagues have had to submit to McCracken's dictates? And what would the board of trustees, with Turner Murray as chairman, have done when there were protests from the faculty? Would they have understood what was wrong about the dean and his agenda? How long might it have taken, how much damage might have been wreaked, before the man's madness became evident to them?

The sense of having been unable to defend himself had been devastating. Of course it was never possible to protect oneself totally against misfortune, irrationality, jealousy. No one was ever invulnerable. But, short of that, wouldn't the best thing that someone like himself could possibly do to safeguard his well-being, and now that of his wife, be to make the fullest use he could of his talents, to establish himself as so thoroughly competent within his chosen field that, so long as there was a place for that field anywhere in the scheme of things, there would be a place for him?

And beyond all such calculations of status and stature, in the long run would he ever be able to respect himself if he did not do the best professional work that he, Rosy Rosenbaum, was capable of doing, however excellent or mediocre that best might be?

Sara Jane had seen that, recognized that both intellectually and socially he was too adaptable, too accommodating. Being in love with him, she was ambitious for him. She asked the question that he had avoided asking: was he living and working where he could do his very best teaching and writing? At one point, while they were engaged but not yet married, she had even told him that he ought not to consider himself wedded to the College of Charleston for life.

He had been taken aback. "Leave Charleston? Why?"

"When was the last time you did any work on your book about the narrator in the novel, Rosy?"

"I don't know — let's see. Was it two years ago? I'm not sure."

"If you wrote another chapter of the book, who could you show it to for suggestions and criticism?"

"Nobody locally, I guess," Rosy said. "Horace Hewitt, perhaps — but he thinks prose fiction ended when Charles Dickens died."

"That's exactly what I mean. And would any of your students, no matter how bright, know enough about the subject to understand what you were talking about?"

"Probably not. I'd have to make an article out of it and send it out to a magazine."

"With five different courses to teach and themes to grade every week you might not get around to that."

"That's true, but —"

"But what?"

"Maybe you're right. I'll have to think about it."

Now he was thinking about it.

THERE CAME A Sunday in early February 1941, when the society pages of the *News & Courier* carried the news that Mr.

and Mrs. Wallace Turner Murray were announcing the engagement and forthcoming marriage of their daughter, Elizabeth Inabinet, to Mr. Elliott Simons Mikell, of Charleston. The bridegroom was the son of Dr. and Mrs. Simons Porcher Mikell, of James Island; the wedding was to be held at St. Michael's Episcopal Church on March 5.

"That doesn't allow Mrs. Murray time to put on much of a show, does it?" Mike Quinn remarked to Polly.

"No, it certainly doesn't," Polly said. "But I ran into Annie Holmes on King Street yesterday, and from what she said, it was a case of the sooner the better."

Accidents did happen. Still, it didn't seem logical that Betsy Murray would ever have permitted that particular kind of accident to happen. She was not one to let impetuous nature take its course. To be sure, there had been that first time with him, when her parents were out of town —— but afterward he had read up on such things as biological rhythms and learned that the odds against anything happening at that particular time were extremely slight. So if Betsy were now with child, he would be willing to bet that she had seen to it that conditions were propitious for that to happen. As was said of her father, when Betsy Murray wanted something, she usually got it.

Whatever the circumstances, surely the change in choice of husbands must have been greatly preferable to Betsy's father and mother. No Roman Catholic from the mountains this time, but a certified, pedigreed Low-country gentleman, one who moreover rode to hounds.

AT THE PORTHOLE one evening not long after the announcement appeared, Mike asked Jim Igoe what he thought of it. Jim laughed. "Well," he said, "Murray's taken his lumps lately, and when they hold the congressional hearings next month he'll take more of same, but at least his darling daughter's managing to get an authenticated descendant of the signers of the Declaration of Independence safely installed in the bedroom. So now he'll have the in-laws he needs to do favors for, if he's ever going to get into the social circles he covets."

"What do you think the hearings will turn up?" Mike asked.

"My guess," Jim said, "is that when they get the information on all those corporations out in the open, they're going to find various kinds of payments made to Poinsett's law firm and Murray's construction company for services rendered —fat payments, lots of dough. I'm sure Poinsett had sense enough not to be holding stock in any corporation actually selling property to the government, but that doesn't mean he couldn't own part of any outfits that those corporations do business with. There are all kinds of ways to divvy up the take. I wouldn't be surprised, for example, to learn that he owns a chunk of Murray Construction Company. That's what McCracken's father was all het up about — he figured that Poinsett and Murray were receiving too much gravy, while as a stockholder he wasn't getting enough.

"Franklin Poinsett will probably get himself rebuked for improper use of privileged information as a member of a congressional committee — and that will be it. When he comes up for reelection in 1942 the good people of Charleston and the First Congressional District will show their outrage at his failure to observe the highest ethical standards in public office by giving him only a five-to-three margin in the voting, instead of the usual two-to-one.

"As for Turner Murray, he'll have to settle out of court with those people that he bought the property next to the Army hospital from — but when you consider what he stands to make from developing the property once the hospital's under way, it'll still be a colossal bargain.

"You know, I was thinking the other day that I wouldn't be surprised if Turner decides not to run for reelection to City Council. Being mayor pro tem's not worth that much, and with the defense business booming like it is, he doesn't really need to keep a finger on what's doing with the city government any more. With the kind of money he's going to be raking in over the next few years, he'll have what it takes to operate statewide, regionwide, just about anywhere. He won't get into high gear until the war's over, but eventually the barefoot Clemson College drop-out from Upstate is going to be a genuine Grade-A, *Wall Street Journal*-certified, Standard and Poor's-registered multimillionaire. Then we'll see what happens Below Broad Street.

"Who knows, perhaps he may make it into the Saint Ceci in time to celebrate his grand-daughter's debut, and get fuddled on champagne at Hibernian Hall.

"Speaking of which, let me tell you something, kid. I've known the young lady you now got on the string — and vice versa — since before she took her first communion, and she and her parents are worth several dozen of any combination of the heirs, heiresses, assigns, and relatives of W. Turner Murray you could come up with. On any scale except future per capita income, you can count your blessings."

IN MARCH, ANOTHER announcement of a forthcoming wedding appeared on the society pages:

QUINN - MORRISON
WEDDING PLANNED

Mr. and Mrs. Henry Mitchel Morrison, of 34 Rutledge Avenue, announce the engagement to be married of their daughter, Mary Lucille, and Mr. Michael Redmond Quinn, of Charleston and Roanoke, Virginia.

Miss Morrison is a graduate of Memminger High School and a member of the senior class at the College of Charleston. Mr. Quinn, the son of Mrs. and Mrs. Willard James Quinn of Roanoke, is a graduate of Washington and Lee University and is assistant city editor of the *News & Courier*.

A June wedding is planned.

36

L'Envoi

AT THIS POINT we take leave of our friends — except for one item of unfinished business to be saved until the very last. Before then, however, those readers who have journeyed this far might like to know what became of them afterward.

As the reader may have suspected, when Polly Morrison Quinn registered for graduate study at the University of North Carolina in the fall of 1941, her husband Mike did the same — in English rather than history. The journalistic career that had been his goal from childhood onward went by the boards. But events at Pearl Harbor that fall had the result of sending him into Naval Officers Training the next summer, followed by four years of service, the last three aboard landing craft in the Southwest Pacific. When he returned home to Chapel Hill in January of 1946 to resume his studies, his wife Polly and daughter Sally (for Sara Jane) were there to welcome him. Polly, having completed her course work, by then was well along with her doctoral dissertation. In the years to come the Doctors Michael and Polly Quinn were to be found teaching on the faculties of Georgetown and George Washington Universities, respectively, and writing their numerous books, while living in Fairfax with their four children. "You know, it's absurd," Mike wrote to Rosy on one occasion in the late 1960s, "but even today, twenty-five years after I left the *News & Courier*, I still feel, particularly on election nights, that in not sticking with journalism I somehow failed."

Mike's dissertation director at Chapel Hill was, of all persons, Rosy. For when in 1942 Rosy's long-delayed book on the role of the narrator in the American novel was published, it received notably favorable reviews, with the result that he was offered a professorship at the University of North Carolina — which he accepted after an appointment as reference librarian at nearby Duke University was offered to and accepted by his wife Sara Jane. Oddly enough, in the early 1950s Rosy began reviewing books for the *Charlotte Observer*, and these proved so popular that they were syndicated to other newspapers as a column, on a regular basis. Later he expanded the scope of the column to include other subject matter, and even touched on the political situation sometimes. In the 1960s he took early retirement from his teaching, and devoted his full attention to writing his column and his books. So it turned out that Rosy ended up as the journalist, and Mike the professor.

The Rosenbaums never moved back to Charleston, not even after their retirement, but in the 1970s their oldest son, Thomas, became professor of French at the College of Charleston. He was named after Tom Lowndes, who did not come home from the war. A rifleman in the Twenty-Ninth Infantry Division, he was killed instantly when a German artillery round landed squarely upon the point at which he was engaged in an attack near St. Lo in Normandy.

Dolf Strongheart's extensive work with warm-weather fauna and their habitats gave him a highly desirable specialization for a Navy that was fighting a war in tropical Pacific waters. Commissioned and dispatched to Hawaii and then Midway Island to help develop methods for combatting marine growth on submarine hulls, he took part in several extended combat patrols in the Philippine and South China Seas, one of which was savagely attacked and depth-bombed by Japanese aircraft, and was awarded the Navy Cross. Returning to the College after the war he was instrumental in the creation of a marine biological research station at Fort Johnson, and he also became an avid sailor, skippering his Herreshoff sloop, the *Tartaruga*, in regattas up and down the coast from the Chesapeake Bay to Florida.

Page Carter, who had served in submarines in the First World War and was a physicist, was recalled to active duty in the summer of 1942 as lieutenant commander. Stationed first at the Navy Yard, he was later sent to New London, Connecticut, and after that transferred to Admiral Lockwood's staff in Honolulu as chief underwater propulsion engineer. When he returned to Charleston in 1946 he wore on his uniform collar the two stars of a rear admiral. Before resuming his duties as president of the College, however, he and Tennie went on a six-month journey aboard their ketch, circumnavigating the continent of South America. "From here on in," he wrote Rosy and Sara Jane before departing on the trip, "we shall travel upon water only as wind and wave permit. Not unless we find ourselves in dire straits (such as those of Magellan) and about to be driven upon the rocks, will we call upon our auxiliary engine for assistance."

When war was declared in December 1941, Jim Igoe surprised all his colleagues by showing up in the news room clad in the uniform of a captain in the Army. It turned out that he had been on counterintelligence surveillance duty in the Charleston area for the past five years, even while working as a reporter. In arresting three German spies the day after Pearl Harbor he had "blown his cover," he explained. Thereafter he was transferred to Washington, and after the war remained in the Army, retiring in 1955 with the rank of colonel. To the astonishment of all who knew him he simultaneously married the head nurse at the Stark Army Hospital and accepted a position as commandant of cadets at the Citadel, the Military College of South Carolina.

Igoe's prediction of what lay ahead for W. Turner Murray proved accurate. His construction business proved enormously profitable during the war and thereafter; among other things he developed practically the entire eastern half of the Isle of Palms for residential use. By the late 1950s he was operating on a national scale, developing a chain of elegant office plazas and shopping malls throughout the country. In 1960 he dropped dead of an attack of apoplexy. Three years later residents of Charleston, particularly those who resided south of Broad Street, were astonished when his widow married Allen Faucheraud Grimball. Soon after the marriage they purchased Gwenby Plantation, on the eastern branch of the Cooper River, and resided there and in the city.

As for Betsy Murray, her marriage to Elliott Mikell was followed by the premature advent of a son and heir just seven months after the wedding. Just over a year later, she was granted a divorce under the laws of the State of Nevada, on the grounds of adultery and desertion, her husband Elliott meanwhile having joined the U. S. Marine Corps and also been sued for breach of promise by a nightclub performer in Coronado, California. Mikell was killed in the attack on Tarawa and was awarded the Distinguished Service Medal posthumously. In 1944 Betsy remarried, this time to Billy Hugenin, then a first lieutenant in the Army. That marriage too ended in divorce following the husband's return from duty in Iceland in late 1945. Indeed, Polly Quinn, visiting her parents that Christmas while awaiting Mike's arrival from the Central Pacific, heard from Annie Holmes that a considerable sum of money was said to have changed hands before Hugenin was induced not to press charges of adultery but instead to accept a divorce on the grounds of mutual incompatibility. In 1948 Betsy was married for a third time, this time not to anybody from Charleston but to an Italian diplomatist stationed at the Embassy in Washington. Thereafter she maintained residences in Rome, Washington, and Charleston.

The summer after Dean N. Joseph McCracken left Charleston he secured an appointment as associate director of the educational testing program for the West Virginia Department of Correction. Some months later he was named acting director, and shortly thereafter resigned that office. No one is sure what happened to him thereafter. He was reported once as having been seen wearing a Navy Shore Patrol uniform in Bremerton, Washington. In the mid-1950s Dolf and Linda Strongheart, visiting relatives in San Francisco, read a news story in the *San Francisco Examiner* having to do with a Swami Gjògluv Nadj Krahjynh, Ph.D., who was implicated in the investigation of a faith healing institute for allegedly fleecing elderly women suffering from incurable diseases. The Swami's photograph, Linda wrote to Sara Jane, seemed oddly familiar.

FINALLY, THIS. WHEN Rosy and Sara Jane left Charleston for Chapel Hill, they sold the *Gilmore Simms*. Wartime gasoline rationing had by then brought an end to its use. But prior to that, back in the summer of 1941, they were able to solve, to their private satisfaction, a riddle that had for some time vexed authorities in Charleston. They did not reveal their solution to anyone, and so far as the public is concerned, the mystery remains to this day among the unsolved legends of a legend-prone community.

The notorious Cooper River Ghost, the mysterious watercraft which had been materializing on stormy nights in Charleston harbor, had put in yet another appearance. Reading about how it appeared as usual in the lower harbor following thunderstorms, on nights when as always there was no moonlight and when the tide was at flood-high stage, Rosy had a thought.

It was generally agreed that the Ghost could have reached the harbor neither from the Navy Yard upstream, nor from the Ashley River that flowed into the harbor from the west, nor from the harbor's mouth beyond Fort Sumter, nor yet from either the Wando River or Shem Creek along the eastern shore of the harbor. So seemingly there was nowhere from which the mystery boat could come, or disappear into following its swift but brief circumnavigation of the harbor, without being readily seen by numerous people.

The only break in the solid carpet of salt marsh along the James Island shoreline at the southern rim of the harbor, flanking the ship channel and leading into the Ashley River, was the creek leading to and beyond Page Carter's place — the selfsame creek that Rosy and Sara Jane had aimed for and almost miraculously reached on that momentous occasion when the hurricane had brought about the stunning alteration in both their lives.

Rosy remembered how the bend in the creek looked when they had approached it that morning after the wild ride across the harbor, and how welcome it had seemed through the rain — the dock, the green-hulled ketch moored at the edge of the channel, the Carters' house up on the bluff, the long, low boat house at the creek's edge.

What was that boat house used for? He had never been inside it, had seen it only from outside, with the electric line angling down to it from the garage and utility building behind the house atop the bluff.

One of the numerous theories advanced to account for the propulsion of the mystery boat was that it was powered by a motor driven by electric storage batteries, just as submarines were powered when submerged. The objection to the theory was that electric engines were able to move boats only at very slow speeds, and for a boat of the reported length of the Cooper River Ghost to be propelled by storage batteries rapidly enough to plane over the surface rather than displace the water, so many batteries would be needed that the boat would have to be of very deep draft.

Rosy consulted Mike Donahoe, who was also a physicist. Would it be possible for a storage-battery-powered boat to trade endurance for speed — to be able to operate at a quite high speed, but only for a brief period?

Theoretically, yes, Mike told him. But it would take a great many storage batteries, and would thus draw considerable water.

Tracing the route out on a harbor chart, Rosy estimated that for a boat to circle the harbor from the creek leading from Page Carter's place on the shoreline along the south channel, northward up the waterfront to the upper tip of Drum Island, and then back along the eastern rim of the harbor to the creek again, traveling at a speed of about thirty knots, would take about twenty to twenty-five minutes.

The question was whether batteries of sufficient storage capacity and strength to move it at high speed for as long as that could be fitted into the hull of a craft generally agreed to be approximately thirty feet in length. It would have to be deep-hulled. At mean low water the creek leading to the Carters' place was certainly deep enough to float their forty-foot ocean-going ketch, which must have a keel drawing at least five feet. Add to that another five feet of water at flood tide, and it should be possible for a boat to carry batteries that would weight it down quite deeply when not on plane, and yet negotiate the creek.

SO ON A DARK night in the last week in August, with the moon hidden behind heavy clouds, the incoming tide close to flood stage, and a thunderstorm approaching from the southwest, Rosy and Sara Jane cast off the lines and the *Gilmore Simms* left Adgers Wharf and headed down the waterfront toward the south channel. Angling across the mouth of the Ashley River, as the thunderstorm drew near, they dropped anchor just beyond the south channel range light, let out an extra long scope of anchor line, and — in violation of regulations, to be sure — doused all lights, including the anchor light.

Soon the thunderstorm, coming down the Ashley River from the west, moved in. For twenty minutes or so there were gusting wind, salvos of thunder, flashes of lightning all about them. The engine of the *Gilmore Simms* was kept running in neutral in case the anchor dragged. Then the wind and waves began to subside, and there was only the steady falling of the rain. Rosy went out onto the bow, Sara Jane eased the boat ahead, Rosy snubbed the anchor line, and the anchor broke free of the bottom.

They were a half-mile upstream from the mouth of the creek. He turned off the engine. With the rain still coming down, they could see very little. Presently they heard, off to the east, a whining sound. It seemed to move from the James

Island shore off in the direction of the city.

Rosy cut on the engine, and they steered for the edge of the marshland; at flood tide they could get in quite close. The rain had slackened considerably. Reaching a point down the way that he had marked on the chart, they edged into a break in the marsh grass that would permit them to move somewhat closer toward the shore, while placing a broad reach of marsh between them and the mouth of the creek several hundred yards downstream. All illumination doused, they waited in the blackness.

Far across to the east the lightning from the departing thunderstorm flared occasionally along the horizon. The red lights of the Cooper River Bridge blinked across the northern sky. The lights of the downtown city cast a reflected glow upon the lowlying clouds. Five minutes passed in silence, with only the wavelets lapping against the wooden hull of the *Gilmore Simms*.

Just over twenty minutes had gone by since the whining noise had been heard, when the sound became audible once more, faintly, off to the east across the harbor. It grew in volume. Then, through the light rain, they caught sight of a white bow wave, and then a boat, speeding directly up and across the south channel. Binoculars trained, they watched in the darkness as a thirty-five foot motorboat, unusually deep-hulled, swung into the creek mouth, a figure in white at the wheel, cap upon his head, wearing goggles, and planed swiftly along the creek, until abruptly it cut its speed, whereupon the hull dropped low into the water.

At very low speed they moved out of the cove and into the harbor. Glancing back, they saw a light come on approximately where the boathouse was located. It shone for a minute, then was extinguished.

Rosy pointed the bow of the *Gilmore Simms* toward the Charleston waterfront. Halfway across the channel he turned on the running lights and, the mystery of the Cooper River Ghost solved, he and Sara Jane stood side by side at the wheel and steered for Adger's Wharf.